TARGET: REDACTED

THE COVERT ASSET SERIES BOOK 1

BRAD LEE

PART 1

WEDNESDAY

1

THE DREAM

71 Ocotillo Street
Sands, Arizona

Every night, the dream was the same.

Thomas was always back in Afghanistan.

The smell of the desert at night. The crisp, cold air. The brilliant stars.

The enemy advancing—an overwhelming force focused on killing them all.

And his brothers getting shot, their blood black in his night vision goggles.

Despite the chaos, the gunfire, and the pain, the Team maneuvered, communicated, and fought for their lives with calm focus...

Followed minute by minute by soft curses, gasps of pain, and the final, strangled breaths of dying men.

The sounds were what always woke Thomas.

This morning was no different.

He sat up in bed, gasping. His head snapped around, looking for muzzle flashes. If he could see where the gunshots were coming from, he could shoot back. He already held the pistol he kept holstered on the nightstand.

Instead of the valley in Afghanistan, though, there was only his bedroom and the faint hint of dawn through the window.

It took a long second for him to blink himself present.

It was just the dream.

He lowered the weapon and fought for control, breathing in, holding it, and breathing out.

Gradually his pulse slowed and the adrenaline coursing through him dissipated.

He slid the pistol back into its holster and flopped onto his back.

The sheets were drenched with sweat, so he rolled to the other side of the bed, welcoming the dryness.

His head throbbed from the booze at the bar the previous night. His mouth tasted like he'd had a midnight snack of rancid roadkill. But at least he was awake.

He'd made it through another night.

He was safe. The past was over.

The enemy was gone... And his buddies were all dead.

Thomas swung his legs out of bed and made a trip to the bathroom. He bent to slurp water straight from the faucet before staring at his face in the mirror. The dim light of the coming dawn showed his full beard could use a trim, but his shorter brown hair didn't need a cut for another week or two. The dark bags under his eyes would fade later in the morning, and he'd take care of the redness with drops before school.

There wasn't much to be done about the long, narrow face and haunted look that appeared when he let his true spirit show. He smiled, revealing the crow's feet by his eyes. At only thirty-five, they were deeper than his father's had been later in life, but at least he wasn't going gray yet.

And he still had the lean musculature from his active-duty days.

Though the smile didn't often touch his eyes, this was the face he showed to the world. Normal. Put together. Functional.

A lie.

He splashed warm water on his face, wiped his beard on a towel, and returned to bed. Like every morning, he prayed that this time he could get another hour of rest.

It rarely worked.

He'd likely toss and turn for thirty minutes before giving up, slipping into running gear, and driving to his favorite trailhead for his daily long-distance run.

The exercise in the desert reduced the intensity of the dream.

As did drinking at the bar after work.

Between the two, he managed a few precious hours of sleep each night.

But no matter what he did, he found himself back in Afghanistan, his mind replaying the memories in a futile attempt to process the tragedy of losing his brothers.

Afghanistan

Seven Years Ago

The interpreter bent at the waist, heaving his guts out onto the tarmac.

Thomas watched along with the other seven members of the Team going on the mission. They were geared up and ready for battle. Knives hung from plate carriers packed with extra magazines of ammunition. M4s were in hand or slung ready for use. The air base was well protected, but better safe than sorry.

Some of the SEALs watched the 'terp's plight with amusement, others with sympathy, but no one could tear themselves away from the gross spectacle.

"Oh, look, chunks!" a SEAL called.

Thomas—callsign T-Bone or just Bone—chuckled. He'd been about to say the same thing, but his best bud Mark—Tank—had beaten him to it.

"Get it out of your system, Zia," Bossman called, standing next to Thomas. He was an excellent leader. Smart. Situationally aware. Calm under fire.

"We'll hold another minute," Bossman said quietly to the Team. "We might need him tonight."

The mission involved an insertion on the far side of a valley, followed by a long hike to a decent-sized village whose residents were friendly toward the Western forces helping bring peace to their chaotic country. Because of that, they had recently come under increased harassment.

Intel claimed a group of Taliban was hiding out in caves near the village.

Bossman's team—Tank, Bone, Baldy, Sneaky, Biscuit, Iron, and Dizzy—would go in and take them out.

"I am fine," Zia called, still bent over, and wiped his face with the sleeve of his US-issued desert-camo fatigues. He was in his mid-thirties, several years older than all the SEALs except for Bossman. He had thick dark eyebrows, a perpetual three-day growth of beard, and was everything they could ask for: fit enough to keep up, quiet on the hunt, and he related well to the locals wherever they went. Before war came to the country, he'd run a restaurant in Kandahar. Now he risked his life nightly with the Team, smoothing ruffled feathers with Afghans, interrogating detainees, and acting as the mouthpiece for the warriors.

Zia straightened and took a few steps toward them before stopping abruptly, spinning, and hurling again.

"If it's food poisoning, he's going to get worse," Sneaky muttered behind Bone. "We don't want him barfing all over the chopper or slowing us down. He's noisy too."

The rest of the SEALs nodded. There would be no hiding the sound of Zia's illness.

"And if he's caught a cold or the flu, he's not sitting next to me," Baldy grumbled. The burly, flat-out ugly guy was a bit of a germaphobe. All the guys knew. Something like that couldn't be hidden in a tight unit.

Tank grunted in agreement, which turned into a small cough that he aimed toward Baldy.

A second later, they were all coughing right at him.

"Very funny, assholes," Baldy said with a scowl, taking a step back as they laughed.

"I can interpret," Thomas announced without much thought. He'd been working with the interpreter, studying the language their whole tour. He was finally getting the hang of it.

"Seriously?" Bossman asked. He looked Thomas squarely in the eye. "We might have to communicate with the village elder or question detainees. How sure are you?"

Bossman went along with the unit's usual banter, but when it came to the mission, there was no room for error—or playfulness. He had the lives of the men in his hands.

"I got it," Thomas said. "Seriously."

For another few seconds, Bossman stared at him before nodding. "Congratulations, you're our interpreter for the night. Zia, get back inside and take care of yourself."

Zia waved weakly and staggered toward the barracks building, which was surrounded by a double-row stack of sandbags and held the nearest bathroom, stopping twice on the way to hurl.

"I'll get him to stay near the radio. If you have a question, he'll be a call away," Bossman told Bone.

Thomas nodded, confident it wouldn't be needed. The last few weeks, he'd easily followed Zia's conversations while on ops. It might take him an extra second to find the right word in some cases, but tonight's mission would be straightforward. They weren't about to have a long sit-down with a local leader. They'd fly in, hunt the bad guys, and take them out. Easy.

Along with the rest of the SEALs, Bone finished a final check of his gear. In the group of stocky men with bulging muscles, Bone's leaner frame looked out of place. If the rest of the guys were pit bulls —like Tank—and mastiffs, he was a Doberman.

Back in the real world—civilization—Bone's above-average musculature would stand out. But he could also pass as an average twenty-eight-year-old: messy brown hair short enough to be low-maintenance, thick beard just like all the other guys, long, narrow face, and gray eyes.

Physically fit, but normal looking. An ordinary guy compared to the rest of the team and their hulking frames.

Bossman signaled the pilots of the helo, who started the engines—a familiar, comforting sound in the cold night air.

"All right, time to do it again," Bossman called over the noise.

They mounted up. Bone followed Tank into the chopper with Baldy right behind him.

They'd done so many missions—sometimes two or three a night—for months. They were at the top of their game, lightyears beyond the enemy in training, tactics, and equipment.

Bone settled into his spot near the door of the helicopter, feeling calm and relaxed. With his M4, night vision goggles, plenty of ammo, and his brothers surrounding him, it was just another night at the office.

An easy gig. They'd go in, kill the bad guys, and get home in time for breakfast.

Ninety minutes later, they were in the fight of their lives.

2

THE BATTLE

Afghanistan

Seven Years Ago

Bullets zipped past Bone's head as he lay in the desert sand, partly shielded by small rocks. He returned fire. The hill to the sorth of the village swarmed with armed men shooting at them. Some pressed close to the dirt. Others charged forward, firing while running.

Bone killed two with quick shots to their bodies before ducking behind cover.

Baldy sprawled on the ground several feet to his right, not moving.

Closer, behind other small rocks, Tank grunted in surprise and stopped firing.

"You okay?" Bone yelled as he shot another tango on the hill.

"Not good," Tank replied. "Took one to the arm."

As Bone switched magazines, Tank rolled over. He pulled out a tourniquet and wrapped it around his arm above the lower half that dangled, partly torn off.

"There's a damn good sniper out there," Tank said through the pain of applying the tourniquet.

Bone helped him tighten it. "You're going to be fine," Bone told him while the other SEALSs returned fire. "Hang in there, okay?"

Bone snagged Tank's extra ammo, returned to his position, and shot another tango. He was pinned down but still in the fight.

One by one, the other SEALs stopped firing until Bone was the last one putting rounds downrange.

Things weren't looking good.

Bodies of the enemy littered the hillside in the distance. Several more lay at the edge of the nearby road where they had played hero, storming the SEALs' position only to end up dead.

"Tank?" Bone called. "How ya doing?"

A quick glance showed Tank slumped in the dirt, chin to chest.

"It's been real, Bone," Tank forced out over the noise of the battle. Only his mouth moved. "See you on the other side."

Bone made the last magazine count, killing several more of the enemy while avoiding accurate sniper fire by rolling left and right to change shooting positions, staying behind the small rocks he'd initially used as cover.

When the last mag ran dry, he rolled to check on Tank.

He wasn't moving. The tourniquet was wrapped tight, but there was so much blood…

3

THE AFTERMATH

71 Ocotillo Street

Sands, Arizona

Present Day

As always after waking from the dream, sleep wouldn't come.

It was time to hit the desert trails. The morning runs and the nightly drinking kept him sane enough for his job as a special education teacher at the local elementary school.

Though he wasn't sure living with the ever-present nightmares could technically be called "sane."

Maybe "somewhat functional" would be a better term.

He made a difference at the school, survived the nights, and refused to feel sorry for himself. He had more of a life than—

Thomas made a conscious effort not to think about the many brothers who hadn't made it out of the Sandbox alive.

He'd go for a long run and spend the day at school, followed by the night at the bar.

Just another day in paradise.

Thomas pushed himself out of bed and put one foot in front of the other, repeating a quote from his time as a SEAL.

"You don't have to like it, you just have to do it."
The rough part—the night, the dream—was over.
Things couldn't get any worse.
It had to be downhill from here.

4

THE GAME

Yucca Elementary School
Sands, Arizona

It was as hot as usual in the late spring of the high desert.

Thomas felt better after his morning run. On the trails, working his body through miles of sandy twists and turns, ups and downs, he detoxed his system. The pent-up trauma his mind tried to work through in his dreams faded in the sunshine.

Showered, beard trimmed, semi-sincere smile plastered on his face, he looked presentable in khaki chinos and a light-blue button-down shirt.

He was ready for the best part of his life.

A few hours later, Thomas surveyed the day's battlefield: Yucca Elementary's playground at recess.

Chaos reigned. The warring factions ignored the heat as they struggled against each other. Screams of victory—and defeat—filled the air.

He shifted his body to catch the eye of one of the combatants and gave him a stern glare. The enemy held the gaze momentarily in defiance before frowning and offering a small, reluctant nod.

On the battlefield, Thomas' buddy Simon stood with his head down, staring at a spot in front of his feet. His body danced with nervous energy as he awaited the enemy's next move.

The playground was fraught with danger for Simon, one of Bone's young students with special needs. Most of the kids understood Simon's situation and were cool, but a few jerks would have gladly tormented him, were it not for Thomas' diligent watch.

The pitcher of the kickball team called out. "Ready? Let's do this!" He rolled the red rubber playground ball toward Simon, who stood at home plate. It came much slower and more gently than any other "pitches" thus far in the kickball game.

With great concentration, Simon kicked, making contact with the ball—a minor miracle. He usually missed.

The ball sailed nearly straight up.

"Run, Simon!" Thomas yelled, unable to contain his excitement.

Simon looked back at Thomas, confused for an agonizing moment before he remembered the next step in the process. He shambled toward first base at a pace that counted as running for him.

"I got it!" yelled the pitcher Thomas had made eye contact with. He raced forward, hands out, face tilted up, locked onto the ball.

Please... Thomas thought.

The ball slipped through the kid's arms on purpose, but he did a decent job of faking it. He grabbed the ball, fumbled it again, and threw it to first base only after Simon had made it safely there.

"Nice job!" Thomas called, aiming the remark at Simon. The pitcher would understand Thomas meant it for him too.

Simon's huge grin lit up his face.

The rest of the fielding team took their cue from the pitcher's actions and Thomas' presence. The kids put Thomas on a pedestal, probably due to whatever stories their parents told them about Thomas fighting in the war as a SEAL. His missions were all classified, and he never mentioned his years in the Teams. For all anyone knew, he could have spent his entire military career in Coronado, California as a SEAL instructor, as he had for the last year of his service, not in the thick of the action as he'd spent the majority of his years.

Simon eventually made it around the bases and safely home to the cheers and congratulations of his teammates—but no high-fives. Everyone knew Simon hated physical contact with people.

A few minutes later, the bell rang. Recess was over.

Simon rushed over to Thomas. "I won the game, Mr. Marks!"

Thomas bit his lip hard, fighting back tears. The kid rarely showed much emotion besides confusion and uncertainty. That short sentence was the most he'd ever spoken at once.

He had made a ton of progress this year—and at least some of it was because of Thomas.

"I saw—you did great, buddy!"

Simon didn't say anything more. His demeanor abruptly returned to the usual—head down, eyes fixed on his feet, lost somewhere inside himself.

But as they walked toward the school building, Simon reached over and slid his hand into Thomas', holding on tightly.

5

THE AMBUSH

Southeastern Yemen

Hani didn't question who had provided the surface-to-air missiles. Miracles happened.

He didn't wonder how anyone knew when the big helicopter, filled with American special forces, would appear over the mountains to their east. Allowing timely, actionable intelligence to "accidentally" slip into an enemy's hands to stage an ambush was a proven tactic if not overused.

He and his brothers merely accepted the blessings and prepared for the mission. They followed orders.

Hani and another true believer—Imad—lay on a mountain ridge. They had been provided a large silver blanket and ordered to keep themselves—and the missile—covered until the last minute.

The two of them had only a vague understanding of America's ability to see their bodies in the dark but didn't question the directive. They were at the end of a long chain of command. Their job was to shoot the first helicopter and escape to Al-Mukalla—the nearest small city—where they would hide amongst their people.

They rested on the rocky ground, covered by the thin silver blanket, the missile launcher between them, and waited. This was the third night they had made the trek from Al-Mukalla in the old white pickup belonging to their militant organization, hauled the rocket launcher up the mountain's switchback trails, and prepared for the Americans.

Perhaps tonight the Americans would finally take the bait and fly into the ambush.

A faint *thump thump thump* echoed through the valley. A helicopter was coming.

"I am starting the camera," Hani said. "No speaking from now on," he reminded Imad.

Under the cover of the noisy silver blanket, Hani fumbled for the proper buttons and selected the large cell phone's camera feature. A moment later, a green light appeared on a square orange device the phone was connected to that would send what the phone saw to… somewhere. It was the most high-tech device he'd ever seen, aside from the missile. As far as he was concerned, they both were gifts from the heavens.

Through the tented opening of the blanket, he pointed the phone up the valley, where the helicopter should appear, doing his best to keep the viewfinder properly aimed with his shaking hands.

Imad prepared the missile exactly as practiced over and over in the security of the small safe house in Al-Mukalla. His hands moved with ease and he was ready in seconds.

The helicopter came up the valley, heard more than seen, though its dark solidness could be made out by looking closely.

Hani checked the cell phone's screen. It showed only the blackness of the valley but was transmitting—"streaming," his trainer had called it. All was ready.

The helicopter was close. He lightly tapped Imad on the shoulder and flung off the silver blanket.

Imad fired the missile.

With an explosive *whoosh,* it streaked into the night.

The Americans never had a chance.

One second, they were flying toward a mission to kill or capture several Al Qaeda leaders supposedly meeting in a nearby valley.

The next, the missile slammed home, blowing up the helicopter.

Small bits of wreckage rained down on the valley below.

Hani and Imad shared proud smiles in the glow of the phone's screen as it streamed the video of the burning helicopter pieces on the ground.

They had killed Americans.

Hani kept the phone pointed at the destruction for another minute before he turned off the camera and gathered up the small brick that sent the signal into the air.

It was time to make their escape. They would drive the truck to Al-Mukalla, lose themselves in the narrow streets of the historic Old Town, shelter in one of its many mud-brick buildings, and enjoy the feast promised to them upon successful completion of the mission.

The hike down the narrow game trail was easier and faster without the missile launcher.

The truck—and soon the feast—awaited them.

Their job was done.

The other team's was just beginning.

6

THE TOC

Commander Jerek kept his eyes glued to the radar as a specialist spoke urgently into the radio.

"Shadow 2-1, come in. Shadow 2-1, how copy?" she repeated.

Jerek didn't have a headset on, but the specialist's hunched shoulders and repeated calls told him the story. There was no reply.

"Sir, we've lost contact with Shadow 2-1," she said several seconds later from her workstation.

Jerek had an instant gut feeling but didn't want to believe it. "What happened?"

"A short broadcast, sir. All the pilot said was, "Missile!""

"Do we have them on radar?" he asked. He didn't see anything, but hoped…

"No sir," another specialist said. "They were here." He pointed to his screen. "They passed point 'Denver' about sixty seconds before dropping off."

"Scramble the QRF," Jerek ordered, calling for the backup

helicopter standing by as a quick reaction force. "And send two gunships as an escort. What else do we have to give us a picture of the crash site?"

Everyone in the command center knew the chopper hadn't crashed, but no one would say that. They held out hope that the eight SEALs and two pilots might be alive.

"We have a drone that can be there before the QRF, sir."

"Vector in the drone. Get me a live feed. Let's find any tangos in the area so no one shoots down the next group."

7

THE DRONE

"Sir, the drone is arriving on station," a specialist called.

"Put it on the big screen," Jerek ordered.

Before he finished the sentence, the visual popped up on the huge high-definition screen of the TOC.

The view switched to shades of gray—infrared—without him giving the order.

Several small, bright blobs appeared in the middle of the valley.

"Signs of possible wreckage sir," a specialist said in a hushed voice, failing to hide the distress in her tone. "Very small pieces, consistent with a missile impact on a helicopter."

From the shapes and heat signatures, the blobs weren't people. Just small chunks of a twenty-million-dollar helicopter. Its priceless cargo —America's warriors—had likely been instantly killed when the missile hit. Unlike the pilots, the fighters in back probably hadn't even realized the danger.

"We'll search for possible survivors in a moment," Jerek said.

"Give me a full circuit of the valley, focusing on the ridgelines. Look for heat signatures. Let's find who did this and see if they're prepping for another shot."

The view on the screen changed as the drone banked.

A specialist spoke up. "Sir, what looks like two foot mobiles are fleeing the area on the downslope of the mountain on the north side. Permission to vector the drone five degrees off course to confirm?"

"Granted."

A minute later, the screen showed two white blobs moving slowly across the base of one of the valley's mountains.

"The drone pilot is requesting permission to fire on them, sir."

"Denied. For all we know, it's two goat herders running from the explosion or a couple of lovers running back to town after their night got interrupted."

No one believed that for a second, but the rules of engagement were clear. They couldn't just blow people up because they were in the area of an attack.

"Mark their position and direction. Vector one of the attack choppers to them," Jerek continued.

"Copy that, sir."

"Three minutes until the QRF arrives in the valley, sir."

"Tell them we haven't seen any other threats, but warn them about the two foot mobiles fleeing the area. There might be more teams with missiles. Tell them to be careful."

8

PATIENCE

The waiting was the hardest part. Having the opportunity to strike at America made Ghassan want to jump up and down with joy, not lie motionless on the ground holding a surface-to-air missile launcher.

Next to him under the large silver blanket, his cousin and fellow fighter held a cell phone connected to a small orange device that, he'd been told, could send whatever the phone's camera saw straight to someone else half a world away, moment by moment. He marveled at the technology.

Another large American helicopter was right there, circling the burning wreckage of the first, directly across the valley from them. Its powerful engines drowned out the faint buzz of the drone that had flown over them minutes ago. They'd been told to expect it but not to worry—if they were detected, they'd never feel the missile that killed them.

A small helicopter escorted the larger one, and a second had flown over the mountain to the north, hunting the other team.

Ghassan had wanted to shoot that one down, but it was more maneuverable and had better defenses. The high-tech missile could probably still destroy it, but saving his brothers wasn't the priority. Killing Americans was.

Besides, his life and those of his countrymen were cheap.

The lives of Americans—and their expensive helicopters—were worth far more.

And the larger helicopter would have fighters inside, unlike the smaller attack aircraft.

While his cousin used the phone to send the video around the world, Ghassan waited, ready to fire, looking for the perfect moment as the helicopter banked to the north, away from his position.

With barely a thought, he fired, destroying part of the silver blanket and blowing back its remains, exposing them to the night sky.

The missile streaked toward the helicopter.

In seconds, it closed the distance.

The pilots likely never saw it coming.

The helicopter exploded into a huge orange fireball.

It was the most beautiful thing Ghassan had ever seen.

His eyes weren't adjusted to the darkness again after staring at the explosion, but he heard the change in the engine of the second attack helicopter.

It was coming toward them.

Tactical Operations Center
USS Ramage
The Gulf of Aden

The white bloom of the explosion overloaded the drone's IR camera, blanketing the screen in white.

"Damn it!" Jerek yelled before getting himself under control. They'd lost another bird—and more men. "Did Killer-2 see where the missile came from?"

Only a few seconds passed before he received the reply from the attack helicopter.

"Yes, sir. Somewhere near the south side of the valley, on a ridge."

The drone operator, on an air base outside Las Vegas, had already banked the drone.

"There!" the specialist said.

Two white blobs lay in a narrow gap on the mountain's ridgeline.

"Tell Killer-2 to take them out," Jarek said. "Weapons free."

The energy of the room changed. They were all still shocked and angry, but at least they were killing one group of men responsible for the deaths of Americans.

Vengeance wouldn't bring back the warriors or pilots, but it would feel damn good.

Southeastern Yemen

The remains of the silver blanket fluttered down the back slope of the mountain.

The Americans had incredible technology that seemed like the power of the heavens, but could they truly see two human-size specs in a narrow gap on the ridgeline of a mountain range? It didn't seem possible.

Yet the helicopter gunship came straight toward them like a beast that could smell its next meal.

Bright orange tracers lit up the night.

The line of death marched toward them.

Ghassan didn't panic. He had accomplished his mission. Paradise awaited.

Tactical Operations Center
USS Ramage
The Gulf of Aden

"Targets destroyed, sir," a specialist announced in a steady voice, without remorse.

"Spin up another QRF," Jarek ordered. "Get me more attack choppers and another drone. I want the two foot mobiles in custody—not shot. We're going to flood the area with forces, secure the crash sites, and recover our people. Get a move on."

He picked up a handset and prepared to report to his superiors, who were undoubtedly already aware of the situation. They would have questions, as would the president, and would make every resource available to find out what the hell had happened tonight—and punish those responsible.

9

THE PRINCIPAL'S OFFICE

Yucca Elementary School
Sands, Arizona

Being called to the principal's office at the end of the day made Thomas feel like a kid again—and not in a good way.

Today he had no reason to worry but still felt uneasy. The principal might want to talk about his drinking.

Thomas never drove home drunk. Not even close. If he had more than one beer, he left his car in the bar's back parking lot and walked home. No way was he risking his job, his life—and someone else's—by believing he could safely drive under the influence. The next morning, he would end his run at the bar to drive home before showering and getting to work.

But he was at the bar a lot. Probably more than he should be. Maybe word had gotten around. It was a small town.

The drinking didn't impact his job, though. By the time he got back from his daily run, he was always sober and good to go.

Thomas pulled open the glass door to the school office. At this time of day, after the last class, only the principal's assistant—a pleasant, talkative woman about his age—was still at work.

He stopped at the worn Formica counter where decades of kids and parents had stood, substitute teachers signed in, and parents signed their kids out for doctor's appointments.

"She's finishing up a call," the principal's assistant—Lauren—said. Her normally friendly voice was cold. Thomas had known her casually for the four years he'd worked at the school; they were colleagues.

She refused to meet his eyes.

Something was definitely up.

He was careful never to drink excessively on a school night. Well, maybe not never. Rarely. And he gave one hundred percent every day in the classroom.

Why was he standing outside the principal's office like a kid about to be expelled?

The light next to one of the phone lines winked off on the assistant's desk. "You can go in," Lauren said, still without looking at him.

When he entered her office, Principal Cathy Kaeler's face only confused him more.

She glared at him from behind her desk like he'd kicked her puppy. While her short gray hair was perfectly in place, her lips were pressed together in a sharp line, her brows furrowed, and her face red. As a principal and person, she was normally calm and even-keeled. Nothing got her spun up. To see her this way meant something bad had happened.

Thomas' combat senses tingled for the first time in ages. His eyes swept the entire office, focusing on the corners, looking for threats.

No one else was in the room. Everything looked normal. Outside the windows, the school buses were long gone. Only a few staff cars were in the parking lot.

There were no threats. And yet the feeling wouldn't leave him.

"Cathy? What's wrong?" Thomas moved to the guest chair but didn't sit until she gestured.

Her grim look didn't soften. "We're occasionally audited," she said, jumping right in without pleasantries. "Our employment roles are checked to make sure no one has been arrested, we haven't hired any undocumented immigrants, that sort of thing," she said, sounding like she was barely holding her anger in check.

"Okay…." He felt a bit of relief. It didn't sound like she was pissed about his nightly trips to the bar. And he'd never been in legal trouble. What could have happened?

"Maybe this is some kind of mistake," she continued, but it didn't sound like she believed it. "You're a hard worker and you're great with the kids. They love you…" She trailed off and glared at him.

Her beating around the bush was driving him nuts.

"Whatever you have to say, please just get it out," he said with a grin, trying to break the tension. "We'll deal with it."

She didn't smile.

"The employment audit came back. Everybody's exactly who they say they are with all the right documentation—except for you. I was just on the phone with them going round and round. They are adamant. 'Thomas Alan Marks,' with your Social Security number, is dead. So either there's a huge mistake—or you're not actually Thomas Marks." Her glare challenged him for an explanation that might change her mind.

"I'm dead?" Thomas asked, eyes wide as he fought back a smile. "I knew it felt harder to get out of bed this morning than usual," he joked, trying to control the dread that had sprung up inside him.

He knew exactly how this had happened.

He felt himself spiraling downward. The view of the principal's office flickered. His best buddy—Tank—lay on the floor, which was suddenly covered with sand and rocks. Thomas ducked low as bullets filled the air. He tightened the tourniquet around Tank's dangling arm.

"You're going to be fine!" Bone told him while the other SEALs returned fire. "Hang in there, okay?"

Tank's face contorted in pain and they shared a look. Though Tank said nothing and his eyes were hidden behind the night vision goggles, they'd been buds for long enough to practically read each other's minds.

They both knew Tank was dying.

10

THE RETURN

In the elementary school office, the principal was still talking. Thomas didn't hear the words, but he caught Cathy's tone: angry and frustrated.

His eyes unfocused as he drifted farther away. A heavy tiredness gripped him and he lost control of his body. His head drooped, chin falling to his chest as if he were a puppet whose strings had suddenly been cut.

Realizing that the post-traumatic stress disorder was triggering a dissociation episode didn't help him. Thomas was locked into the memory of the battlefield. Only a small percentage of his consciousness was awake and partly aware that he was sitting safely in an elementary school in Arizona.

A bullet kicked up dirt in front of him as he ducked down to reload.

"See you on the other side," Tank called in a pained voice.

By the time Bone had fired his last round from the M4 and rolled to check on Tank, there was so much blood…

"Come on, bro, you're going to be fine!" Bone yelled.

He sensed danger, pulled his sidearm, popped up, and shot two men rushing across the dirt road toward the rocks. "You have to be strong and fight, okay? Never give up, right?"

There was no reply from Tank.

"Tank? Tank! Stay with me!" Bone adjusted the tourniquet, his hands coming away thick with Tank's blood.

Bone wanted to tell him to fight, to hang on, but held back. It was too late.

"See you on the other side, brother," Bone said, but Tank was already gone.

"Thomas! Thomas!" Bone heard faintly in the background. The sounds of the battlefield mostly drowned out the voice. There weren't many remaining fighters, but they were pouring it on—probably covering fire as a few more advanced. Bone was out of his ammo and Tank's. He'd risk rolling to Baldy's body, but there wouldn't be much cover. This was the end.

"Tell me how many blue items you can see in this room," a female voice commanded from a distance. "Tell me!"

There was no blue in the desert night. Only hot-white tracer fire. The world painted green through night vision goggles, and Tank's blood black in the NVGs as it saturated the ground.

Definitely no blue.

What made him think of blue at a time like this?

Tank's face faded for an instant, replaced by a gray-haired woman with dimples sitting behind a desk, wearing a dress with small blue flowers. Bone came back to reality.

"Your... dress... flowers..."

No—he had to work on Tank. Get on the radio and find out how long until the QRF arrived. Roll to Baldy, reload, and return fire.

The woman faded.

Bullets ricocheted off the rocks next to him. He had to get to Baldy's ammo.

"Yes, my dress," Tank said. "Well done! Tell me two more."

That wasn't right. Tank couldn't talk. He was gone. It had to be the woman he'd seen a second before.

Bone blinked. The woman was there again. A vase on her desk was a deep cobalt blue.

"The vase," he muttered, impatient to get back and help Tank.

Tank... who was dead.

Bone's attention was drawn further to the room. He was at school, not in Afghanistan.

"The file folder on your desk is blue," he added.

Thomas blinked repeatedly and took a deep, shuddering breath as he came fully back, though the feeling of Tank's blood coating his hands lingered long enough for him to unconsciously wipe them on his chinos.

Cathy looked at him with concern, at least some of her anger gone. "You okay now?"

He nodded, unable to speak for several seconds. "How did you know to do that?" he mumbled while he got himself under control.

Cathy's expression softened. She took a big breath and released it slowly, leaning back in her desk chair. "My brother is a Marine veteran. It happens sometimes, same as you, at family gatherings—especially where there are fireworks like the Fourth of July. His wife taught me how to bring him back if he gets triggered."

Thomas was too drained from the experience to be embarrassed. He felt physically, mentally, and emotionally wrecked. "Thank you," he managed to get out.

Once more, the memory threatened to overwhelm him, but he slowed his breathing and maintained his connection to reality. He wanted to make Cathy understand that this hardly ever happened. He wasn't a danger to her or the students or anyone.

"Thomas, you're a good guy," she said softly. "I don't know what's going on, but after seeing you like this"—she gestured to him as he sat slumped in the chair—"there's no question you saw combat and might actually be who you say you are. I'm reluctantly willing to give you the benefit of the doubt." Her eyes flicked toward her office door and Lauren, the talkative school secretary on the other side. "Others won't."

Lauren was the school—and town—gossip. The news would be all over by tonight.

She was probably out there right now, texting people about the man who was getting fired for impersonating a war hero.

Thomas tried to muster the energy to care about what others might think but didn't have it in him.

"My name and my buddy's were—" He started before she held up her hand and cut him off.

"I don't need the story. The only thing that matters is proof that you are who you claim to be—and that you're not dead. I'll give you the number to call and the name of the person I was talking to, or maybe you should call the Veterans Administration to get this worked out. We'll hold your job open as long as we can. I've got a few substitutes I can call. Just…" Her eyes narrowed in suspicion, the anger and doubt returning to her face.

"Am I really some jerk using a dead Navy SEAL's identity?" he asked.

Cathy nodded, her eyes hard.

He sighed and forced himself to sit straight in the chair. "I really am Thomas Alan Marks, retired Navy SEAL. I think I know how this mix-up happened and it should be pretty easy to fix. I just have to make some calls."

The principal nodded with a tilt of her head, neither agreeing with him nor arguing.

She hesitated—there was more to say.

"What else?" he asked.

What was worse than thinking you've been working with either an identity thief pretending to be a hero or a real SEAL with severe post-traumatic stress disorder?

"You're not going to get paid for the past two weeks," she said.

"That doesn't make any sense! If I died in a car accident last night, my heirs would still get my final paycheck, right?"

"Yes. The problem is, according to the audit you've been dead for years. Which indicates fraud. Payroll will run but the district will hold the money until they investigate further."

He remembered Tank's face from an earlier time, long before the ambush and the blood. Tank had a twinkle in his eyes. He had a boyish charm, easy smile, muscular body, light hair, and a handsome face that the ladies loved. He was going to get rich someday and never have to worry about money again.

Bone had come home from Afghanistan.

Tank hadn't.

Thomas pushed the image aside and focused on the current problem.

Somebody had messed up the files.

Bone was Thomas Alan Marks.

Tank had been Mark Alan Thomas.

The names were different enough. But they'd dealt with confusion several times before when their names were input incorrectly into computers. Some clerk in a hurry would see the two names, figure someone else had messed up, and enter one or the other in the database or report—not both.

It was annoying, but a few calls from the CO always straightened it out.

In social situations, if people noticed the similarity between their names, the two of them had a little comedy routine worked out. "We're brothers from different mothers," one would start.

"Who weren't very creative!" the other would add.

"Your mother just stole the name from mine and switched it around," the first would tease.

They had a lot of fun with it.

Because of the similarities, everyone on the Teams exclusively used their call signs. Thomas Marks was T-Bone—usually just Bone for short—and Mark Thomas was always Tank.

"Thomas?" the principal asked, bringing him back to the present yet again.

"Yeah, sorry," Thomas said with a half-smile. "I'm fine. I'll get my personal items and clear out right away. Don't worry, I should have this fixed in a day or two. By Monday, for sure."

Passing through the office, he was ready to quickly explain the problem to the town gossip before she spread around that he was a fraud.

As he stopped by her desk, though, she gave him a livid glare—and literally turned her back on him.

It was too late for damage control.

He walked out.

Action was better than words, anyway. He'd clear it up quickly. By tomorrow afternoon, she'd have a story to tell about how a government clerical error nearly ruined his life.

Thomas went to the classroom to gather up his personal items, planning out the operation. He'd get to his car and start making calls. Explain the problem. Get it fixed.

How hard could it be?

11

THE NEWS

Sands, Arizona

Before Thomas could leave the school's faculty parking lot, the news on the car radio made him put the hatchback in Park so he could focus on the report.

"We have received information that there have been multiple attacks on helicopters in Yemen. While neither the Pentagon nor the White House has released statements, video footage of the destruction has appeared online. Experts have confirmed that the footage appears to be authentic and shows—from two different cameras—missiles being fired at two Blackhawk helicopters commonly used by the United States and its allies. The helicopters would each normally have two pilots and up to twelve soldiers.

At this time, we have not confirmed they are American helicopters, nor that there have been any American casualties. However, the information supplied with the videos claims that more than twenty Americans have been killed, and the videos have been geo-located to Yemen. We're working on confirming the details. At this time, we're joined by…"

Rage filled Thomas at the thought of Americans being killed.

If the report was correct, the men in the choppers had probably been SEALs.

His brothers.

If he were still a SEAL...

He wanted to make calls and finagle a way to get back in uniform. Screw calling the VA to straighten out the stupid mix-up with his and Tank's names. Someone at the Pentagon had to be planning more ops in Yemen against whoever was behind this.

Bone wanted in.

The idea was ludicrous—he'd left that life behind five years before. It had been almost that long since he'd fired one of the weapons in his gun safe, though he maintained them regularly.

At this point, he was on the outside looking in.

Would a private military contractor take him on?

That option merited looking into, but in his heart he knew he was too long away from the fight—and too damaged—to get back to it and make a difference.

He turned the volume down on the radio as the horrible news continued, put the car in gear, and drove to the bar, the phone call to the Veteran Administration offices forgotten. His misfortune paled in comparison to the loss of the lives of America's warriors.

He thought of Tank, Baldy, Bossman, Sneaky, Biscuit, Iron, and Dizzy.

Of the desert ambush seven years before.

And the men on the helicopters in Yemen, their lives gone in an instant.

12

THE VIDEOS

33 Gold Road
La Jolla, California

The last kernels sputtered in the large glass-enclosed popcorn machine on the wheeled cart at the back of the home theater room.

Prince Rafiq Al-Najjar used the stainless-steel scoop to shovel popcorn into a round paper container. The butter came next, melted in the microwave in a small glass bowl by whichever one of his bodyguard-servants had started the popcorn for him.

Finally, plenty of salt.

A soda from the full-sized refrigerator gave him everything he needed to watch the premier.

Rafiq loved movies. Happy or sad, short or long. Thrillers, action movies, horror, comedy, it didn't matter. He'd fallen in love with the cinema at an early age, and it had become his passion.

But he hated watching them with others, especially Americans. The whispers—or, worse, full-voice commentary—enraged him. On occasion, he'd share the home theater with Khalid, Nasir, or Basoul, the three bodyguards who had been with him longest. They knew to sit silently, barely moving, and enjoy the movies.

Usually, he watched alone.

Especially the movies he financed—or the special ones he secretly funded.

Like today's.

He sat in one of the comfortable leather recliners in the first of three rows. He wanted to be as close to the 170-inch projection screen —as close to the action—as possible.

The popcorn went into the oversized cup holder on the left; the soda on the right.

Rafiq took a handful of popcorn, savoring the buildup. The anticipation was the second-best part.

With a tablet computer from the seat next to him, he selected a series of options. First, the lights faded off. Next, the projector turned on, quickly brightening. Finally, he pressed the button to start the first video.

Sitting close to the screen, Rafiq felt like he was lying on the ground of a high mountain pass overlooking a dark valley.

The room's surround-sound speaker system, which brought the *thump thump thump* of a helicopter, helped the illusion of being on the mission.

Unconsciously, Rafiq took another handful of popcorn, engrossed in the recording.

The crinkle of a metallic blanket competed with the rapid breathing of two men.

Rafiq imagined he could hear their hearts pounding.

The camera shook in the holder's hands as a dark shape appeared in the distance—the helicopter.

After a few moments, the blanket rustled, followed by the *whoosh* of a missile being fired and the bright flame of its propulsion.

Rafiq's hand stopped halfway to his mouth. A few pieces of popcorn fell on the chair and bounced to the floor.

The roar of the helicopter's explosion made the room shake. The video went white, the smartphone's sensor overloaded with the brightness of the destruction before getting back on track quickly enough to capture the fiery rain of pieces falling from the sky.

Rafiq shoved the popcorn into his mouth, grinning as he chewed.

Of all the movies he'd seen lately, this was by far his favorite.

A few minutes later, when it ended, he stood and applauded.

The men who had made the video were either dead or in hiding. They would never know how much Rafiq valued their efforts, but he had to show his appreciation anyway.

He sat and enjoyed a long, cold sip of soda. He'd watch this video once more—or maybe twice—savoring it, before turning to the next.

The mission had been a huge success—an excellent return on investment. Killing twenty Americans and destroying two helicopters had cost him relatively little. Had he not been rich, he still wouldn't have thought twice about the cost. There were plenty of people in the world with a hatred for America, a desperate need for a small amount of money, or both. Khalid, Rafiq's right-hand man and long-time bodyguard, dealt with the shell companies, cutouts, numbered bank accounts, and all the rest of the details that made the operations work.

Rafiq merely had to decide who he wanted dead...

And enjoy the streamed videos that came soon afterward.

It was enough—for now. But soon he'd be able to watch in person.

The thought sent a thrill through his body.

Khalid would attempt to talk him out of it, of course.

He would cross that bridge when he came to it. Khalid was getting older. Perhaps it was time for Basoul or one of the younger bodyguards to step up to a new position.

In the meantime, there was this video to watch again, plus the next.

And later, one last night with the prize in the playroom.

Life was good.

Rafiq pressed a button on the tablet. The video started again, transporting him to the mountain in Yemen.

He grabbed another handful of the buttery popcorn and ate, his eyes never leaving the movie screen.

13

THE BAR

The Bar

Sands, Arizona

Steph walked the length of the bar, checking her watch. There were men waiting impatiently on the other side of the solid steel door. Despite their desperation, she always opened the bar at 4 p.m. sharp.

They still had thirty seconds.

"We know you're in there, Steph!" one of the regulars called as he did every afternoon. He didn't mean anything by it. He also knew nothing he yelled would make a difference.

She ignored him. As an MP in the Army, she'd had plenty of experience with mouthy drunks.

When she finished her service, she had traveled for a few months, enjoying no one ordering her around. She'd met a guy in this half-sleepy, half-touristy high-desert town, fell in love and stayed.

"Come on, Steph," the same man said, more quietly, the need plain in his tone. He must have his mouth right near the door. He had gone from playfully belligerent to pleading.

"Hang in there, Henry. Almost time."

She glanced over her shoulder to take in the long, dark bar—her daily ritual.

She'd had her final drink sitting at a table near the back on the right. An Army girlfriend passing through had looked her up. The two of them got together for a glass of wine. Except that her formerly hard-drinking Army buddy had sparkling water and told Steph her story—then took her to a meeting.

Steph hadn't had a drink since.

3...2...1...

Steph clicked open the deadbolt, raised the metal bar that provided extra security, and opened the door to the bright sunlight of the hot spring day.

Henry was the first through the door, as usual. He went directly to his spot, a stool at the bar three-quarters of the way down, his long skinny legs taking huge strides across the freshly mopped floor.

Steph already had a glass of beer and a shot waiting for him. Henry wouldn't bother to sit on the stool. His hands would be shaking too much with need to pick up the shot.

He'd bend toward the whiskey—she always filled the first one to the brim, going the extra mile to make it easier for him—and slurp as much as he could. A few gulps of beer would be next—he could handle the glass, which she purposefully didn't fill to the top because he'd just spill it on her clean bar. After "taking his medicine," as he called it, he'd slide onto the stool, no longer as desperate.

Hours from now, he'd be the last to leave, never stumbling out or looking drunk—just at peace.

She greeted the other "breakfast club" regulars by name, standing at the door like a hostess at her home—which wasn't far from the truth of it.

The place had a certain run-down charm. It had a fancy name for the tourists, but the locals all called it "The Bar." There was a small menu of homemade food: meatloaf, burgers, a few sandwiches, and a daily special. The place was part dive bar and part diner; more like an English pub where the locals gathered nightly to socialize over a beer or glass of wine and have a solid, inexpensive meal.

Well-behaved children were welcome—they had their own table in the corner, the official kids' table—and were taught from the start that both they and their parents would be uninvited if they whined, acted up, or were otherwise annoying.

There were two TVs—not twenty like in the sports bars—and an honest-to-God pinball machine that still only cost a quarter per game.

The jukebox had switched to digital a few years back, but it offered decent background music without costing an arm and a leg.

Steph ran the place for her ex-husband's parents. She had needed a job after the divorce. They loved the idea of keeping Steph in the family—and blamed their son for the breakup.

He left town.

She didn't.

She was the bartender, bouncer, big sister, hostess, comedian, and —whenever possible without being too annoying— a subtle preacher, therapist, and sponsor.

It was a living, she was good at it, and she made a difference. Maybe it wasn't as important as serving her country, but with vets like her making up about a quarter of the regulars, it still felt that way.

With the breaking news of American servicemen dying in a far-off land, tonight would be busier than usual with former warriors gathering together for support, war stories, and memories.

14

THE HOME

Stepping inside the bar always brought Thomas a sense of peace. It was his home away from home.

Both TVs were tuned to the 24-hour cable news shows and muted. Closed-caption text popped on the screen. Each channel showed different talking heads and experts reporting on the attacks.

The usual assortment of drunks sat at the bar. More would fill the tables after work. He didn't count himself among them; he wasn't that bad. The bar gave him a place to socialize, eat better cooking than he could do on his own, and helped keep him sane—or as close as he could get to it.

Even in the shoulder season before the main influx of summer visitors, a sprinkling of tourists managed to venture away from the hip downtown area with its overpriced sports bars and sushi restaurants to slum it here. A few couples sat at tables along the wall, their backs to the TVs, taking in the atmosphere as they waited for their dinners.

He bet at least a few of them took pictures of the meatloaf to post on social media.

"The usual, Steph," he said, sliding heavily onto a barstool at the far end, under one of the TVs. He rubbed his beard. The days were getting hotter.

He nodded to Henry, a few seats down. Nice guy—another veteran. He would chat if you were in a talkative mood or keep to himself otherwise.

The vibe of the place was one draw. The simple, quality food another. But the main attraction brought the various pieces together into a cohesive whole: Stephanie—Steph to her friends; 5'8", pale skin, muscular arms, short, punky hair dyed bright red, or purple, or blue depending on some unknowable reasoning and schedule. The last few weeks, it had been a bright green, almost fluorescent.

She had served in the Army and took no shit.

"Thomas," Steph said, setting a glass of a draft beer on a small white bar napkin. "You see the news?" Her voice betrayed the same anger he felt—along with the usual undercurrent he convinced himself was there.

They had dated—three very fun Saturdays in a row, nothing special, just trips to the farmer's market or walking around town chatting, having coffee.

He'd started falling for her.

She hadn't fallen for him.

It was as simple as that. It ended before it started. He'd never even held her hand, let alone kissed her.

"I saw."

"Bad day."

"Terrible," he muttered, but didn't mention his own news, which meant little compared to the events of the day.

"Burger too?" she asked. The bar wasn't busy yet. Bertha, in the kitchen, was an excellent cook, but it was just her. Dinner took longer and longer as the night built.

"Yes, please," he said, his eyes on the television.

And like that, hours flew by.

At some point, he staggered to the bathroom and had the bright idea to keep going into the relative quiet of the back parking lot.

He fumbled his phone out and had just enough composure to do a search for the toll-free number for the U.S. Department of Veterans Affairs.

After navigating annoying prompts and pressing number after number, he eventually got the option to leave a message.

He let them have it.

It felt good.

As he turned to go inside, he had another great idea. It would get things moving a lot faster than the VA.

He found two phone numbers for the White House.

The guy who answered the switchboard wouldn't put him through to President Heringten, so Thomas hung up and called the number to leave a comment.

After ranting and raving until the recording timed out and hung up on him, he felt a lot better.

He pocketed the phone and staggered back into the bar.

Finally, he was drunk enough—and the news of the attack on Americans less raw after several hours—to tell whoever would listen about the massive screw-up that had gotten him fired.

The next thing he knew, Henry was by his side at the bar. Steph had announced last call fifteen minutes before.

"You can't drive," Henry said. "Give Steph your keys."

Thomas grinned at him, enjoying the irony in Henry being the voice of reason.

"Don't worry," Thomas told him. "No way I'm driving. But I'm not so bad I can't stagger home." He slipped his keys out of his pocket and slid them down the bar to Steph. "The cool air will sober me right up."

He wasn't sure the words came out exactly as he'd intended—they sounded slurred even to his ears. He might be further gone than he'd realized.

"Don't worry, Henry," Steph said as she pocketed his keys. "I'll drive him home."

Thomas grinned. That was a great idea!

Yes, he was definitely wasted if he thought anything was going to happen between them.

"We can get him home, no problem," a voice called from across the room. Youngish sounding. Cocky with a hint of menace.

Thomas glanced over his shoulder. Three guys in their mid-twenties glared at him. They were as tall as he was, lean, muscular, and tan. Ranchers or farmers, maybe, or former high school football players who had kept in shape as they grew up.

"We heard all about you, you... phony," the leader said, fishing for the word.

Thomas laughed. "Dude, stick with looking tough, okay?" His words were definitely slurred, but he pushed through. "You can pull that off. Don't talk, though. It ruins it."

"We don't have to talk," one of the others said. "Coward."

That one stung.

Thomas slipped off the barstool, stumbling as he turned to face them head-on.

All three stood from their table and stepped toward him.

"Settle down, you assholes," Steph said, her voice commanding. It made Thomas come to his senses.

"Sorry, Steph," he said, looking back across the bar at her.

With his head turned away, he sensed the guys rush him, exactly as he'd hoped they would.

15

THE FIGHT

The Bar
Sands, Arizona

Thomas moved a moment too late to avoid the solid punch to his face. His head snapped back. Without the barstool and bar to fall into, he would have been on the ground.

He was much drunker than he thought.

Drunker than he'd been in a long, long time.

And slower than he should have been.

Protecting his head with his arms left his stomach open.

At least one of the guys knew what he was doing. A fist—or maybe a foot—slammed into Thomas' stomach, doubling him over.

The next strike would be to his chin or the back of his head. The fight would be over before he could land a hit.

That was unacceptable.

The only option was to attack.

A fight was exactly what he needed tonight. Work off a little aggravation.

With a roar, Thomas slammed his body forward. Punches and kicks landed hard.

But he took two of the assholes to the ground, knocking the wind out of them and himself.

It didn't matter. Plenty of times—both when sparring and in life-and-death situations—he hadn't been able to catch a breath.

As one guy kicked at his head, Thomas caught the man's ankle and twisted savagely.

The sound of bones breaking was music to his ears, as was the scream of agony that came an instant later.

One down.

Still on the ground, Thomas slammed the faces of both gasping attackers lying near him, knocking them out.

Numbers two and three were down.

A darkness grew inside him, a rage so hot it burned.

The feelings of pain and loss, grief and bitterness, sorrow and guilt that Thomas had been holding back for the past seven years ripped through him.

He got to his feet, the rage-fueled adrenaline stripping some of the drunkenness away, or at least providing more coordination than he'd managed only seconds before.

The two knocked-out enemies could wait.

The other guy lay screaming and cursing about his broken ankle, vulnerable on the desert sand.

"Hang in there, Tank!" Bone called over his shoulder. "I've got this!"

No one attacked them and got away with it.

Bone bared his teeth. He didn't have to look to see Tank's broken, bloody body. He didn't have to ask permission to take the fight to the enemy—he was the only one still conscious. His Teammates were dead or dying—watering the dry earth with their gushing lifeblood.

Yes, the three tangos had to die, but nothing said Bone had to do it quickly. He'd start with breaking this guy's other ankle and take out the knees, followed by both hips and work his way up from there.

The tango's head would be last.

Bone wanted to hear him scream until the very end.

With any luck, at least one of the other two would have woken up by then. They would hear their buddy's cries and know they'd made a huge mistake ambushing Bone and the Team.

He was going to enjoy this.

"You deserve everything coming to you," he muttered, getting the words in Pashto mostly correct, he thought, or at least the intention.

If there were other tangos around, so be it. He'd do what he could and go out avenging his brothers.

They'd all meet in the afterlife soon.

As the enemy clawed at the sand, crawling away, Bone shifted his weight, preparing for the first stomp.

16

CEASE FIRE

The Bar

Sands, Arizona

"Cease fire!"

The sergeant's commanding voice rang in Bone's ears, easily heard over the pleas of the man crawling away in the sand.

He hesitated at the order before its ridiculousness made him look for whoever was alive after the ambush to yell at him.

A woman with short bright green hair stood about ten feet away, behind some kind of wooden barrier. Her eyes were narrow, her brows so close together they almost touched, and her jaw was set. "Two steps back—right now!" she growled.

Bone's training took over. The part of his mind used to following orders without thought made him immediately step back two paces. But he stood on the balls of his feet, leaning forward, ready to attack.

The rage fought with his drunkenness. While they battled, a tiny, rational part of his mind made him blink and look around.

The desert night slipped away.

A dim bar took its place. Tables, chairs. A couple of TVs. A long bartop with a woman standing behind it. A lone older man on a stool, sipping the last of his beer.

Bone shivered, the hair on his arms springing up at the sudden drastic change in location.

"Stand down, Bone," the sergeant ordered—Steph, he realized now.

He nodded and stepped back until he could grab the bar and hold on tight. The rage slithered back into its hole at the core of his being, leaving a trail of dark slime and the shocking realization of what truly lived inside him.

Two of the men on the bar's wood floor—not the desert sand that Thomas had clearly seen a moment before—groaned. The third whimpered, eyes closed, holding his ankle, and dragged himself another few inches toward the door.

Sirens wailed in the distance, coming closer every second. The bar was only a few blocks away from the town's only police station.

Thomas shook his head, trying to piece together what had happened, what he'd done—and what he'd wanted to.

Stephanie hopped over the bar and stood between Thomas and the three guys. "You were yelling at them," she said, more quietly now. There was an edge to her voice but with a note of concern underlying it.

"In Pashto," she added.

Thomas couldn't look at her. He glanced at Henry instead.

"Son," Henry said, gently setting his empty beer glass on the bar. "Hope you don't mind me sayin', but you got some serious issues."

Thomas nodded slowly and collapsed onto a bar stool.

"Yeah. No shit," he muttered.

17

THE APPRENTICE

Central Analysis Group (CAG) Headquarters
Arlington, Virginia

Day 1—Six Months Ago

Wyatt struggled to focus on the briefing from the young intelligence analyst training him in the ways of the Central Analysis Group.

He sat in a double-wide cubicle next to the most attractive and intelligent woman he'd ever met. She was ten years younger than him and out of his league in every area—looks, brains, and—he had to reluctantly admit—intelligence analysis.

His slim frame, the wild curly dark hair that he kept long in a fruitless effort to hide ears that stuck out too far, and pale skin from too much time inside sitting at a computer wouldn't interest her.

He didn't have a chance in hell.

"Are you with me?" Haley Albright asked him. "Are you getting what I'm telling you?"

He nodded, hoping he wasn't blushing too hard.

"I am."

He put aside his dream of them falling in love and living happily ever after to refocus on the screens. What Haley was showing him flew in the face of all his previous training and experience.

He absolutely loved it.

Her approach was right up his alley. It was what he had wanted to do at the CIA: be free to roam through any top-secret database, read all the raw intelligence reports he wanted, watch debriefing and interrogation videos from around the world. After which he could sit back and let the intel roll around inside his head until a path became clear.

He wanted to follow the trails of breadcrumbs wherever they led. Without distractions, without interference.

That isn't at all how they did things at the CIA. Everyone had their "desk"—their assigned area of expertise. Each analyst specialized in a part of the world or, in some cases, particular threats like Al Qaeda, the Taliban, or other terrorist organizations.

He was a generalist. At the CIA, he'd fit in about as well as a clown at a funeral.

His "lateral promotion" to the Central Analysis Group had been the gift of a lifetime.

Haley explained another one of her intel analysis tricks—a more formal version of one he'd gotten in trouble for using at the CIA.

It was only the first hour of his first day, but if this was how they really worked, he was in his element.

Here, his unorthodox approach was welcome.

He had found his work home.

"I get it," he told Haley. "This is exactly my style."

Wyatt wanted to share his more rudimentary approach with her but reined himself in.

Maybe it was all too good to be true. Did he dare ask whether it was?

He took the chance and leaned closer to Haley—not to get cute, but because he didn't want people on the other side of the cubicle walls to hear if he was reading the situation wrong.

"Following the intelligence trail..." Wyatt started. "Going where it takes you, no matter if it crosses the lines of continents or organizations... That's allowed? Only the results matter, no one cares how you get there?" He glanced around quickly to check if anyone could overhear them. "Or is this, you know, only how you do it and I should"—he lowered his voice to a whisper—"keep it to myself?"

A few strands of fine, long blond hair slipped from behind Haley's ear. She quickly brushed them back with a finger. Her nails were closely trimmed with no polish and her hands looked strong. Weathered.

"What matters are the results. Period," she said. She stared over his head into space, long enough for him to glance over his shoulder and check if someone was standing at the entrance to the cubicle.

Her attention snapped to him. "Though you have to be able to back up your conclusions. We don't do half-assed guesses or vague warnings. Whether your assessment relies on logical inferences or leaps of intuition, you have to be able to make your case. Then it'll be a matter of how often you're right versus how often you strike out. In baseball, you get three strikes. Here…"

"One strike and you're out?"

Haley shrugged, her eyes hard. "Ideally, we don't swing and miss. Ever. If we're not sure, or we can't back it up, we say so. We can work with other elements to gather more intel and get our questions answered. Get someone out in the field with eyes on so we can be sure —or as close to sure as possible before we make a recommendation."

Wyatt had a fine-tuned sense for BS and lies. Working at the CIA was a master class in detecting deception—whether from sources, coworkers, or management.

There was something Haley wasn't saying.

He'd barely detected the change in her voice, but the way she had mentioned working with outside elements—which he assumed meant field assets and operators—raised a red flag.

Was that something to bring up now?

At the CIA, his questions, impulsive nature, and occasional inability to read social cues got him in a lot of trouble. Landing at the Central Analysis Group was an incredibly lucky turn of events. He didn't know how it had come about and hated the idea of messing it up on day one.

Still, he had to ask. It was his nature. He couldn't help it.

"If I need clarification or have a question, what's the process for getting answers from an asset or sending an operator into the field?" Wyatt asked. "You don't have direct action elements, right? Or do we just grab weapons and slip into the field ourselves?"

He meant it as a joke.

The drop-dead stare from Haley caused him to shiver.

The woman before him had transformed from a supermodel-caliber beauty to an apex predator in an instant.

Wyatt wished he had a gun, or at least a bulletproof vest under his shirt and tie.

Before he could stop himself, his heels pushed the rolling chair away from the woman in front of him, though the close confines of the cubicle stopped him from getting far. Haley now seemed less like a young, attractive, smart intelligence analyst and more like...

The best he could come up with was a great white shark.

There had been rumors at the CIA about the Central Analysis Group. How they'd single-handedly managed to not only discover the last several terrorist plots against the United States but also stopped them using assets and operators that they—in theory—didn't have.

The consensus was that they had off-the-books help or unofficially tapped into the CIA's network of spies and paramilitary assets.

But with a leap of intuition of the kind that had so infuriated his CIA superiors, he had it.

The Central Analysis group didn't have operators—they were the operators.

Including Haley.

He stared into her cold, dead eyes, knowing without a doubt he was right.

They shared a moment before Haley's look returned to normal and her eyes softened.

"Why don't we cross that bridge if we come to it," she said in a mild tone, the deadly stare gone so easily Wyatt wondered if he'd imagined it.

18

THE FEED

Central Analysis Group (CAG) Headquarters
Arlington, Virginia

Day 8—Six Months Ago

Wyatt slid two frozen burritos from their wrappers onto a cheap white ceramic plate in the breakroom's kitchen area. Tonight both were filled with chicken, though all the varieties tasted about the same.

The microwave in the office kitchen was more powerful than the one in his tired apartment an hour's drive from the CAG HQ, but he had the timing down to a science. The wrapper said two minutes per burrito, but if he let them go that long, they'd be tough and rubbery before cooling enough to eat.

He pressed three minutes on the microwave and waited, staring through the doorway at the night-shift workers in the warren of gray cubicles of the large, impersonal main CAG room. Everyone had their heads down, eyes glued to their computers. Most wore large noise-canceling headphones or smaller earbuds, though the only noise in the office was the faint hum from the too-bright fluorescent overhead lighting and the clicks of fingers on computer keyboards.

Even after only a week at the job, he felt right at home.

The men and women at the Central Analysis Group were both nicer and more professional than Wyatt had expected. There was none of the in-fighting, lying, or jockeying for position he'd hated at the CIA. Here, people kept their focus on their screens as they looked for holes in the country's defenses and hunted for threats other agencies might have overlooked.

They protected the country, but it wasn't as exciting as he'd hoped.

The CIA hadn't been either.

Intelligence gathering and analysis sounded fun, but most of the day—or night, in his case—was spent reading reports, looking at maps, and trying to sniff out danger from too little information and too few clues.

At least here he got to follow his gut.

And no one had given him a hard time about working insane hours. Gregory, the boss—a man of about sixty who looked as fit as a forty-year-old—wore fashionable black glasses and had graying hair longer than Wyatt had expected for a career analyst turned manager. He only cared about results.

Wyatt's coworkers on the night shift never questioned why he stayed late. If they thought he made them look bad with his eighteen-hour days, they didn't show it.

It was a one-hour commute to his crappy apartment—if traffic was good. He didn't have a girlfriend or social life to speak of. No cat or dog to get home to. All he cared about—all he'd ever cared about, for the ten years he'd been in intelligence since starting at the CIA straight out of college—was protecting the country.

The microwave dinged. He already had the paper towel folded and used it to grip the edge of the hot plate. He took it to one of the small round tables in the breakroom.

The other analysts didn't like him eating the smelly burritos at his desk, so he ate them here, taking as little time as possible away from his computer.

After training with Haley, he'd been assigned the night shift. From day one, he arrived before his shift started, worked a few hours, and had two dinner burritos at 7 p.m. He stayed past the end of his shift, ate two breakfast burritos at 7 a.m., and put in a few more hours before shuffling home for what could at best be described as a long nap.

The rest of the time, he was at his desk.

Even that didn't feel like enough.

He'd done good work at the CIA, despite the bad habit of getting distracted from his assigned part of the world—the Middle East—whenever an interesting tidbit of intel intrigued him.

Since coming to the CAG, he'd gotten into the swing of things but hadn't found anything to help the country.

What he needed was a big intelligence score.

He wanted to make a difference. To use his mind, reasoning, intelligence—hell, even luck—to keep the country safe.

It wouldn't happen working forty-hour weeks. Or, well, it might, but he'd double his chances by working eighty. And if he snuck into the office on his days off, even better.

After scarfing down dinner, he washed the plate, dried it, and returned it to the stack. People at the CAG cleaned up after themselves.

Wyatt poured himself a coffee, topped off the large mug with cream and sugar until the drink was practically a liquid dessert, and returned to his cubicle. No one looked up. All the other analysts were in their own little world.

Back at his desk, he eagerly sat down to see what he'd missed.

After basic training with Haley, he had customized his intel interface. Other analysts, including Haley, set up searches based on their assignments, focus, interests, and concerns.

He'd tweaked the system until it worked like a social media news feed, showing him real-time posts. Each new entry in the many top-secret databases he had access to appeared at the top of his screen as they fed into the system, while the summary lines for the previous report marched downward.

With the flood of data from so many agencies in the USA's extensive intelligence network, the format was completely impractical...

Unless someone sat at the computer screen for hours—skimming the headlines, speedreading at a super-human level—there was simply too much to digest, and much of it would be irrelevant for any one analyst. There were reports from each of the one hundred and ninety countries where the USA had an intel presence.

Many reports were mundane. Others had sections he would need higher-level permission to fully access.

There was only one reason to have a system set up this way—to see every scrap of intel possible.

Which is exactly what Wyatt had always dreamed of.

Being away from his machine for a ten-minute dinner meant he'd missed row upon row of summaries.

And new ones appeared on the screen in a constant stream.

He quickly scrolled down, skimming the ones from ten minutes earlier. One lead line caught his eye.

Bounty Program Rumor
Near East/South Asia—HUMINT—8/9

The second line of each entry showed a string of data numbers and letters: the region, the source of data—Human Intelligence (HUMINT), Signals Intelligence (SIGINT), and Cyber Intelligence (CYBINT) were the most common—and a string of numbers. Wyatt was most interested in the first two: Threat Level and Reliability

This entry's Threat Level was a very low 8 out of 10. Along with a Reliability of 9 out of 10, the report was barely worth noting for most analysts. The data represented a tidbit to be logged and found someday if a threat warranted further examination.

Wyatt barely had the bandwidth to read the titles of each report as they appeared on his screen and quickly scrolled down, replaced by a never-ending stream of others. There was no time to click on any but the most intriguing summaries—but this one he had to read.

Something about it spoke to him.

And it was exactly the type of report that everyone else would ignore.

19

THE COINCIDENCE

Central Analysis Group (CAG) Headquarters
Arlington, Virginia

Before the report summary could tick off the bottom of his screen, Wyatt selected it with a click, nearly missing the moving target.

Istanbul, Turkey — Source 29X43RC19 reported that a drunk, mid-40s male in a bar was recently overheard quietly bragging to a second male (mid-40s) about helping to "bring death to Americans" in Afghanistan and Iraq years ago. Other snippets of conversation made it appear to the source that the man could have been a money courier both in the past and currently.

The second man became suspicious of Source 29X43RC19 and both men left the bar.

Useless, vague descriptions of the two men followed, and a final note from the case officer.

Source 29X43RC19 had no further information. No surveillance footage is available from the area to identify the two males. There is no confirmation from other sources.

Wyatt clicked on the Source Identifier (SI), which linked to an electronic file. The location was a bar frequented by mid-level criminals, from drug dealers to human traffickers. If Wyatt had to guess, he thought the source might be a server, a bartender, or a local barfly.

Another click brought Wyatt to the code name of the case officer who handled the source, with few details attached.

The high level of secrecy was enough to confirm the case officer was important and highly placed—probably in the country as a staff officer with diplomatic cover.

The idea that a courier could be moving money to terrorists to finance the killing of Americans was interesting, but the vagueness, the reported unreliability rating and lack of further confirmation doomed the report. And the Afghanistan-Iraq connection was practically ancient history at this point.

Weeks, months or years from now, if there was a terrorist attack or further intel became known, this information might be helpful to piece together a profile.

Otherwise, only analysts with extra time or a desire to make a name for themselves would follow up on a longshot like this and see what they could find.

It reeked of a local case officer with interesting but non-urgent information filing a report to cover his ass in case the impossible-to-verify intel ended up being accurate and important somewhere down the line.

The possibility that a courier got drunk and let details slip which were overheard by an asset seemed far-fetched on the surface. But thankfully, people were people. Fallible. Egotistical. Criminals made mistakes. They talked, especially when drinking. And at times, the good guys caught a break—especially if they worked hard, developed an extensive network of local sources, and followed protocol when a tip came in.

Wyatt's pulse raced. His gut rumbled from more than the cheap frozen burritos and coffee loaded with milk and sugar, his usual after-dinner drink.

If there was a hint of truth in the intel, it could be huge.

It was exactly the type of report he'd been hoping for.

A chance to look into a longshot and make a name for himself. Do some good. Save the lives of his countrymen.

And if it didn't pay off? No harm, no foul.

He clicked the back button on his system window.

His computer froze.

"No!" he said, too loudly, knowing that other analysts must have heard but not caring. He was on the hunt—he could feel it. Now was not the time for an IT issue.

ERROR #404: UNKNOWN REPORT

Strange. He'd never seen that error before.

Refreshing his screen didn't help.

Hitting the forward button to return to the source file got him the same error message.

Another click moved him forward to the case officer's information, which remained.

Odd, but Wyatt wouldn't be thwarted. A quick search and...

Nothing.

The original report had vanished.

Or it had been deleted.

He chuckled quietly. Several of his college friends had been paranoid conspiracy theorists, both on the progressive and conservative side. They'd have a field day with tonight's computer glitch, blaming it on whatever or whoever they thought was running things behind the scenes that week.

Wyatt focused on the problem, opening an error ticket with the IT people in charge of the database where he'd seen the report.

It was entirely possible the case officer had deleted the file, thinking it was too flimsy. Or he could be actively editing it—maybe that would show it as an unknown.

Following a hunch, Wyatt switched to a public search engine and looked up Istanbul.

This led him down a rabbit hole, researching the city. He switched between the public search and government databases, reading about the area's criminal elements and looking for the location of the bar from the report.

A few hours later, his senses tingled as he read a news story from the night before.

Fire Reported in Kadıköy

An entire city block burned near Bahariye Street overnight. Fire crews battled the blaze, which may have started in a local bar before spreading to the surrounding buildings. Sources report several victims may not have escaped before the fire engulfed the bar. Authorities recommend avoiding the area until the situation is resolved and the investigation is complete.

Wyatt worked his computer, wondering if the bar from the vanished intel report and the bar that had caught on fire could be the same.

He eventually sat back in his chair.

It had to be a coincidence... right?

20

THE BRIG

Present Day

Thomas hadn't been this hungover in years. Besides his pounding head, he'd have to vomit before too long. He pushed the feeling down, trying to convince his stomach to hang in there for at least a while. He didn't think he could make it to the bathroom quite yet.

His bed was surprisingly uncomfortable this morning. He lay face down, eyes tightly shut against the blazing sun. His whole body ached.

Hell, even his face hurt.

For once, though, he felt surprisingly rested. The sun through his window was bright—he had slept in. He must have forgotten to pull the shades down when he stumbled home last night.

He hadn't dreamed. There had been no nightmares.

It had been years since he'd slept an entire night without waking up screaming, back in Afghanistan.

Back in the fight.

His stomach rumbled and flip-flopped. No matter how much he told himself he could hang on, it was all coming out—soon.

Thomas swung himself up, ignoring the pain in his head. He couldn't let anything keep him from getting to the bathroom. His stomach wouldn't have it.

When he opened his eyes, though, the churning in his gut temporarily became a secondary concern.

Where the hell was he?

The small room's concrete floor and block walls were painted a hideous puke-green—which didn't help his stomach. A stainless-steel toilet bowl and a tiny sink were in the corner, only a few feet away from the bed. The metal door had no knob. Bars covered the small high window in one wall.

He must be in the brig.

His stomach couldn't wait a second longer. He rushed to the toilet and knelt.

A few minutes later, he felt better and his mind had started to clear.

He was no longer in the Navy, so he couldn't be in the brig.

Some of the previous night came back to him. He'd been at the bar and gotten into a fight.

And apparently, he'd been drunk enough to black out. That was a first—and very bad.

On the other hand, there had been no nightmares.

Which had done that—the fight or the extra booze?

He rinsed his mouth with a handful of water from the faucet, stumbled to the thin, vinyl-covered cushion on the concrete bed attached to the wall, and immediately fell into a restful sleep.

21

THE CAPTIVE

33 Gold Road
La Jolla, California

The older homeless man in the playroom hadn't been much of a challenge so far and wouldn't be tonight.

He sat slumped on the thin mattress against the far wall, head down. It looked like he had given up and surrendered to his fate.

That was no fun at all.

"Give me the key," Rafiq ordered, holding his hand out to Khalid, who stood next to him in the security room.

Screens showed the outside of the house from multiple camera angles. One showed the inside of the playroom—yet another concession forced upon him by the overly protective Khalid. The sixty-year-old bodyguard—twenty years Rafiq's senior—wore casual clothes as usual when they weren't in public: black ripstop cargo pants and a tight, black long-sleeve t-shirt that stretched over his muscles. His gray hair was cropped so short he was almost bald, so different than Rafiq's thick, wavy black hair. And while the prince sported a carefully trimmed beard, Khalid was clean-shaven, which showed off his narrow face and sharp chin.

"Sir," Khalid started.

"No arguing," Rafiq said, cutting off Khalid. "I am in no danger."

Khalid nodded once and said no more. He removed a small padlock key on a ring from his pocket and handed it over, taking his sweet time. Rafiq didn't let it bother him. His day had been exceptional so far, spent watching the videos of the helicopters blowing up and reading countless news stories, wondering which military or terrorist organization had orchestrated the ambushes.

He'd chuckled at the endless speculation. If they only knew that he lived among them for four months every year, pretending to enjoy their country.

Pretending he didn't hate them.

"You'll enjoy this one," he told Khalid and Nasir, another of his bodyguards, who was short, squat, and bald. He nodded at the screen. "Just watch."

He left the small dark room and moved across the carpeted hallway to the nondescript playroom door.

Basoul, his other long-time bodyguard, waited, door key in hand, ready to unlock it for his prince.

Khalid stood in the home's security room, unable to look away from the video monitor.

In the soundproofed playroom across the hall, the prince stood before a scruffy White homeless man. Khalid didn't know his age—they had stopped asking those details when they realized the prince didn't care—but with his long, graying, matted hair, he looked like he'd lived sixty or more very rough years.

He was hardly the prize the prince wanted but was the only person the other security team had been able to procure. There had been little to choose from last week, they reported.

The homeless man looked like he had lost all hope, but he could be faking it. The captives did that, thinking it had never been done before and would fool the prince—and his bodyguard waiting outside the door, ready to rush in at the slightest sign of a problem.

22

THE CHALLENGE

33 Gold Road
La Jolla, California

Rafiq approached the dejected homeless man carelessly, hoping the man was faking and would spring up to fight, but the captive didn't move. Rafiq quickly slipped the key into the lock at the back of the collar around the man's neck and unbuckled it.

The collar dropped to the vinyl tile floor.

The man didn't budge.

"I'm going to give you two big advantages tonight," Rafiq said as he moved out of reach. "You're unchained from the wall, and I'll fight with both hands behind my back."

From beneath a mass of white, tangled hair, the man looked up, eyes narrowed.

Rafiq made a show of putting first one hand and then the other behind his back.

When the man refused to rise, Rafiq dropped the upbeat act. "You have ten seconds to stand and fight," he said, his voice quiet, calm, and menacing. "After that, I come beat you where you sit." He barely paused before starting the count. "Ten. Nine. Eight."

The man glared at him, waiting out the count, and stood abruptly at the count of one.

"That's better. Now—fight, or die."

Rafiq hid the smile which threatened to break out. It wasn't a true either-or proposition. The man's life ended tonight whether he fought or not.

Rafiq had been looking forward to it all afternoon.

———————

Khalid tensed. There was little chance that Prince Rafiq, with all his experience fighting, could be overwhelmed by the old man in the room. But the prince took more risks than prudent. Fighting without using his hands was merely the latest example.

Nasir shook his head from the chair in front of the screens. "He's crazy," he muttered.

He muted the sound on the monitor. No noise would reach them through the soundproofed walls and doors of the playroom and security room.

Neither of them needed to hear the prince taunt the captive, talking about his mother, his country, his looks, his bravery, or his status in life —whatever it took to get him fired up enough to fight hard.

They certainly didn't need to hear what came after.

"And," Nasir added, "he's getting worse."

"Yes," Khalid said. This was not the first time they'd started this treasonous conversation. Tonight, however, Nasir wouldn't let it go.

"He wasn't so bad ten years ago," Nasir said. "Even eight. It was the ambush in Afghanistan. Allowing him to go and get a taste of killing was a mistake."

"He is the prince. I did not 'allow' him to do anything. He wanted to go, so he did. He wanted to shoot the Americans, so he did. It was not for me, for any of us, to object. Our job was to protect him, which we did."

"And now?"

Both kept their eyes on the screen, unable to look away. There was always a small chance the prince would get into a situation he couldn't handle. It would be up to Khalid to have Basoul enter and save the prince. It had only happened once before, years ago, before the prince improved his technique. Still, one never knew.

Khalid shifted his weight. His leg always ached this time of year, here in the humid air close to the ocean. He preferred the dryness of the Middle East in the winter. His leg hurt less then and the prince had fewer opportunities there for what was about to happen in the room across the hall.

"Nothing has changed," Khalid said. "He is the prince, we are the help. What are we to do?"

"Tell the king?"

Khalid grunted. This was the first time that solution had been mentioned, though surely they both had thought it. "I would be blamed —and we would all be killed. The prince would be taught a lesson and assigned bodyguards loyal to the king to keep him in check. You know this."

"You are like an uncle or older brother to him."

"Like one, yes," Khalid said. "A step above a servant, maybe, but not family."

Onscreen, the prince kept his hands behind his back and headbutted the homeless man, who staggered backward, hands cupping his broken, bloody nose.

The prince wiped a splash of blood from the scar on his left cheek before returning his hand to his back.

"You know as well as I that he is too far gone," Khalid said, voicing his true concern for the first time. "He enjoys the killing too much."

They sat with the painful truth for several seconds.

"And us?" Nasir asked after a time. "What happens when the authorities catch up to us?"

On-screen, the prince continued to "play," though the so-called fight was over. True to his word, he savagely beat the man but used only his feet and knees.

"Nothing will happen to us," Khalid said, "because we make sure not to get caught."

"And what of our souls?" Nasir whispered.

Khalid had no answer to that question.

Rafiq savored the moment.

The defeated look in the man's eyes.

The realization that tonight had been his final fight.

The fear of what came next.

"Americans," Rafiq whispered, his voice filled with venom.

The country had people who made such exceptional movies, yet most of the citizens were loathsome. Lazy, cowardly, ignorant.

Every single one deserved to die.

With a twist of his hands, Rafiq snapped the man's neck and let the body fall.

The moment gave Rafiq the exquisite rush he so desperately craved. He sighed, savoring the moment, once again relaxed and at peace...

But already looking forward to the next captive.

He wanted more.

So much more.

This one had been a pleasure at the end—they all were—but a disappointment overall. He needed a younger opponent next time. Someone with many more years to live. Who would fight harder for that time, no matter how bad the odds.

It wouldn't change the outcome but would be much more fun along the way.

PART 2

THURSDAY

THE PACKAGE

MV *Horizon Breeze*
Port of Long Beach, California

A crane moved the ocean-blue shipping container steadily from its place on the tall stack on the boat's deck to the ground storage area.

Inside, carboys—4.6 gallon, 35-pound boxed cans of olive oil—were arrayed four wide and five deep on wooden pallets.

The shrink-wrapped pallets were stacked to the ceiling, held in place with straps and load bars.

In the center of the shipping container, cleverly taking the place of several carboys across two pallets, sat a homemade wooden box, six feet long by three feet wide.

The box had no markings on the outside to identify it.

The inside was filled with straw, sawdust, and a package carefully wrapped in thick plastic.

Beneath the plastic, a Russian-made man-portable surface-to-air missile waited to be claimed.

THE REPORT

Central Analysis Group (CAG) Headquarters
Arlington, Virginia

Day 10—Five and a Half Months Ago

Wyatt was, for lack of a better word, obsessed.

His clothes were wrinkled, his face unshaven, his eyes bloodshot. He badly needed a haircut, more frequent showers, and a day off. Or several.

It wasn't a good look for the newest member of the team on a regular day, let alone when standing in his manager's office after a little over a week on the job.

Gregory hadn't invited him to sit.

"This is an interesting way to start your time here," Gregory said. He sounded more intrigued than annoyed, and not judgmental. His fashionable black-rimmed glasses made him look intelligent and oddly hip, as did the gray hair flowing to his shoulders. With his muscular physique, he seemed more like an executive of a tech company than of a little-known clandestine government spy agency.

Gregory's wooden desk was spotless. It held only a medium-sized monitor on an adjustable stand in the far right corner, a sleek white keyboard and mouse in front of it. The monitor screen was dark either because Gregory hadn't logged in yet this morning or because he'd turned off the screen to hide... something.

In addition to being obsessed, Wyatt had started to stray toward paranoia the last few days.

When Wyatt didn't respond—he hadn't been asked a question and wasn't sure what he should say, anyway—Gregory slid open the wide middle drawer of his desk and removed a file folder with the words *Top Secret* in large, bold letters on the front.

Carefully centering the folder on his desk, Gregory flipped it open. Wyatt recognized the two sheets of white paper as the report he'd sent to Gregory five days ago detailing the scent he'd caught.

Gregory placed page one on the left side of the open folder and page two on the right, nearly touching.

While Gregory skimmed the report with his head down, Wyatt made a belated attempt to clean himself up. He ran a hand through his unruly curly hair and tried to smooth the wrinkles out of his button-down dress shirt, but it was hopeless.

He guessed he'd get chewed out first. If he was lucky, he'd get a warning. If not, they'd shuffle him off to a backwater department somewhere in the bowels of Washington.

The CIA wouldn't take him. The day the Central Analysis Group requested the CIA to release Wyatt for a lateral transfer to the CAG, his manager had looked like he'd hit the jackpot.

Gregory's face revealed nothing as he looked up from the report, leaving the two pieces of paper on the desk. "This is five days old. What's new?"

Wyatt blinked repeatedly. He'd expected to be transferred, not asked for a progress report.

He pulled himself together. He was living and breathing the details of his file. If Gregory wanted an update, he'd knock his socks off.

"The bar that burned down was, in fact, where the CIA's local source worked as a server. She died."

Gregory nodded for him to continue.

Wyatt did, warming to the story. "The cause of the bar fire, officially, was faulty wiring, but there's no way. I can get into it if you want—"

Gregory gave a subtle shake of his head.

"Right. So—it was arson. There's no physical proof the people were locked in, but I suspect chains on the doors' exteriors or metal wedges holding them in place—all removed in the time between the fire raging out of control and firefighters arriving. As I mentioned in my report, there were two car crashes that night on both ends of the road where the bar was located. They were quickly cleared away but slowed the response of the rescue crews. Additionally..." Wyatt gulped, thinking about the people in the bar. "The fire victims' remains were found near the two exit doors. Including the CIA's source. As if they tried to escape but couldn't."

Gregory sat stoically, waiting for more.

"What's new," Wyatt continued, lowering his voice before realizing how stupid he must sound, "is that the case officer handling the source at the bar died walking to work the morning after the fire. Hit by a car driven by a middle-aged woman who said the man ran off the sidewalk right in front of her. Police do not suspect foul play."

Gregory's expression didn't change, but Wyatt knew he had the man now.

"The local CIA Station Chief investigated," Wyatt said. "They released their findings the day after I wrote my preliminary report to you," he said, gesturing at the papers on the desk. "They ruled it a tragic accident."

Wyatt paused, thinking Gregory would ask a question or defend the CIA, but he only sat there waiting.

"It could be a coincidence, yes," Wyatt said as if Gregory had argued with him. "Stranger things have happened. But taking into account the case agent's report—"

"Which no one besides you has any knowledge of, correct?" Gregory asked.

Wyatt wasn't an idiot. He knew exactly how the whole thing sounded, which was why he'd delayed writing a second report while he consulted with the IT professionals and frantically looked through other database entries for that timeframe, one by one, hoping to find a rewritten or mislabeled file.

"Correct. Though the computer logs show a report was entered and deleted a few minutes later," Wyatt said. "No one else that I know of read the report. My guess is the case officer deleted it because of how flimsy it sounded. Maybe he planned to gather more data before filing an in-depth report. But..." He was going out on a limb here but couldn't help himself. "Someone must have been suspicious, followed his source, and saw their meet. They couldn't kill them right then; it would be too suspicious. The case agent files the report, has second thoughts, and deletes it. Someone stages the fire to take out the source at the bar and either pushes the case officer into the road or the driver was in on it and ran him down. The tracks are covered. The server is dead, and they killed an American spy to stop the pursuit of the lead. If the report had been in the system, it still might not have gotten any attention because of its vagueness and the nature of the 'accidents.'"

Maybe he was paranoid. His desire to make a name for himself, to find a big intelligence case he could work, might have led him to misinterpret facts and twist a report into what he so hoped to find.

"And since then?" Gregory asked. "It's been days—or nights, rather. You've barely left the building." He frowned. "We have showers in the gym locker room. You're aware of this, right?"

Wyatt glanced down. "Um, actually, no. I didn't even realize we had a gym."

"Sorry about that. Get someone to show you where it is."

Wyatt stared. "I can stay?"

"I don't like coincidences," Gregory said. "What else have you found?"

"Given the reference in the report to killing Americans and the suspected connection to a money man or courier, I've been digging into the so-called 'bounty program' during the Afghanistan war."

Gregory frowned and shook his head. "Others have looked into that and concluded that the initial reports of the Russians making cash payments to the Taliban, Al Qaeda, or ordinary goat herders to kill American troops were bogus."

"Yes, sir." Wyatt hesitated. No one would want to know what he found, not years after the war in Afghanistan had ended. It was over and done. He'd learned at the CIA that sometimes it was better to let sleeping dogs lie. There seemed to be no immediate threat against the country, so Wyatt should be happy to let the past be the past.

"But?" Gregory prompted.

Wyatt gulped and locked eyes with Gregory. "They were wrong on all accounts, sir. There was definitely a bounty program… but it wasn't the Russians who were responsible."

25

THE IMPLICATION

Central Analysis Group (CAG) Headquarters
Arlington, Virginia

Day 93—Three Months Ago

Wyatt was in his element. He had Gregory's official permission to spend all his time on the Afghanistan war's bounty program.

He lived and breathed forensic accounting, shell companies, cutouts, money laundering, cash transfers, couriers, arms dealers, and black-market weapons.

Rumors, innuendoes, and vague intel reports.

Plus—all too real—the records of dead American warriors.

After-action reports from battles.

Descriptions of random, unprovoked attacks from common-seeming citizens.

Along with well-planned and executed ambushes.

Wyatt stood in front of Gregory's desk. It was a familiar routine by now. Every week, he'd be summoned. He still hadn't been invited to sit.

Wyatt was more excited than usual. He'd taken five minutes to change into a clean shirt—and add fresh deodorant—in the men's locker room of the gym. Though he left the building for only a few hours a day, he'd recently made more of an effort to present a professional look. It kept his fellow coworkers from eyeing him with a combination of concern and disapproval.

"What's new?" Gregory started, as he often did.

Wyatt took a breath and gave a quick smile. "I made a breakthrough today." Technically, it had been last night, as he was still assigned to the night shift, but it didn't matter.

He plowed on. Gregory didn't stand on social niceties like question and answer. He just wanted a report.

"I have it mapped out," Wyatt said, tilting his head in the direction of his cubicle, out the door, and down the long hallway to the open room where the analysts worked. "It's as irrefutable as intelligence gathering and analysis can be. In my opinion," he added. He was still the new guy with no track record of success here. "Mostly thanks to your... note."

A week earlier, Wyatt had hit a wall and could go no further. He'd reluctantly asked Gregory for help. He needed access to a foreign computer system for one of the final puzzle pieces, but he had no way to get in. "Maybe the NSA has access?" he asked.

The next morning, Gregory gave him a piece of paper with handwritten instructions on how to access the system. Across the bottom, Gregory had written, *Work fast. You'll have less than five minutes before you're booted off.*

Wyatt hadn't asked, nor wanted to know, how Gregory had gotten the login details. But getting inside the computer system pulled everything together and opened up a brand-new avenue of the hunt.

"I still don't have a name," Wyatt admitted sheepishly. "Or, at least, a real-world one. But combining all I know so far, it's my contention that the person ultimately responsible for the bounty program is already in our system."

Gregory didn't have many tells, but Wyatt had learned to read what little there was. Gregory leaned forward imperceptibly as he did when he was intrigued or excited.

"But I can't access his file. The classification is too high. All I see is the code name."

Wyatt blurted out the reveal instead of waiting for Gregory to ask for it. "It's 'Hollow Star.' There are a few entries about him—or her—in our databases. Small things—meeting with a few fringe characters, millions of dollars being moved around, connection to other Code Name-level individuals. If I could have access to that file…" He trailed off.

There had been a subtle change in the energy of the room.

Gregory leaned forward slowly, putting both hands on the edge of his desk like he was about to climb over it to get to him.

"What? What did I do?" Wyatt asked.

"You think Hollow Star financed the bounty program during the Afghanistan war?" Gregory asked. His voice was level, but there was both a coldness and a warning note in his tone.

Instead of scaring Wyatt, Gregory's reaction only confirmed his extensive research. "I would prefer to have access to the file to do more digging, including being able to match the target's actual name with normal, everyday activities in the real world. Travel itineraries, other financial statements, and the movement of money to see if they cross paths with the more clandestine activities I've uncovered. But otherwise, yes." He took a breath and stood tall. "It is my hypothesis that Hollow Star provided financing to kill our troops in Afghanistan and Iraq, from approximately 2016 to 2020."

Gregory stared at Wyatt. The seconds dragged on. Most humans aren't accustomed to staring at each other without speaking, but Wyatt's time at the CIA had trained him well. Every second he'd been there, for ten long years, had been uncomfortable. The Central Analysis Group was a piece of cake in comparison.

Finally, Gregory spoke in a voice so low Wyatt could barely hear it. "Are you willing to bet your career on this?"

The hair on Wyatt's arms stood on end as he shivered. His whole body tensed. What had he gotten himself into?

But he spoke without hesitation. "Yes, sir."

Gregory stared over Wyatt's shoulder, thinking—and not hiding that he was making an important decision.

"We follow the intel wherever it goes," Gregory mumbled, barely loudly enough for Wyatt to hear.

Gregory's eyes returned to Wyatt. "You have temporary clearance to view Hollow Star's file. I'll handle it in the system," Gregory said with a nod at the computer sitting dark on his desk. "Move your computer into Conference Room 4, the small one. Close the blinds, lock the door, and don't tell anyone about this. Only you and I are read into it, clear?"

"Yes, sir," Wyatt said. His excitement at the possibility of completing the hunt was tempered by the chilling realization that he'd stumbled upon something much bigger than even the bounty program.

Gregory spoke in a low voice, though Wyatt hoped there was no way anyone in the world could listen to what was said in the director of the Central Analysis Group's secure office. "Hollow Star is the code name for Rafiq Al-Najjar, a minor prince of Saudi Arabia. But he has a closer-than-average relationship with one of his distant cousins: the new ruler of Saudi Arabia.

Wyatt held perfectly still, as if not moving would erase any tracks he'd surely left behind in his search over the last three months.

"You've indirectly implicated the country of Saudi Arabia in the sanctioned, paid deaths of American servicemen and women," Gregory added as if Wyatt hadn't already put that together on his own.

26

TARGET: REDACTED

The White House Oval Office
6:01 A.M.

Two and a Half Months Ago

By prior arrangement, Gregory worked out in the basement of the White House a few days a week. The schedule had originally been set up as a way for the director of the small, specialized intelligence agency—the Central Analysis Group—to keep the commander-in-chief apprised of various unofficial actions the agency was taking on his orders.

It continued when President James Heringten seemed to enjoy having him as a pre-dawn workout buddy.

Today's intelligence, though, was too monumental for an informal discussion between weightlifting sets.

Gregory sat on a couch in the Oval Office. On another couch across from him, President Heringten sat with a mug of coffee that matched Gregory's own. When it was just close advisors in the room, there was a standing order to skip the small, fancy china cups and go with full-size mugs.

Behind and to the right of the president stood Chad David, the chief of staff.

Both men were dressed in dark suits. The president's shirt was white, as usual. Chad's was light blue. Their ties were each a mix of patriotic red, white, and blue in unmemorable patterns that didn't catch the eye or draw attention away from the men.

The similarities ended there. President Heringten had short dark hair, going gray at the temples. His muscular physique came from lifting heavy weights every week. He looked like the former Navy SEAL he was: white teeth, serious eyes that could light up with a joke or a jab to relieve tension when needed, and more stress lines around his eyes and on his face than Gregory had noticed during the president's first term.

Chad David was about ten years younger—early-fifties—with longer, brown hair, less gray, and a blocky face that reminded Gregory of an all-American football-player type. He was almost as muscular as the president, but Gregory had no idea how he found time to work out. From everything he'd heard and seen, the man barely slept, dedicating nearly twenty-four hours a day to helping the president with every important detail.

One of which was national security, the topic that brought Gregory to the White House this morning.

"It's never a good sign when you schedule an Oval Office meeting with me," the president started after a quick sip of coffee. "Especially so early in the morning. How bad is it this time?"

He meant it half as a joke, so Gregory offered a hint of a smile.

"The situation is delicate, Mr. President, but we shouldn't have to rush to the safety of the bunker for this one."

President Heringten chuckled for a second before his eyes went hard. The joking was done. He was ready to get down to business.

Gregory handed a top secret file to the president. Chad waited a second before moving closer to read over his shoulder.

They either had some kind of signal for when Chad could read along or had worked together so long that the chief of staff just knew. Chad had been James Heringten's right-hand man since they were on a SEAL Team together.

Gregory guessed he wouldn't have to wait long for their reaction—and he was right.

The president glanced up only a second after opening the folder. "The name of the target is redacted," he said, his tone curious with an undercurrent of annoyance. "I'm the president. I read the unredacted version of reports, not this."

"Yes, Mr. President," Gregory said. "If I could ask, sir, please keep reading. I'd like you to see the report free of any bias from the target's name."

Gregory had to suffer the president's scowl, but he held firm.

The president's eyes flicked back to the report in the folder. At the same moment, Chad's eyes met Gregory's. The younger man kept his face under control, but Gregory knew how he must have felt.

The report was a one-page powder keg, ready to blow.

It didn't take the president long to read it.

He slowly closed the cover of the folder, absently handed it to Chad over his shoulder, and reached for his coffee mug to take a thoughtful sip.

"I recruited a new analyst from the CIA," Gregory began. "A ten-year veteran who didn't fit in over there. Every quiet complaint I heard about him made me think he'd be perfect at the CAG, so I got him. He's spent the last three months working non-stop—almost literally—on this. He's like a dog with a bone; he doesn't let up." Gregory gestured to the report in Chad's hand. "That's as close to gospel as I've seen in my years in the business. The CIA, us... every agency has made mistakes over the years. But this, Mr. President, is unfortunately very solid."

The president stared at him as he placed the coffee cup slowly back on the table.

Gregory spoke softly as if his voice could lessen the impact of the intel. "We have strong indications that, over many years, the redacted target paid bounties to several different groups and individuals in Iraq and Afghanistan to target and kill Americans."

"These indications..." the president said.

"Are compelling but not admissible in a court of law. Some,"

Gregory said with a note of contrition, "were obtained via a…
whistleblower."

"By whistleblower, do you mean a hacker who illegally accessed
computer systems?" Chad David asked.

Keeping his face still, Gregory ignored the question. He wouldn't
answer unless the president asked himself. They both were aware of a
hacker Gregory had access to, but the less said about his involvement,
the better.

"We have no knowledge of the so-called bounty program still being
active, Mr. President. But a person like that, dedicating so much time
and resources to killing Americans…"

"Wouldn't be likely to walk away as the war wound down," the
president said, finishing the thought.

Gregory nodded. It was why he'd given Wyatt so much leeway to
pursue the lead.

"To be clear, we have no intel that the individual has continued to
target our people—service members or civilians," Gregory added. "But
you had to know about this, despite it being several years in the past."

"America doesn't forget," the president said, his voice cold and
hard.

"Exactly, Mr. President."

President Heringten reached back. Chad handed him the folder as if
he knew the move had been coming.

The president opened it again. His eyes flicked to the top of
Wyatt's report, where it had a large black block printed over the
target's name.

"Who is it?" President Heringten asked.

"Prince Rafiq Al-Najjar, a minor prince of Saudi Arabia and distant
cousin of the new king."

For a moment, no one moved.

After a few seconds, the president slowly closed the file and once
again handed it over his shoulder. He reached for his coffee cup, which
he'd left on a coaster atop the antique coffee table between the two
couches, and sipped thoughtfully from his mug.

"There's no indication that the new king—or his father, the former
king—was aware of the bounty program?"

"None that we have found, Mr. President. Yet," Gregory added, under his breath but loudly enough for both men across from him to hear.

"So he could have been acting alone, without the knowledge of the Saudi monarchy," the president added, ignoring the last part of Gregory's answer.

"That is one of the possibilities, sir." The other possibilities were more harrowing to consider.

"And you said there's no intelligence that suggests the prince is still engaged in the same behavior—paying others to target American troops or citizens?"

"That's correct. Not that we have found, Mr. President."

After a few seconds of mulling it over, the president spoke again. "Where is Prince Rafiq Al-Najjar these days?" he asked, going exactly where Gregory had hoped.

"He's obviously quite rich, sir, so he is all over the globe. He is currently living in his mansion in La Jolla, a part of San Diego. For the last several years, he has lived there in late spring through the summer. He is a big movie buff and uses the San Diego home as a base to travel frequently to Los Angeles for movie premieres. He finances movies—it's one of his passions."

"How much contact does he have with his cousin the king?"

"Limited, sir. They run into each other at the odd sporting event—they are both big soccer fans. It does not appear that they are particularly close as family or have much interaction with each other. However, if there was a person the Saudi family wanted to use as a front, for a bounty program, Prince Rafiq Al-Najjar would make an excellent, deniable cutout."

The president nodded, his face blank, before glancing back at Chad, who leaned forward and whispered in his ear.

President Heringten listened to his advisor's words without comment, took two more slow sips of his coffee, and finally looked at Gregory.

"Thank you for bringing this to my attention. Excellent work. If I need further assistance from you or your agency on this, I'll let you know."

Gregory nodded and stood, leaving his mug of coffee untouched.

"Thank you, Mr. President." He nodded to Chad and left the two men alone to, undoubtedly, discuss what moves to take—if any.

While the United States had a strict policy against assassinations, the War on Terror gave wide latitude to a commander in chief.

Gregory could only guess where President Heringten would go with the information he'd received, but he had his preference...

Which was why the only printed copy of the top secret report had every reference to the name of the individual responsible for the bounty program blacked out—and the report's heading was simple:

Target: REDACTED.

27

THE IDEA

Present Day

Haley Albright, intelligence analyst, sat in a small cubicle at the far end of the cube farm that made up the bullpen—the warren of desks where a few dozen very smart people sat in shifts, working to keep America safe.

At twenty-two years old, Haley was the youngest member of the team but had already proven an insightful analyst who used her intuition and unorthodox methods to piece together puzzles no one else could.

As a reward for her diligence and uncanny ability to discover danger before others, her boss had directed all unusual intelligence activity to her desk. If a rumor struck an analyst at the CIA or another agency as weird, she got flagged. If a report didn't fit the normal expectation or conventional wisdom, an alert flashed on her screen. All the outliers and bizarre incidents were funneled her way.

And at her direction, if a report had anything whatsoever to deal with Navy SEALs, active, retired, or deceased, it hit her inbox.

This morning, she brushed back stray blond hairs, tucking them behind her ear as she stared at her two huge computer screens, reading the minor report flagged for her.

There was no cause for alarm; no missiles were heading toward the country. No terrorists were active. But the report was interesting, anyway.

The United States Department of Veterans Affairs—the VA—had received a drunken phone message from a man claiming to be a retired Navy SEAL with enough details—and heartfelt pleading—to open a ticket and log a report for follow-up or investigation if warranted.

It took Haley thirty minutes of digging to figure out the situation, though she had access to more databases than the people who worked at the VA. Solving the problem would take them much longer because of their bureaucracy and unfortunate lack of adequate staffing due to underfunding by Congress.

Haley displayed two Navy SEAL personnel files side by side on her screen.

Thomas Alan Marks on the left.

Mark Alan Thomas on the right.

The names were different enough but easy to mistake.

Their social security numbers were similar as well.

She could guess what had happened.

A few months before, various departments in the government had begun transitioning from horribly outdated personnel management software to modern, high-powered databases. Given the similarity in the two men's names and social security numbers, either the artificial intelligence tasked with making the process supposedly smoother had messed up, or a human had seen the two entries, assumed there had been a mistake, and "fixed" it by merging the two files into one.

Given the huge undertaking of the millions of files being moved, there were bound to be problems like this.

Errors could be fixed—it would only require time, resources, and someone to take ownership of each problem.

In this case, that someone could be her. It would certainly make a world of difference to retired Navy SEAL Thomas Alan Marks, whose life had to be a mess this morning. If she didn't jump in, there was a decent chance the situation wouldn't be resolved for months.

As Haley poured over Thomas Alan Marks' file, though, she had an idea.

The new guy—Wyatt, who she had trained a few months ago—stayed late into the day shift.

And he did it locked inside Conference Room 4.

She knew exactly what that meant, having camped out in a larger conference room herself plenty of times. Wyatt, a transfer from the CIA and a quick study the few days she'd spent training him, had to be working on a top-secret assignment for their boss, Gregory.

Haley considered the angles of her idea—a solution to a long-standing problem she'd been wrestling with.

It could work. The very-much-alive Thomas Alan Marks—call sign T-Bone or just Bone—was an experienced, decorated, solid Navy SEAL. Brave. Smart.

While on active duty, he went above and beyond—even more so than other SEALs, which was saying something.

He had learned Pashto, the language of the area in Afghanistan where he'd spent much of his last deployment.

She continued reading his file, including the report of the ambush and final firefight, written by the team leader of the quick reaction force who arrived too late to save the Team.

It was a brutal story.

Haley considered the things she'd been through out in the field—and what that had done to her.

The occasional nightmare.

The hypervigilance.

It didn't make sense to compare one person's experience to another's. Yet she couldn't help but wonder about Bone's demons—and how he dealt with them.

She had access to countless databases, from highly classified to public searches, and she couldn't find any proof Bone had spoken with a professional about what he'd been through.

It meant nothing, really. Medical records were very tightly locked away. And look at her team—they got together frequently to drink beer, eat pizza, and tell stories. Catharsis through camaraderie.

There was no indication the events of that final battle negatively affected Bone. After the ambush and recovery, he'd taught at the Navy's Basic Underwater Demolition/SEAL (BUD/S) training program for a year, then returned to school after leaving the Navy. He earned a teaching certification and started work in a small-town Arizona school.

Yesterday, he'd been fired from his job because he was, according to a computer, deceased.

Haley didn't know what Wyatt and Gregory were cooking up, but they might need a dead-but-not-dead former Navy SEAL for some off-the-books fieldwork.

If they didn't, maybe she could recruit Bone for the next crisis she and her direct-action team had to face.

It could be a win-win for everyone.

She had some calls to make.

28

THE JAIL

"Wake up, sleeping beauty," a gruff male voice said.

Thomas opened his eyes slowly, his body, mind, and soul at peace. All he wanted to do was to sleep, to stay in the warm embrace of the pleasant dream he'd been having.

"Thomas! Wake up," the man's voice said. "We're not running a bed and breakfast here."

The puke-green walls reminded Thomas of his situation as he cracked his eyes open. He was in jail.

The realization propelled him up. His head still hurt, but he felt rested for the first time in years.

A stocky man in slacks, a cheap but well-fitted sport coat, a dress shirt, and a loosened unfashionably wide blue tie stood at the open door to his cell, gesturing impatiently for him to get a move on.

As Thomas stood, it all came rushing back. Losing his job over a government accounting or database error. The attack on the Americans in helicopters in Yemen. His bar fight. Getting arrested.

And having the best night of sleep in a decade.

Detective Devon, the town's only investigator, stared at him with barely hidden anger. "You want out or not?"

Sands was a small town, so Thomas knew Devon in passing—enough to nod at in the grocery store. The man didn't have any kids in school, and Thomas hadn't ever been in trouble, so they'd had no cause to speak before.

"Yes, please," Thomas said. He wondered if the look on Devon's face had to do with word getting out about Thomas supposedly impersonating a Navy SEAL, being a blackout drunk the night before, or getting into the bar fight.

Probably all three.

"Am I free to go?" Thomas asked as he walked to the door.

Devon nodded. "I reviewed the security camera footage from the bar and talked to Stephanie. Pretty clear-cut case of self-defense. The delay came from the District Attorney, who had to sign off on everything.

"Delay?"

"It's 6 p.m. You slept all damn day."

Thomas took a second to process that, then asked, "What about the three assholes who jumped me?"

Devon led the way down a wide hallway, past three other cells and into the main work area of the small police station. It didn't look that different from the school's office area, with relatively tidy desks, modern but not fancy computer workstations, budget black roller chairs, and worn vinyl flooring.

"They'll be fine. You want to press charges?" His tone made it clear it wouldn't be a good idea. He glanced back, only partly hiding the same look of disgust from a minute before. He must have heard about the name mixup and thought Thomas an identity thief at best.

Or a cowardly blowhard pretending to be a SEAL at worst.

"No. No charges. Simple mistake. They thought—"

"Save it," Devon said, interrupting him with a frown. He unlocked a drawer in one of the neater desks, took out a brown manila envelope, and handed it to Thomas. "Everything you had on you last night. Sign here for receipt." He offered Thomas a cheap pen and a piece of paper that confirmed he was getting back all his stuff.

Thomas signed without opening the envelope. He could feel his wallet, phone, and sport watch inside. He had a vague memory of giving Steph his keys right before the fight. He hadn't carried a knife or gun in years, so unless the arresting officers last night had stolen the few dollars in cash he'd had on him, there was no need to check.

"It's a good thing you didn't stomp on that guy last night or go after them when they were down," Devon said. "They were clearly out of the fight. Had you done that, this would be going differently for you."

He leaned a few inches closer to Thomas and spoke under his breath, which smelled faintly of onions. "Steph vouched for you," the detective said as if he couldn't believe anyone would stick up for him. "And your driver's license checks out in the system. According to the state of Arizona, you're Thomas Alan Marks. So I don't know what to think." He took back the pen and paper. "But if we find out you've been pretending to be a hero in our little town..." His look said it all. Thomas would be on the shit list of the police. They'd make his life a living hell until he got smart and moved away.

Thomas opened his mouth to explain, but Devon cut him off. "Not a word. No one wants to hear it. If you're who you and Stephanie claim you are, better fix it quickly. Otherwise..." Another threatening look, then a tilt of the head toward the front door of the police station. "Now get out."

Thomas nodded and glanced away, but before he turned to go, he couldn't help himself. He slowly raised his head and gave Detective Devon a look of his own. One that Thomas hoped showed the danger in his soul. The part of him he'd kept under wraps for the past many years. A spark that revealed who he really was—an ass-kicking, death-dealing, absolutely fearless, won't-stop-till-I'm-dead Navy frogman.

The two of them locked eyes. The seconds ticked by with neither of them willing to give way.

Finally, Detective Devon blinked and gave a small nod. His anger seemed to drop a notch or two, and he looked away.

Thomas stared at Devon a moment longer before turning and walking to the door, the envelope with his belongings in his hand.

Staring down the detective—and letting out the warrior within that had been held in check far too long—had felt damn good.

29

THE HOUSE

71 Ocotillo Street
Sands, Arizona

Thomas ran. His body felt good. Rested. His soul, too, despite the mess his life had suddenly become yesterday.

As his sneakers pounded the pavement of the town's back streets, leaving the police station behind, he fell into the zone. The dry, hot air felt good as the sun set, even in his button-down dress shirt and chinos —dirty and torn from fighting the night before.

He had every intention of going to the bar to get his keys and car, but he wanted to sweat the impurities from his body, and he desperately needed to brush his teeth and take a shower before spending time around other people, even the regulars at the bar.

And especially Steph.

After a few miles, Thomas turned onto his dead-end street at the edge of town. He slowed to a walk to give his muscles a chance to cool off. It felt great to have energy for a change, the product of sleeping all day.

As he neared his house, his senses tingled. A closer look showed why—his front door stood open several inches.

There were no cars on the street or in his driveway. His house stood at the end of the road. The nearest neighbor was a few hundred yards back.

For the first time in a long while, he wished he carried a pistol instead of leaving them locked in the gun safe in his bedroom closet.

His soul stirred—the part brought to life the night before during the fight.

Going inside unarmed and confronting what he guessed would be the three assholes from the bar wasn't smart. They could have brought friends—or weapons.

If his phone's battery weren't dead, the logical move would be to call the police. Or to go to the nearest neighbor and ask for backup or to use their phone and call 911.

But that's not at all what he wanted. He hadn't been trained to retreat.

He'd been trained to fight.

Thomas changed his angle of attack, moving so he wouldn't be easily seen from the front window, hoping he was still too far away for anyone inside to have noticed him in the dusk.

He had to consider whether the intruders had left the front door open by mistake or to herd him toward the back.

The door at the rear of the house opened into the small kitchen. If several people were waiting inside, the kitchen would be better for him. The tight confines would work to his advantage. Only one or two people at a time could fight, and they'd get in each other's way.

But if they meant to shoot or stab him as he came through the door...

His gut told him to go through the front.

Thomas eased up on the wooden slat front porch, carefully placing his steps to avoid the areas that would squeak. Ducking low, under the window, he approached the front door and stood listening.

Nothing.

He extended his senses, tapping into his old ability to—for lack of a better term—feel if danger was nearby.

Still nothing, but that might be because of how rusty he was and how uncomfortable it felt to trust a skill he hadn't used in years.

He planned out the assault as if the men were inside, ready for him.

They'd be waiting in the living room or the front bedroom where they could watch the street. Maybe one guy would be in the kitchen, just in case.

Thomas would go inside and straight to the left. Through the hallway and into the back bedroom.

His gun safe was in the closet. If he could get there and open it without taking a bullet, he'd be in much better shape.

Anyone waiting in the kitchen would have a shot at him as he entered the front door, but if he surprised them and moved fast enough, he'd be out of their line of fire before they could aim.

Just like back in Afghanistan and most of the dangerous places he'd served, it was rare to face an enemy who could calmly aim and fire in the middle of combat. It took a high level of training and a ton of experience to do more than "spray and pray" when fighting for one's life.

Local yokels in backwater Arizona shouldn't be a problem...

Unless they had shotguns or saw him coming.

Thomas mentally shrugged. There was only so much he could do. If he was outgunned and faced a superior opponent, he'd get injured or killed.

It was how he'd lived for years.

It was what it was.

If they didn't take him when he rushed in, though, the enemy would die. Thomas would see to that.

He focused his mind and body...

And moved.

As he slammed into the front door, Thomas belatedly considered the possibility of a booby trap—a shotgun pointed at the opening, the trigger primed to pull via a string attached to the door or some clever trick like that.

There was no blast from a shotgun—either in a trap or held by a tango.

He crashed into the living room, every sense on high alert.

The smell hit him first, but Thomas didn't identify it as a threat. He kept running through the living room—the most likely kill zone—and made it to the hallway unscathed.

The house was dark. The remnants of the day's sunset didn't reach inside.

No one shot him as he reached his back bedroom.

No one tackled him.

No one shouted an alert.

He slammed the bedroom door closed, sensing no one, pushed in the doorknob and turned, locking it.

It might buy him a few seconds.

As he rushed to the closet and entered the code for the gun safe, it smelled like his toilet had backed up. This far outside of town, he wasn't connected to city services.

That was all he needed—bad guys trying to hurt him and his septic tank acting up.

The sewage was a problem to deal with after killing whoever had dared break into his house and wait for him to come home from jail.

He wanted the shotgun standing upright in the rack but couldn't spare the time to load it. He grabbed a pistol instead. It felt good in his hands.

Sliding in a magazine, Thomas breathed more easily. He was armed, knew his house better than the enemy, and certainly had far more combat experience than anyone in the town, county, or possibly the entire state.

No matter what the government's computer systems claimed, or the bullshit story Lauren the chatty school secretary was spreading to the community, he was an experienced killer.

Anyone wishing him harm was now as good as dead.

Thomas stood in the closet, pistol ready, and extended his senses.

He could be wrong—it had been seven years since he'd been in a combat situation like this—but his gut told him the house was empty. Nobody scrambled to get to the bedroom, no one ran away after chickening out of a confrontation, and no whispered conversations about what to do drifted from the living room.

Still, he had to be sure.

Crouching low, he peeked out of the walk-in closet.

No one in the bedroom, obviously.

The smell made his eyes water, but he pushed that to the back of his mind.

An old clock radio gave the room just enough of a red glow for him to see.

It was dark under the bed, but no man-sized shapes lurked there.

Sneaking into the bathroom, he expected a flood of sewage from the septic system, but the floor was dry. The white shower curtain with a design of seashells and fish an ex-girlfriend had given him hung in tatters, showing that no one hid in the shower.

Thomas efficiently cleared the rest of the house. The close-quarters combat skills came back in a rush. His steps were sure, his movements fluid. It was like he'd been transported back in time to his heyday as a warrior.

The only things missing were his Teammates.

And an enemy.

The house was empty, though the assholes had been there.

Keeping the pistol just in case, Thomas moved back through the house room by room, flipping on the overhead lights and surveying the destruction.

In the living room, his nice leather sofa was ripped to shreds. So was his old easy chair. The TV was smashed, the coffee table broken in half.

Everything that had once been in the kitchen drawers or cupboards now lay jumbled on the kitchen floor. Boxes of food had been dumped. Utensils were broken or bent. Cans of soup had been splattered on the counters and cabinets.

The rest of the rooms were the same. Anything that could be broken had been—except the lights.

They wanted him to see.

His bedroom looked fine, but several people had used his bed as a toilet.

Others had picked spots in each of the other rooms to go.

They'd used their filth to write on at least one wall in every room.

Shame on you!

Fake

Coward
Loser
Poser
LEAVE!

If any furniture had survived, Thomas would have collapsed into it, mourning the little house he'd bought cheap and fixed up over the years. The first place he'd been able to call home as an adult, aside from wherever he'd been stationed in the Teams.

Instead, he stood straight and tall, his resolve hardening.

It was hard for him to face, but his townspeople, his community, thought he was an asshole who had duped them and pretended to be a hero. He didn't agree with their methods of expressing their displeasure at what they wrongly believed, but he understood where they were coming from.

Thomas wouldn't let their mistaken understanding break him.

He would come back from this. He'd fix the problem, show he was who he claimed to be, and win them back.

The only easy day was yesterday, and he was never out of the fight.

30

THE MOVIE PREMIERE

The Hollywood Theater
Los Angeles, California

As the vehicle slowed, one of the bodyguards sitting across from Yousuf in the back of the stretch limousine spoke.

"It is time, Your Highness," Syed—the thin, smarter one—said, sticking with the charade.

They might know he wasn't actually Prince Rafiq Al-Najjar, but neither of the bodyguards ever acknowledged that Yousuf was anything less than the prince.

Yousuf nodded once and said nothing, as expected of him. He focused on the street outside the slowing car: the famous movie theater, the huge spotlights shooting into the sky, the crowds of people around the sturdy—though decorative—barricades lining the red carpet, and the group of press and paparazzi with priority access so they could take pictures.

Squeals of excitement came from several gorgeous young women, their eyes wide in anticipation.

They couldn't see past the vehicle's heavily tinted windows.

They didn't know how disappointed they were about to feel when he stepped out instead of a movie star.

Yousuf suppressed a sigh and unconsciously touched the jagged scar below his eye—the one he'd been given to match Prince Rafiq's.

As one of the early financial backers of this movie, he—or rather, the prince—had received credit as the executive producer. An invitation to the opening night red carpet came with it, and here he was.

The attendant at the curb knocked lightly on the glass. Yousuf smoothed his thick hair and put on his pleasant but knowing smile just in time for the door to open.

Syed stepped out first. A second later, he gestured. Yousuf emerged to a dazzling array of camera flashes and a chorus of cheers that quickly faded as no one recognized him. Despite his tailored suit, perfect dark hair, carefully trimmed beard, and toned physique, he was a nobody.

He chuckled good-naturedly, gave a quick wave, and walked up the red carpet, the convincing smile still on his face. Turning toward the cameras closer to the theater's main entrance, he slowed for a few steps. Several diligent photographers took his picture. They'd ask the movie's publicist who the well-dressed, confident, relatively handsome man was—and if he was important. The picture would appear in a few obscure movie industry publications—the movie's publicist would make sure of it to keep him happy.

None of the sexy young women waved or asked for his autograph.

Yousuf hadn't expected their attention, and the lack of it didn't bother him. This was his life.

Inside the theater, he was warmly welcomed by the movie's hands-on producers and director. Yousuf had hoped to meet a famous star, but the movie was a smaller one with no big names. Still, it was someone's dream, and the people outside were excited. The movie might be enjoyable.

Yousuf shook hands, smiled, nodded, and said little. Many would assume he only spoke Arabic.

As one of several thousand minor Saudi princes in the royal family, Prince Rafiq had much money, no fame, and little power.

But he loved financing movies, being a small part of the business.

It was all part of his carefully cultivated image as a wealthy benefactor of the arts. And frequently, Yousuf understood, the carefully selected movies made him a decent return on his investment.

Over the weekend, the real prince would receive a copy of the movie or a link to stream it privately in his home cinema. He wouldn't watch it in a crowded theater full of horrible Americans and be forced to hide his hatred for them.

That's why Prince Rafiq had Yousuf.

Yousuf didn't mind. It was a good living, going to movies and appearing in public at the events Prince Rafiq didn't want to attend or where the security wasn't to the high standards of Khalid, the prince's chief of security.

His life could have been much, much worse.

Yousuf shook yet another hand, nodded his greeting, and was escorted to his seat in the last row of the large movie theater, on the aisle, as requested.

Syed stood near the doors to the lobby, at parade rest, "protecting" Yousuf.

As always.

31

THE DEBATE

71 Ocotillo Street
Sands, Arizona

Thomas retrieved a pair of old rubber gloves and other supplies from the small padlocked backyard shed the intruders had either overlooked or hadn't bothered to ransack.

He crammed his soiled sheets, blanket, and pillows into trash bags, and hauled his bed into the back corner of the yard.

It took several trips to carry out all the broken furniture.

After using two rolls of paper towels from the shed to clean the worst of the filth off the walls, he filled a bucket with water and bleach and scrubbed them clean.

He used a utility knife to cut the ruined carpet into strips, rolled them up, and started a new pile next to the stinky bed. The carpet pad came next. He'd have to rent a dumpster to haul away everything, but getting it out of the house was a good start.

There was little to salvage from the kitchen. It all got bagged and thrown onto the growing mound of trash.

With all the windows opened to the cool desert night air, the house smelled more like bleach than a sewer, though he'd need to prime and repaint the walls—and probably treat the concrete slab too—before the smell would be entirely gone.

He set the pistol on the soap shelf while he showered, finally brushed his teeth, and got dressed.

His hand trembled as he combed his hair.

He was going on twenty-four hours without a drink.

Thomas took two energy bars from his go bag in the large gun safe in the closet—along with several guns, his cleaning kit, and one of his emergency bottles of whiskey—and moved to the living room. The large window on the north side and the kitchen windows to the south allowed a light cross-breeze to clear the air better here than in the other rooms.

He made himself eat both energy bars first, debating whether he should skip the drink. He could risk leaving the house unguarded to run to the bar for some company.

But he didn't want to wait—and wasn't sure he could.

An hour later, the bottle was getting low…

And his resolve to find a solution to the government's computer problem and prove himself to his community wavered.

He methodically cleaned the weapons and wondered about his life.

What the hell happened to him?

He'd been a Navy SEAL. A trained killer. One of the country's elite warriors. A true hero—not that he needed or wanted the recognition, but it was a damn fact. He'd saved lives. The work he'd done—and that of the rest of the men and women who served, whether on the front lines or in the rear—had kept the fight from coming to America's shores. For years, he'd helped give the people of Afghanistan and Iraq every opportunity to rebuild their lives and their countries. He and his men, among others, had taken a lot of bad guys off the face of the earth. The world was better for it.

Yes, he'd turned his back on that life. But when he did, when he left it all behind, he remade himself into a teacher. He brought smiles and laughter to kids, saw the glow of realization in their eyes when a lesson clicked. After a few years, he transitioned to helping special needs kids get through their days with a little extra grace.

He made a difference.

And what had he gotten?

Undiagnosed but pretty damn obvious PTSD.

Quite likely a drinking problem.

And right now, no job, a messed-up permanent record, and a community that thought his entire life was a lie.

The gun oil smelled good. Like coming home.

The bleach from the walls and floors competed with it, though, ruining the feeling.

Thomas looked up from the guns at a movement across the room and almost had a heart attack.

Tank, Baldy, and Bossman sat against the wall to his left where the couch used to be. Directly below the remaining faint outline of *Shame on you!*

"What the hell?" he asked them.

They sat with their legs out, relaxed, dressed in their dusty everyday desert fatigues, alive as they'd been years ago, before the ambush, and smirked at him.

Bone blinked several times, and they were gone.

Along with the nightmares, now he had to deal with waking flashbacks and—what? Hallucinations?

He looked away, then back. The guys weren't there, which was a relief.

He really didn't want to be crazy.

Thomas swore. Here he was. Literally at the end of a road, in a small, cheap house—now trashed and smelling like the enemy's shit.

His life was in ruins.

He took another drink.

And he was a drunk. He couldn't forget that part.

He had the nightmares to look forward to tonight, even with the whiskey.

Before him stretched a long, uphill battle to clear his name.

He was so tired of this life.

The guns were spread out on the smooth concrete floor in front of him.

He took a long pull from the bottle, thinking it through.

Mistakes happened all the time.

Not to SEALs, true, but the locals no longer believed he'd served his country, anyway.

Sure, they'd wonder, but…

Would they be generous and call it an accidental discharge while he was drunkenly cleaning a weapon?

Or would they see through the ruse?

He picked up his favorite pistol, instinctively checking to ensure it was empty and safe. It felt good in his hand.

Who would even care that he was gone?

At school, Simon was too young and had plenty of other issues to deal with. He'd never hear about it.

Henry at the bar? He was a nice guy. He'd raise a toast to Thomas' memory, but no. Henry wouldn't miss him.

The vision of Stephanie came to mind, her short, bright green hair collecting the dim light behind the bar. In his memory, she was laughing at something he'd said, her dark eyes on him, crow's feet crinkled up tight.

Steph would miss him, right?

Maybe. Maybe not. After all, they'd only gone on a few dates before she placed him nicely but firmly in the friend zone. And weren't bartenders supposed to make the customers feel special? Laugh at their lame jokes, fend off their awkward, heavy-handed come-ons?

He took a deep breath. He should embrace the suck, accept the hand he'd been dealt yesterday, and stop feeling sorry for himself. It was unbecoming of a warrior.

But for some reason, the urge to jump in, find a solution, and make it happen wouldn't come like it used to in the old days.

His warrior spirit was completely and utterly gone. Something had changed.

He had changed.

The mag was right there on the floor. All it would take was…

Thomas jumped at the light knock from the door across the room.

In a flash, he'd loaded the pistol, stood, and rushed into the hallway, out of sight of the windows.

The thought of ending it all vanished as he focused on the threat outside.

32

THE BACKUP

71 Ocotillo Street

Sands, Arizona

Thomas held the pistol at the low-ready position. If the same group that had defaced and desecrated his home had returned, he'd be greatly outnumbered. If backed into a corner, he was taking at least some of them with him.

Another quiet knock came from the front door—but who knocks before an ambush?

They could be distracting him in front while entering through the back door—or his bedroom window.

Thomas spun and dropped low, staggering and almost losing his balance before catching himself. He aimed at the bedroom with its wide-open window.

No one was there.

"Thomas? You in there?" came the quiet voice from the front.

"Steph?" Thomas called. What the hell was she doing here?

"You okay? I didn't see you tonight. I brought your car back."

His car. He shook his head as he stood.

Once again, he was drunker than he should be.

Wait. Was it drunker? Or more drunk? He was a teacher, he should know which was correct. Drunker. More drunk. Now they both sounded wrong.

"You decent?" Steph called more loudly. "Want to let me in?"

Damn it. He was very drunk, holding a weapon, trying to figure out grammar. He was in no shape to deal with Steph.

"Thanks," he called, holstering the weapon in the concealed carry holster. "Just leave the keys. I'm too messed up for comp—"

The door opened slowly. "Don't shoot me, okay? I'm alone, it's late, and I'm coming in."

Well, hell. Thomas sighed and walked into the living room.

Steph stood in the doorway in her normal work attire of tight black jeans and a black t-shirt, taking in the bare concrete floors in the blaze of every overhead light. The complete lack of furniture, the array of weapons, and the overwhelming aroma of bleach with the lingering stench of human waste fighting through.

"I like what you've done to the place," she said without a hint of humor in her voice. "Nice feng shui, or whatever they call it. Smart move—get in a bar fight with three asshats, go to jail, and launch a redecoration mission."

Her lips twitched. For an instant, Steph's eyes seemed to dance in delight before she got her face back under control.

"Too soon?" she asked in a softer voice.

"Yeah, a little," he said, trying hard not to slur his words. But her being there to check up on him, along with her dark sense of humor so common in the military, had him feeling lighter already.

"Come in." He gestured at the wall where the couch had been the last time she'd visited, after their third date. Right before she'd kissed him on the cheek and told him she just wanted to be friends. "Have a seat," he said, getting into the spirit of the ridiculous situation he found himself in.

Steph walked straight over to the couch's former position and lowered herself to the concrete floor, stretching her legs out with a contented sigh. "Feels good to take a load off."

He joined her, back to the wall, a decent distance between them. The last thing he needed tonight—aside from an attack from a bunch of locals looking for a fight—was to make a drunken move on Steph and get shot down.

Steph sniffed the air. "Is that one of the new candles from the fancy tourist trap store in town? Highway Restroom, I think they call it, right? 'A delightful blend of bleach and urinal cake with a hint of shit.' I passed on that one but couldn't resist the candle called Grandma's Closet. Mothballs, old lady perfume, and hairspray. I'll pick one up for you tomorrow. Trust me, it'd be better than this."

Thomas tried not to smile but couldn't hold back. It turned from a chuckle into a full-throated roar of laughter that, once started, he couldn't stop until tears were streaming down his face. Not all of them were from laughing, but he hoped Steph wouldn't notice.

"Thanks for coming over," he said finally, wiping his eyes. He felt better. "And thanks for standing up for me with Detective Devon. You didn't have to do that. In fact," he said, turning to face her. "You shouldn't be standing up for me at all. Until I get my situation straightened out, the people of this town think I'm some kind of monster, impersonating a hero at best. Or possibly stealing his identity. You defending me could get the bar blackballed."

Steph glanced away.

It clicked. She hadn't been defending him at the bar.

"I get it," he said.

She gave him a quick apologetic nod. "Sorry," she whispered. "I should—"

"No. No, you're doing it right. Better to not say much. Maybe just, you know, don't exactly badmouth me?"

She stared at him and shook her head. "Never." After a second, she turned her attention to the living room. "They came here while you were in jail, right?"

Thomas nodded and Steph swore under her breath.

"What can I do to help?" she asked.

"Nothing. I'll make some calls in the morning, after my run. My situation should be relatively easy to straighten out. It's not the first time it's happened."

She nodded, glancing at him before looking straight out across the room again. "You look like hell, by the way."

He hoped she was joking again, but couldn't tell.

"Well, I'm dead, remember. It's okay to look like this."

She didn't laugh.

A swing and a miss on that one.

They sat in silence for a few seconds before she turned her body to face him, drawing one of her legs under her. "Thomas?"

That tone was never good.

"You ever think about giving up drinking?" she asked.

He had, but immediately considered the alternative—the nightmares. They were barely in check now. Without the booze…

"No," he lied. "I'm fine."

She smiled slightly, her face kind. "It doesn't have to be meetings, you know. Whatever works. People use long-distance running to stay sober. That might work for you."

"Running helps. The booze helps more." She was a veteran—she'd understand.

He had a sudden inspiration, and his drunken lack of inhibitions allowed him to spit it out. "But… If I stopped drinking… Do you think you and I could date again?"

Her hesitation said it all—it wasn't out of the question. Or, at least, that's how he chose to take it.

"I can't be the reason you get sober," she said. "And the drinking's only a symptom. You've got a lot of shit to heal."

"Sure, but…?"

"Sober and not so messed up? No promises, but I think I'd like that." A hint of red showed on her cheeks. She looked at the living room again, breaking the serious mood. "Just do a better job cleaning yourself up than you did in here, all right?"

Thomas chuckled as he weighed whether a woman like Steph was worth him dealing with all the baggage buried under the pain and grief of losing his Team.

33

FIRST WATCH

71 Ocotillo Street
Sands, Arizona

Steph took the first watch, turning off the lights in the house and loading the shotgun before helping put the rest of the weapons back in Thomas' gun safe.

She encouraged him to lie on the floor where the couch had been. He'd sobered up some since she had arrived but looked like he was about to pass out any second.

There were no streetlights this far out of town on the dead-end street, so the darkness was complete once the lights were out. Her eyes adjusted fast. You don't make it far in the military without getting used to pulling guard duty at night.

Bone's breathing settled.

She stood at the front window, checking the empty street, then moved to each of the bedrooms. From the living room, Thomas snored.

After clearing the bedrooms, she walked lightly through the living room, past the small dining area, and into the kitchen.

Whoever had ransacked the place had left nothing usable behind. Thomas had done an admirable job cleaning up, but the horrible scent remained under the overpowering smell of bleach. Her anger flared for a moment before she got it under control.

The guys were too cowardly to come back tonight.

But if they did, they'd have to deal with her first, then an armed former SEAL—assuming she left any alive for him.

34

JABBER

Afghanistan

Seven Years Ago

Bone sat near the sliding door of the helicopter. Around him, seven of his brothers relaxed in the chopper.

It was another nice night for a helicopter ride and killing bad guys.

They'd been at this as a team for months—this deployment. All but one of them had been on previous deployments together. Bone knew them better than his family. Better than any girlfriend he'd ever had.

Below them, the mountains and valleys of Afghanistan came and went.

He wondered if he'd miss this someday.

He shared a smile with his buddy Tank, sitting across from him.

Years from now, the two of them would be the ancient guys at the bar, drinking beers and telling stories about the good old days.

Younger guys would be convinced the two retired SEALs were making shit up when they were only telling it like it was.

Bossman gave them the five-minute signal and soon the helicopter slowed. A few minutes later, it landed, and they slid into the darkness, game faces on.

The hike to the village was just like any other night. They were careful and quiet. Ghosts in the darkness. No one was out.

Bone figured the chances were fifty-fifty tonight's mission was a bust. The Taliban fighters wouldn't have the guts to stay in the area and risk American special forces dropping by to root them out.

The war was winding down. America and the Western forces had definitely not won. Anyone willing to be honest would admit the country was too messed up to ever have an organized, effective, top-down government like a Western country. There were too many tribes, too many feuds. The area didn't have a history of central government. It had been crazy to think an entire country, a whole population, would suddenly embrace a democracy run by a leader in a city hundreds of miles away that most of the citizens would never see in their lifetimes.

The people didn't want or need what the West was offering.

Instead, they had families, tribes, regions, and an informal system of government they'd been using for centuries longer than democracy had been around.

The Western coalition had done some good. They'd killed a bunch of genuinely evil guys who would have taken terrorism first to Europe, then the USA.

Now human rights had improved, especially for women.

And overall, people seemed happier.

One of these nights, the Team was going on its final mission, but they wouldn't know it ahead of time.

They'd fly in one last time, hike to a target like they were doing now, take care of business, and get back to base. A few days later, they'd learn the politicians had called it. They would all head home.

Tonight, as they neared the village, they slowed, moving carefully. The village had been harassed recently by Taliban forces. If the bad guys were still around, they'd be in the hills on the other side of the village—but you never knew.

The eight SEALs—with eight more on standby fifteen minutes out as a quick reaction force—were taking the fight to the enemy.

They were on the outskirts of the village when the man in front of Bone raised a fist. Immediately, Bone halted, holding up his hand for the man behind, and scanned his sector.

"Terp up," Bone heard through his headphone.

It took half a second to remember the call was meant for him.

He moved forward, passing three other guys before he got to the front of the column.

The point man—Bone's buddy Tank—gestured at the mud-walled village several hundred yards ahead. The local village elder had proven helpful in the past to other American troops.

Right by the side entrance, an old man sat slumped in an ancient wooden chair against the six-foot-high wall surrounding the village, wrapped in a thick blanket.

"Think he's out here waiting for us?" Tank asked Bone and Bossman, who moved up to crouch with them. "Want to talk to him, see what's what, 'terp'?" Tank whispered with a grin, teasing Bone about his new role.

Bone glanced at Bossman, green in the glow of the NVGs. "Are they supposed to know we're coming tonight?"

"Nope—but it's not hard to guess," Bossman said. "They had to know we'd come help them out—just not when. I bet he's been out here for at least a few nights."

"You two, go talk to him—quietly," Bossman ordered.

The rest of the SEALs, already spread out in a defensive formation, found what little cover there was along the rutted dirt road leading toward the village, extremely aware of the potential for improvised explosive devices.

Bone and Tank were halfway to the elder when his head jerked and he sat up. He looked around as if unsure of what had woken him.

Bone raised a hand in greeting.

Despite the darkness, the old man caught the movement and mumbled something Bone couldn't make out.

Shit. What had he been thinking, volunteering to be the interpreter?

"You following that jabber?" Tank muttered.

Bone shook his head. "He's too quiet and his accent is—"

The elder used one hand on a walking stick to push himself up from the chair. The other waved and he called out, more loudly this time.

It only took a second for Bone to translate: ambush.

The elder's chest exploded and his body slammed against the wall. An instant later, the sound of gunfire filled the night.

35

THE VICTIM

Downtown San Diego, California

Present Day

Syed drove the white panel van. With his clean-shaven face and good looks, he fit the profile of a successful tradesman, getting a very early start to the workday instead of being the junior bodyguard of a Saudi prince on a mission to abduct a homeless person.

Next to him, Fahad looked like the assistant or apprentice: full, bushy beard and more muscular than Syed.

Their well-worn ballcaps would allow them to blend in at the local big-box hardware store or on any job site.

They turned right, off a main road downtown. They focused on back alleys and side streets to avoid security cameras—a necessary precaution that got more difficult each year.

Fahad had the syringe filled and the cap back on. It wouldn't be good to accidentally inject the sedative into his own muscle.

"There," Fahad said as they cruised slowly through a deserted intersection. "Up the road, a man going through a garbage can near the curb."

They both pulled their baseball caps lower to better hide their faces.

The back street was quiet for the moment but well-lit.

"More public than usual," Syed muttered.

"Not much to choose from," Fahad argued quietly. They hadn't seen many homeless. Volunteers and the local police had been encouraging the unhoused to sleep in shelters.

Los Angeles was the better place to hunt, but Prince Rafiq needed a fresh playmate soon. If they could safely acquire one nearby, it would limit the exposure a few hour's drive would bring, save time, and keep the prince in a good mood.

The man with matted, long hair up ahead dug through a trash can and placed an aluminum can into the worn trash bag on the sidewalk near him. He glanced their way before he returned to his work.

"Cameras?" Syed asked.

"No."

They were in the middle of a block. Graffiti covered every flat surface. Tired storefronts, many of them with roll-down metal shutters, sold lower-end food and merchandise in the daytime. Some might have cameras, but they weren't likely to be viewed unless a store was broken into.

"Hit his bag," Fahad said.

Syed smiled, seeing where his partner was going. "It will work."

He turned the van toward the middle of the road, into the empty oncoming lanes before jerking it hard to the right—directly at the trash can.

At the last second, the man looked up. Syed slammed on the brakes and turned onto the sidewalk just in time to avoid hitting him as the van hit the full trash bag before stopping.

His black bag exploded. Soda cans and bottles flew.

"I told you! You're too drunk to drive!" Fahad yelled. He threw up his hands.

"I'm sorry," Syed said, loudly enough for the man to hear. This street person looked younger than the last one—perfect for the prince. Maybe in his late twenties, with the same overgrown beard and dirty, tangled hair of the older man from two weeks before. He had brown hair and beard, though, not gray.

Syed stepped out of the van at the same time as Fahad. "I'm sorry," he called again, keeping his head down.

"I will drive," Fahad said to Syed. "I'm sorry," he added to the man who had already started to pick up his bottles and cans.

"Help him," Syed said. "Then, yes, you should drive."

Fahad picked up the cans nearest him while Syed leaned against the hood of the van, acting drunk while subtly keeping watch.

The man began putting cans into the trash bag. Fahad helped.

When the homeless man turned to pick up another can, Fahad slipped the syringe from his pocket and jabbed the man's arm.

"What the hell, dude?" the guy said. He squared up to Fahad, slid one foot back, and let the can in his hand fall.

He was a fighter.

The prince would be very pleased.

"I'm sorry," Fahad said.

"What did you do?"

Syed straightened from the hood of the van, dropping the drunken act. "A mild sedative. We're from the city. We have orders to round up all homeless and take them to shelters. There's a bad disease going around and everyone needs to be checked out—whether they want to go or not. We're sorry—we are just doing our jobs."

They had perfected the lie over the last few years. The sedative needed between one and three minutes to kick in, depending on the health of the victim. The explanation made no sense, especially tonight, given the drunken driving act. But confusing the men they targeted made them easier to deal with. Blaming the government worked best, they'd found. The targets were often suspicious of the authorities, but less likely to outright fight them. There was often arguing and bluster, but since Syed had first used the lie, not one had run away or attacked them.

"That's bullshit," the man muttered. It didn't look like the drug had started working. He backed away, leaving behind the bag, cans, and bottles.

"No, sorry, it's true," Syed said. Fahad grabbed the trash bag and hurried to pick up more cans.

The homeless man stumbled into the street.

Syed jumped back in the van while Fahad opened the back door and threw the bag inside—they left no trace of their victims.

The man stopped in the center of the two-lane back street, swaying.

As long as no cars drove by, they were fine.

Fahad jogged ahead and caught the man as he fell.

Syed moved the van, stopping when the rear doors were next to Fahad and the passed-out homeless man.

A few seconds later, both were in the back of the van. Syed drove away, pleased with the night's hunt.

The prince would have a lot of fun with this one.

PART 3

FRIDAY

36

PAYBACK

The President's Weight Room
The White House
5:15 A.M.

Gregory's arms were trashed from the exertion of the morning, but the burn felt good.

Holding out on telling the president his news, however, was a strain.

President Heringten finished his last set on the bench press. As he sat up, Gregory handed him a small white hand towel, complete with the presidential seal, from a stack near the door.

"Thanks for waiting," the president said. "I needed a good workout this morning, free from distractions. But I can see it in your eyes. What do you have for me that doesn't need to be discussed in the Oval Office?"

"We may have an opportunity, Mr. President."

"For?"

"Payback."

It only took Heringten a few seconds to get where Gregory needed him to go.

"The bounty program? Prince..."

"Prince Rafiq Al-Najjar, sir."

Gregory, the president, and Chad David had discussed the situation only once in the months since Gregory's initial presentation. As the man posed no current threat to the country, and it was such a political can of worms, their hands were tied.

Left unsaid was the true problem: they had no means by which to punish him. He couldn't be arrested or brought to justice in the usual manner. The politics were too risky—an arrest would cause a political firestorm, and too many secrets were at stake, not the least of which was Gregory's use of a hacker to illegally access documents that helped put the puzzle together.

While they could have tasked one of the other intelligence agencies with a capture/kill mission, there was too much to explain.

The risk of such an operation was too damn high.

"What's changed?" the president asked. "Do you have new intel? Is he up to something?"

"We have no new intel at this time, sir. And there is no indication of him continuing the program. This is preliminary, but—"

"The helicopters shot down in Yemen," the president said, putting it together. "Someone had to organize and finance the attack."

"Yes, Mr. President. Again, we have nothing that connects Prince Rafiq Al-Najjar to the attacks."

"But it feels like it could be him, doesn't it?" the president asked, his voice quiet.

"It does, sir. Someone had to finance and coordinate it. The local Al Qaeda cells aren't organized or funded enough to pull it off. However, regardless of how that investigation shakes out, I believe you always prefer to take the fight directly to the enemy. We have the solid bounty program intel blaming Prince Rafiq Al-Najjar, but you have lacked the resources—a true dark asset who would give you complete deniability."

"You've found such a person? Someone reliable who isn't going to mess this up and get us in a world of political trouble with Saudi Arabia?"

"Yes, sir."

It was clear that the president wanted to ask for details but wisely held back.

"Totally off the books?" the president asked, half to himself.

"Yes, sir. But legal, if you give the word and jump through one or two very simple hoops."

"Give me something."

Gregory had planned for this scenario. "We have a deniable candidate who has no current connection to any intelligence agency or the government. No one would look at him as an asset. He's perfect for this mission—for several reasons I would rather not get into with you."

President Heringten pondered the answer, struggling with whether the information was enough or not. "I need a little more before I give the green light. What makes him so perfect?"

"His experience and deniability, sir," Gregory said softly. "And... he's already dead."

37

THE MORNING AFTER

71 Ocotillo Street

Sands, Arizona

Thomas woke empty-handed, frantically scrambling for his pistol on the nightstand.

He had to return fire. He had to save Tank and the rest of the guys.

It took a few seconds to realize he was at home, lying on the living room floor. The sun was barely up, but enough light shone into the empty room.

There was no nightstand. And no gun.

"Thomas?" A woman's voice came from the hallway.

Someone was in his house.

His head pounded and he felt like he'd been run over by a bus, but he had to find his weapon.

He felt the weight of it at his waist and drew it without thinking.

"It's Steph," the woman called. "I'm in the hallway. Don't shoot me, okay?"

Steph—from the bar? She was here?

He tried and failed to remember the previous night.

"It's okay," Steph said from the hallway. "You were dreaming. You're at home. I took first watch, remember?"

Steph appeared slowly in the entrance to the hallway, one hand holding a bottle of water, the other holding a shotgun—his shotgun—pointed at the ground. In the dawn light, she looked more attractive than ever, though he could barely see straight with his head pounding so hard.

"I've got water from the gun safe, and aspirin. Bet you need both."

She stood there waiting for him to catch up.

The events of the previous night finally came back to him. He sat up, wincing, and holstered the pistol. "Yeah, right. Sorry."

She moved toward him with the graceful walk of a warrior who knew how to cover ground quickly yet quietly.

"Take these," she said, handing him the bottle of water and three aspirin. It came out as an order from a superior officer, and he followed it without question.

"You're well supplied in the gun safe. Go bag, food, water. Booze."

His eyes locked on hers. "You didn't—"

"No," she said, interrupting him. "I'd never do that."

He had a slight recollection of them talking about his drinking last night but couldn't come up with the whole thing. Just the general sense that it would probably be a good idea for him to cut back or quit. It would come to him during his run. That's usually when he put together the events of the previous night.

Thomas was contemplating whether he needed to throw up immediately, wait, or could hold it in when he realized it was Friday. If he was going for a run to get himself together before work, he had to move.

He was up from the floor and stumbling to the bathroom when the memories came crashing in.

The government thought he was dead and the school had fired him.

He had no job to rush off to. No kids to help.

Simon would be in the hands of someone new—and he'd hate that.

Standing in the middle of his empty, stinky living room, Thomas had a moment of clarity as he contemplated all he'd lost: Tank and the rest of his brothers, and now Simon.

"You okay?" Steph asked from behind him.

He nodded, not trusting himself to speak, or to turn and face her.

"I'm not here to rescue you," she said quietly. "You're a big, bad Navy SEAL and I'm a little old Army MP. But if you need backup or a friend, I'll be there. Copy?"

He cleared his throat before replying. "Got it, and thanks."

"Great. Now get cleaned up so you can drive me home." Her voice still had the hint of a sergeant's command, though tempered with the tone of a concerned friend. "I've got to get some sleep before opening the bar this afternoon. You have a trail to run—and a lot of calls to make, right?"

"Copy that," Thomas said, feeling a renewed sense of purpose.

A few phone calls and this would all get straightened out. How hard could it be?

38

THE TRAIL RUN

Snakeridge Trail
Outside Sands, Arizona

Thomas wasn't used to running with a gun, but he wasn't going anywhere these days unarmed. He had to tighten the drawstring on his shorts and adjust the holster a few times, but the weapon rested comfortably against his abdomen and his shirt hid it.

It helped that he'd chosen the smaller 9mm pistol from his safe. If he got into a firefight, he wanted a chance—but he wasn't going to war.

He'd left that life behind.

All he needed now was a long trail run to work out the kinks from sleeping all day on the thin mattress of the jail and a few hours last night on the cold concrete floor of the house.

Plus, he needed to distract his mind with the ups, downs, twists, and turns of the trail so it could sort out the next steps to getting his life back.

He'd call the VA every hour if he had to. Drive to Washington, DC, and camp out in person until someone agreed to help.

But he was going to succeed.

The area outside of town where he preferred to run was high desert. There were rocks galore, from small boulders to massive, house-size blocks, and cliffs soaring to a hundred feet high. The gravel and sand trails could be slippery if one lost focus, especially on the countless dips and rises. In the entire six-mile loop Thomas liked best, he swore the only flat spot was an overlook about two-thirds of the way through the loop. He often stopped there for a quick breather, taking in the magnificent view of the valley below and higher mountains fifty miles away.

He ran the same as always: not slow, not fast. His legs chewed up the miles and he worked up a sweat, enjoying the quiet solitude of an area where few people went, especially just after dawn on a school day.

Thomas avoided a chunky rock in the middle of the trail at the top of a small rise, right before the narrow trail took a sharp turn to avoid huge boulders on the left.

The sudden change in direction allowed Thomas to catch a glimpse of a person about a mile back wearing a bright white t-shirt. Thomas slowed to a walk. In his years of running here, he'd encountered only a handful of other people in the morning, and none on the longer six-mile loop.

His combat senses had been rekindled over the last few days, but Thomas didn't pick up any danger from the fellow desert lover. He resumed his run—but increased the pace. He didn't need or want company, whether a threat or not.

A few minutes later, after dipping down into a narrow slot canyon, the trail climbed again and turned back in the opposite direction, giving Thomas another view back up the trail.

The man in the white shirt ran smoothly and efficiently—and he had gained ground on Thomas.

Thomas didn't believe in coincidences. He'd either been followed or someone who knew his love of running had staked out the favorite trail.

Neither was a good sign.

Thomas picked up the pace again, putting extra effort into it. At this speed, his mind had to focus too much on the trail to work through the government's computer problem, but that could wait. If the man trailing him was a threat, Thomas wanted to get out of the potential kill zone and back to his car. Shooting someone was the last resort. He didn't need to further complicate his life. Better to escape, figure out who was after him—and why—and deal with it without gunfire.

If possible. If not, he'd handle it.

Trail running, especially the longer distances that Thomas enjoyed, wasn't about going fast. The key was relentless forward progress and never giving up.

All things SEALs were good at—even retired ones.

The boulders and twisting trail didn't allow a clear view back for several minutes. The faster pace chewed up the distance. Thomas sweated, cleansing his system of the booze.

The four-mile mark was approaching, with an expansive view he wouldn't stop to enjoy today.

Breathing more heavily than usual, Thomas slowed as he crossed the sole flat spot of the loop, glanced behind him, and slowed further in surprise.

The man in white had gained more ground despite Thomas' increased pace.

Enough was enough. Thomas was being pursued, but he was done running.

The overlook would make an excellent place for a confrontation. Man-sized boulders on the other side of the trail would provide cover if the situation devolved into a shooting match.

Seven years before, Thomas would have waited patiently, hands at his side, confident in his abilities. Today, under the bright sun turning the desert hotter by the minute, he gripped the pistol without drawing it and prepared himself for a fight.

He didn't have to wait long. The man in the white shirt slipped in and out of view more frequently as he worked his way along the trail. Thomas couldn't place the brief glimpses of his face. He wasn't from town.

The man had the bearing of a guy in the military, though he seemed much too old for active duty. Plenty of warriors kept up the punishing physical fitness workouts long after their lives depended on them. This guy could be one.

Thomas admired his running form. He floated over the ground, moving like he could run all day and night.

He ran like a SEAL.

39

THE MEETING

Snakeridge Trail
Outside Sands, Arizona

Thomas kept his hand on the weapon, not relaxing for a moment. He wouldn't let his guard down until he understood the situation.

He thought of the drunken phone calls he'd made outside the bar two nights before.

That had to be it. He'd mouthed off, sounded crazy, and they sent someone to deal with him—or at least make sure he wasn't dangerous. Maybe even help with his situation.

And what better place to confront an off-his-rocker former SEAL than out in the middle of the desert?

Thomas had to commend the thinking.

He reluctantly released the grip on the pistol and waited.

Long before he came into view, the man's panting breath reached Thomas. He had to be making plenty of noise to show he wasn't a threat.

Several seconds later, an older man rounded a bend in the trail and slowed to a walk, a pleasant smile on his face. He raised one arm in a cautious wave. "Thanks for stopping," he called. "I thought I'd have to chase your ass all the way back to the parking lot."

He was in his mid-sixties, with military-short gray hair, and a narrow face tanned from plenty of time outdoors. His physique was more than wiry but less than muscular. He wore faded, tan running shorts cut shorter and tighter than people wore these days. And though the thick t-shirt was drenched in sweat, its whiteness shone. Either it was brand new or expertly laundered.

The face, outfit, demeanor, and voice all came together for Thomas.

"Admiral Nalen?" he called as the man approached, still breathing heavily.

Nalen's smile broadened.

During Thomas' active-duty days, he'd seen the admiral in person at a few events but they had never formally met. Thomas had been one of many SEALs in Nalen's chain of command, and yet here he was on a trail in Arizona, with his hand out to shake.

Thomas stuck his hand out automatically, frantically searching his memory.

What the hell had he said in those phone calls?

Was the admiral here to help, or was Thomas in a lot more trouble than he realized?

40

THE VIEW

Thomas waited for Admiral Nalen to begin, but it looked like the former SEAL was in no hurry.

"Stunning view," Nalen said. The bright morning sun lit up the sand, rocks, and scrub. There were no clouds in the sky. "The desert here feels different than Afghanistan." In the far distance, tall mountains shimmered. "I like this better," he muttered.

Thomas said nothing, easily falling back into the old routine of not speaking unless asked a direct question.

"Where's your truck?" Admiral Nalen asked.

Thomas looked at him blankly.

"I followed you from near your house. You're driving a car. Is it your girlfriend's? You're incognito?"

The last two days had turned Thomas' life upside down, but this conversation took the cake.

Where was the admiral going with this?

"No, sir. It's my car. The hatchback."

Nalen stared at him expectantly for several seconds as if waiting for the punchline. "Seriously?" he eventually asked.

"I'm retired, sir. What the hell do I need a big, gas-guzzling truck for?"

The admiral just shook his head and looked at him like he was crazy.

After another long look at the view, Admiral Nalen turned to him. "You were pretty drunk on the voicemail you left at the White House. And you didn't leave your name, which was smart. But paired with the other drunken phone call to the VA right before, a clever intelligence analyst friend of mine put two and two together—and here I am."

Thomas closed his eyes for a moment, regretting that he had to ask the next question. "What did I say?" It came out in a whisper.

"I can play it for you, but you don't want that. Trust me. We can only hope they don't tell the president—the country's commander in chief—the rude names you called him."

This week couldn't get any worse.

Thomas stared at Nalen, not knowing where to begin, so he went with the first thing on his mind.

"I'm sorry, Admiral, but what the hell is going on here?"

Admiral Nalen's mouth moved into a tight smile, but his eyes showed no amusement.

"I take care of my men. No matter what else happens this morning, I will personally move heaven and earth to get you your old life back. The VA would fix the name mix-up problem on its own, but it might take a while. I'll make sure it happens much quicker than that."

Thomas felt like a heavy burden had been lifted off his back. Before he could offer his thanks, though, the admiral continued.

"Now, on the cons side..." Nalen shook his head. "Calling the President of the United States what you did won't necessarily bring the Secret Service to your door. Let's hope not, at least. If they come, though, that's on you. You'll probably be able to talk your way out of it. You might not. We'll see. If they show up, no matter what, you don't mention me or this visit. Clear?"

"Yes, sir," he answered automatically.

He waited for more, but Admiral Nalen seemed to have finished for the moment and turned to look at the mountains far in the distance. "Damn, that's a nice view," he mumbled.

"Sir, I appreciate any help you can give me," Thomas said, "but that doesn't really explain why you came all the way out here. You could have called."

Nalen glanced at him for a second before returning to the view.

"You'll figure it out," Nalen said half to himself.

The run had helped, but Thomas wasn't thinking as clearly as he wanted. It took him a few more seconds.

What had the admiral said? "No matter what else happens this morning"?

"You need me for... something?"

Nalen turned back to him slowly, all business. "Back in the day, you were willing to give your life for your country, right?"

"If necessary, yes. But none of us, you know, wanted to run to our deaths," Thomas said, referencing a common SEAL saying.

"Understood. What about now?"

Thomas searched Admiral Nalen's face for a sign he was yanking his chain in the way of the Teams, where joking was an art form.

The man seemed completely serious.

In his car outside the school only two days before, listening to the news report of his countrymen losing their lives in helicopters half a world away, Thomas had wondered how he could possibly reenlist or, barring that, join a private military company. He could fight as a contractor instead of a SEAL.

His answer to Nalen's question was easy. Thomas nodded. "Yes. I'd still give my life for my country. Do you have the pull to get me back in the fight? I'm rusty, but with a little time—"

"Glad to hear it," Nalen said, cutting him off. "You're not going to Yemen, Syria, or anywhere like that. But you have all the skills needed for a clandestine mission essential to the United States of America, which is what I'm here to offer you. It's dangerous in two ways. One, of course, you might die. And two—you might get caught, arrested, tried, convicted, and go to jail."

The admiral frowned. "Either way, you'd be entirely on your own. No one's coming to save you, no one is going to step in and say you're with us, he's just doing his job. This is a very sensitive operation. One hundred percent legal, but completely off the books and entirely deniable to the powers that be—including yours truly."

This wasn't at all what Thomas had expected to hear. They had worked with plenty of "Company Men" in the Teams—CIA spies who were normally other paramilitary people—mostly guys—but also sometimes regular men and women who didn't spend time in combat zones. Most of the SEALs had grudging respect for the ones who could handle themselves, and everyone appreciated solid intel that helped take the fight to the enemy, but the general consensus was that "spy shit" was beneath the men of the Teams. It wasn't what they were trained or equipped for.

"I'm sorry, admiral, but I'm not a spy. Besides," he started, then faltered, not sure if he wanted to admit to the man—or himself—how messed up his psyche was. It was just too much to put into words. Too much to voice. Too much to explain.

Nalen must have read the look on his face because his expression softened. He nodded gravely. "I get it, son. We all have our demons. Running from them doesn't make them go away. Sometimes, confronting them is the only way to ease the pain."

They shared a long silence, warrior to warrior.

"Never forget," Nalen said. "You're Thomas Marks: Frogman. Remember what's inside of you. It may have been years since you were that person, but I believe you still have that spark. The will to never quit. You only have to tap into it."

"How?"

"I can't tell you. No one can. You have to discover it yourself. Dig deep, Bone, and get back to who you were."

"Yes, sir," he said after a second, with much more conviction than he felt.

Before he could second-guess himself, Bone blurted out the question on his mind. "What's the mission?"

41

THE TARGET

Snakeridge Trail
Outside Sands, Arizona

Bone immediately regretted asking the question.

He should just say no, thanks, accept the admiral's help, and get his life back.

Maybe he could look into therapy. Stop drinking so much. Ask Stephanie to go out on a date with him again.

Live his life.

"There's a man, forty years old," Nalen began. "He's rich and travels extensively but lives in San Diego for part of the spring and most of the summer. Based on rock-solid intel, he has a history of financing terrorists. The president has authorized two things. First, on-the-ground recon by a capable asset to find out what, if anything, the target is up to these days. Could he currently be involved in funding terrorists domestically or overseas?"

"Sounds like a job for the FBI."

"Nothing against the FBI, but they can't handle this. An undercover operation would take years. There's also some concern that the upper management might not have the guts to risk their careers and lives to go after this target. If he is who and what we believe, his wealth and extensive connections require the utmost secrecy. Dropping this into the bureaucracy of the FBI or any similar organization is a recipe for failure and potential exposure, which would be politically catastrophic. I won't say more about that unless you commit to the mission."

Bone nodded slowly. "I see your point. You said the president authorized two things."

Nalen nodded, his eyes hard. "The president has authorized the neutralization of the target with particular focus on limiting collateral damage. Unofficially, it would be nice if the target was eliminated in such a way to seem like an accident, though that is not an absolute requirement of the mission."

Bone finally understood why the admiral had followed him to the desert and pushed hard to catch up with him on the trail. This conversation couldn't happen anywhere people might see or overhear, no matter how unlikely.

There were several problems, but Bone started with the most obvious. "I'm not an assassin."

Admiral Nalen shrugged. "You had sniper training and experience. You shot first, long before anyone knew they were in your sights or under attack. Same thing here, though if possible we'd prefer you not just set up and shoot the guy from a mile away. But if that's how it has to go down, it's fine," he said, his voice hard.

Bone shook his head. "And 'rock-solid' intel?" he said, not hiding the skepticism he felt. "How many times have we heard that? Hell, rock-solid intel sent us to the wrong damn town for a raid!"

"You were on that raid? I authorized it, so I'm partly to blame too. In the intel team's defense, there were two towns with the exact same name. They were fifty miles apart. We sent you to the wrong one, but no one died. Shit happens. But the intel on this guy is tight, I've been told. I know the person in charge of the analysts that came up with this. If he says it's real, it's solid. I'd do the mission myself if I wasn't an admiral and known to the world."

"But me?" Bone asked.

"If you get caught or killed, you're expendable. And..." The admiral paused, looking like he was trying to find the right words. He took a breath and glanced at the mountains in the distance again before returning to look Bone in the eye. "They've had this intel for several months—I don't know exactly how long, but they sat on it. Waiting for the right time—and the right asset."

"What makes me..." Bone trailed off. "You think I have some personal connection with this guy? If he's not a clerk somewhere who switched my name with my dead buddy's, or someone at the VA purposefully messing with my life, there's no one I want to kill."

Nalen looked at him like he was once again waiting for Bone to catch up, which only pissed Bone off.

"I'm sorry, Admiral, but I don't get it. I've had a rough couple of days. Just spit it out, would you? Tell me what you're here to tell me."

Nalen nodded. "Sure. Sorry. I thought it might be better if you got there on your own." He paused for a second, giving Bone one last chance before continuing. "We're convinced the target funded a bounty program in the Middle East. He—"

It hit Bone. "The helicopters in Yemen? He financed the attack?"

Admiral Nalen shrugged. "Maybe. We're looking into that. More directly related to you, however, is that the target provided the source of funds for an ambush in Afghanistan where eight SEALs were killed —though one was brought back to life after technically being dead for quite a long time."

Bone used every ounce of willpower not to stagger backward. Nalen meant him and his Team.

The sunlit desert landscape wavered, held for a second, but soon faded to darkness.

As Bone slipped from the present into the past, Tank lay on the ground, muttering a pain-filled curse tinged with fear.

He fought the darkness, not wanting to relive the trauma, to dissociate, in front of Admiral damn Nalen.

42

THE DECISION

As he faded, Bone heard Nalen's voice. "Stay with me, Marks. Focus on your breath. In four, hold four. Out four, hold four."

Bone breathed as ordered. Tank and the darkness faded, turning into Admiral Nalen standing closer than he had before. "You with me, son?"

Still breathing in the way that helped focus attention, Bone nodded.

"How long's that been happening?" Nalen asked, sounding interested but not overly concerned.

"While I'm awake? Only the last few days. But the dreams... every night," Bone said as he returned to breathing normally. The danger of slipping away had passed.

Nalen nodded thoughtfully. "Let's get you some help when this is done."

Bone looked at Nalen, sure his face showed his surprise. "You still want me after seeing that?"

"You're the only one that fits, Bone. If you're caught—before or after completing the mission—we can blame it on PTSD and a delusional belief that the target was a bad guy of some sort. We might even be able to quietly leak that you had good reason to take him out. Unconfirmed rumors or suspicions. Still, I'd rather not trade you for him. I don't think it's likely, but it's a risk we're willing to take if you are. If you agree that killing the man who paid others to kill your fellow SEALs, along with countless other American servicemen and women, is worth doing."

"Easy answer, sir. Definitely worth doing. But by me? This is different from reenlisting or going to work for a private military company where I'd have time to train and be part of a team. I haven't shot a gun in years. I'm a teacher now!"

"Didn't the school fire you? That's what I heard." Admiral Nalen grinned. "I thought you might have an unexpected opening in your schedule."

They stared at each other for a second before Bone answered. "Thanks, Admiral," he said dryly.

"Come help us out. It'll be good for you."

Bone nodded. Maybe this was exactly what he needed.

He drew up straight, looked the admiral in the eye, and again nodded. "Yes, sir. I'm all in."

43

THE TRAIL

71 Ocotillo Street
Sands, Arizona

The house was exactly as Thomas had left it—empty and smelly.

He showered, thought about trimming the beard but decided against it, and put on clean clothes from the go bag in the safe.

It was time to prepare for the mission.

A full-size 9mm made sense, but he wouldn't take his favorite pistol. He might have to dismantle and dispose of it. No matter how careful he was, holding on to a weapon used in a crime—what the authorities would consider a murder—would be stupid. He selected one of his older weapons he'd be willing to part with if necessary.

A backup pistol could also come in handy, so he kept the smaller 9mm and grabbed an ankle holster.

Extra magazines for both, but he had to travel light. He wasn't planning on a protracted shootout. If he couldn't get it done with the rounds available, he was out of practice—or fighting for his life.

A fanny pack and fixed-blade knife in a horizontal sheath he could strap to his belt rounded out the gear.

He wished he could take the shotgun, hunting rifle, and or the civilian version of his trusty M4, but they were harder to conceal—and he didn't want to have to ditch any of them. Besides, Admiral Nalen didn't want a sniper shot. Thomas would have to risk getting in close.

The large go bag was already packed with other essentials: energy bars, large, thin bottles of water, lock-picking tools, spare clothes—all black—a balaclava, and emergency cash. He set it on the floor of the still stinky bedroom, sat down next to it, and prepared the most important item: the trail.

In case he was captured or caught, he had to leave a logical backtrail for the police to follow. Nothing he did could lead back to Admiral Nalen or the president.

Since he had just been fired, it made sense that he might consider getting away for a few days. And what better getaway than a trip to the ocean?

As Nalen had instructed, he started looking for things to do in Los Angeles. That led him to search for movie premieres. There were several options. He eventually came to the one the admiral had told him to find.

Thomas drilled down as if he were truly interested, reading about the movie until he found an article in an industry trade magazine reporting on the people behind the film.

Right there on his smartphone screen, he saw what he'd been told he would.

Saudi Prince Finances Award-Winning Movie

Prince Rafiq Al-Najjar, a distant cousin to the new King of Saudi Arabia, was the major backer of The Velvet Reverie, *which recently won the Best in Show award at the prestigious Lincoln Film Festival. Prince Rafiq has been a generous arts benefactor for many years, helping young directors bring their creative vision to the screen.*

The article went on to describe the film, which didn't sound at all like Thomas' type of movie.

Along with the article was a collage of pictures. In one, a tall man with a full head of wavy hair, wide-set eyes, and a closely trimmed black beard, maybe forty years old, wearing dark slacks and a dark shirt unbuttoned to the middle of his chest, stood next to a group of happy younger people. A scruffy thin man in the center smiled widely while holding a small trophy.

Thomas used his fingers to zoom into the picture. The man identified as Prince Rafiq Al-Najjar had a bump on the bridge of his nose and thin lips.

Thomas couldn't tell for sure given the resolution of the image, but the prince certainly looked like he had a small but noticeable scar on his left cheek, just under his eye.

Staring at his empty bedroom, Thomas faded into the past.

Seven Years Ago

Afghanistan

The three enemy soldiers arrayed in front of him didn't seem to care about Bone's night vision goggles, so he left them down over his eyes.

Other enemy fighters emerged from firing positions behind boulders in the hillside and hurried down the slope, excited for the confrontation. A large man with a thick, bushy beard shaped into a point stopped three meters away in the half circle of gathering men.

Bone fought to keep his balance as his body oozed blood from several gunshot wounds. Only sheer stubbornness and spite kept him upright.

He refused to cower.

He was still in the fight. SEALs always have contingencies, and Bone had a plan. One last "screw you" for the enemy, to show them what Americans were made of.

If Bone hadn't already used his grenades, he would have pulled the pin and rushed the sniper and his bodyguards—or at least that's what Bone assumed they were, as they stood protectively close to the man with the sniper rifle—blowing himself up along with them. But all he had left was a throwback to his childhood. Before he dreamed of being a Navy SEAL, Bone had wanted to be a ninja.

The original cheap throwing stars he'd saved his allowance money for were long gone, replaced by a custom-made, razor-sharp star from a buddy's machine shop back home. Bone carried it to remember his friend, occasionally throwing it at the plywood walls of whatever base where he happened to find himself. The only way it could be at all dangerous in battle was through a lucky shot to an enemy's eye or as a brief distraction. Tank often joked, "If I ever see you holding that stupid thing on the battlefield, I'll know we're out of time."

Tank lay dead a few feet away. Bone would die in a few minutes even if the enemy didn't shoot him again.

If there was ever a time for ridiculous, last-ditch efforts, this was it.

Bone had the star hidden in his palm. The brutally sharp points dug into his skin, allowing him to hold his hand open. It looked like his hands were empty and he was unarmed.

Bone heard the quick reaction force's helicopter at the same moment the enemy soldiers did.

He'd been expecting it.

They hadn't—or at least not this soon. All three glanced west as if they could see the bird in the darkness from so far away.

For maximum effect, a star should be thrown overhand, like a knife or an axe. Unfortunately, that movement would draw the eye. One of the two bodyguards surrounding the sniper would notice and deflect it or knock the sniper aside.

Instead, Bone took his shot, flicking the star at the sniper's face like a frisbee.

No one saw it coming, but Bone's aim was off. The sharp points missed the man's eye but slashed his left cheek just below it.

Bone lunged forward, following the throw. He would get close, wrestle the pistol from the sniper, and take one or more of the men with him before the darkness came.

Bullets tore into Bone before he could complete a step.

44

THE PREPARATION

71 Ocotillo Street
Sands, Arizona

Present Day

Thomas sat on the cool concrete floor of his bedroom, remembering. At least this time he hadn't full-on dissociated. He'd remained present—mostly—as the memory came.

He blinked away the Afghanistan desert and returned to his phone.

After all these years, he would have his revenge.

The movie premiere the prince was scheduled to attend wasn't until tomorrow night. Thomas could make a stop Admiral Nalen had suggested.

Time to visit an old friend—or a person complicit in the ambush—and figure out whether to add him to the list or let him be.

After doing all he could with the phone's search history to portray himself initially as a clueless, newly fired person planning a vacation, then a surprised, vengeful lone gunman, Thomas turned off the phone and put it on a shelf in the gun safe. He didn't need the smartphone tracking him. If he succeeded in the mission and got away with taking out the prince, Thomas didn't want to leave a trail of breadcrumbs for an industrious detective to follow later.

Assuming Admiral Nalen was true to his word, in a few days Thomas would have his life back. No need to get arrested and lose it again.

He locked the safe, grabbed the go bag, and hoped the house would be fine while he was on his unexpected "vacation."

He had one more stop to make—and this would be the hardest goodbye of all.

The bar beckoned.

45

THE GOODBYE

The Bar

Sands, Arizona

Bone sat in his car under a spreading mesquite tree that offered a bit of shade a few blocks from the bar.

The backseat was filled with a sleeping bag from his gun safe and his large go bag.

He'd locked the booze in the safe—along with all the guns except for the older full-size 9mm and the smaller one on his ankle.

The bar was his last stop before he started the mission.

Bone debated going inside. It was early, but Steph was probably already there and would let him in.

A part of him longed for the dark, cool comfort of the bar. A couple of guys to chat with. And Steph.

But the less she knew, the better.

And if he were honest, he didn't trust himself to walk in, have a drink, and leave before closing time.

He grabbed a small pad of paper and a pen from the glove box and wrote.

It took him several tries, but he finally got a note he could live with.

Steph,

I'm going away for a while to straighten out a few things.

Take care,

Thomas

He folded it in half and wrote her name on the outside before driving the rest of the way to the bar.

Henry stood at the bar's front door, hands clenching and unclenching. He looked at his watch every few seconds. None of the other breakfast club members, as Steph called them, had arrived yet.

Bone rolled down his window, letting in a rush of dry, hot air. Henry walked the few feet from his position at the door to the car.

"Sorry about the other night," Bone said. "Hope it didn't put you out too much, talking to the police and all."

Henry shook his head and glanced at the go bag in the back seat of the car. "No problem. Clearing out?"

Bone couldn't tell from his tone whether he approved or not.

"Got a few things to take care of." He handed Henry the note. "Can you pass that to Steph for me?"

Without bothering to wait until Bone had driven off to snoop, Henry opened the note, his hands trembling, skimmed it, and folded it in half again. "You got it." He glanced up. "Make sure you don't drag her down into your bullshit, son."

For a second, Bone saw the toughness still inside the Vietnam veteran.

"Yes, sir," Bone said. "That's exactly what I'm hoping to avoid."

With one last look at the bag in the car, Henry leaned closer to Bone. "Take no prisoners," he whispered before returning to his post by the door, waiting for the bar to open.

46

THE DIRECTIVES

Motel Grande

San Dimas, California

The hotel in an eastern suburb of Los Angeles was a long way from Omar's college campus, but it was cheap and out of the way—perfect for his needs.

Omar didn't consider himself a radical, and he certainly wasn't a terrorist. He was a college sophomore with a bright future.

But he was smart enough to admit to himself that what he'd gotten involved with would change his life forever.

He might die.

If he lived, he would likely be arrested and spend the rest of his days in prison.

If he got away with it, though…

He smiled at the thought. He would no longer be tall, skinny, pale Omar. He'd be important. A hero.

More missions would surely follow. Someday, he would form his own group and lead others.

Raise an army.

No matter what, he would deliver a great blow to the country—his homeland, technically, though he felt nothing but revulsion for the United States.

Over the past year, what he'd learned first from new friends at college and read about online had been confirmed by an elderly friend of his father's.

How the United States constantly undermined Middle Eastern countries—politically, economically, and by invading them when lesser measures didn't work.

How the US corrupted its young people, encouraging immorality and promiscuity.

About America's aggression against the entire world—and that it must be stopped.

Others could demonstrate, protest, meet and talk endlessly, or post information online to help people discover these truths.

But his father's friend had chosen Omar. He was special, they said, which finally confirmed what Omar had felt in his heart for years.

He had been selected for a very important—and risky—assignment.

Details were sketchy at first. He was put through a series of tests to prove his dedication.

Spray painting anti-American graffiti around Los Angeles.

Beating up a homeless person he'd been told was an American veteran—a man who had surely killed innocent Afghan or Iraqi civilians.

Stealing from rich, filthy capitalistic Americans' homes.

Finally, he was in the cheap hotel far from school and home with his suitcase full of clothes and a brand-new computer he'd bought from the big box electronics store with his own credit card.

He had settled into the small hotel room and installed a Virtual Private Network on the computer—used to prevent any of America's many spy agencies from tracking him or his internet use.

Dinner came from delivered pizza; for breakfast, he ate the leftovers straight from the small refrigerator that reminded him of the one in the dorm room he'd abandoned the previous week.

The friend of his father's had passed along a list of sites on the dark web and two directives.

He was to pray five times per day...

And learn how to aim and fire a Russian-made, man-portable surface-to-air missile.

47

THE DELIVERY

San Diego, California

Daoud climbed out of the semi and unlocked the regular door into the warehouse. His gray beard fluttered in the breeze.

It only took him a minute to unlock the two padlocks on the huge overhead roller door, use the chain to slide it up, and get back into the truck.

He expertly backed into the narrow loading bay inside the small warehouse.

When the rear of the flatbed trailer touched the black bumper of the dock, he put the semi in Park, shut it off, and hurried to close the roller door, hiding the truck, trailer, and bright blue shipping container from view.

The single-level warehouse looked like the others in the neighborhood. It had seen better days, with peeling white paint in places, and four large, dented, metal roller doors on its south side.

No one in the surrounding buildings had given him a second glance as he drove his precious cargo through the area. Trucks and trailers came and went all day, delivering materials and picking up finished products.

It was American industry at its finest and most common.

The semi, the white panel van backed into the next loading dock, and his old, beat-up car in the third bay fit right in.

In the late afternoon, inland from the ocean, the non-air-conditioned loading dock was hot, but it didn't bother Daoud. Growing up in the blasting heat of Saudi Arabia and his time in the army had made him immune to much of what most people considered uncomfortable.

He hopped onto the flatbed, much more nimbly than an American in his sixties would, to double-check the combination lock and cable seal on the container's locking bar. Everything looked fine. Few shipping containers were ever inspected or scanned when they arrived in a country. If anyone had discovered its secret cargo, they would have arrested him the moment he took delivery.

Not unloading the olive oil to inspect the cargo was a risk, but Daoud had plenty of time. The missile inside wouldn't be needed for several days. It was best left safely hidden for now.

His contact overseas—an old army buddy and informal Al Qaeda member—had supplied men in Yemen with two missiles to shoot down the American helicopters.

Daoud had no doubt the third missile would be inside the container as promised.

Given the neighborhood and the cargo hidden in the shipping container, Daoud wouldn't leave for the next several days until Khalid messaged him the location to bring the missile.

Other men might be tempted to sell it, but not him. Khalid was another old army buddy, and as his long-time fixer, Daoud was paid very well. Aside from the occasional assignment or request, his time was his own.

He had a good life.

Daoud moved to the warehouse office, right off the loading dock, and flipped on the lights. An air conditioner unit stuck through the wall, quietly cooling the small room.

A large window gave him a clear view of the shipping container from a comfortable couch where he'd watch television, play on the older game console he'd bought for the occasion, read, and sleep. The refrigerator, microwave, and toaster oven would keep him well-fed. He'd be comfortable, though he'd miss running on the beach each morning.

Selecting a soda from the refrigerator, he picked up one of several novels he'd bought from a used bookstore and settled on the couch. Aside from being stuck inside, he was looking forward to a relaxing several days.

He only hoped Khalid knew what he was doing this time. America was much different than Yemen. The missile, even if all went perfectly, would bring the authorities down on their heads. With luck, the stupid young man they'd recruited would take the fall, but there would still be a desperate search for how a surface-to-air missile had made it into the United States.

Daoud would be long gone by then, and he'd likely never be able to return to the United States. It would be too risky.

A shame, really. He liked it here.

48

THE REUNION

Pacific Oasis BBQ & Smokehouse
San Diego, California

It was nearly closing time at the small barbecue place a few blocks from the beach, but there was still a steady stream of people going in and out. And it looked like the type of mom-and-pop place that would stay open a little late if sales were good.

The burner smartphone Thomas had picked up at a rest stop along the interstate had led him straight here. If Admiral Nalen's intel was right, the mission started with some recon—and a confrontation.

Before leaving the car, parallel-parked just up the road from the BBQ joint, Thomas fought for the mindset that used to come so easily each night. He put his game face on, focused his mind, and left Thomas behind. From now on, he was Bone. Frogman, warrior, killer.

Bone stalked down the sidewalk, the old way of walking—smooth and silent—falling back into place.

He didn't pause when he reached the restaurant. He was ready for this.

It might have been a pizza or hamburger place in a former incarnation. Red tables were bolted to the floor on the left side, with bench-booth seating. The middle of the room was only large enough for five four-top tables in a row, parallel to the booths along the wall.

On the right, a long countertop had a glass display case where Bone bet people used to be able to pick slices.

Now, a young woman—college age, wearing jeans, a t-shirt, and a blue ball cap with the place's name embroidered in white over her dark hair—prepped food.

A man at the counter picked up his food and paid as Bone moved further inside. The woman glanced up and smiled in a friendly if tired way, ready to take his order, but a short, dark-haired man stepped over from the cash register.

"What will it be tonight?" the man asked. He was in his early forties, with dark, thick eyebrows. His short hair had flecks of gray and had started to thin. He looked fit, except for a soft belly of about five extra pounds. He hadn't shaved in a few days, and a thick beard was already coming in. The hint of an accent could have come from anywhere—San Diego was an international melting pot—but Bone recognized it easily as being from Afghanistan.

"The fish is fresh. It comes with rice and Dahl," the man continued. "Specialty of the house. But if you like barbecue, try the dry rub ribs." The man smiled pleasantly as he'd undoubtedly done dozens of times already that day. He squinted at Bone as if his face was familiar but he couldn't place it.

Bone stared at Zia, unable to speak. The man's face brought back the night of the ambush in an overwhelming flood of emotions, much stronger than Bone had expected. Here was the interpreter—a valued member of the Team—whose bad stomach one night seven years earlier had caused Bone to volunteer to do a job he thought he was good enough for but wasn't. That had helped get seven of his buddies killed.

Bone breathed in, held it, and breathed out, doing his best to keep it together.

"Sir? Are you okay?" Zia asked. "You want to order or you need some time?"

Going for dark humor, Bone blurted out the first thing that came to mind. "What do you have that won't leave me on the tarmac throwing up?" He didn't mean for it to come out so mean, but he sounded angry, bitter, and full of pain even to himself.

Zia chuckled good-naturedly. "Sir, nothing here will…" He trailed off, leaning forward a fraction. Zia's mouth dropped open in shock and his eyes widened. "Bone?" he whispered. "Oh my God." He rushed to the end of the counter. "Tiffany, take over, please," he called over his shoulder.

The young woman nodded, set down a meat cleaver, and peeled off rubber gloves. "What can I get you?" she asked to a man who had come in behind Bone.

Once around the corner, Zia moved toward Bone with his arms wide. Tears streamed down his face. The smaller man grabbed Bone and wrapped him in a bear hug worthy of a long-lost brother SEAL. "I am so, so sorry," he said, his voice choked with emotion. "It was all my fault. I should have been there that night." He mumbled something more but Bone couldn't make it out over Zia's sobs.

There was so much Bone wanted to say. "Damn right you should have been there." "If you had been along, maybe we would have had enough warning to fight off the ambush." And, "I thought I could do your job—and instead, I got my Team killed."

In the end, Bone said nothing. After a few seconds, he hugged Zia back. And as much as he tried to fight it, the tears came for the first time since that fateful night.

49

THE OFFICE

Pacific Oasis BBQ & Smokehouse
San Diego, California

Bone and Zia were drawing stares from the diners, but San Diego had a large population of military personnel. People had seen reunions between veterans before.

"Come with me," Zia said, wiping his eyes. He latched on to Bone's upper arm with a vice-like grip and practically dragged him toward a back hallway. "Tiffany, prep us a rib dinner, please," he called over his shoulder as they walked into a back room.

Nothing was out of place in the small office. An older computer and monitor took up room on the desk. Plain file folders stood neatly in a black wire rack to the right. A dented four-drawer file cabinet sat against the far wall.

Zia swept his hand over a folding chair just inside the door as if the impeccable room had any dust. "Sit, sit, please."

He pulled out a cheap black office chair. One of the wheels didn't roll properly, so he had to lift the chair an inch to position it in front of the desk, facing Bone.

Zia closed the door. He pulled open the bottom drawer of the file cabinet and produced a small bottle of whiskey. He showed it to Bone, thick eyebrows raised.

Bone stared at it hungrily for a second before looking away. "None for me, thanks. No offense—I need to stay sharp."

Zia nodded, turned to put the bottle away, but stopped. He grabbed an upside-down coffee cup from the top of the file cabinet. His hands shook as he poured a generous amount of alcohol. "Bad American habit I've gotten into," Zia said before downing the drink in one pull. He put the bottle away and left the empty mug on the file cabinet.

"I'm glad you're here," Zia continued. He bit his lip and wiped his palms on his plain black pants. "I have a story to tell you," the interpreter said. He gulped and his eyes darted away from Bone's before looking back. "You're... you're not going to like it."

Bone stared at him, a feeling of dangerous foreboding settling in.

Maybe Zia had been in on the ambush—or had at least known about it.

Bone sat silently, expressionless, letting it play out.

Besides, the less he had to talk right now, the better. Seeing Zia brought his time in the Sandbox and the night of the ambush back strongly. At any moment, he might slip into a waking nightmare that was a dissociative flashback. The breathing trick he'd learned as a SEAL was the only thing keeping him grounded in reality.

He could also smell booze on Zia's breath in the small room. Bone ached with both a physical and emotional need for a drink. He fought it the same way he had gotten through BUD/S training. All he had to do was get through this... whatever it was—reunion, meeting, therapeutic chat. He could postpone drinking until later in the night, or the next morning, or after lunch, and on and on until—he hoped—someday his need wouldn't be so overwhelming.

Zia seemed to be waiting for Bone to say something, so he managed a response. "Let's hear your story. I can handle it."

The words seemed to float between them in the room. While Zia wasn't a SEAL, they'd spent enough time together for both to know Bone was exaggerating at best, or lying to himself and Zia at worst.

The alcohol must have kicked in, giving Zia the courage to begin.

"It's about that night. The night of the ambush." He stepped to the desk chair and sagged wearily into it.

Bone took a deep, steadying breath before returning to his four-count breathing. He could keep it together. Whatever the story, Bone needed to hear it.

Once they got through what Zia had to say, Bone could figure out why Admiral Nalen had suggested he pay Zia a visit.

And whether Zia was an old friend or a traitor.

50

THE BEARD

Pacific Oasis BBQ & Smokehouse
San Diego, California

"This is impossible," Zia mumbled, staring at his feet.

He wiped his palms on his legs again, took a deep breath, sat up straight, and looked Bone in the eye. "On the night of the ambush, I—"

Three quick, light knocks came from the office door, cutting off Zia's story before it began. The door opened and a man popped his head in. "Zia, we need—"

Time slowed to a crawl.

The man in the doorway with the thick beard shaped into a point had changed little in the last seven years.

His widening eyes showed that he recognized Bone too.

The office faded.

The large Afghan stood thirty feet from Bone outside the Afghan village, his rifle lowered.

Afghanistan

Seven Years Ago

The ambush had been much more effective than other lame attempts where a handful of bad guys would hide behind rocks, in windows on the second floor of homes, or at the edges of rooftops. They were predictable; Bone and the others would see a spot, raise their weapons at the obvious position for an ambush, and fire when the tangos popped up thinking they had the drop on the Americans.

This time, none of the SEALs saw it coming. No movement or preliminary peeking around cover had given it away. The ambush positions had been well-hidden and not obvious.

Instead of the usual "spray and pray" method of targeting their enemy, the tangos had waited until the ambush had been sprung by the sniper shot to the village elder's chest.

Other shots from the sniper had done the most damage to the Team, but the accurate, overwhelming fire from more tangos than usual might have done the job without it.

For once, the SEALs had been caught by surprise. The enemy had been disciplined and effective.

They must have been trained and led by someone much more capable than the warriors the SEALs had faced to date.

Bone lay in the sand, shot multiple times in his extremities and bleeding profusely, but the body armor had stopped several shots that would have killed him immediately. None of his wounds on their own was life threatening or debilitating. Taken together, they were overwhelming his system. Blood flowed, but for the moment, he was alive.

His brothers were all dead.

He was out of ammunition for his M4, as well as the pistol which he'd re-holstered out of habit.

A man advanced across the battlefield. He was taller than the other fighters, with a distinctive look: thin, carefully trimmed dark beard, a nose with a small bump on the bridge, thin lips, and wide-set eyes. A sniper rifle was slung across his back. He wore Western fatigues and a top-of-the-line plate carrier with extra magazines in the chest rig. Modern, pricey night vision goggles were flipped up on his helmet, like he was too important to use them.

In his right hand, he carried a pistol, held casually at his side. Bone had no doubt it was the warrior who had planned and led the ambush— and that he was coming to deliver a final shot, a coup de grâce.

Two men, also in Western battle rattle, including helmets, escorted the sniper. Their AKs were up and ready, aimed steadily at Bone. They kept their NVGs over their eyes.

Bone struggled to stand. Every part of him burned with pain, but he would die on his feet. He refused to raise his hands in surrender, letting them instead hang at his sides. Hidden in his right hand, his lucky throwing star from a friend back home dug into his skin.

In the background, the rest of the ambushers gathered in a loose half circle, staying back but eager to watch the final spectacle—a fitting end to their successful attack.

Bone glanced around, taking in the last things he'd see before he died.

In the green glow of his night vision goggles, his men lay dead.

Dozens of the enemy fighters sprawled on the battlefield. Bone and his Team had held their own and might have come out ahead if not for the sniper.

The village in the distance was quiet with its inhabitants hiding inside.

The village elder's body slumped against the mud wall.

The approaching sniper moved with an arrogance that suggested complete belief in himself. His two bodyguards were alert and wary.

In the ring of foot soldiers who had pinned the SEALs down while the sniper picked them off, one stood out. He was taller than most Afghans. Sturdier. His beard was full and bushy, like that of most of the area's men, but shaped into a point. He hulked there, AK held casually at his side, ready to watch Bone die.

The same man stood in the doorway of Zia's southern California barbecue joint.

51

THE ENEMY

Pacific Oasis BBQ & Smokehouse
San Diego, California

The slamming of the office door jolted Bone out of his memory.

Time resumed its normal speed as Bone leaped from the chair to chase the enemy.

"No!" Zia cried. "Wait. Stop! I can explain."

Zia would have plenty of time to explain—Bone would make sure of that—once the bearded man was dead.

Bone didn't bother working out how the tango had gotten from Afghanistan to San Diego or what he was doing sticking his head into Zia's office. All that could wait. Bone's warrior instincts took over. Now wasn't the time for stories or healing old wounds.

It was killing time.

By the time Bone made it through the office door, a door down the long hallway to a back exit slammed closed. The man moved fast for a bigger guy.

Bone sprinted down the hall, avoiding boxes of supplies stacked along the wall. He cranked down the handle as he hit the door at full speed.

The door slammed into something heavy blocking it outside.

He threw his weight at it. The door moved a few inches.

Outside, tires squealed as a vehicle shot away.

When Bone finally pushed the door all the way open, moving a small rollaway dumpster from its place blocking the door, there were only distant taillights of a car turning the corner at the end of the service alley behind the restaurant.

Rage coursed through Bone's body, making him feel alive, but it could cloud his judgment. He suppressed it, controlling his emotions, just like he used to back in the day.

The feelings got put into a box to deal with later. He hadn't used that technique in years, but he did now.

The mission was always the priority. What could be done to salvage the situation? How could he succeed despite the setback?

SEALs adapted and overcame, flowing smoothly around issues that might have bogged down other units.

Bone had one clear next move. He would confront Zia over what the actual hell was going on here—and get the truth out of him, one way or another.

52

THE CONFESSION

Pacific Oasis BBQ & Smokehouse
San Diego, California

Bone returned to the restaurant.

Zia sounded desperate as he called from his office door. "Come back. Let me tell you the story. And please," he asked as they stared at each other down the long hall. "Do not kill me until after you've heard the whole thing."

As Zia spoke, Tiffany, the counter helper, stepped into the hallway carrying a red plastic tray with a paper plate piled with ribs. Smaller containers held side dishes. A tall cup with a straw poking out, paper still attached to the end, completed the meal. She froze at the words. A quick look from Zia calmed her only a little.

Bone stalked back up the hallway, his face set, feeling more like his old self every second. He had the assignment from Admiral Nalen, but directly before him was an equally important—and more personal—mission. One of the foot soldiers who had ambushed his Team was in San Diego, probably less than a mile or two away at the moment, but out of Bone's reach tonight. The quickest way to him was through Zia and whatever bullshit story he had to tell.

Eating Zia's food while listening and gathering intel would put Zia at ease. It would make him believe Bone wouldn't destroy him in a second if necessary. He had to act reasonable, reassure both Zia and Tiffany, and bide his time.

Besides, the ribs smelled amazing. Bone would need his strength for the rest of the mission. He felt it in his gut—tonight was the start. From long experience, he knew that once an operation began, it could go non-stop until the objective was reached.

After hearing Zia's story, Bone could decide whether to kill him tonight in the back office and risk getting arrested before completing the primary mission, or play it safe and return in a few weeks to put an end to Zia and the man who had run.

Either way, eating now was a solid plan.

Bone took the tray from Tiffany with a forced smile. "Thanks," he said.

She looked up at him with wide eyes and gulped.

"Thank you, Tiffany," Zia called. She took it as permission to turn and hurry back to the main part of the restaurant with one last fearful glance over her shoulder.

"She won't call the police," Zia said.

"Unless I kill you," Bone muttered, as he turned and followed Zia into his office.

"You won't. Not after you hear the story."

"We'll see," Bone said as he nudged the office door closed and set the tray on Zia's desk. He picked up the ribs but didn't sit. "You have until the time I'm done with these."

Zia remained standing as well. His nerves seemed steadier after the momentary distraction. "I don't need that long," he said, sounding sure of himself.

"Fine. Make it good. Let's hear it."

As Bone bit into the ribs, Zia took a quick breath and began. "That was my cousin. The night of the ambush, he poisoned me so I wouldn't be with you on the mission. I had no idea the attack was coming. He did. He and many others from the region were recruited and paid by a man for a mission to kill Americans. My cousin needed the money. He was in the ambush and fired his weapon, but claims he shot no one—

he purposefully aimed poorly. He was sickened by what he saw that night. He wasn't a warrior—he was a cook, working in a restaurant like me before I became your interpreter. He regretted his decision from the start." Zia glanced away, then back to Bone. "It has taken years, but I have forgiven him." Zia paused again. "Mostly," he muttered.

He cleared his throat and looked back at Bone. "In part, I've forgiven him because he saved my life by having me to lunch that day and putting something in my food to make me sick later. Also..." Zia paused, his eyes hardening. "Together, we have spent the last four years tracking down the man who paid him. I know who ambushed your Team and paid to have so many other Americans killed. I know where this man lives. Now that you're here," Zia said, his voice fierce but quiet, "you can help my cousin and I kill him."

The first bite of ribs had been delicious, but that's all Bone had managed. He held them in his hand, all but forgotten, as Zia finished.

"Prince Rafiq Al-Najjar?" Bone asked in a voice as quiet and cold as Zia's.

Zia gasped. "How...?"

Bone took a last bite of the ribs before setting them on the plate and wiping off his hands on a thick napkin. He pulled over a chair and gestured for Zia to sit too.

The story could be bullshit, but it made sense. Afghanistan had been like that. People changed sides all the time. Loyalty was a moving target. Everyone looked out for themselves first and their family second. Their country and duty came in a distant third and fourth.

Bone's long-dormant gut instincts told him Zia's story was true.

And if it was all a lie, there would be plenty of time later to take care of the problem.

For now, Bone needed to hear what else Zia had to say. Maybe he had a plan better than waiting in the audience at the movie premiere tomorrow night, hoping for an opportunity to shoot the prince that would still let Bone escape with his life—and freedom.

53

THE ROOM

When the sedative had worn off, Matthew came to on a bare mattress. He didn't know how long he'd been out, but he'd been washed—or at least rinsed. His long hair and beard still felt dirty and hadn't been combed. They probably couldn't be, with all the tangles and mats. At some point, he'd have to just shave it all off.

It was the first time he'd been clean and had fresh clothes in weeks.

He wore brand-new black boxer briefs, new gray sweatpants without a drawstring to use as a garrote or to hang himself, a black t-shirt, and no shoes or socks.

Now he stalked the empty room, searching for anything he could use to escape. A thick leather collar locked on his neck chafed his skin. A heavy-duty steel chain locked to the collar ran to a bolt embedded in the wall. It rattled as he walked.

He could reach the halfway point of what seemed like a rather large bedroom. The chain also allowed him to enter the ensuite bathroom.

All the walls were glossy white.

As a teen, he'd help his dad paint their house. Dad had chosen glossy paint for the kitchen and bathrooms—it was easier to clean.

Matthew took the pristine white walls of the room as one of many bad signs.

Aside from a security camera in the far corner of the room, right above the door, there was only a thin, vinyl-covered mattress on the floor. In the bathroom, he could only reach the toilet—not the sink or the walk-in shower.

Nothing in either room would serve as a weapon. No pen, broom, or television. The lighting was recessed into the ten-foot ceiling—and the bulbs where the chain allowed him to walk had been removed. There wasn't even a toilet seat.

Another bad sign.

A homemade turkey sandwich on a paper napkin and a sealed bottle of water had been waiting next to the bed when he woke up. He'd eaten and drunk. If the two men who had abducted him wanted to poison him or give him more sedatives, they wouldn't need to spike his food or water.

While he used the bathroom the first time, a guard had entered and collected the water bottle. Matthew had caught a glimpse of him as he left. It was a different man than the two who had picked him up.

This one didn't wear a mask, either.

Matthew took that as the worst bad sign.

They didn't care if he saw their faces.

They weren't worried about him going to the police.

He wasn't getting out of this alive.

He paced. The chain rattled. It was heavy enough to be an effective weapon if he could get the guard to approach.

At the very least, he'd go out fighting—and take as many with him as he could.

54

THE HIT

33 Gold Road
La Jolla, California

"What happened earlier?" Rafiq asked as he walked into the security room. Monitors lined the wall. On one, his newest opponent paced in the playroom. Others showed the exterior of the house, from the deserted sidewalk outside the ten-foot-tall security gate at the bottom of the driveway to the brightly lit backyard pool.

Khalid stood behind Nasir—the other long-time bodyguard—who sat at the security desk in front of the TV monitors.

"Sir," Khalid said, using the more casual title Rafiq allowed. Around strangers or lesser staff, Rafiq would be addressed as "Your Highness," of course. If it had been only the two of them in the room, Khalid had permission to address him as Rafiq; Khalid had known his father and served both of them long enough to dispense with proper etiquette when the two of them spoke privately.

But Khalid had never called him by his name in the entire time they'd been together.

"The report came in moments ago," Khalid said, turning to face him.

From the tone and serious expression, it was more bad news. "Not again," Rafiq muttered.

"I'm afraid so, sir. This time, as the men were about to start the fire, the larger man—Lamar—fled the restaurant. Since your orders were to ensure both targets were inside, the men—"

"Fled?" Rafiq interrupted. "What do you mean? Were our men discovered?"

Nasir ignored the conversation, diligently monitoring the screens.

Khalid shook his head. "They don't know why. The dumpster was almost in position to fully block the door, left there for a moment in case one of the workers took the trash out before closing time. One man was nearby, ready to start the fire in the back hall. Another man was in front.

"The back door flew open. Lamar pushed the dumpster the rest of the way in front of the door, as the man we hired would have, except he did not think to lock the wheels. He jumped in his car and sped off. Our man hid.

"Several seconds later, someone tried to open the door and eventually succeeded, moving the dumpster out of the way. They must have been unusually strong; the dumpster was very heavy. The door then closed. That is all I know so far. We are waiting to see if Lamar returns, though the hired men have backed off. The police have not come and nothing unusual is happening in the restaurant."

Rafiq frowned. The scene at the back door into the alley was unusual enough. "I do not like it."

"Yes, sir," Khalid said. "It is an anomaly that we cannot explain."

"Could it have anything to do with..." he trailed off, trying to remember if Nasir knew about the important upcoming mission.

Khalid shook his head and frowned. He had disliked the idea from the start and had fought him every step of the way. Rafiq finally had to order him explicitly to do his bidding. The man argued too much for a servant.

Rafiq had had nearly enough of him.

He brought his focus back to the present as Khalid answered. "No, sir. I do not believe it is about the mission. It could be unrelated. Perhaps the two had a disagreement."

"That would be unfortunate," Rafiq muttered. His plan to kill the two cousins worked best if it looked like an accident—or at least gang-related violence, hence the hired muscle Khalid had negotiated with a local gang. American police were overwhelmed and understaffed, especially the detectives responsible for handling murders, but they could get lucky or decide to throw more resources than usual at an investigation if the deaths were high-profile enough. Killing a local businessman and his cousin, the chef responsible for the restaurant's much-loved barbecue, could be one such case. Especially when it became known the one was a hero of the Afghan war who had helped American soldiers as an interpreter.

"What about the surveillance?" Rafiq asked.

"Still gone," Khalid said.

The loyal bodyguard had been the first to note the presence of excess joggers, bicyclists, skateboarders, speed walkers, dog walkers, and fishermen passing their house the past few weeks. Despite the exclusivity of the neighborhood just north of La Jolla, the streets were public, not gated. People parked in the area to walk and jog surrounded by multi-million dollar homes as if they lived in one of them. Others parked there to access the beach via a short, steep, winding road gated to prevent vehicular use by all except the residents, who were granted a highly coveted access key upon purchase of a home in the neighborhood.

The area was busy—but it defied logic that so many would show such an interest in his home. Rafiq agreed with Khalid. He was being investigated.

The watchers weren't professionals. It was not the FBI or another organization, whether law enforcement or spy, American or foreign. His long-held secret—the activity in the playroom—was likely safe.

The surveillance had the air of an informal yet well-directed operation: volunteers asked to pass in front of Rafiq's home occasionally. They might have gone unnoticed if not for one bicyclist slamming into a parked car while trying to use his phone to take pictures of the gated driveway—all caught on the security camera.

The crashed bicycle rider had eventually led back to the barbecue place several miles to the south near one of the city's most popular beaches.

Further investigation revealed the owner of the restaurant had served as an interpreter for American forces in Afghanistan.

More research—and bribes to Khalid's contacts in Afghanistan—proved that the interpreter had fallen ill the night of the first—and only —ambush Rafiq had participated in.

Rafiq fingered the scar on his cheek, right below his eye. He remembered the excitement of the night.

The thrill of taking the lives of the SEALs.

His rage when the American's stupid weapon had nearly taken out his eye and left an impossible-to-hide scar.

There was also the frustration of later having to admit Khalid was correct; personally killing American troops with the sniper rifle was too risky.

Seven years later, the interpreter and the cousin—the co-owner of the restaurant—were snooping around.

Had they somehow discovered Rafiq's identity as the sniper that night? Did they know Khalid was the one who had organized and paid for the ambush, along with the rest of the bounty program?

The answers weren't clear until Khalid staked out the street near the restaurant.

A large Afghan man at the restaurant with a long, pointed beard—the cousin—looked familiar to Khalid from training the fighters for the ambush, leading them away afterward, and meeting later to pay them for their efforts.

Khalid wasn't sure—it had been years—but Rafiq didn't like the coincidence.

Something was going on.

He wanted the two men dead, just in case.

"Tomorrow night?" Rafiq asked.

"Yes, sir. The hired men will try again. The cousins never take nights off. It would be very unusual for them to not both be there tomorrow."

Rafiq nodded slowly, a glorious idea coming to mind. "Fine. I will go along."

Immediately, Khalid opened his mouth to protest, but Rafiq raised his hand sharply. "There will be no discussion." He said the last word with all the disdain he had.

His bodyguard was an indispensable part of the operation, but increasingly took his role of advisor too far. He was, in the end, not an equal. Khalid was a servant and needed to be reminded of his place once in a while.

"Yes, sir," Khalid said quietly. "What about the movie premiere?" he asked in a suitably submissive tone.

Rafiq had forgotten. He refused to sit in theaters with the disgusting Americans while they chomped on popcorn, slurped soda, whispered to each other, and checked their phones. The body double would go in his place. The director would deliver a copy of the movie in a day or two for Rafiq to watch "again," this time in the home theater downstairs, supposedly with other wealthy people who were interested in financing movies.

Unfortunately, the event in Los Angeles would prevent Rafiq from assisting at the barbecue restaurant or enjoying the spectacle from a suitable location nearby. He couldn't be in two places at once, no matter how unlikely it was to be noted.

"The body double will attend, as usual," Khalid said.

"If this mission is not completed tomorrow, though, I will go along the next night."

"Yes, sir," Khalid repeated.

Finally, the man had stopped arguing so much.

"Now," Rafiq said, rubbing his hands together. "Is my latest opponent ready?" he asked, pointing at the screen that showed the pacing man in the bare room across the hall.

"Yes, sir," Khalid said. "This one is younger and has spirit, as you ordered."

"Excellent." He needed a fun workout—and someone to take out his frustrations on.

55

THE DOSSIER

Pacific Oasis BBQ & Smokehouse
San Diego, California

Bone marveled at the folder in front of him.

Calling it a file didn't do it justice.

The collection of information was a dossier, filled with details about Prince Rafiq Al-Najjar that Bone bet the man would prefer others not know, including drawings of the prince in full battle rattle, looking exactly like the man who had stood in front of Bone that night outside the village, ready to finish him off.

"The first several years here in the US," Zia explained, "we worked eighteen-hour days. Two jobs, sometimes three. We lived frugally, saving every cent for two purposes: one, opening this restaurant. And two, for Lmar—my cousin, who we call Lamar here—to return home. He lived with the guilt of what he'd done every day. We agreed that as soon as we were able, we would make things right somehow.

"Once we had the money, Lamar returned to Afghanistan. He hired an artist from a city and took him to meet with all the men he could find who lived through the ambush."

Zia pointed at the stack of drawings on cheap, rough brown paper. "The artist drew each man's recollection of the sniper. Lamar went last. You see the results."

Every drawing showed the same distinctive man. There were slight differences—the exact size of the bump on the nose or the thickness of the lips. But all matched closely enough—and synced with Bone's recollection too. Wide-set eyes, carefully shaped beard, nose with a bump, thin lips.

"He was the one who paid Lamar?" Bone asked as he stared at one of the drawings, surprised the face didn't throw him instantly back into his waking nightmare. Instead, he felt in control. Focused. On the hunt.

"No," Zia admitted. "He delegated to this man." Zia opened another file and pulled out more drawings showing a second man. Shorter. Muscular, with a narrow face and sharp chin.

"That's the bodyguard who saved him," Bone muttered.

Zia looked at him questioningly, but Bone waved him off.

"His second-in-command, everyone agreed," Zia said.

"Yes," Bone said, remembering the moment the three men stood before him without losing reality and snapping back to that desert night.

"All three of these men were foreigners, likely Saudi or Iranian, Lamar and the others thought. The second man is the one who passed out the money from a large backpack he carried. The men had to wait, however. According to Lamar, the quick reaction force came faster than the foreigners thought. The second man coordinated the retreat and planned a meeting as they all fled. He returned three nights later to hand out the money.

"Lamar and the other surviving men nearly shot him after the ambush, thinking they were being taken advantage of, but in the end he persuaded them and was a man of his word. All were paid as agreed, but the taller man didn't return."

Other pages of the dossier contained photographs of a mansion inside and out, its address, maps of the area, ideas for infiltrating the grounds, and the man's movements: where he went and what types of things he did. He was quite active, going out to eat several nights per week and attending art gallery openings. He also frequently flew to Los Angeles via a chartered helicopter—for the movie premieres, Bone figured.

"We've had people staking out his home and following him for the last few weeks," Zia said with pride.

The statement sent an alarm through Bone. If the man's security detail was halfway competent, they would have spotted amateur surveillance attempts.

He'd have to deal with that later.

Bone held up the artist's sketch of the man who had killed his brothers. "How did you put this man's face with the name of Prince Rafiq Al-Najjar?"

Zia shuffled the papers in the folder until he found what he wanted. It looked like one of the sketches had been turned into a photograph. "We hired an artist online to make this photorealistic image from the best sketch. I think they used one of the newer artificial intelligence programs. Only twenty dollars and delivered the next day."

He showed the receipt clipped to the back of the image. They had saved everything.

"We thought the next steps would take months or years. We had a plan to hire remote workers in Bangladesh to look at the faces of Arab men on the internet, or to pay hackers to access databases. But I found an online service. We paid thirty dollars for a month's worth of searches and found him on the first attempt. The technology is amazing. We uploaded the photorealistic picture and a few seconds later it showed us this." Zia slid a paper from the thick folder.

It was the page Admiral Nalen had alerted Bone to and ordered him to find.

"We used a computer at the library to send an anonymous tip to the FBI via their website, but nothing was ever done."

One of Admiral Nalen's intelligence analysts must have put two and two together and guessed the interpreter was somehow involved, which is why he'd wanted Bone to visit Zia.

"In the end," Zia continued, "we decided we had to handle it ourselves."

Bone held the printout of the web page and stared into the face of his enemy.

The man he would kill in less than twenty-four hours.

56

THE PLAN

Pacific Oasis BBQ & Smokehouse
San Diego, California

"Bone? Are you okay?"

Bone nodded. He must have gotten lost for a moment. "I'm fine. Just remembering. I can confirm that the man in the picture and the drawings is the sniper from that night. He killed the guys."

The two of them shared a moment of silence for the men of the Team.

After a few seconds, Bone raised an eyebrow. "How were you going to take care of it yourselves?"

"The prince is going to a movie premiere in Los Angeles tomorrow night. It's been on his schedule for a while—he financed the movie. He'll get out of a limo, walk a red carpet, stopping once or twice to get his picture taken. He does a few of them each year. Lamar scouted the location. There is a hotel with a rooftop terrace less than two blocks away that is closed for renovation. It is across the street to the west of the theater."

"That's a very public location."

Zia nodded. "It is the only place we can be sure the prince will be, where we know he will stand still, and in a location that we can also get away quickly. There will be so many people in the area. It will be easy to blend in and slip away."

It was Bone's turn to nod. "You've got it all figured out, huh?" Zia talked as if shooting a man in cold blood from an elevated position were a walk in the park.

"What about a weapon?"

Zia's eyes flicked to the office's closet in a subconscious tell. "Lamar went to Mexico, spoke to several dangerous people, and eventually bought a rifle. An AK. He purchased a scope for cash at a store in Arizona and shot the gun in the desert. It is a good weapon. There is no paper trail. And now, with you here…"

They shared another long look.

"You thought I would take the shot instead of Lamar?" Bone asked.

"Don't you want to?"

Bone didn't hesitate. "Hell, yes."

57

THE LET DOWN

Pacific Oasis BBQ & Smokehouse
San Diego, California

Bone debated the wisdom of taking a mission plan from amateurs, but he had to start somewhere. He picked Zia's brain and studied the file, memorizing every detail he could.

Their idea probably wouldn't work, but it was a better one than the rough plan he had.

"I'll go and check things out," he said. "No promises, though. I'd prefer a less public attack," he said, remembering Admiral Nalen's preference. "It makes sense to blend in to escape, but police will be on the scene quickly. It would be very easy to get trapped in the hotel or seen leaving. It's extremely risky."

"Lamar thought he might get caught. It didn't matter. The truth would come out about what the prince did..."

"And he could stop feeling guilty?"

Zia didn't answer. He didn't need to. "We can change the plan for you to take the shot. Or we can find a position further away. With your skills, we can—"

Bone interrupted him, dropping the bomb. "Neither of you can come along."

"But—"

Shaking his head, Bone held up his fingers one by one, counting off his reasons. "One, there's no interpreting to be done. Two, I don't know Lamar except as a guy who ambushed me. Three, the more people around, the more conspicuous we would be." He paused and took a deep breath, not wanting to say the next part aloud but forcing himself to. "And last, I can't risk more people dying next to me."

"We're not going to die…"

"Getting arrested and thrown in prison? Same thing. It's losing your life. No, this is my responsibility now."

"What can we do to help?" Zia asked after a few seconds. He didn't like it, but he was smart enough to see how much sense it made.

"You two stay here. Mingle with your staff and customers. You'll be safe and have rock-solid alibis in case anyone comes looking. If I get caught, say I looked you up to talk about the old days. I seemed really depressed. Don't mention the prince, and deny anything that suggests you were a part of what I'm about to do."

Bone gathered up the papers and stuffed them back into the folder. His hands trembled slightly. He ignored it.

"Destroy all this," he said. "Shred them, then burn it, then get rid of the ashes. Destroy and trash the computer or phone used to do the research. You don't need proof any longer. You have me."

58

THE PLAYROOM

33 Gold Road
La Jolla, California

As soon as Rafiq entered the playroom, his heart rate went up with the thrill of the game. He forced himself to calm down. It was only the first night.

He wanted to make this one last.

Rafiq stood inside the door to get a sense of his latest opponent. The man stopped pacing to return the assessment. The chain hung loose behind him, barely touching the floor. It wasn't long enough to use as an effective weapon unless Rafiq got careless and moved much further into the room than usual.

At times in the past, that had been necessary. Men retreated after the first bout, requiring pursuit. Many had the idea that strangling him with the chain would be their way to freedom.

They were so predictable.

Aside from the long brown hair and bushy beard, both tangled and unkempt, the latest captive looked less like a homeless person than the last several, though he had the same dark tan that came from being outside every day.

He was younger too. Maybe in his early thirties. He had smart, wary brown eyes, but he wasn't afraid.

Yet. He'd get there soon enough.

He looked at Rafiq without the usual sputtering anger or frantic pleading.

"Welcome," Rafiq began as always. "I am sure you have many questions. In time, they will be answered. For now, all you need to know is this. We will fight. If you beat me—if you force me to tap out or one of my guards enters to save me—I will release you."

The man didn't move or ask questions. He continued to stand ready and stare.

Rafiq frowned. Perhaps his idiot guards had picked up a deaf person, or one who didn't speak English.

"Do you understand what I have said?" Rafiq asked.

The man's eyes narrowed and his mouth twitched with a slight grin. He lifted one hand slowly and extended his middle finger.

Rafiq smiled himself. This one would be fun.

59

THE DRIVE

Interstate 5
Southeast of Los Angeles

Bone drove north in traffic that was surprisingly heavy for after midnight—the difference between rural Arizona and overpopulated Southern California.

The hatchback's rear seats folded down to make a cargo area. In the space created between the seats, Bone had hidden the AK-47 acquired by Lamar in Mexico.

It looked well-maintained. The scope on it was perfect for the mission—the Afghan had done his homework and chosen well. Thirty minutes earlier, Bone had pulled off the freeway and driven on the highway for several miles to a camping and hiking area he'd visited years before, in his other life as a San Diego-based SEAL.

One shot in the mountains—using a night vision monocular from his go bag—had reassured him of the weapon's usability. The scope was dialed in, but...

His hands trembled on the steering wheel. They'd gotten steadily worse since leaving Zia's restaurant. The minor tremor was now a full-blown shake.

He was sweating profusely off and on, despite the cool evening, and his head pounded. Putting it all together, he had to face the uncomfortable truth: he was going through alcohol withdrawal.

Between the trembling hands, throbbing headache, and sweating, if Zia's research and Lamar's scouting proved accurate, Bone had a big problem.

There was no way he could shoot accurately like this.

60

HOTEL DEL TORO

Tiempo del Toro Hotel
Hollywood, California

The upscale hotel diagonally across the street from the famous old movie theater had an outdoor patio bar on the ground floor. Bone saw no security cameras, but he kept his sunglasses on and hat pulled down despite the darkness and late hour, looking like several other men he'd seen already. Maybe those guys were famous and didn't want to be recognized, acting cool, or intent on hiding their features like he was. It didn't matter; Bone blended right in.

Ordering a soda instead of booze took all his willpower, but he once again fought through the temptation to drink. Being on a mission made it easier. He pushed off the nearly overwhelming need until an indefinite "later"—after he'd completed his assignment, at least.

Hollywood on a Friday night was rocking, even after midnight. Tourists walked the sidewalks and took pictures with buskers dressed as famous characters from the movies working for tips. Some of the costumes were great; most were cheap, embarrassing attempts at scamming tourists out of a few bucks for a photograph.

He'd paid an exorbitant amount to park in a guarded lot a few blocks away, right outside another hotel. Again, he hadn't seen any security cameras—just the three valet lot attendants who looked like they'd be there all night. He couldn't risk the AK being stolen by someone smashing a window.

Bone kept his shaky hands out of sight as much as possible, using the straw to drink while he casually surveyed the area. The night was cool but pleasant, the vibe hip and friendly.

Down the street, less than two hundred yards away, was the ornate two-story movie theater where, according to Zia's file, a movie called *The Moonlight Mirage* would premiere in less than twenty-four hours —Saturday night. The entrance sat well back from the street and the polished sidewalk with its many stars featuring the names of celebrities.

A red carpet would run from the curb to the wide double doors. Depending on the importance of the movie and the fame of the movie stars, there might be bleachers set up for fans. Barricades would keep people back, but plenty of spectators, tourists, press, and paparazzi would fill in the area.

He wouldn't take the shot if there was a chance he'd miss and hit an innocent civilian. The prince's bounty program had caused enough pain and grief. Bone wouldn't inadvertently add more.

The rest of the street, up and down, was filled with restaurants, tourist traps, and other shops. There was a mix of tall office buildings with retail on the ground floor, one- and two-story buildings with many restaurants, lots of clothing stores, and a few pharmacies, all catering to the tourists walking along the street, posing for pictures next to their favorite celebrity's star.

The road was two lanes in each direction, with an unmarked area one-lane wide for busses, but no parking in the block of the movie theater.

Bone was already convinced of the foolhardiness of Zia and Lamar's plan without seeing the rooftop bar under construction.

Lamar might have hoped to get away after the shot, but there wasn't much chance of that. The location must have been chosen primarily because killing the prince from this distance would be relatively easy for Lamar, not for its tactical advantages or the ease of successfully making a quick getaway.

As Bone had told Nalen, he was willing to give his life for his country. But there was dying for a realistic objective—and throwing your life away.

He'd had a dark moment a few nights before. It had passed. He wanted to live—and live free, not get caught shooting a Saudi prince and sent to rot in a cell for decades.

No matter how much the prince deserved to die, Bone would rather get away with it. If the United States of America needed an assassin to take out an enemy, Bone would be the best one possible and get away clean, leaving everyone to wonder why a rich supporter of the arts had been gunned down in Los Angeles.

Having discarded the original plan, Bone worked the problem and drank his soda. By the time he'd finished the sugary drink, he felt almost himself again. His hands still shook, and he had no detailed plan yet for taking out Prince Rafiq Al-Najjar, but he was on the job. There was planning to do, a solution to create—and a man to kill.

He left a tip for the soda and walked away from the theater, up Hollywood Boulevard, estimating the distance as he went.

After only one block, he left the busiest, most touristy area behind. The neighborhood switched from retail to offices and a few restaurants.

On the left were tall buildings that just might work.

He walked, glancing casually at two dark gray ten-story office buildings. They were close together but separated by a single-story connector structure. He stopped at the intersection just past the second building and turned slowly, looking back down the street toward the theater, gawking like a tourist—and a sniper planning his shot.

The distance was four hundred yards, give or take. Easy.

It had been years since he'd had any range time, but he wasn't worried. At that distance, on a calm night, with his training and experience, he'd have to be blind to miss.

He held up his trembling hands and wondered.

If he were sober and shaking, he would miss.

Would the tremors stop with one or two drinks?

He'd cross that bridge when he came to it.

The angle looked perfect from the building closer to the theater, but there might be an angle from the corner of the second building too.

Anyone who thought of a sniper shot would naturally look at the first building—while he snuck away from the second.

It might buy him a few minutes, allowing him to get away clean. The solution wasn't the best—it was specifically what Nalen hadn't preferred. For now, though, unless he could think of something better, it would do.

Bone waited for the traffic light to change, crossed the street, and enjoyed the two-and-a-half block walk back to the theater, checking out the many stars on the sidewalk along the way.

He felt good. He'd made it through the night without drinking and had the start of a mission plan.

All he had to do now was access the roof of the building after dark in a busy, well-lit area while carrying a rifle, remain undiscovered on the roof while baking in the sunshine all day tomorrow, and get himself in shape enough to shoot the man who had killed his brothers.

61

THE ROOF

Hollywood Boulevard
Hollywood, California

Bone ducked into a 24-hour liquor store, keeping his head down to hide his face as much as possible, and bought a bottle of whiskey. He had to be realistic. If the choice was between having a few sips to steady himself or taking the shot sober with shaking hands, he'd risk the booze.

A few blocks further on, he retrieved his car, gave the valet a tip both large and small enough to not be remembered, and drove to a back street to prep what he needed for the mission.

His clothes were fine—straight out of his go bag yesterday morning after his trail run and meeting with Admiral Nalen. Black cargo pants, a black long-sleeve shirt, and a black windbreaker made him look hip on Hollywood Boulevard—and would allow him to slip into the shadows off it.

The larger pistol felt comfortable in the holster inside his pants.

The smaller 9mm in the calf holster, under his pants leg, was barely noticeable.

Tactical gloves went into his pocket. He couldn't leave fingerprints behind.

Once the go bag was empty, Lamar's AK went inside. It was long, but just barely fit on the diagonal once he extended the straps holding the flap over the top. Extra clothes padded the bag to make it look less like he was carrying a rifle.

The bottle of booze went in between the clothes, and he packed a few of the large bottles of water and several energy bars inside too.

An old wool blanket completed his load out.

As he closed the bag, he had another withdrawal sweat attack but ignored it. It was uncomfortable, both physically and as a sign of how much his body had grown to rely on alcohol, but it wouldn't affect him. As a SEAL, he had learned to be comfortable with being uncomfortable.

It had been much too long since he'd used that skill—and so many others. Tonight, though, he was back on track.

Bone drove the car around the back streets several blocks from Hollywood Boulevard, looking for a good place to park the car. He couldn't be too far away from the buildings he'd picked but the spot had to be both safe and legal. Discovering the car had been towed right when he needed to make a speedy getaway would be bad.

He found a space a block to the west of the buildings on a street of apartments, slung the backpack over one shoulder, and locked up the car. Imitating a weary worker coming home after a long night, he made his way along the quiet residential street back to Hollywood Boulevard, head down.

At the second office building, he'd planned on finding a dark corner and waiting until right before dawn for the next stage, but he had a good feeling. The area was quiet, with only the occasional car. The restaurants had closed and there were no bars nearby. No lights were on in the offices. The few retail shops were all dark.

A long gray drainpipe along the back corner of the second building looked freshly added. The city had gotten more rain than usual the last few years. Arizona had too. More rain meant people paid much more attention to their flat-roof houses and office buildings. No one wanted a deluge off a corner of a building or leaks from pooling water that hadn't drained properly. Gutters and drains were installed where they hadn't been before—or cleaned out and made functional for the first time in years.

The office tower had new exterior drain pipes, attached every four feet with shiny silver bands bolted to the building. No one would think of it as an easy way to access the roof.

No one except a SEAL.

Bone's arms went through the other pack strap. He slipped on tactical gloves and didn't even have to jump to reach the pipe. It conveniently ran to three feet off the ground where the rainwater could flow onto the sidewalk and to the street, funneled safely away from the building.

After a quick look around to confirm there were no cars or pedestrians approaching, he started. The eight-inch pipe was smooth, but Bone had no trouble wrapping his hands around it, planting his feet, and clambering up the outside of the wall. The pipe barely moved; someone had done a good job securing it to the exterior.

He felt like a monkey climbing a tree for a coconut.

It took little time to reach the roof. No one yelled at him, asking what he was doing. There were no police sirens.

He'd made it.

If there wasn't an angle for the shot, though, the climb would mean nothing. He'd have to back down the way he came and move to the other building to repeat the process.

Lying near the western corner of the building, Bone pretended to sight Lamar's rifle down the street.

The angle was perfect. He'd be back from the front of the building, behind the low facade at the edge of the roof and partly hidden by an air conditioning unit. No one would see him take the shot.

He was as ready as he could be—but still had fifteen hours before the limos would arrive up the street for the movie premiere.

Bone hated the idea of sleeping, but he needed to rest. If sleep—and the nightmares—came, he would just have to deal with it. As usual.

Ignoring his shaking hands and another surge of withdrawal sweats, he found a place back from the edge of the roof against another

A/C unit, stretched out, covered himself with the blanket from the pack, and closed his eyes. At BUD/S, they'd been taught a sleep technique—as if exhaustion from the constant workouts didn't have them already dropping off to sleep while marching, eating, or swimming.

He used it now, tightening and relaxing each muscle in his body, starting at his feet.

He didn't expect sleep to come, but at least his mind and body would get some rest.

62

THE VISION

Afghanistan

Seven Years Ago

The bullets didn't hurt as they slammed into Bone. Most hit his armor plate. The few that connected hit him in the shoulder and arm and merely added to the devastating damage he had already sustained. With the adrenaline surging through his body and the endorphins blocking the pain, the additional wounds didn't bother him at all.

It would all be over in a few seconds anyway.

The only thing he cared about—the only thing that ever mattered—was staying in the fight.

Bone landed hard in the rocky sand.

His hand reached for the knife hanging from his plate carrier. He drew it and lunged, sensing the enemy within range.

Bone plunged the six-inch blade into the nearest man, directly under the back of the knee—the highest point his depleted body allowed him to reach.

As the man screamed, Bone pulled hard, dragging the knife down the leg, slicing everything in its path as the darkness took him.

Hollywood Boulevard
Hollywood, California

Present Day

Bone woke to a gentle pink sky over the city and an urgent need to vomit.

He tossed the blanket away and low-crawled to the back corner of the building before emptying his stomach on the white coating of the roof.

The lingering images from the nightmare clung to him, but he'd managed at least some rest. Unfortunately, he felt worse than the many mornings he'd awoken after drinking himself to sleep. He was once again sweating profusely despite the chill of the spring morning.

He discounted the idea of a cold or food poisoning from Zia's restaurant. In his heart, he knew there was only one explanation.

The withdrawals were getting worse.

Bone rinsed his mouth with a bottle of water from his pack and slumped with his back against the large, boxy air conditioner. He would go over contingencies to distract himself from his body's reaction to no longer having the alcohol it needed.

On the edge of the roof twenty yards away, seven men grinned at him while shaking their heads in amusement.

A second later, Tank and the others broke out in silent laughter at his reaction to seeing them.

Bone leaned over to heave again, but nothing came out.

By the time he looked back, his brothers were gone.

Over the years, he'd had visions of the men lost that night in Afghanistan. Now they were visiting more frequently.

That was not a good sign.

Before, he'd blamed it on being drunk, but couldn't do that now. The bottle of whiskey was still in the pack, unopened.

"Am I that messed up?"

His voice sounded hoarse in the quiet of the morning. He was talking out loud to himself.

Also not good.

He shook his head and put the fear of being crazy, the grief from seven years earlier, and the concern he wasn't up to the assignment into a box. Those issues could be dealt with another day when the mission was over.

Instead, Bone focused on what he could control. He could take care of himself, eat, drink, stay hidden, and out of the sun. He would rehearse the shot he'd take. Plan contingencies.

And avoid thinking about the whiskey waiting for him if he needed it.

PART 4

SATURDAY

63

THE BEATING

The Room
Unknown Location

Matthew stifled a groan as he rolled over, certain someone was watching via the security camera bolted to the ceiling near the door, out of reach.

He wouldn't give them the pleasure of seeing him in so much pain.

The overhead lights hadn't turned off or dimmed, but he guessed it had to be morning. He felt rested despite the beating he'd taken. The thin mattress, without a blanket, was still more comfortable than the cold hard ground he normally slept on.

The heavy chain rattled as he forced himself up to use the restroom. The more he thought about his situation, the more convinced he became that he was being held in a private residence. There were no windows—Matthew guessed at least one had been drywalled over—and no closet. It had the look and feel of a house, from the HVAC vent above the door to the expensive vinyl plank flooring similar to what he'd helped one of his buddies install in the guy's house, before Matthew had lost his job, his apartment, and—he could admit—went a little nuts, ending up on the streets of Los Angeles.

This type of flooring was normally used in bathrooms and kitchens for one of its most valuable features: it was waterproof. No liquids would seep into it or through the cracks, including the blood the nutjob had beaten out of him last night.

The drops had dried where they fell.

Matthew avoided them out of principle as he staggered to the bathroom, trailing the chain.

He had been in the Navy for six years. He'd had basic training and gotten into his share of bar fights. Those were quickly over, broken up by other sailors, MPs, or by a bar owner racking a shell into a shotgun.

None of it had prepared him for the demented situation he found himself trapped in—bare-knuckle fighting with a guy who knew his stuff. The dude enjoyed the hell out of taking Matthew on, even when Matthew landed one lucky hit.

At the toilet, his urine was tinged red—yet another bad sign. The strikes to his abdomen and lower back had done a lot of damage.

He had no illusions about what would happen to him. He would eventually die in this room.

His body couldn't take many more beatings like last night's. He'd be less strong after each one and spiral downward. With every fight, there was less chance he could get the dude to tap out, assuming the guy was true to his word and would let him go, which wasn't likely.

If he refused to fight, his crazy captor would kill him—and probably enjoy it.

Matthew had to hold out. He wouldn't give up. As long as he put on a good show and fought hard, he'd survive for a few days.

While he lived, there was a chance, no matter how slim, that he would score another solid hit on the dude, wrap the chain around his neck, and kill him before the guard could come in and break it up.

He'd only need a few seconds—and some luck.

64

THE SCOPE

Hollywood Boulevard
Hollywood, California

The day passed quickly for Bone atop the gray office building. The California spring air was pleasant—not too warm or cool—and there wasn't as much smog as he'd expected.

He had made a lean-to with the blanket against one of the huge air conditioners. He planned his escape, what he'd tell Zia and Lamar, and wondered if Admiral Nalen would drop by for a verbal after-action report once he returned to Arizona.

Bone also revised the plan. Instead of assassinating the prince, which Nalen hadn't wanted unless absolutely necessary, he'd woken with an idea. If he shot the prince first, then carefully continued, emptying the rest of the magazine into the limo's engine block, the theater's sign, the building's facade, and the large spotlights sure to be lighting up the sky—targets far from innocent people—the attack might look like an amateur "spray and pray" and get blamed on gang violence or domestic terrorism.

Bone would slip away, the prince would be dead, and no one would suspect he was the only target.

As the sun dipped and dusk settled over Hollywood, Bone returned the blanket, one of the water bottles—and a new pee bottle—to the pack, slung it on his back, and crawled slowly to the front edge of the building. He was on top of the tallest building around, but old habits died hard. Getting into position as a sniper called for stealth, and whether it was essential tonight or not, he'd follow his training.

Throughout the day, he'd worked at settling his mind and, more importantly, his hands. After several hours, he'd had a minor breakthrough. The alcohol withdrawal symptoms had faded and he found himself at peace. The past was the past. His buddies were gone. He had lived, they had not.

It wasn't his fault.

Had he immediately understood the quiet words from the village elder, they might have had a few seconds of warning, but it probably wouldn't have done any good. The enemy ambush had been expertly set up and perfectly executed with overwhelming firepower—plus deadly marksmanship from the sniper.

Nothing he or any of the men could have done would have changed the outcome.

They were dead the moment they landed in that valley.

Being at peace with the memory, though, didn't mean he had forgiven the man responsible.

Bone suppressed a smile. He was looking forward to ending the life of the sniper who had killed his guys.

It had a certain poetic justice. Prince Rafiq would die from a sniper shot he never saw coming on an evening he thought would be similar to many in the past.

Bone stopped at the spot he'd picked out near the edge of the roof. He rolled the pack off his back and removed the large wool blanket. He covered himself with it in case any helicopters flew overhead. A gray and black blanket near the edge of a roof might get a second look, but wouldn't raise as much suspicion as a man lying prone behind a rifle.

The weapon came out next, followed by the whiskey bottle, which he placed nearby, just in case, along with one of the tall water bottles.

The pack went perpendicular in front of him as a makeshift support for the gun barrel.

He settled behind the rifle and pulled the last fold of the large blanket over him and the barrel, using the bottle of water to prop up the fabric. It gave him just enough of a gap to sight up the block to the theater while keeping his body and the rifle completely covered.

He was ready. It wouldn't be long now. The lights were on all over the city. Signs lit the street in front of him, bathing the tourists in reds, yellows, and greens. The sky darkened.

Through the rifle's scope, Bone saw that a crowd had already gathered at the theater. There were no bleachers for people to sit, but fans three rows deep lined both sides of the red carpet that had been rolled out. Metal barriers held them back.

A long row of press and paparazzi stood around looking at their phones or chatting, clearly bored.

Bone's breathing was steady. His hands were still.

He aimed at the curb, where the limos would arrive and let out their passengers.

It was almost time.

65

THE LIMO

The Hollywood Theater
Los Angeles, California

Once again, Yousuf rode in the back of the limousine with the two bodyguards sitting across from him.

These men would keep him from being kidnapped—the biggest but not only threat to an extremely wealthy Saudi prince. They would stay nearby, though the security around the latest movie premiere would be tight as always.

Did they know? Had they been told who he really was, or figured it out on their own? Were they protecting him—or guarding him?

The painful plastic surgery he'd endured to make him an exact copy of the prince was as close to perfection as humanly possible. And Yousuf acted as he'd been taught: aloof, superior, lost in his own thoughts. He asked no questions and made no comments. But surely men who spent much time with the actual Prince Rafiq would notice subtle differences, right?

Unless, as he suspected, this pair was the B-team; the backup guards. There were two others aside from Khalid: Basoul and Nasir. They were older than this pair and Yousuf rarely saw them.

Perhaps they protected the real prince and these two did odd jobs like washing the prince's cars—or escorting the fake prince to movie premieres.

The one with the bushy beard—Fahad, who wasn't as smart as the other guard—spoke. "Your briefing packet, Your Highness," he said.

Yousuf accepted it without a word. He rarely had to speak at these events, but if engaged, it was better to have a few talking points memorized. The right question would get any of the Americans involved in the movie speaking at length. All he had to do was listen.

As he settled back and prepared to study what "his" money had funded this time, Fahad leaned forward. "How was the latest addition to the playroom?" he asked while miming a tiny punch with his fist.

Yousuf acted as he did at every event when he had no idea what people were asking him. He followed his instincts and faked it. He narrowed his eyes and glared at Fahad, expertly slipping into the role of the prince. How dare his bodyguard, the hired help, question him as if they were buddies? Equals?

Fahad froze before lowering his eyes and leaning back. "Apologies, Your Highness," he whispered.

Yousuf said nothing else. He turned to watch the city and the excessive traffic, wondering about the man's words.

He had overheard other mentions of a playroom, but he hadn't put the pieces of the puzzle together.

He'd work on it.

For now, though, he returned his thoughts to the city passing by—and the hands of fate that had brought him to this place, all for being the same height, build, and having similar features to one of the richest men in the world, Prince Rafiq Al-Najjar of Saudi Arabia.

66

THE MOVIE THEATER

The Hollywood Theater
Los Angeles, California

Yousuf waited patiently as the limousine inched its way down Hollywood Boulevard. He'd finished the briefing packet about the movie. For once, he was looking forward to the film. It sounded more entertaining than the one Thursday night, which had been boring.

He recognized the area. They were almost at the theater. Early, of course. Not many people cared about "his" role as executive producer —one of the moneymen of the movie—so he was always one of the first of the VIPs to arrive.

The editor and other behind-the-scenes types who were too important to ignore but not interesting to the general public would arrive shortly after.

The minor stars of the movie would be next, followed by the major stars and the director in an order surely worked out over complex negotiations by their agents. Everyone wanted to be the most important.

The car slowed to a stop with his door perfectly aligned with the long red carpet that would take him inside.

Hollywood Boulevard
Hollywood, California

The whiskey remained unopened. Bone didn't want it. Didn't need it. He was focused. Ready. On target.

The third limo slowed to a stop. Behind it stretched a line of several more, wrapping around a corner two blocks back.

Bone kept his breathing slow and steady. He had slipped back into the sniper zone easily, like stepping into a pair of favorite shoes he hadn't worn in much too long.

His mind was clear, his pulse slow. He was calm and alert.

Deadly.

Zia and Lamar hadn't figured out who arrived when to the premieres. They only knew that the prince would be one of the first welcomed to the red carpet.

Bone was prepared to fire at the man who had haunted his dreams for the past seven years.

When that man stepped out of the limo and waved at the crowd, he would die.

The Hollywood Theater
Los Angeles, California

The attendant at the curb, dressed in a cheap black suit, white shirt, and skinny long white tie, was the same man as earlier in the week at the smaller movie premiere.

The man knocked lightly on the glass as a warning that he was about to open the door.

Yousuf plastered on the pleasant but knowing smile, prepared for the initial screams of excitement as a "star" arrived that would quickly change to boredom and whispers of, "Who is that?"

The door opened. Fahad stepped out first, waited a moment, then stepped away and signaled him.

Yousuf emerged to the flashes from the press cameras and the cheers and applause from the crowd.

He stopped at the foot of the red carpet, smiling at the row of cameras on his left as the cheers died quickly once people saw him, a person none of them recognized.

———

Hollywood Boulevard
Hollywood, California

Prince Rafiq's face was as clear as day in the scope as he posed for the crowd of photographers, a smile on his face.

The carefully shaped dark beard. Slightly wide-set eyes. The bump on his nose.

Tall frame. Thick, dark hair.

The arrogant smirk.

And the scar on his left cheek below the eye.

There was no doubt the man in Bone's sights was the man who had killed his Team in Afghanistan.

Bone thought he was prepared for the shock of seeing him again.

He wasn't.

His pulse rate soared.

He lost control of his breathing.

His hands shook.

If he took the shot, he'd miss.

Bone calmed himself, the years of experience paying off.

The hours on the range.

The nights behind the gun, killing bad guys.

It all helped him now.

He stilled his mind.

Breathed in. Breathed out.

Willed his pulse to slow.

All while tracking the prince as he walked along the red carpet.

Bone got himself under control.

His hands stopped trembling.

A distant part of his mind congratulated himself for the accomplishment.

His finger tightened on the trigger...

... As Prince Rafiq Al-Najjar, killer of SEALs and enemy of the United States of America, vanished into the safety of the theater.

67

THE AUTHORITIES

Pacific Oasis BBQ & Smokehouse
San Diego, California

Zia sat in his desk chair while Lamar paced the small office.

It had been a busy day. The two of them hadn't had a chance to speak other than about work. Zia took and served orders. Lamar worked in the kitchen, prepared the food and supervised the young cooks.

Finally, they had a moment to slip into the back room for a break—and a heart-to-heart talk.

"It should be me," Lamar muttered.

By long agreement, they rarely spoke in their native language, but they had naturally fallen back into Pashto when alone together.

"He is a trained warrior who has much more skill than you," Zia answered. "And it was his men the prince killed, right? It is for him to seek revenge, not you."

Lamar looked down, still not happy.

"He will succeed. If you hadn't run away last night, we could have spoken together. You would have heard his conviction."

"If I hadn't run away, I would be dead. You too, probably."

Zia frowned, conceding the point.

"And how did he come to us at this time?" Lamar asked. "Don't you find it a suspicious coincidence? Could the FBI have traced the anonymous tip from the library computer back to us?"

"I don't know. Bone didn't say. Only that if anyone asked about him, I should say that he had visited unexpectedly, we had a short reunion, and that he seemed depressed. That is all."

Lamar mulled over the words. "Could we be targeted?" he asked. "Arrested for planning a murder?"

"Is that illegal? To plan?"

"I do not know."

"Many American special forces go to work for companies that provide security work for wealthy people," Lamar added.

"You think he is working for the prince? Double-crossing us?" Zia didn't hide his skepticism. "He would not work for the man."

"No, not now that he knows the truth. But before? One of the people watching the prince's movements could have been followed. Perhaps we have been careless."

Zia glanced at the locked office door. Lamar's paranoia was rubbing off on him.

"I don't like it," Lamar muttered. "I sense danger."

Enough missions with the SEALs had allowed Zia to develop a sense of when things were about to go wrong. "I feel the same. But Bone is in Los Angeles. He is likely shooting the prince right now."

"What if he isn't? What if it is a trap, or the government wants to frame two foreigners? Two Al Qaeda terrorists?"

"We are far from terrorists, whether Al Qaeda, ISIS, or Taliban."

"We know that. Most Americans would give us the benefit of the doubt. But not all."

They'd both lived with more than their share of hassles based on the tone of their skin—and especially Lamar's heavier accent.

They glanced at the door as if the authorities would break it down any second.

"We're being paranoid," Zia said, trying to convince them both.

Lamar eventually nodded. "I hope so. I'm going back out into the restaurant. You should too. If Bone is doing as he claimed," he said, with a heavy emphasis on the first word, "we should be seen in public as much as possible."

"I will be right out. I want to go over last month's bookkeeping."

"Don't be long."

Lamar unlocked the door and stalked out.

Zia sat for a moment, debating, then rose to lock the door behind him.

68

THE BOTTLES

Pacific Beach Neighborhood
San Diego, California

Khalid sat in the driver's seat of the luxury electric car, up the street from the Afghan cousins' barbecue restaurant. With the window rolled down, he got a faint sense of the ocean, though he couldn't smell the water or hear the waves crashing on the shore a few blocks to the west.

He was parallel-parked along the most likely route the fire trucks would take from their station four blocks south and one west. When he heard sirens, he would pull away from the parking space and "accidentally" accelerate into the other lane, hitting a car on the busy street.

As the fire trucks neared, the lanes would be fully blocked, slowing the response of the firefighters until a shaken Khalid managed to finally move his vehicle out of the way.

Everyone inside the restaurant would die, including the two targets.

The gang members had been called off—and well paid for their efforts the previous nights.

Desperate times called for desperate measures, and these were desperate times indeed. Khalid had convinced the prince to give them one more night. If they didn't succeed now, he would "assist" them tomorrow.

Khalid couldn't say no, but he also couldn't allow the prince to risk capture in the United States, despite his escalating desire for "action," as he called it.

While the prince was secure in his large suite at the house, Khalid managed the mission to silence the two Afghans.

"I only see the large one," Basoul muttered from across the street from the restaurant. He had drawn the short straw. Not literally—he hadn't actually had a choice. Khalid had chosen Basoul to throw the Molotov cocktails because he had been with the team for a shorter time than Nasir, who had been with Khalid and the prince since before the Afghanistan ambush.

After tonight, Basoul would be shipped back to Saudi Arabia to disappear until they could be assured the crime would go unsolved by the American police. Maybe he would find a wife and settle down. He would receive a handsome bonus and be eligible for more work in the future if all went well.

The earbuds they all wore picked up the sound easily and transmitted it to the three-way chat between Khalid, Basoul, and Nasir, who was hidden in the shadows of the alley running behind the restaurant.

"The smaller one must be in the back office," Basoul added.

If the cousins didn't move soon, Khalid would be back tomorrow with the prince directing the operation.

Khalid wouldn't put it past him to slip on a mask or disguise and want to throw the firebomb himself.

"Block the door with the dumpster now," Khalid said into his earbuds. "Lock the wheels this time. We are no longer concerned with making it look like an accident."

A few seconds later, Nasir grunted. In the background, the dumpster wheels protested. "In place," Nasir said.

"Go," Khalid said. Nasir would take the instructions as permission to leave the area and walk to a car parked a few blocks away.

Basoul correctly took it as the order to begin his part of the operation. He hung up and would turn off the burner phone and drop it in the trash can near him, along with the cheap earbuds.

Khalid subtly glanced toward the restaurant ahead. The thin frame of Basoul hurried across the street, dressed all in black. A black balaclava that he'd worn as a watch cap covered his face. His hands were full, and while Khalid couldn't make out what he carried from this distance, he knew there were two glass bottles filled with gasoline and stuffed with torn pieces of cloth that had also been lightly sprinkled with gas.

Basoul stopped outside the restaurant. The glow of flames appeared as he lit the two pieces of cloth.

69

THE FEELING

Pacific Oasis BBQ & Smokehouse
San Diego, California

Lamar loved to chat with the customers. Being social and recognizing people who returned frequently were essential to the restaurant's success. He no longer cared about his thick accent. The people of the city had welcomed them and their restaurant despite them being foreigners.

His feeling of unease grew as he schmoozed, but he didn't let it show. He knew he wasn't paranoid. He'd had a strong sense for danger since childhood. In Afghanistan, those who learned to honor their intuition survived. Those who didn't ran afoul of the Taliban, local bullies, criminals, or American soldiers.

He'd had a similar feeling at the ambush of the American SEALs.

Late at night, he could admit to himself he'd had a bad feeling from the moment he was recruited and promised a year's worth of earnings for a few days of training and one night of shooting at the Americans.

He was no warrior, but being big and perceived as brave got him the job. Everyone knew his cousin was an interpreter for the

Americans, just as they knew Lamar wouldn't tell Zia what was about to happen.

When he had insisted Zia join him for lunch and poisoned his food —enough to make him ill and not kill him, he hoped—Lamar felt in his gut that what he had agreed to do was wrong.

The Americans weren't the great terror that they were portrayed to be. Yes, they were invaders. Yes, there had surely been many innocent Afghans killed, whether from bullets or bombs. But if left alone, they would leave soon like all the other foreigners over the country's long history.

Fighting them only kept them around longer and brought more agony down on everyone.

Poisoning Zia had been the only way Lamar could think of to keep Zia from being on the raid that night, aside from telling him the truth. That wasn't an option; Zia would immediately inform the Americans, and neither Lamar nor the other men of the surrounding area picked for the mission would get the money they needed.

Lamar had been a cook, not a member of the Taliban or a freedom fighter. He had no quarrel with the Americans. But money was hard to come by, so he accepted the offer, vowed not to kill anyone, poisoned Zia—and had lived with the shame and guilt ever since.

Tonight his hard work would help the only SEAL who had survived that night kill Prince Rafiq Al-Najjar.

Lamar's days and nights of guilt would be over.

70

THE COCKTAIL

Pacific Oasis BBQ & Smokehouse
San Diego, California

Zia considered the routine accounting he had to do on the aging office computer but decided against it. Bone was right. He and Lamar needed to have alibis for tonight. They had to be able to prove they had been nowhere near Los Angeles—and not involved with Bone, should he get caught.

He unlocked the office door, embarrassed that he'd let paranoia get the better of him. With Bone handling everything, they were free of the responsibility that had been hanging over them for years and weighing Lamar down with guilt.

Zia put his best smile on and walked into the small dining area. The restaurant he and Lamar had dreamed of for years was crowded. People on the beach often had a late lunch. After the sun set over the ocean, they wandered the few blocks from one of the area's most popular and crowded beaches to the restaurant for a delicious meal before going home.

He nodded at a few regulars he recognized. Lamar was chatting with one of them at the table closest to the door.

If the traffic kept up, they might have to stay open late again tonight.

Tiffany wouldn't mind. She was a student at one of the local colleges, paying her own way through school. She took all the hours she could get—and the unlimited barbecue that the employees received while working.

They'd let Jack, one of the cooks in the kitchen, leave on time. Lamar would take over as he finished prepping for tomorrow. Sunday would be just as busy as today.

For the first time in several years, Zia let himself relax. The big hunt for the prince had ended. Neither he nor Lamar had to be involved in the man's death. They could focus on the restaurant, maybe take a day off for once. Enjoy the beach a few blocks away. Bring over family from Afghanistan.

The front door opened.

A thin man dressed in black, wearing a mask over his face, stepped inside.

The restaurant had been robbed twice before. They had been quiet, almost civil. Each time, a masked man had entered, holding a gun, and demanded the cash from the register. All of the workers knew Zia's thoughts—it was only money. Hand it over quickly and quietly. One day's worth of cash wasn't worth anyone's life.

Neither of the previous robbers had carried a flaming bottle in each hand.

Zia instinctively started toward the counter. He had to protect Tiffany. He could never live with himself if the young woman, who was like the daughter he'd never had, got harmed.

"Go back to your own country!" the man yelled. He sounded more scared than angry.

The thin man drew back his right arm and threw a Molotov cocktail directly at Lamar.

71

THE AGONY

Pacific Oasis BBQ & Smokehouse
San Diego, California

When the thin man wearing a black mask stepped into the restaurant carrying two Molotov cocktails, Lamar knew in his gut it had to do with the prince.

Somehow, they'd been caught. Whether Zia's friend the SEAL had betrayed them or they'd made a mistake in their search didn't matter.

Saving Zia, the staff, and the customers was the only thing he cared about.

Lamar rushed toward the man as he threw the flaming bottle. It bounced off his chest and didn't break until it hit the floor.

By then, he had the man in a bear hug, propelling him backward. The glass front door broke under their weight as they slammed into it.

They tumbled to the ground. Lamar landed on the smaller man and thought he had a chance of coming out of the night alive.

The second bottle hit the sidewalk, igniting the fuel.

Flames burnt the beard he'd carefully cultivated and shaped over his entire adult life. Even as he screamed, in his heart he knew he deserved all the agony the fire brought.

72

THE AFTERMATH

Pacific Oasis BBQ & Smokehouse
San Diego, California

For Zia, it all happened so fast.

One second, Lamar rushed at the man with the flaming bottles. The next, they were outside.

Burning gasoline covered the floor, the flames waist-high.

Lamar was outside the front door, engulfed in flames.

Tiffany jumped over the counter, a big red fire extinguisher in her hands.

Two bursts smothered the flames with a light-yellow powder.

A second later, she was outside, spraying the writhing body of Lamar.

The thin man in black slapped at flames on his arm as he ran away.

Zia picked up the landline phone from the counter, dialed 911, and efficiently relayed the information. His eyes never left Lamar. Tiffany knelt next to him. His body smoked, but his clothes, hair, and skin were no longer on fire.

The attacker had vanished up the sidewalk.

Pacific Beach Neighborhood
San Diego, California

Khalid watched the attack with dread. It had all gone wrong.

He never should have assigned his men to the mission. They would all be lucky to get out of this without going to prison.

Basoul sprinted toward the car, his arm smoking.

They had contingency plans, of course.

Nasir would be the one to risk apprehension, not Khalid.

Khalid put the car in gear, quickly made sure the road was clear, and pulled away from the curb, driving straight past a panicked and pained Basoul. At least the thin man had the sense not to wave or try to get in the car. He kept running down the block, toward the ocean.

"Pick him up as planned," he said into the phone to Nasir. "Escape and evade."

Nasir would take the unregistered junk car—purchased for cash by Khalid's army buddy and fixer Daoud—to a poorer part of the city and switch it for another one parked on a little-trafficked back street. He would leave the keys in the first car and the windows down. It would be gone within an hour.

If Basoul was badly hurt, they would take care of him at the house in the same manner they'd used with the homeless captives over the years.

As Khalid drove past the restaurant, a young woman knelt next to the big man lying on the ground. The cousin had to be dead, or at least very badly injured.

The other man—the smaller one—might be hurt, but given the immediate response from the bigger man rushing at Basoul, Khalid suspected that the operation had failed.

The only thing left to do was save themselves—and hope the prince would give up now that at least one of the men after him was dead.

73

THE SECOND CHANCE

Hollywood Boulevard
Hollywood, California

Bone kept his breathing steady.

His mind clear.

His hands still.

There was always the chance the prince found the movie boring.

Or he had somewhere better to be.

At the very least, the man had to eventually leave the theater and get back into a limo. There would be no pausing, no stopping to wave to the crowd, but if Bone kept himself together, he could manage.

He'd taken harder shots from longer distances.

Back in the day.

For three hours, Bone lay prone, barely moving, the rifle aimed at the theater, ready to fire.

At last, the doors opened.

A few people trickled out, then a larger surge.

The prince wasn't one of them.

Finally, he emerged in a small group of tuxedo-clad men and women in black gowns—others involved in the movie, Bone guessed.

They shook hands all around.

Bone didn't have a clean shot.

A bodyguard in a respectable-looking suit stepped forward as the prince left the small group of people. He was glued to the prince's right side, directly in Bone's line of fire.

Other people milled about, crossing between Bone and the prince as the bodyguard walked the man to the curb and a waiting black limo.

The door opened, the prince ducked inside, followed by the bodyguard, and the long vehicle drove off.

Only after it turned right at the first intersection did Bone sag in defeat.

He wanted to scream, to scamper down the drainpipe, run to his car, and chase down the limousine. Smash into its bumper, pull over as civilized people do when there's a fender bender, and hop out, guns blazing until everyone inside was dead—especially the prince.

Instead, he sighed, dropped his head to the rooftop, and remembered that night.

Afghanistan

Seven Years Ago

Bone awakened for a moment, lying face down in the sand, still clenching his knife.

No one was around. The enemy fighters were gone.

The shock and adrenaline must have worn off. He was in agony. Breathing hurt. Every beat of his heart pumped blood out of more bullet wounds than he could count. He was in bad shape. As much as he wanted to roll over, grab his med kit, and patch himself up—then get back in the fight—he couldn't move.

He closed his eyes in defeat. There are some things you just know: when you've found the love of your life. When you've discovered your calling.

And when you're about to die.

He didn't question it. There was no more fight. He was fading. Not in an "I'll be fine once they fix me up" way, but more along the lines of, "This is the end."

A helicopter landed nearby. The quick reaction force was here. There would be medics who could save him.

It was too late.

He knew it, through and through.

A sense of peace came over him as he heard Tank's welcoming voice.

"Took you long enough, brother," Tank said from somewhere nearby. "But good job—that guy will never walk right again."

Bone wanted to speak but couldn't.

"Give it a minute," Tank said, his tone quiet and kind. "You're almost here."

The bright white light confused Bone for a second. He could have sworn his eyes were still closed.

He felt the rest of the Team waiting for him.

"Here he comes," one of them called.

Bone had the sudden urge to fight the light, to stay and get the job done, but he was being yanked forward, like one of those slingshot rides at the state fair that pulls you back, back, back, until it suddenly flings you up in the air with no way to stop or slow down.

The thought of Tank and the guys already out there, together, waiting for him, allowed Bone to let go.

And then he died.

74

THE QRF

Seven Years Ago

"Clear!" came the calls from Ben's men around the area. "No enemy nearby. Looks like they escaped into the mountains or those caves."

Ben—call sign Big—stood in the middle of a massacre. Eight unmoving SEALs soaked the ground with blood.

"What about our guys?" Big asked his second-in-command, call sign Gator. Asking was a formality. He knew the score just from looking. Two medics were checking the dead SEALs, though, just in case.

As the quick reaction force, Big and his men had been airborne seconds after getting the call for help. The chopper pilot had flown the bird like he'd stolen it, completely disregarding normal operation. The thing's engines would probably have to be rebuilt.

"Looks like all eight dead," Gator reported.

They didn't speak for a second. Big needed time to put the rage and grief into a box deep in his soul. He could deal with those feelings later. Right now, they had a job to do.

"Upwards of forty enemy killed in action," Gator said. "Our guys went out fighting. One—Bone—died with his knife in hand, coated in blood."

"Always in the fight."

"Always in the fight," Gator repeated quietly.

"What about the village?"

"The village elder is dead," Gator said. "Sniper shot to center mass. The rest are huddled in their homes. Don't get the sense they were involved. My guess is the village elder tried to warn our guys, but it was too late."

"Come on, come back!" a medic cried from nearby. He was screaming at one of the dead SEALs—the one with a knife clutched in his hand.

"Bone?" Big called, rushing over. "His name is Bone."

"Bone, get your ass back here right now!" the medic yelled, spittle hitting Bone's face.

"I thought they were all dead," Big said.

"He is," the medic called, frantically working on Bone. "But just barely. Come on, Bone! It's not your time yet."

Big and Gator exchanged glances. Some medics got like that after seeing too much death.

They couldn't let go.

Then again, if there was any chance at all of saving one of the guys, Big was all for it.

"Can we get the bird here?" the medic asked without looking up from his work on Bone. "Like right now? I... I might be able to save him."

It would mean leaving the rest of them in the field without the protection of the circling chopper, but it was worth the risk.

"Absolutely," Big said, and got busy on the radio.

75

THE LIGHT

The Light
Afghanistan

Seven Years Ago

Bone was happier than he'd ever been before. In the light, it felt like Christmas, his birthday, and falling in love all wrapped up in one.

An instant later, all that was gone. In its place was more pain than he thought possible, and a loud noise of...

It sounded like a helicopter.

"Holy shit, it worked!" someone yelled. "Welcome back, Bone. Stay with me, okay? You're going to make it!"

Bone faded again, looking forward to the exhilaration of the slingshot ride to the warm, safe, white light, his buddy Tank, and the rest of the Team...

It didn't come.

He was going to live after all.

As he passed out from the pain, fading into darkness instead of the light, he wasn't entirely happy with the way this was working out.

76

THE PUZZLE

Hollywood Boulevard
Hollywood, California

Yousuf had enjoyed the movie and stayed late after, smiling and asking the occasional question of the director and editor.

They had left together, saying goodbye in the plaza in front of the theater, until Syed had escorted him to the waiting limo. They would reverse the earlier process, riding to a private helicopter terminal nearby, flying to San Diego, and taking the waiting SUV to the mansion.

Yousuf usually loved this part. His work was done for the night, aside from being silent and acting aloof in front of the guards and helicopter pilot.

Easy.

Tonight, though, his mind wasn't on the tourists milling about, the brightly lit city, or the ever-present traffic.

His mind turned over Fahad's earlier question.

"How was the latest addition to the playroom?"

Followed by Fahad pretending to punch something.

Someone?

It started coming together as he thought it through.

Fahad's question.

The screams he'd heard his second season at the house—before the contractors had come and banged around for several days. Soundproofing rooms, he guessed now.

The whispers he'd overheard the past few years.

How hard Yousuf was required to work out—to make his body look as toned and as fit as the prince's.

How the first season in San Diego, years before, Khalid had made him punch a concrete block until his knuckles were raw and bruised.

Since then, the rare cuts on the prince's face he'd had to replicate on his own.

One thing seemed clear: His Highness got into fights. But with whom? The prince would never go to a boxing gym or martial arts studio. He was Saudi royalty; he wouldn't mix with normal Americans like that, not even the wealthy. He wouldn't allow any of them to touch him.

Khalid might find tough men or fighters to compete with in private. That could explain the "playroom" reference—but not the conspiratorial nature of Fahad's question.

Whether the prince won or lost, he wouldn't want it mentioned. People could talk.

No, it would be better to just abduct people…

Yousuf kept his breathing under control and continued to stare out the window as if nothing was wrong—and he hadn't just figured out the puzzle.

The clues fit, though the idea was horrifying.

Could the man be so bold, so brazen, as to kidnap American citizens and force them to fight?

And dispose of them when he was finished?

The answer came quickly. Yes, of course. He was Prince Rafiq Al-Najjar.

The realization sent a shiver down Yousuf's spine.

If he was right, the man he'd been impersonating all these years was a monster.

PART 5

SUNDAY

77

SAN DIEGO

Pacific Oasis BBQ & Smokehouse

San Diego, California

Bone dreaded speaking with Zia and Lamar. All night, as he slipped out of Los Angeles and drove to San Diego, he rehearsed various ways to tell them he'd failed without having to say those exact words.

He debated lying and saying he didn't have a shot, or that he couldn't take the risk of hitting nearby innocent bystanders. Both were technically true. He didn't have a shot—because he had lost his focus with the prince centered in his sights.

He didn't want to risk killing other people, but only because he'd missed the best opportunity to shoot the prince with no one around.

SEALs rarely failed. With all the focus, training, and skills acquired over the years, mistakes were minimized. And yet, there it was. He'd blown the shot and the mission.

By first light, he was on the beach a few blocks from the barbecue restaurant. The dawn was chilly with a light breeze, but the clear sky promised another stunning Southern California day.

As he watched surfers ride the waves, Bone thought things through.

Yes, he'd missed the chance to kill the prince and likely get away clean. But there would be more opportunities. The prince might attend other red-carpet movie premieres at the same theater. With the initial recon done, Bone would have the same shot—and not choke this time.

Zia had intel of the man's house only a few miles north. An infiltration there could be made to look like a home invasion, satisfying Admiral Nalen's preference for the assassination to look accidental—and less public.

The prince traveled too. Perhaps it would be better to kill him in another country. A remote-detonated improvised explosive device on a rarely traveled stretch of road could work. Let the blame fall on one of Saudi Arabia's enemies.

By the time lunch rolled around, Bone felt better about the situation. Maybe it had all happened the way it needed to. Everything would work out in the end.

It was the SEAL way: take a setback and turn it into a new opportunity.

He was always in the fight.

Bone made his way to the restaurant, feeling better about the talk he'd have with Zia and Lamar. The three of them could brainstorm a plan. Bone could work on forgiving Lamar. They would move forward.

Adapt and overcome.

His plan went out the window the moment he saw the wide yellow plastic tape fluttering in the breeze. Several pieces blocked the entrance to the restaurant, but one end had come loose, the words easy enough to read as the strand danced in the wind.

POLICE LINE DO NOT CROSS

Bone stopped outside the door. The tables inside were out of place. A pale-yellow powder coated the floor near the entrance.

And though it had been cleaned up on the sidewalk, some residue remained.

So did the smell, familiar to anyone who'd spent enough time in combat zones: the stench of burned human flesh.

78

THE TALK

San Diego General Hospital
San Diego, California

Bone sat in the car near the front of the hospital, using his mirrors to keep an eye on the entrance. He sipped coffee and nibbled at a sandwich from a restaurant several doors down from Zia's barbecue joint. One of the workers there had been happy to talk about the attack, which led to Bone driving to the hospital. At least one person—it sounded more like Lamar than Zia—had been taken there with severe burns.

Given the circumstances and police involvement, Bone elected to wait outside and catch Zia coming or going. The less they were seen together, the better.

The mission would go on, with yet another good reason to eliminate the target.

Bone had no doubt: whatever happened at the restaurant had been ordered by Prince Rafiq Al-Najjar. The attack might have been undertaken by a local gang or hired thugs of some sort, but it surely had been paid for and arranged by the prince.

Zia and Lamar must have spooked him enough for them to be eliminated.

Walking slowly, his head down and shoulders slumped, Zia emerged from the front door and made his way to a beat-up car. For the first time, Bone noticed the thinning hair at the top of his head.

Bone followed him out of the parking lot. Before Zia could get far, Bone pulled up next to him, honked to get his attention, and gestured for him to turn into a convenience store ahead.

He led the way into the lot and parked far from the door, near a dumpster area enclosed by a dingy wooden fence that had been white years before. Once Zia parked, Bone got out and slid into the passenger seat of the Afghan's car.

"Tell me it is done," Zia said, getting straight to the point. He was exhausted and sad, but his dark eyes burned with anger. His knuckles were white from gripping the steering wheel so hard. "Tell me he is dead."

Bone thought of the rooftop. The prince in the crosshairs of his scope. The shaking hands. The lost moment.

"No. It..." For all his planning, Bone was suddenly at a loss for words. "I couldn't take the shot," he mumbled with a glance out the window at the ugly old fence hiding the dumpster. This close, the smell of garbage hung in the air—a welcome distraction from the reek of burning flesh in front of the restaurant that still lingered in his memory.

"Is Lamar..." Bone stopped, waiting for Zia to fill in the missing pieces. The kid at the sandwich place hadn't known if the burnt person would make it or not.

"He's alive but badly hurt," Zia said, his voice heavy with pain and fatigue. For the moment, the anger was gone. "He saved my life." He wiped his eyes with his thumb and finger. "Again," he muttered.

"I'm sorry." It was all Bone could think to say.

They sat staring out the window for several seconds, both lost in thought.

"What do you need to get the job done?" Zia finally asked.

Bone nodded slowly. It's what he was thinking about, too. "Tell me more about the prince's house in La Jolla."

79

THE NEW PLAN

The Glider Port
La Jolla, California

The glider port perched on a bluff overlooking a miles-long stretch of beach that sparkled in the setting sun. The wind had picked up all afternoon, leaving only the most skilled pilots fighting the offshore breeze, staggering toward the cliff one by one, canopies up, until just the right moment when they could launch and be swept into the air.

Once flying, they easily rode the air currents upward, traveling back and forth along the cliff edge, south to north before turning in the distance to repeat the trek, gaining altitude with every yard.

The paragliders made a stunning picture in the late afternoon sun. The dark blue ocean, the scattered clouds, the sunset, men and women wearing colorful helmets steering equally colorful gliders.

Bone hung back, off to the side, away from the main launch area. It had been years since he'd spent time there, but he didn't want to risk being recognized. Not with what he had planned.

According to Bone's cheap burner phone, the strong wind was supposed to continue all night. It would make the start of the mission challenging, especially considering Bone's rusty skills, but if he got into the air, he'd be set.

On active duty, when Bone and the rest of the Team weren't deployed, they were training. It never stopped. They had to be ready for war at a moment's notice, so they kept their skills sharp. They jumped out of airplanes, swam, went SCUBA diving, and shot tons of rounds on the range.

They could also make requests for specific instruction to improve their fighting abilities. If they convinced the brass that a skill would make them better able to accomplish their mission, the approval was nearly guaranteed.

People sometimes considered SEALs cocky or arrogant, but that wasn't at all accurate. They were merely extremely knowledgeable and capable.

Those who were neither often felt threatened or jealous of the SEALs' skills.

Bone could fly an airplane well and a helicopter in an emergency. He had learned how to sail boats from small to large, navigate by the stars, fish, spearfish, and survive at sea. He could forage for wild food in many different parts of the world, collect and filter water for drinking, and create shelter from sticks, grass, logs, dirt, sand, or snow.

And among many other skills, he could paraglide.

The classes at the glider school just north of their San Diego base had been an easy sell. The SEALs were already expert skydivers. With a slightly different approach, they easily picked up how to soar under the canopy instead of floating to the ground.

They had taken a series of classes at the school connected to the glider port, starting with tandem lessons and eventually flying on their own.

Each day after training, they had carefully packed up the gliders and helped move them into the storage room attached to the main glider port building.

Now, as the afternoon wore on, Bone confirmed that many pilots still stored their gear in the back room.

He'd use the remaining hour of the day for recon. Bone jogged down the steep, sketchy descent trail to the beach below. He continued south along the shore before cutting back inland and up a winding emergency access road to the neighborhood he'd fly into later. The heavy-duty lock and chain securing the gate at the top attested to its infrequent use, likely by lifeguards or other first-responders.

Continuing around the area of high-end homes like several other joggers and bikers, he kept his head down and barely glanced at the prince's large white house. A dense privacy hedge screened a formidable fence. An imposing, ten-foot-tall metal gate prevented anyone from seeing the inside of the compound.

An exfil out the driveway might be best if the gate was programmed to open automatically as a person or vehicle approached.

Leaving the same way he got in would be unlikely. He wouldn't be able to launch from the rooftop of the home.

Instead, he'd have to risk getting caught on cameras that surely ringed the house—unless he destroyed the entire system after taking care of the prince. If it meant taking out a few more of the man's guards, so be it. They had to have known what they were signing up for—and what kind of man employed them. They, too, would get what was coming to them.

The rear of the house was a no-go. It backed to an imposing tree-filled ravine with steep, crumbling cliffs that led to the ocean. He'd seen it during the run along the beach. If he were in charge of the prince's security—and money were no object—he'd install a hard-to-climb fence there. He'd add plenty of security cameras, full-time guards to watch the screens 24/7, and, if possible, a dog or two to patrol. Given the prince only lived in this house a few months a year, some of it—especially the dogs—might be overkill, but there would definitely be cameras.

His plan felt good. Bone ran out of the subdivision, along the main road, and back to his car in the emptying glider port parking lot. He had several hours to eat, rest, and prep for his second try at the prince.

This one, he vowed, would succeed.

80

THE PIZZA

Motel Grande
San Dimas, California

Omar missed his friends, and, if he was being honest, his family. Sitting alone in the cheap motel for the last few days had finally started to get to him. He fiddled with the scraggly beard that was taking forever to grow.

When he had his friends to talk with, to debate which of America's many atrocities was the worst, he felt alive. Invigorated.

When his father's friend took him aside to tell him what a wonderful job he had done with the spray paint and graffiti, or beating up the homeless man, his life had meaning.

Watching videos to learn how to aim and fire the missile had been fun at first. With no mockup for practice, though, the thrill quickly wore off. He knew everything about the weapon—but he had too much time on his hands to consider the ramifications of what he had been tasked with learning.

He was far from stupid. Shooting at any aircraft in the United States would bring the authorities like bargain shoppers at a Black Friday door-buster sale.

Nothing had been mentioned about how he would escape.

Where would he go?

Did they expect him to casually slip back into his life at the college while the police, FBI, and every other agency hunted the person who had shot down a plane?

In the movies, someone was always offered up as a sacrificial lamb.

Was his faith strong enough to endure life in prison?

He used the hotel phone to order yet another pizza, opting to cheat and get his former favorite.

He'd watch TV tonight instead of exploring the dark web. He needed a break from the accurate but overwhelming anti-American rhetoric he'd been immersed in lately.

Feeling guilty at his decisions, he unrolled his rug and prepared for the prayer done just after sunset—but didn't call and change the pizza order.

If these were his last days of freedom, he wanted pizza topped with forbidden pepperoni before a life of prayer—and solitary confinement.

81

THE NIGHT

La Jolla, California

With a balaclava rolled up on his head like a cap for now, Bone ran. The black tactical pants and black long-sleeve shirt from his pack didn't look exactly like what a jogger would wear, but people in California seemed to live and let live. At least the outfit looked athletic; he wasn't running in jeans like he had just robbed a convenience store.

If anyone saw him as he jogged north toward the glider port, he'd barely be noticed. He was just another guy getting his miles in before bed.

He'd left his car in a twenty-four-hour pharmacy parking lot a few miles away, grateful for a hatchback that blended in. No one would think anything of the older car there all night, unlike the beast of a truck Admiral Nalen thought he should drive.

The stars were bright in the moonless sky. The wind had stayed strong; it might have picked up a bit.

Bone felt good. This plan fit him better. He'd scoped out the target. Come up with an approach that would be hard to defend against. It felt better than the sniper shot from the office building.

Lamar's AK was in his car, wedged in the compartment under the hatchback area that held the spare tire. If anyone broke in, they wouldn't find it in the limited time they had in the busy parking lot.

The AK wouldn't be as useful in the close confines of the house as his pistols, especially with only one magazine. While Bone wouldn't mind the extra firepower, it wasn't the right weapon for the job.

Instead, he was going in fast and lean, with only a fanny pack of tools, his two pistols, the extra magazines, and a fixed-blade knife.

The way to kill the prince was up close and personal. Bone wanted him to know who had finally come for him. Longed to twist the knife, bringing him more pain as his life slipped away. Needed to look in his eyes as the prince died.

He hadn't realized how much he burned for vengeance until he saw the prince in the crosshairs of his scope.

But first he had to get to the target.

As he ran down the long approach road to the glider port, Bone kept his head down and stayed in the shadows as much as possible.

He slowed as he left the paved road and walked, hoping he looked like he was cooling down from a long run.

Bone had timed it well. At 01:00, the lot was empty. The van lifers abandoned the lot by midnight, after which no parking was allowed. The police probably swept it around 12:30 hours, Bone figured, so thirty minutes after that was perfect.

He expected another patrol around 02:00, by which time he'd be long gone.

Of the many training opportunities offered to the Teams, one of Bone's favorites had been lock picking. They'd learned the ins and outs of all kinds of locks, been given proper lock picking tools, and practiced, practiced, practiced.

After a lot of grumbling—most of the men were happier to set a breaching charge or shoot out a door lock with a shotgun—all had learned to be capable lock pickers.

Only then had the trainer brought out the lock pick gun. The guys who were all about blowing the locks instead of employing the subtle picking techniques had been pissed that there was an easier way than the finicky tools they had "wasted" days on, but everyone loved the simplicity of the new tool.

Bone pulled the balaclava over his face, slipped on his tactical gloves, and removed his lock pick gun from the fanny pack as he neared the back entrance to the glider school building. The solid metal door had two heavy-duty locks—one in the handle and a deadbolt. Ignoring the tiny blue light of a security camera set on a high pole, he slid a tension tool into the lock and turned, then slipped the gun's pick into the lock and pulled the trigger several times.

He had both locks open in less than a minute.

A red light on the wall across from the door flashed quickly, accompanied by a warning *beep beep beep*. The glider port was at the end of a long road, above a beach, and next to a golf course. Aside from the police patrols to keep the van-lifers from camping in the parking lot, no one was around. The strong door, expensive locks, and security camera would deter most ordinary thieves, and the monitored alarm would send the police to the location more quickly than anyone could steal the large packs of gliders or the limited snacks and drinks sold to the pilots and tourists each day.

Bone had easily defeated the locks. The security camera would record a male figure of average height and weight wearing dark clothes who had lock-picking experience.

The only real worry was the alarm.

Years ago, the place had used the phone number of the main information line for the glider school as their code. Poor security, but it was a different time. They were more worried about kids or random strangers breaking in than professionals who had given the code some thought.

Bone was hoping for the same lack of concern.

He entered the code he and the rest of the Team had memorized out of habit while they trained there.

The alarm control box gave an angry tone and kept beeping.

If necessary, he would run down the steep trail to the beach instead of getting caught by the police, but it wouldn't be ideal. He couldn't steal one of the gliders and launch before the police responded, nor could he run fast with one of the bulky packs. He could be spotted and apprehended. The police would call in reinforcements to catch him on the beach. He could swim for it if they didn't see him go into the water, but a late-night swim in cold water presented its own problems.

If he somehow managed to escape, he'd just have to return and try again, or find another way into the prince's house.

No, he had to disarm the system now.

He tried the phone number but in reverse order.

Another angry tone.

How many tries did he get?

At some point, maybe after three attempts, the alarm would be triggered. People who knew the code didn't need four tries to get it right.

Bone flipped the sequence, entering the last four digits of the phone number first, followed by the first three.

The red light stopped blinking and turned green. A happy *chirp* came from the system.

He was in.

82

THE ANIMAL

The Room
Unknown Location

As the door unlocked, Matthew stood, rolled his shoulders, and prepared.

He'd already been served dinner. Noise from the door meant only one thing: his crazy captor had returned. The weirdo had some kind of fight-club fetish and wanted a partner he couldn't control. Needed the danger of a bare-knuckle, drag-out fight with a stranger kept chained and locked in a dungeon.

The dude poked his head around the partly open door like a kid playing hide and seek. His wide-set dark eyes were bright with anticipation, and he didn't bother to hide his grin.

"Ready for more, are you?" Matthew asked with an air of nonchalance. He couldn't resist trash talk. He had only barely started to recover from last night's beating, but had to put up a good front.

The longer the guy wanted him around, the longer Matthew got to live—and search for an opening or weakness he could exploit.

Matthew interlaced his fingers and cracked his knuckles.

Matthew had dubbed him "the Tyrant." With his arrogant attitude, cruelty, perfectly arranged dark wavy hair, and toned physique in tight-fitting black t-shirt and high-end sweatpants, he seemed like a young ruler who hadn't gotten enough love as a child.

The Tyrant dropped the smile and narrowed his eyes. He had thin skin and didn't like being taunted.

Matthew could use that.

The nutjob said nothing. He put on his fighting face and jumped up and down lightly on his feet, warming up while staying well out of reach. The chain only allowed Matthew to get within about five feet of the door.

The Tyrant was by far the better fighter. Matthew figured his only real hope was to get inside the guy's head. Sooner or later, his captor would make a mistake.

Matthew would be right there to exploit it. He'd wrap the chain around the Tyrant's neck, take him hostage, and use the threat of killing the guy to get free.

If the guards didn't cooperate, he'd strangle the dude and take his chances.

At least he'd go out with a bang.

The Tyrant switched to jumping jacks.

Matthew imitated him, exaggerating the movement, mocking the guy.

The captor stopped after a few seconds. Matthew suppressed a smile. He was definitely getting to him.

"You enjoy playing games?" the guy said in his perfect English, with the slightest hint of an accent. "I didn't beat you hard enough last night?"

"Dude," Matthew said, coming right back at him, "my mama beat me better than you when I was five and stole cookies out of the cupboard."

The Tyrant's lips pressed together in what was an attempt at a smirk, but there was no hint of amusement in his eyes.

He advanced.

Matthew retreated, the chain rattling behind him.

Tonight wasn't the night for Matthew to go for the capture or kill, though he would if the opening presented itself. He would play the long game, fight defensively, stay alive, and put up another decent fight while getting his ass kicked again.

He'd gather intel and find the opening he needed.

So far, it looked like taunting the Tyrant might be the way to go. Make fun of the situation the guy took so seriously and get him pissed off.

He'd make a mistake. Matthew would exploit it...

Or get the guy so mad he'd kill Matthew prematurely.

One way or another, the ordeal would be over.

Last night, Matthew had fought conventionally, boxing, trying a few awkward kicks, showing skills but not revealing his true abilities, speed—or the dirty tricks he'd learned in the Navy.

"Come on, let's do this," Matthew called. "I took it easy on you last night. Get ready to have your ass handed to you, crazy."

The Tyrant liked that even less. He stalked toward Matthew with hard eyes and his teeth bared like a wild animal.

83

THE LAUNCH

La Jolla, California

After retiring from active duty, and given the unlikelihood of ever again being in a battle at night, Bone had only purchased a monocular night vision goggle for his go bag.

He regretted that decision now.

A higher-end—and more costly device—would have come in handy tonight. But at least he could see well in the dark out of one eye.

The glider port launch area as seen in the green glow of the night vision goggle comforted him in the same way the knife and pistols did. He was back where he belonged.

At war.

In the stiff breeze, Bone staggered across the glider port's wide grassy takeoff and landing area, hands on the toggles, the glider in the air above him. He struggled, trying to get to the edge of the cliff. If he wasn't close enough, he would launch into the air but not get the lift he needed to go anywhere.

He'd never flown in such a strong wind, but the principles were the same. Once aloft, with the wind coming off the ocean and blowing up the slope of the cliffs along the beach, he should be able to gain plenty of altitude to safely travel the several hundred yards inland to the flat roof of the prince's house.

If he could get into the air.

After several minutes of carefully controlling the glider and making incremental progress toward the cliff edge, he was in position.

With a final lunge, he was airborne.

The familiar drop in his stomach made him smile as he tucked his legs into the leg pod and soared over the wide beach three hundred feet below. He pulled on the toggles, turning the glider north, gaining elevation immediately.

He flew about a mile, consistently rising higher. After passing the vast, dark expanse of the golf course on his right, he turned back, hugging the cliff line. He was at least four hundred feet above the beach—one hundred above the cliff.

He needed more elevation.

Adjusting course, he found the best lift by feel, reveling in the night. He was on a mission.

Focused yet relaxed.

Soaring free, like a bird.

As a SEAL, he had frequently trained for insertions via parachute, but in Afghanistan rarely had the chance to use the skill. It made more sense to helicopter to a safe area and hike in stealth mode to the target. But there was a lot to be said for a silent approach from the air, whether it meant jumping from an airplane or taking off the edge of a cliff to soar.

After passing the golf course again, Bone scouted the parking lot of the glider port but saw no police activity. As he left, he had rearmed the alarm and locked the doors behind him. The person whose glider he had stolen would be pissed, but it might take a while to figure out what happened. Sooner or later, though, some smart detective would put together the coming bloodbath at the prince's house with the case of the missing paraglider.

Bone would be long gone by then.

Flying over the hazardous trail down to the beach made it look like an easier path than when running it several hours earlier.

A few seconds later, he passed the first house of the exclusive La

Jolla subdivision on his left, an enormous two-story building with what had to be a few acres of land, away from the edge of the cliff by a couple hundred yards. Hiking trails crisscrossed the area of brush and trees between the house and the cliff, making a home worth tens of millions of dollars much less private than the owner undoubtedly preferred.

He soared past several more houses before that portion of the bluff curved toward the ocean. Other even grander homes filled the area, but with less land surrounding them.

Why anyone would pay millions of dollars to have another house practically on top of them was beyond him. He had more room between his house and his nearest neighbor than these had. Of course, if the homes were fifteen thousand square feet, maybe it was less of a big deal. Half of these houses were probably second, third, or fourth homes and only occupied part of the year anyway.

Gliding a few hundred feet above but only thirty feet past the edge of the nearest house, Bone approached the long ravine behind the prince's house. He turned inland, flying over the deep, dark, impassible ground.

His target lay ahead. Like all the houses in the area, the large pool in the backyard was lit by underwater lights. Other decorative lamps illuminated the grounds, making the night vision monocular unnecessary.

The wind carried him as he lost altitude. He silently approached the northern edge of the house's flat roof, which had to be seventy-five yards long. It bent in the middle and looked like a wide boomerang.

Bone timed it perfectly, flaring to a soft landing at the northwest corner of the roof.

Zia had found pictures from the last time the house was sold, which Bone had looked at in Zia's office that first night.

The house had two primary suites, one above the other, both in the center of the house where it bent in the middle. This allowed astounding views to the north and the south, and straight out at the ocean, though it created an awkward interior layout. The designers had solved that by making one half of the huge primary suite on the second floor the main bedroom and the other half a sitting room with a small workout area.

Prince Rafiq would be in the upstairs section at the midpoint of the house, with its spacious balcony overlooking the pool, the yard beyond, and the ravine dropping away before the ocean came into view. The other houses in the area, including the pricey ones he'd flown past, wouldn't have the vista the prince had. Sure, they'd see the ocean, but none of them would get the full picture of land, beach, waves crashing, and the swells beyond.

The house and views were one of a kind. Perfect for the man who had everything.

Bone gathered up the glider quickly and quietly, moving as little as possible in case he stood over occupied staff quarters. From what the floor plan had revealed, he should be above one of the house's bedrooms—ten in total, counting the two primary suites. But if the prince had guests, or the layout had been changed, it paid to be careful.

He looked around for a place to stash the large bag carrying the stolen paraglider and froze.

Three feet away, a small black security camera was anchored to the northeast corner of the roof.

84

THE BLOOD

The Room

Matthew lay in the middle of the room where he had fallen, cheek to the cool floor, eyes closed, gasping. Blood from his split lip and broken nose pooled beneath his face. He turned his head to the other side, slowly, not faking the pain, so the camera mounted on the ceiling near the door couldn't see his face.

Tonight's fight with the Tyrant hadn't gone well. Matthew had gotten his ass handed to him. Again.

He didn't want to move from where he'd fallen for fear his captor would return and continue the beating.

Matthew had been forced to put up a better fight than planned. If he hadn't, he might be dead now—or rapidly on his way.

Lying on the hard floor, he reviewed the fight, cataloging what he'd learned.

The Tyrant often led with a left-hand jab before coming in strong with his right.

He was easily provoked by the mildest trash talk, becoming more aggressive and less careful.

Most interestingly, he switched from punching to kicking after a few good hits, maybe concerned with hurting his hands.

Matthew could use all of it.

He'd be ready the next time the captor came; there would be no surviving another round like tonight. He would switch from defense to offense—and fight as dirty as he knew how. Biting, kicks to the groin, thumbs to eyeballs, whatever it took.

As long as he got a day or two to recover, he might have a chance. Not much of one, true, but more than the Tyrant expected.

Assuming Matthew was successful, the guards would rush in and negotiate for the release of their leader—or Matthew would die a few seconds after killing the dude.

But so what? He'd do the best he could and let the chips fall where they may.

He fell asleep on the cold floor, his back to the camera, smiling through the pain.

85

THE VIEW

Security Room

La Jolla, California

The nights were long but quiet for Syed. When he wasn't escorting the prince to Los Angeles or hunting for fresh fighting opponents, he worked as the night shift security guard, taking over from Nasir or Fahad, who manned it during the day.

He got to sit in a two-thousand-dollar ergonomic chair in a quiet second-floor room and watch twenty security screens. His job was essential on the off chance something happened, but nothing ever did.

Who would attack the prince anyway? The man supported the arts and lived the typical life of a forty-year-old rich guy, going to movie premieres in Los Angeles, and to art galleries, book signings, and fancy restaurants in San Diego.

Yes, Prince Rafiq also had them abduct homeless people so he could beat them to death. Syed had to watch onscreen from time to time when the fights bled into his night shift.

But no one looked for or cared about those men. If the police ever suspected His Highness, they would come with lawyers and a search warrant, not ram the main gate at 3 a.m. They would have time and, hopefully, a chance to escape the country before being arrested.

And one of the reasons the bodyguard job paid so well was to make up for the risk of apprehension by the Americans.

Not that it mattered. As a loyal Saudi, Syed would have served Prince Rafiq for free. Just because Rafiq was one of many lesser princes didn't make him any less royal. Syed flew around the world, working for a prince. He got to live in California every spring and summer, Europe in the fall, and in the Middle East during the winter.

He could look the other way when the prince engaged in his "playtime" every season in southern California.

He also knew not to ask questions about the irregularities he observed. There weren't cameras inside the house, but Syed saw things that didn't make sense. The prince acted differently at times, especially in Los Angeles. There was something not quite right about him then, especially when compared to the fierce, almost crazy man who beat up the prisoners in the playroom.

The only rational explanation was that the prince had a body double. A stand-in to attend boring events in the prince's name—and act as a target if danger came near. Syed figured the man was a younger brother or a cousin, maybe, which likely made him royalty, too.

Syed put it out of his mind; it wasn't for him to be concerned about. If no one mentioned it, neither would he, not even to Fahad. The Americans had a saying he'd heard on TV during his off hours a few years before that immediately became his motto: "Go along to get along."

Syed's eyes flicked over the wall of monitors in front of him.

Each of the twenty screens could show any of the security camera feeds, but Syed had them set up logically.

The first —bottom—row had the most important cameras: the garage exterior, main entrance, back entrance off the prince's ground-floor exit to the pool, and a screen devoted to the prince's playroom.

The next row up showed the front cameras, including the fenceline, the front gate, and the street view. He enjoyed watching the street.

Several neighbors had luxury cars. Seeing them come and go helped him stay awake.

The third row of five screens showed the back and side fenceline. They were interesting because raccoons, feral cats, or other critters wandered by from time to time. He glanced at these most often and would run back the recording if he caught movement out of the corner of his eye but hadn't seen what kind of animal it was.

Technically, he should pay the most attention to this row of screens. Any attack from an enemy of Saudi Arabia in general or the prince in particular would come from the back. The ravine was difficult and dangerous to use as an approach but would offer a group of enemy fighters the most cover and concealment. Men coming for the prince wouldn't be worried about how challenging, time-consuming, or dangerous the ground was.

The final cameras, across the top row of screens several feet above his head, displayed the pool and his favorite views—the rooftop.

He watched one of them now.

After a brief distraction on the back fence monitor when the raccoon he'd named Rocky wandered by, Syed returned his attention to the camera positioned near a skylight on the roof.

Syed took the job seriously, but there was only so much staring at the same, unchanging images he could handle. Tonight he didn't want to look at the bleeding pile of flesh lying on the middle of the playroom floor. The latest homeless man he and Fahad had abducted fought well, but Prince Rafiq was stronger and better trained.

It would be a few days before the prisoner recovered enough for the next "round," as His Highness called it.

Syed didn't like watching the new arrivals. They were too nervous, always pacing, or they tried to get his attention by waving at the camera.

With a tap of a key on the control panel, he switched the playroom screen off. He wouldn't hear any screams or cries for help; the walls and doors of both the playroom and security room were too well soundproofed.

As usual, once the rest of the house was asleep, Syed used the controls on his console to tilt the roof cameras straight up as he'd done an hour earlier.

The wide-angle view and 4K resolution made it feel like lying on the roof and staring at the stars all night. His favorite memories from childhood were going with his father into the desert a few times a year, spreading a blanket on the sand, and being taught the constellations.

Each clear night in California, he got to relive those memories, study the sky, and watch for shooting stars.

He hadn't had the grades to be an astronomer, but he loved the four months per year in California when he could spend hours watching the stars from his little room.

As dawn approached each morning, he'd tilt the cameras east and watch the sunrise before setting them back as they were meant to be: covering the approach to the house and every inch of the rooftop.

Syed settled in now, smiling at the view of the sky. He tilted his chair back to see better, put his hands behind his head, and enjoyed the view.

86

THE PROBLEM

33 Gold Road
La Jolla, California

Bone had been stupid for not anticipating cameras on the roof. Of course someone as rich as the prince would have them there.

He'd made yet another mistake.

He had lost his edge. Let himself go soft.

He was rusty.

Shoving those feelings down for now, he focused on the task at hand.

Had he been visible to the camera as he glided in?

It had only been a few minutes since landing, but no floodlights had come on. No one came to investigate.

Crouched low and barely moving, he used the night vision monocular to check out the nearby camera.

It pointed straight up.

He hadn't flown over it, so he couldn't have been seen as he glided in.

A careful examination of the rest of the roof—as well as he could from his vantage point crouched on the north side—revealed another camera at the inner angle of the bend in the house, near a skylight. It was hard to tell for sure, but it looked like it pointed straight up as well.

A third small camera, too far away to make out clearly, was attached to the southeast corner of the roof.

Did it also face the sky? And if so, why?

Bone tilted his head up, wondering what could be above him.

Nothing but stars—and it clicked into place.

Guard duty was boring. There was nothing to see, nothing to do. It happened all the time—people got complacent and followed the spirit of their jobs, not the letter of the assignment.

Men would be near their posts but congregate and chat instead of focusing their attention in the direction of a potential threat they figured would never come.

They might walk a patrol pattern, physically showing up while being lost in thought and oblivious to the real world.

Or they would sit in a small dark room, dreaming of freedom, looking at the stars on the screens.

He'd seen it many times while on active duty. If the enemy had paid half as much attention as they should have, the SEALs' job would have been much harder. But human nature was what it was.

Tonight it worked in Bone's favor.

He moved the glider bag so it would be hidden when the guard repositioned the camera.

Staying low, he moved to the west side of the roof and leaned over the edge to check the balcony directly below.

Nothing stirred.

Almost as smoothly as he had done on active duty years before, he slid over the edge, lowered himself slowly, and dropped lightly onto the balcony.

The deadbolt lock on the glass French doors didn't stand a chance against Bone's lock pick gun.

In twenty seconds, he was inside a vacant guest room and on his way to kill the prince.

87

THE RESULT

33 Gold Road
La Jolla, California

In the vast white marble bathroom of the ground-floor master suite, Rafiq examined his knuckles. Though Khalid begged him to use boxing gloves to protect his hands, he enjoyed the feel of pummeling his opponents with bare skin.

His only concession was to stop using his fists before the skin was torn up too much.

He'd grown to enjoy the challenge of only kicking and kneeing his opponents.

The latest man collected by his bodyguards had at least some experience fighting. Rafiq suspected he must be a veteran—they were the most challenging and fun, despite often being out of shape or past their prime.

The captive had done well tonight, putting up a spirited fight. Rafiq had to work for the victory, which made it sweeter.

He'd get at least a few more nights out of the opponent before the end. Eventually, Rafiq wouldn't be able to hold himself back. The need would get too strong; he could already feel the compulsion lurking in the pit of his soul, demanding release.

After showering—carefully scrubbing his knuckles—he toweled off, not caring about the faint pink of blood his hands left on the thick, perfectly white towel.

He slipped on black silk pajamas and climbed into bed, reliving the pleasure of the evening. The lights went off with a tap of a button on the nightstand. The thick curtains were already closed. He'd sleep until his body was rested. Only poor people woke to an alarm clock.

Lying on his back, eyes closed, he thought of his opponent bleeding in the playroom.

Rafiq would enjoy the next part even more than the fighting.

He liked seeing the expression on their faces when they realized it was the end.

Would this latest one beg? Quietly accept death? Or go out fighting, mustering one last desperate attempt at besting Rafiq?

No matter what they did, the result would be the same.

Rafiq sighed with pleasure at the thought. Tomorrow night, or maybe the next. Certainly before Thursday. It had to happen before the much more exciting event soon to come.

Because killing a homeless man would be anticlimactic after killing a few hundred Americans at once—along with one specific, exciting target he'd had his eyes on for years.

88

THE DOOR

33 Gold Road
La Jolla, California

Bone saw no security cameras in the guest bedroom—a good thing for his sake and anyone who stayed there—but the hallway might be another story.

He tested the doorknob—unlocked—and turned it slowly, inching the door open. As expected, he was at the end of a dark hall. A door directly across from him likely led to another guest bedroom. Dim, widely spaced nightlights plugged into wall receptacles lit the thick, lush carpet that stretched into the distance.

With the door cracked, Bone couldn't see any cameras. He pulled it open farther, staying back and out of sight.

Nothing.

He hadn't expected interior cameras. No one—rich or poor—wanted to risk people hacking a camera inside a house to watch their private moments, or have a recording of themselves stumbling around in the morning, hair a mess, starting their day.

Then again, he hadn't expected security cameras on the roof either, and look how that had turned out.

He vowed to take it slowly and carefully. He debated pulling the pistol. In his mind, any guards were now fair game. They had to know who employed them and at least some of what he was up to. If not, that was on them.

No one would stand in Bone's way of accomplishing the mission tonight.

The problem with using the pistol was the noise. He didn't have a suppressor, often mistakenly called a silencer. He'd left the warrior life behind, and what civilian needs to shoot as quietly as possible? Certainly not him. Any shot he took inside the house would be an instant signal of an intruder. He'd have seconds to accomplish what he came for and attempt an escape.

He left the weapon holstered and kept his hands free. This was an exclusive, ultra-rich neighborhood of southern California. It wasn't likely the prince would have guards patrol inside, fingers on the triggers of rifles, ready to shoot intruders. If he encountered anyone, there would be a second or two of confusion followed by a confrontation. In that amount of time, Bone could attack, drawing his knife for a silent kill or the pistol for a noisier solution from farther away.

Nothing stirred in the hallway as he made his way toward the bend at the middle of the house—where the prince would be sleeping away the last few minutes of his life.

He stopped at a sturdy wooden door. It had a gold knob and, unusual for inside a house, a matching gold-plated deadbolt.

The prince would be in the primary suite on the other side of the door.

The deadbolt was of a much higher quality than most locks.

It made Bone pause. Getting past it, even with the pick gun, would be challenging and time-consuming.

He had a heavy-duty ten-inch pry bar in the fanny pack that might be better. If the door, frame, and screws were as good as the lock, though, getting in would still be tough, slower, and noisy.

A breaching charge would have been perfect here, but unsurprisingly the Navy didn't allow SEALs to walk off with them when they retired.

He chose the quiet route, removed the lock pick gun, and got to work.

It took a few minutes—much longer than any lock so far—but both locks finally slid open.

He'd been quiet, but not silent. Had anyone heard? Was the prince or a bodyguard waiting on the other side, ready to shoot him as he walked through?

Or was the door to the inner sanctum alarmed? Would the stargazing guard stationed in the dark security room elsewhere in the house get an alert when the door opened?

There was only one way to find out.

Bone returned the lock pick tools to his fanny pack, slid the night vision monocular down over his eye, and opened the door.

89

THE BEDROOM

33 Gold Road
La Jolla, California

The dark bedroom glowed green in Bone's night vision goggle. It was as large as Bone's living room and both bedrooms put together—and that was only the half right in front of him. To his left, through open double doors, a kitchenette lined the wall, and workout equipment filled the floor of an equally large space.

To Bone's right, about fifteen feet away, a king-sized bed with a plush padded headboard sat against the wall in a fancy shallow alcove. A figure lay on the bed, its back to Bone.

Thick curtains covered what must be a door to the balcony another fifteen feet from the bed, and windows to the left of the door. A seating area with one wingback chair and a side table piled high with books arranged haphazardly atop each other faced the curtains, and a fireplace—stacked with perfect white birch logs but unlit—was to the left of the chair.

Instead of a reading lamp, an ornate chandelier hung from the high ceiling. A similar one hung in the middle of the room. Small lamps sat on the nightstands on both sides of the bed, along with short goose-neck lights built into the headboard, pointed down for reading in bed.

Bone took a steadying breath. It was time. He'd kill the prince, go out onto the balcony, jump to the ground, sprint across the wide yard, climb over the fence, and risk the ravine.

Tumbling down steep slopes was much easier than scaling them, and exfilling to the deserted beach and ocean would be safer than trying to escape the subdivision that had only one way out.

His exfil decided, Bone slid the long, fixed-blade combat knife from its horizontal-carry sheath at the small of his back and stalked silently across the thick carpet to the bed.

At the edge of the nightstand, closest to the bed, a large button glowed. It was green in the night vision goggle, but red without it. A plastic lid covered it as a safety feature preventing it from being pressed accidentally.

A panic button.

There was a matching one on the other nightstand.

They didn't matter. The prince wouldn't have a chance to reach for either of them.

Standing over the sleeping figure of the man, Bone took another deep breath. Losing himself to a flashback now would get him killed.

The hand holding the knife was steady; he no longer had the shakes. In fact, he felt like his old self again, from before he left the Teams. He wasn't as sharp as he'd been back in the day, but he was on a mission and doing well.

This time, he wouldn't choke. He'd finally avenge Tank and the others, get away clean, go home, and reclaim his life.

The smart move would be to reach over and slit the prince's throat. The blood would spray forward—Bone would be in the clear.

The prince wouldn't think about the panic button; he'd wake up to pain and instinctively grab his throat in a pointless attempt to stop the bleeding.

A few seconds later, he'd be dead.

As much sense as it made, Bone couldn't do it. The prince had to know death was coming—and who had brought it.

Bone leaned forward, careful not to bump the bed, slipped his left hand over the prince's mouth, pulled him onto his back, and held the knife blade to the man's throat.

"Wake up, Your Highness. It's payback time."

90

THE REVENGE

33 Gold Road
La Jolla, California

Yousuf had been dreaming of the ocean. It was so close to the house—
he watched it from the window because he wasn't allowed on the
balcony—but unless the real prince had a good reason to go, Yousuf
would never again jump in the waves or feel the sand beneath his feet.

He was under no illusions. When the job ended—because the
prince no longer needed a body double or something happened to the
man—he would not be useful.

A person who looked exactly like Prince Rafiq Al-Najjar wouldn't
be allowed free. At best, he'd be imprisoned in a similar fashion to
now but not allowed out for any reason.

At worst, he'd be dead and buried somewhere no one would ever
find his body.

He awoke to a gloved hand covering his mouth and a sharp blade
drawing blood on his neck. The future he had long feared had arrived
much earlier than he imagined. His life of quiet isolation, confined to
this large bedroom suite except for the few times a week when he
appeared in public pretending to be the prince, was over.

Irrationally, the thing he regretted most was a book. He was nearly done with a gripping novel and would never know how it ended.

He froze and kept his eyes closed, waiting.

The end didn't come.

He opened his eyes. The room was dark except for the ever-present red light of the panic buttons on the nightstands. A man's shape loomed over him, dimly lit in the glow.

Did he have a chance? Whoever had made it this far into the house —past the many security cameras outside and the locks on the doors— had to be talented. They must want something or they would have killed him while he slept.

His duty was to fight. Yell. Hit the alarm button. Anything to give the guards time to defend the prince or rush him to safety. It was the very reason the prince had paid his family so lavishly years before. But Yousuf's parents dying too young had changed the equation. The prince no longer had leverage over him. Not that it mattered. When not locked in this spacious bedroom, he was surrounded by guards. They never left his side. He'd never had a chance to escape or a reason to.

Until tonight. Figuring out the puzzle in the limo had planted the seed in his mind.

Yousuf composed himself, ready to exploit any opportunity he got.

Bone scooted onto the bed, risking leaving DNA or other clues for the inevitable investigation to follow, but he needed to be close enough to control the prince and whisper in his ear.

"This is for Tank," Bone whispered, speaking quickly. "Baldy, Bossman, Sneaky, Biscuit, Iron, and Dizzy. Remember that night in Afghanistan? You got them, but not me. I'm the one who gave you the scar on your cheek," he said. "And now it's time to die."

It felt so good to finally say that.

He waited for the prince's reaction, wondering if he'd fight, resign himself to death, or struggle cowardly for the panic button.

Instead, the prince didn't react. He lay still on the bed. Not resigned; he hadn't given up. But he wasn't fighting either.

Something was wrong.

Crouching over the guy, Bone felt no anger from him and saw nothing on his face. No panic. And most disconcertingly, no recognition at Bone's speech.

What the hell was going on?

Could Bone be in the wrong room? He'd consistently made small mistakes he never would have years ago.

He had to see for himself.

With his elbow, Bone flicked the switch on the headboard for the gooseneck lamp, keeping one eye shut to avoid the brightness through the night vision goggle.

In the better light, without the night vision goggle, it was definitely the prince, the man from the ambush seven years before. The bump on the nose. The dark beard, close-cropped the way it had been in Afghanistan and last night in his scope. The thick, wavy hair. The small but recognizable scar on his cheek below his eye. The wide-set eyes...

... That didn't recognize him.

The man whispered. Bone's gloved hand covering his mouth was just loose enough for the words to be understandable.

"I'm not the prince."

They stared at each other for several seconds.

The face showed concern and desperation—but still no hint of recognition.

"I'm his body double," the man mumbled into the glove.

Bone didn't want it to be true, but in his heart, he believed the man. It felt real—and no one was that good an actor.

He had to hand it to whoever had planned this. Giving the prime bedroom to the decoy was very clever. But it didn't make any difference.

The prince still had to die.

He was somewhere in the house. This guy might not be the one behind the killing of the Team or the bounty program, but he was a part of the inner circle. If Bone let him live, it would ruin yet another perfect chance at the target.

He refused to fail again.

The man must have seen something on Bone's face. He didn't fight, didn't lunge for the panic button. He merely closed his eyes, relaxed, and accepted his fate.

Bone willed his right hand to dig the knife more deeply into the man's throat. To drag it from left to right, opening up a deep wound impossible to close. To watch the man die and get on with his hunt for the actual prince.

He couldn't do it. Something held him back. A spark inside himself wouldn't allow his hand to move.

91

THE BARGAIN

33 Gold Road
La Jolla, California

Yousuf prepared himself for death, but the end didn't come. After a few seconds, he opened his eyes. The warrior grimaced as he wrestled with himself.

"I can help you," Yousuf whispered. The man's gloved hand wasn't as tight as before, making the words easier to understand.

"I'll help, then you decide what to do," he continued. "If I help enough, please let me live." He didn't have a lot of leverage, but maybe there was a solution that would benefit them both.

The hand loosened more, cupping his mouth instead of pressing against it, allowing him to breathe and speak better.

"Prince Rafiq's actual bedroom is directly below this one. There is a staircase in the other section of the room," Yousuf said. He gestured with his eyes, careful to not move his head with the knife already drawing blood at his neck. "It has an electronic lock and needs a thumbprint, however. More secure than the door to the hallway."

The soldier took in the information. "How else can I get in?" he whispered back.

Yousuf considered lying but didn't want to risk it. "I don't know. I'm not allowed there, but I believe it to be impossible. My room is meant to be easily broken into, I think. My guess is the doors to the prince's room from the exterior or the hallway are similar to the access from here. Without a fingerprint and code or explosives, you won't get in. I am sorry."

The soldier didn't like hearing that.

Yousuf had one additional card to play—his only chance at escaping.

"There is another consideration. I think there is at least one man held captive in the house." Yousuf had thought of little else since the conversation in the limo, going over and over the clues. The inadvertent comment from Fahad the previous night had been the last piece of the puzzle.

"The prince beats them. Or maybe they fight." Yousuf paused, wondering what extremes the prince was capable of. "I believe he kills them when he is done."

92

THE SITUATION

33 Gold Road
La Jolla, California

Bone frantically worked through the angles. The operation was taking too long. Each moment in the house and every second he dealt with the body double put him at greater risk of capture or death.

Failure. Again.

The fake prince could be lying, but Bone didn't get that impression. Which put him in an impossible position.

He was no longer risking only his life to take out the prince.

If Bone failed, an innocent man held hostage somewhere in the house would die too.

His conscience wouldn't let him tempt fate.

He had to rescue the captive, get him into a vehicle, and take his chances after that.

Maybe he could use the escaping prisoner as a distraction, drawing the prince out once the guards raised the alarm.

It might work.

"Where is he?" Bone asked.

The fake prince offered a tiny shrug. "I do not know. I am not allowed out on my own. My guess, though, would be this floor. The prince would not want to share a floor with a prisoner. There are guest rooms at the end of the hall on each end. One of those, perhaps."

"What about guards? Do they patrol the interior?"

Another shrug. "I am sorry, I do not know that, either."

Bone made his decision. "Thank you. I won't kill you, but I have to tie you up and gag you." He had zip ties in his fanny pack. "Don't make noise or you die, understand?"

The man nodded but whispered as Bone reached for the cuffs. "I'd prefer you kill me. If you tie me up and do not succeed, they'll know I betrayed them. The prince will kill me slowly and quite painfully."

The situation was going from bad to worse.

Maybe the best move really was to kill the guy.

"Take me with you," the fake prince said.

"What? No way!"

"Then slit my throat. I am serious. You have to kill me fast or take me with you."

This was a disaster.

Bone missed having a team. One or more guys could set up here—in case the guy was lying and he was the real prince, along with being an exceptional actor—while Bone and the rest of the team went room to room killing bad guys until they had the whole mansion secure and knew the truth.

He carefully moved the knife away from the man's throat, backed off the bed, and stood, watching for the guy to lunge at the panic button or yell for help.

Instead, he scooted off the bed and stood near Bone. He extended his hand. "Thank you. I am Yousuf."

Bone switched the knife to his other hand and shook, going along with the crazy twist the mission had taken.

Yousuf dabbed a thin trail of blood from his neck with the back of his hand before adjusting the black silk pajamas he wore. "I will lead the way down the hall if that is acceptable? Yousuf is locked in his room and cannot escape, so if someone sees me walking the halls at night, I must be the real prince, yes?"

Bone saw the logic and gestured to the door, half convinced that any second Yousuf would betray him. The other half of him held out hope the mission hadn't gone off the rails—that he now had an ally who could cover for him if things hit the fan.

He'd soon find out which was correct.

93

THE FINAL FIGHT

The Room

Matthew painfully forced himself to his feet at the sound of the key in the lock. He had fallen asleep—or passed out—but it didn't feel like he'd been out for long. His ribs hurt where he'd been kicked. His head rang from several well-placed hits that had slipped through his defenses. His lip was split and his nose probably broken.

He resigned himself. The Tyrant was back to beat him again.

As much as Matthew's body hurt, it was now or never.

He'd mock the dude mercilessly. Insult his mother. Call him a dog. Whatever it took to wind him up.

Once the guy rushed in, Matthew would give him all he had, use every dirty trick he'd heard of, move as fast as he could.

He stood as tall as possible, putting on a good front that the Saudi would see through immediately.

Matthew was battered and hurting.

The lock finally clicked open. The weirdo stuck his head around the door, exactly as he had earlier.

Except the Tyrant wore black pajamas and looked surprised to see him.

"Back for more?" Matthew said in a casual tone. "I knew you couldn't stay away. Come on," he said. "I bet your mother's a better fighter than you—and she has a fuller beard!"

The captor ducked away and the door swung open wider—a bad sign. He'd pushed too hard.

The guards were coming in to finish him off.

A different face appeared in the doorway. A White guy with a trimmed beard and short brown hair. Mid-thirties. Tired, sad, haunted eyes. There was something about him...

Matthew knew before the man spoke—he was a warrior.

"Friendly coming in," the soldier whispered, checking him out as he moved into the room, holding a lock pick gun in one hand and a knife in the other.

Matthew refused to let himself sag in relief, but he couldn't hold back a sigh. "Man, am I happy to see you."

94

THE EMERGENCY

33 Gold Road
La Jolla, California

"He's a body double," Bone explained to the beat-up guy—Matthew—
as he used the lock pick gun on the padlock keeping the thick leather
collar around the guy's neck.

"I figured after you popped in," Matthew said. "That, or he had a
split personality or something."

The double waited in the hallway. If the security camera in the
room was being monitored at the moment, they would have a warning
that trouble had arrived. Bone's guess, though, is that no one watched
the prisoner sleep. The guard would be focused on the stars.

"We'll get you out, but I have to look for the real guy," Bone said
as the lock opened and Matthew removed the collar. He had to make
one last try at the prince. Maybe he'd get lucky. Maybe he'd die trying.
But he hadn't come all this way to give up.

"No problem. I'm not in much shape to help at the moment, but do
you need backup?"

"No. You and Yousuf—the double—wait in the kitchen. He says

it's right next to the garage. If I make it, we'll grab a car and take off. If
I don't come back…"

"You'll make it," Matthew said.

Bone hoped he was right.

Yousuf led the way. Bone followed, desperately hoping they were
actually on the same team and the double wasn't leading them into a
trap.

Matthew shuffled along behind him, moving as quickly and quietly
as he could, which wasn't much of either. He had taken quite a beating.
His lip was puffy and cut and his nose looked broken, with caked
blood under both nostrils. The area around his eyes had just started to
turn black.

As they crept down a plain staff staircase at the end of the hall,
Bone prepared for the second part of the mission.

A wide, unadorned service hallway led to the kitchen. As they
approached, Bone sensed danger. He put a hand on Yousuf's shoulder
to keep him from continuing forward. Behind them, Matthew's painful
shuffling stopped.

None of them moved for a moment.

A whisper of movement came from the kitchen.

Someone was there—and had heard them.

Bone drew his pistol and stepped smoothly past Yousuf. He moved
his head around the corner just enough to see into the kitchen.

A man with close-cropped gray hair, no beard, and a sharp chin,
dressed in black tactical pants and a black, long-sleeve shirt stretched
tight over his muscular frame, stood behind a stool at the far end of a
massive granite kitchen island. An open half-gallon of ice cream sat in
front of him, a silver spoon on the counter next to it.

The man locked eyes on Bone and the years fell away. Bone saw
him as he'd looked seven years earlier outside a small village in
Afghanistan, a second before the bodyguard had pushed the sniper—
Al-Najjar—out of the way, saving him from Bone's knife attack.

A full second ticked by as they stared at each other.

The prince's bodyguard reacted first, drawing a pistol from the
holster at his waist quicker than Bone could bring his to bear.

Instead of firing, Bone drew back and dropped as bullets tore into the drywall corner.

"I'll cover you. Go to the garage!" Bone whispered behind him, hoping Matthew and Yousuf could handle themselves.

Bone fired blindly around the corner. As Yousuf and Matthew ran the few steps into the kitchen and down the hall, he kept up the covering fire, staying crouched as he followed them. The bodyguard stopped shooting.

Bone backed down the entrance hallway, firing steadily into the small part of the kitchen he had an angle on.

A return shot tore a small hole into the wall near Bone before he made it out the door to the garage and slammed it shut.

The overhead garage door nearest him was a quarter of the way up and rising quietly on a well-oiled chain.

Bullets slammed into the metal door but didn't penetrate it.

Would the bodyguard follow and engage or rush to check on the prince?

Bone changed magazines, backing away from the door until he felt the bumper of a vehicle behind him.

An engine started and two doors slammed shut. Yousuf and Matthew were ready to go, and so was Bone. He had no way to lock or bar the door from the garage side. At any moment, the bodyguard could push it open and start firing. He might not hit Bone or the other guys—but then again, he could. Enough bullets sent downrange fast enough, whether aimed or not, was too dangerous to risk.

"Let's go!" Matthew called.

Bone kept the pistol trained on the doorway as he moved to the driver's side rear door of a large black SUV, which had been backed in for a quick exit—solid work by the prince's bodyguards—and hopped in. The engine roared as the truck shot forward before he could close the door.

The huge gate at the end of the driveway opened automatically, rolling back slowly while they waited. Bone aimed at the garage, too far away to hit anyone accurately but willing to try if the bad guys came through the door after them.

When the gate had rolled back enough, they shot through, scraping the passenger side of the SUV, and turned onto the quiet early morning street of the subdivision.

There were no gunshots, no squeal of tires as any of the other vehicles in the garage followed.

"Slow down—don't make a scene!" Bone called to Yousuf, who had the SUV careening past the large houses. "We're safe for now," Bone added. The SUV braked sharply, eased off, and slowed.

"Sorry," Yousuf said. "I haven't driven in years. Where do we go?"

"Pull over right before the exit onto the main road from the subdivision. We'll switch places."

"I think that was Khalid," Yousuf said, sounding calmer by the second. "The chief of security and Prince Rafiq's longtime bodyguard."

"Yes, I'm aware," Bone said, remembering the night in Afghanistan years before. Yousuf glanced at him in the rearview mirror. "Does he walk with a limp?" Bone asked.

Yousuf looked again, holding his eye for a second. "Watch the road," Bone said.

The double focused on the dark streets lit by well-spaced street lights. "How did you know he limped? You've been watching us?"

"Something like that," Bone muttered. "Here, pull over."

They quickly switched seats.

"What's the plan, bossman?" Matthew asked as they rolled forward again.

Bone's last view of Bossman—his team lead—had been of the warrior slumped over his M4 with a bullet to his face.

"Not 'bossman,'" Bone corrected. "Thomas. Or T-Bone. Or Bone."

He paused, contemplating Matthew's question and refusing to think of tonight as a failure. He'd rescued an innocent captive and a different sort of prisoner in Yousuf, the fake prince.

No plan survives first contact with the enemy. Tonight had been no exception.

While he'd lost the element of surprise, the prince and his team would be in emergency mode right now. They would be wondering if Bone's infiltration had been an attempt on the prince's life, a mission to rescue Matthew, or if somehow Yousuf had managed to pull one over on them.

People made mistakes when the pressure was on.

The prince's mistakes—or Khalid's, who was in charge of making the recommendations—would be opportunities for Bone.

"Does the prince have tracking devices on his vehicles?" Bone asked.

"I don't know for sure, but I think no," Yousuf answered. "He would never allow it. He is too concerned with his privacy."

"Good. He won't know where we are. Now," Bone said, stopping at the intersection of the subdivision and the rest of the town, "I'm still in the fight. What I need to know is..." He glanced in the rearview mirror at Yousuf before looking over at Matthew. "Are you two with me or not?"

95

THE CONVERSATION

La Jolla Grace Community Church
La Jolla, California

A car drove by on the main road, cutting through the dim yellow glow of the regularly spaced lights on the street. No other cars were in sight, not unusual for this late—or early—hour.

Bone turned left, then took an immediate right into the parking lot of a small church. He tucked the SUV in behind low, thick shrubs. They didn't completely hide the vehicle, but it would be hard to see in the dark.

Neither Yousuf nor Matthew had jumped to answer Bone's question. And as much as Bone hated the idea of risking their lives by allowing them to come along, he could use some help. Yousuf's insight into the house, the bodyguards, and the prince's thinking would be invaluable.

Matthew couldn't do much physically yet, but he seemed to be moving better. Adrenaline did that. Plus, the body—when pushed—could handle much more than the mind thought it could. Matthew was finding that out now.

"Before you say anything," Bone said, turning off the SUV and the headlights, "let me spell it out. I'm going to kill the prince."

Bone paused, his eyes never leaving the only road leading into and out of the subdivision, and reassessed the situation.

He'd had two excellent opportunities to kill Prince Rafiq and failed both times.

But he wasn't ready to admit defeat.

Still, was he making the right choice?

There was persistence—slamming against a wall until you finally broke through.

And there was stupidity: destroying your life by not learning quickly enough to just give up already.

After a quick gut check, he thought he was on the right path.

The prince had to die for what he'd done in the past: for the ambush on Bone's Team and the bounty program, and for his more recent activity of capturing a homeless man—and possibly others—to use as living punching bags.

Bone was the person best positioned to kill him.

If they could figure out a way.

"Both of you can hop out right now. Go to the police if you want, or disappear into the night. That's the safe play. But..." He hesitated, not wanting to ask. "I could use the help," he finally said. "How much risk are you two willing to take?" Bone turned to the homeless man in the passenger seat.

This time, Matthew didn't hesitate. "I'm all in."

From the back, Yousuf spoke quickly as well. "I am with you, too. If he lives, I die."

96

THE AGREEMENT

La Jolla Grace Community Church
La Jolla, California

Bone stared across the street, willing the prince to appear. He had the window down and the pistol ready.

He regretted not having the AK now—it would have come in handy here—but there was no time to drive to his car and pick it up. The prince had to be coming any second.

In the few minutes they'd sat watching, only two cars had driven by. Though the rich neighborhoods in the area likely had a rapid response time from the local police, Bone could unload rounds from the pistol into the prince's vehicles—targeting the drivers—and rush over to finish the job. They'd get away long before the authorities appeared. It would be tight, but he would risk it. They all would.

"You're waiting for him to rabbit?" Matthew asked from the passenger seat. With dried blood below his nose and on his cut lip, he looked like he'd gotten his ass kicked but he sat up straight—alert and ready.

"Rabbit?" Yousuf asked.

"Run away," Matthew explained. "Someone broke into his fortress and rescued me. You escaped. What, he's going to keep on with normal life? No way. He bolts to an airport and flies to..." He glanced at Yousuf.

"Saudi Arabia."

"What do you think?" Matthew asked Bone.

"He has to run. It's too risky for him to stay. We could be talking to the police right now, or the neighbors could have reported the gunshots."

"No," Yousuf said. "The guns were fired only in the house. I believe it is well-insulated and soundproof. Two of my guards were talking about being able to play music loudly in their quarters and not worry about the neighbors outside or the prince inside. The prince had work done the summer after he bought it." He paused. "It was after I heard screams coming from down the hall one night. I..." He looked down, ashamed. "I didn't know what it was. I only put the clues together last night and guessed he was keeping hostages." He shook his head. "I have a question if you don't mind," Yousuf said, changing the subject.

"Go ahead."

"Why didn't Khalid follow us—because he didn't want gunfire outside to alert the neighbors?"

Bone nodded. "Partly. His primary responsibility was to protect the prince. Once he'd exchanged shots with us and we left the house, he would have gone to the prince and made sure he was safe. Now, my guess is they're getting dressed and hoping they can get out before the police arrive to arrest them for taking Matthew captive. That road is the only one in and out of the neighborhood. Any time now, he's going to leave. If they're smart, they'll split up and take all the vehicles from the garage. We won't know which one has the prince, so we'll have to take out the drivers—and quickly mop up after that."

He pulled the smaller of his two pistols from his ankle holster, handing it to Matthew. "Can you handle this?"

After expertly checking it over, Matthew nodded. "Definitely."

Bone glanced in the rearview mirror. "I only have one extra, sorry."

"It's okay. I don't know how to use a gun, anyway," Yousuf said.

"I get first shot at killing him," Bone told Matthew, his voice firm and cold. "It's a long story, but it's personal. You only step in if I go down, no matter how much you want to take him out. Understand?"

"Copy that," Matthew said.

From the backseat, Yousuf spoke up as well. "Agreed," he said.

97

THE ARGUMENT

33 Gold Road
La Jolla, California

Rafiq couldn't contain himself. He paced across the kitchen, spun when he reached the refrigerator, and returned, glaring at Khalid as he passed the side of the kitchen island where he stood. "First the fiasco at the restaurant. And now someone broke into my house. My house!" he yelled.

"Sir, please," Khalid said, his voice pleading. "I am sorry. We will learn how he accessed the house later. But we must leave immediately."

"You keep saying that. I have said it already. I. Am. Not. Leaving." He couldn't go. In Europe, he didn't dare have his guards kidnap people off the streets. The places he most enjoyed visiting—Paris and London—had too many surveillance cameras, police, and social systems in place for the homeless. America made it easy. San Diego, Los Angeles, Las Vegas, San Francisco, all were havens for people who had nowhere to live except the streets.

If he left San Diego now, he wouldn't be able to finish in the upstairs playroom.

He had been nearly done with his latest opponent. He would have killed the younger man with the taunting words in a day or two. It would have been exquisite. He was looking forward to making the captive suffer for the words he'd spouted.

No one spoke to Prince Rafiq Al-Najjar like that.

But more importantly, Rafiq would miss the conclusion to the operation he and Khalid had been planning for over a year.

Which, in a rare moment of honesty with himself, he had to admit was the key.

It had started in Yemen but would finish in America.

The prospect of pulling the trigger and killing an American president made him not want to leave yet.

"A few more days," Rafiq said, hating the plea in his tone.

"Staying is not an option," Khalid said. "We must leave, sir. Your double is gone. The captive has escaped. The police will be on their way very soon—maybe as we speak. Given your stature in the community and your heritage, they will be kind at first. They may even discount the homeless man's story for a while. But with the word of the intruder, the captive, and your double, they will listen."

"They can do nothing to me. I will be released on bail within an hour of arrest," he said, sounding more like a little boy with every sentence.

"Not if they search the house."

Khalid's comment made him pause. "There is no evidence left," Rafiq said, part statement, part question.

"My men and I have done all we can," Khalid said. "But a look at the playroom, or one tiny drop of blood elsewhere, a scrap of flesh, or a single hair and…"

Rafiq glared at the man who had kept him safe all these years, struggling to reconcile the sensible advice with the urges he felt deep inside.

"Your Highness, the plan was never to allow a thorough search of the house. We agreed. At the first sign of suspicion, all of this would stop." Khalid waved his hand in the direction of the playroom upstairs, along with the room in the garage where so many bodies had been drained and broken down for careful disposal over the years. Rafiq had only been allowed to watch that part; Khalid refused to let him handle the saws for fear of leaving trace evidence behind.

"If we leave now," Khalid said, his voice softer, "we may try again elsewhere. Turkey, perhaps. Albania. We will find you a suitable location—and 'playmates.' But if you are arrested, it all stops. Even if you are under suspicion…"

"I will be confined to Saudi Arabia and other allied countries." Rafiq stared at the spreading puddle of ice cream leaking from the container on the kitchen island. Had it not been for Khalid's desire for a late-night snack… Rafiq couldn't contemplate what might have happened. Would the electronic locks have prevented access to his suite, or could the intruder have thwarted them as he had the rest of the security system?

Khalid interrupted his train of thought with a delicate cough. "The American police are not my primary concern." Rafiq paused his pacing, meeting his bodyguard's eyes. The man wanted Rafiq to figure out his meaning, to get there on his own so Khalid didn't have to say it.

He was too angry to play these games. Too upset about the possibility of missing the action this Thursday. "What are you talking about?" he asked.

His bodyguard glanced around the kitchen. The other men searched the house and grounds, inspecting every room to ensure there were no other intruders hiding out. Busy work—it was merely an excuse for the two of them to speak alone so Khalid could convince him to abandon his favorite house and the fighting he looked forward to all year.

"The king," Khalid whispered.

Rafiq sucked in his breath and stood straighter as if his distant cousin and Saudi Arabia's new king could walk in any moment.

Khalid was, as usual, way ahead of him. Rafiq hadn't considered what the king would do if he brought shame upon the family.

Whatever the king decided, it wouldn't be pleasant for Rafiq. A lesser punishment would be the confiscation of all his wealth and every source of income he had access to. No other family members would support him. He would be given a tiny stipend to live meagerly on in a small apartment in a backwater town. The king would delight in banishing him there.

A more realistic punishment would be locking him in a bare room and sending soldiers to fight him as part of their hand-to-hand combat training.

The king would enjoy the irony of Rafiq being forced to suffer endless beatings at the hands of his captors.

Rafiq's attention returned to the kitchen when Khalid spoke again. "If you escape now, you are a free man. Wanted, perhaps. The police may have questions, but you will be far from their jurisdiction. Out of their reach. Your lawyers would handle it, and perhaps something could be worked out with Basoul." It took Rafiq a moment to remember that one of his bodyguards had that name. "The guard was bored," Khalid said, warming to the idea. "He abused your generosity, vehicles, and a part of your large home—rooms you never visited—to fulfill his own perverted desires. You had nothing to do with whatever happened. And, unfortunately, your busy schedule does not allow you to return to America to be interviewed. The security guard…"

"Has honor," Rafiq said, considering. "He would of course come forward and confess his crimes." He paused, frowning. "For the right price," he muttered.

Khalid nodded. "If all of us are gone when the police arrive, perhaps they don't come in. It would take time to get a search warrant, and with no one to speak with, the process might take longer or not happen at all."

Rafiq nodded his understanding.

Khalid's shoulders relaxed. "Thank you, sir. Please, change your clothes. I will—"

"No," Rafiq said. "Your argument makes sense, but I am not leaving."

98

THE APPEASEMENT

33 Gold Road
La Jolla, California

Khalid stared at the man he had protected for decades.

He was at a loss for words. The prince had been difficult as a young man, a greater challenge to manage in his thirties, and now was nearly impossible. He seemed intent on pushing the limits to the point where Khalid wondered if he wanted to get caught.

Khalid couldn't allow that. He'd been tasked by the boy's father to protect him at any cost. And at this point, whatever happened to the prince, whether at the hands of the American police or the king and his men, would be twice as bad for Khalid.

He would have failed in his sworn duty to keep the prince from harm—from others, the outside world, and his own worst impulses.

The prince's father must have known or suspected what the prince would become.

Rafiq resumed pacing across the large kitchen, more like a stubborn child stomping back and forth than a wealthy, grown man considering what the right course of action was.

As the pieces fell into place, it all made sense. The outburst, the refusal to leave the country.

"This is about—" Khalid said, pausing to make sure they were still alone. "Thursday?"

Did the prince want to be there in person this time? Was he no longer content to watch the camera footage of missiles streaking to their targets and killing people? Did he want—or perhaps need—to take a more active role?

The conversation with Nasir in the security room Wednesday night came to mind.

"He's getting worse."

The first year, it had been enough for the prince to pick a fight in a low-rent biker bar in the middle of nowhere—with Khalid and other guards sitting nearby as backup.

But not for long.

Antagonizing American Marines at bars near their base in San Diego had come next.

By the end of the season, an occasional Navy SEAL had succumbed to the prince's taunting.

Sometimes, the prince lost the fights. Other times, he won.

He improved with each.

One night, Khalid had watched in horror as the prince knocked out a biker behind a bar and stomped him to death.

That had been the first of many bodies Khalid and the team had disposed of for the prince.

Abducting homeless men from larger western cities had been Khalid's plan to minimize the risk of the prince's predilections. If anyone was caught, it would be Syed and Fahad, who were well compensated for the risk the men took.

The killing of American soldiers overseas continued through the years, too, with Khalid carefully funneling the prince's money to organizations that were happy to help—and to make videos of the attacks for the prince to watch in his home movie theater.

There had never been a hint the prince wanted to participate further —until now.

"You cannot watch in person, sir," Khalid said.

The prince stopped his pacing, spun, and glared at Khalid. "I want it!" He slammed his fist on the kitchen island. "You can't take this from me!" He had gone from childlike insistence to rage in an instant. "You are my servant. You should do as I say and not constantly question me!"

The outburst startled Khalid.

The prince was crazed.

"Your father, on his deathbed, ordered me to look after you, to protect you," Khalid said, hoping the mention of the man would calm the prince. "This—"

"My father is gone and has been for years. You serve me, not him." The prince had calmed slightly.

Was it enough?

"We will all be in jail by Thursday," Khalid said, nearly whispering, hoping the contrast in tone and volume would break through the prince's madness.

They stared at each other, locked in a silent battle. For a long moment, Khalid feared for his life.

The prince was leaner, twenty years younger, had spent years fighting desperate strangers bent on saving their lives.

Khalid had army training and a lifetime of sparring with highly skilled warriors.

Could the prince beat him to death over this?

The thought sobered Khalid—and the prince must have seen it on his face.

"We leave when it is done," the prince said, a low, quiet growl.

Khalid thought fast, weighing his limited options, grasping at straws.

"What if we moved up the timeline?" he asked. "A different target?"

Would the prince agree to abandon his dream of killing an American president—even a retired one?

The current president would always be much too well protected and Air Force One had too many defenses—one man-portable surface-to-air missile would never blow it up.

But the retired president flying to Los Angeles for a speaking event made a juicy target. His plane could be destroyed with the missile.

But if there was another target for the prince, sooner than Thursday...

"Perhaps a different plane—with more passengers?" Khalid asked, desperately fishing into the prince's broken psyche for the right button to push. He had to accomplish two immediate goals: getting the prince safely out of the house—away from the police—as well as limiting his exposure to future trouble—or death.

"More people?" The prince's eyes widened and seemed to sparkle in the bright LED lights shining from the kitchen ceiling.

"Yes. Many more. And we could do it later today. But not the former president Thursday. You have to choose."

It took only a moment for the prince to nod. The gleam never left his eyes. "That is acceptable. Let me change my clothes and empty the safe. Five minutes at most. Then we leave."

Khalid nodded in relief, but the prince had already turned toward his suite.

Instead of the angry stomping of before, he practically skipped down the hallway.

The plan had been risky.

Now it was suicidal.

PART 6

MONDAY

99

THE GATHERING

Gold Road
La Jolla, California

Khalid quickly called the men to the kitchen. One way or another, whatever happened next would greatly impact them all. They would be risking their freedom to give the prince what he most wanted, or—if His Highness somehow managed to see reason while packing—they'd be leaving immediately on a chartered flight to the Middle East.

He shared a subtle, worried look with Nasir, suspecting the man had been close enough to hear at least some of the argument. Nasir raised an eyebrow but said nothing.

Basoul cradled his arm gingerly, still in pain from the burns he had suffered during the attack on the barbecue restaurant.

Syed and Fahad looked uncertain. They were kept mostly in the dark about the operation. They abducted the homeless men and knew what happened in the playroom, but Nasir and Khalid took care of the disposals— though they at least had to guess what happened when the prince finished with his "opponents," since they monitored the playroom security cameras.

They looked at Khalid, but he said nothing. He didn't want to make an announcement only for the prince to change his mind.

True to his word, though, His Highness didn't take long. Five minutes after going to his bedroom suite, he emerged dressed in black jeans, a black silk dress shirt, and a black sports coat, carrying a brown leather duffel bag filled, if the past was any indication, with the prince's emergency cash.

Instead of exhibiting his earlier rage, the prince was all smiles, as if the intrusion violating the sanctity of his home had never happened.

"We have one errand to run," the prince announced. "We leave the house this morning and we may not return for a while." He paused and the facade slipped, revealing underlying anger. "Unfortunately, because of tonight's incident, we must leave immediately. You have four minutes to gather your passports and other personal belongings. Go now."

The team dispersed. All knew the drill. While the prince normally stayed in one country for several months, a few times a year he would decide on a whim to journey to another city.

The men would grab their always-packed go bags and be back quickly.

Khalid pulled aside Nasir as he left the kitchen. "Erase the computer server," Khalid told the guard.

"What about—"

"Yes," Khalid interrupted. "Including the prince's 'special' files."

Nasir glanced at the kitchen where the prince had started humming what sounded like an old American show tune.

"He will kill me," Nasir whispered. "Then you."

"The American police may be coming. His Highness will understand—eventually."

He hoped.

Nasir saw the logic in the argument and nodded. "Yes, Khalid. Let us hope so."

"Go now."

Too much time had gone by since the intruder left with Yousuf and the captive, but at last Khalid had everyone moving in the right direction. And the proof the Americans needed about the prince's playtime would soon be erased.

Right now, the homeless American must be explaining to the police how he'd been abducted and escaped the multi-million-dollar house. The soldier would back him up.

And Yousuf? Was he also at the police station?

He was the least of Khalid's worries. The body double knew nothing—including, probably, the address of the house. He would be no help to the Americans.

Five minutes later, they left the house behind in a caravan of cars.

Khalid would pay the bills and have it cleaned weekly until it was safe for a team to sanitize it, return the playroom and the special room in the garage to their original condition, and move out, keeping the prince's artwork and disposing of the rest.

Assuming they made it out of the country without being arrested.

He had work to do as they drove. First, get Daoud—his former lieutenant—on the way to pick up Omar, the radicalized college student.

Second, pick a large commercial jet to shoot down.

Last, charter a last-minute yacht to sail to Baja, Mexico so they could make their escape.

There would be no flights out of LAX—or possibly all American airports—for a few days.

Maybe longer.

100

THE ESCAPE

Gold Road
La Jolla, California

Khalid rode in the passenger seat of the smaller SUV—the intruder had stolen the large one. Nasir drove. Basoul, his bandaged arm smelling of burnt flesh, sat in the backseat next to the prince.

They followed the red electric sedan carrying Syed and Fahad.

The caravan stopped a half-mile from the house. Khalid slid out and hobbled ahead to the gate blocking the narrow side road, his leg flaring with pain in the pre-dawn humid air. He used a key to open a large padlock, unwound a chain from a post, and swung the gate open. The sedan drove through first and stopped just down the hill as backup in case they were attacked.

After Nasir drove the SUV through, Khalid closed and locked the gate. Ownership of a house in the neighborhood had many perks: being surrounded by other ultra-wealthy people, proximity to the ocean, and easy access to one of the area's best beaches through a locked gate. Aside from the local lifeguards, only current area homeowners had the key and could drive down the long, steep, windy road to the most exclusive parking lot on the west coast, mere steps from an uncrowded beach.

But for Khalid, the location of the little-known and difficult-to-access emergency escape route had been the entire appeal of buying a house in the neighborhood.

He climbed back into the vehicle and they continued down the road. A pre-dawn fog had rolled in, haunting the darkness and hiding the view of the ocean.

Despite the beauty of the area, Khalid wouldn't miss Southern California. It was too cool and too humid. And as much as the prince disregarded the danger, America's police, warriors, and intelligence services were smart. Khalid and his team had been extremely careful, but limiting the targets to homeless men was the big reason they hadn't been caught. And, perhaps, some luck.

One couldn't discount luck.

At the bottom of the hill, they turned down a short ramp to the beach used only by lifeguards.

The sand didn't slow them down, and the tide rarely rose high enough to block the beach going north. After about two miles, they'd be able to turn off the sand and into a parking lot outside the town of Del Mar.

From there, it was a straight shot to the freeway and the prince's first—and hopefully last—in-person attack on the United States of America.

101

THE MISTAKE

La Jolla Grace Community Church
La Jolla, California

Something was wrong, but Bone couldn't put his finger on it.

Wisps of fog slipped in from the ocean as Bone, Matthew, and Yousuf waited in the church parking lot, ready to spring their ambush. They had the windows of the SUV down to better hear approaching vehicles, but in the twenty minutes since they'd escaped, only a few cars had passed by on the main road; no one had left or entered the subdivision.

Bone had been on a roll, feeling like his old self, but the firefight with the man in the kitchen had rattled him. At least he hadn't slipped into a flashback at the sight of one of the faces from his nightmares. Freezing at that moment would have gotten them all killed.

But since leaving the house, he couldn't shake the look on the bodyguard's face—Khalid, Yousuf called him. Khalid had recognized him but not known from where. Would the prince know him after all this time?

Could Bone live without Al-Najjar knowing who was about to kill him?

"What's taking so long?" Matthew muttered from the passenger seat, a steady hand holding Bone's smaller pistol. "Shouldn't they have been here by now?"

Bone nodded. "I'm wondering the same thing." He glanced quickly at Yousuf in the back seat, who shrugged.

"I don't spend much time around him, but I pretended to be him. He is arrogant. He may think he is invincible. Or that we are happy to get away and won't go to the police."

It didn't feel right to Bone.

What was he missing?

"We'd have heard a helicopter, right?" Bone mumbled.

Matthew nodded. "Definitely. Too quiet not to have. But what about an escape route? You said the house is near the ocean, right? A ladder down the bluff? Or—"

"Damn it!" Bone said, cutting him off.

The winding road with the locked gate. He'd run up it during his recon of the area and thought it was an access road for the lifeguards. But what if the prince's men cut the chain or rammed it open?

He'd made another mistake.

Bone started the SUV and floored it, spinning out on gravel in the parking lot. They fishtailed onto the main road and accelerated into the subdivision.

He slowed a half mile into the neighborhood, peering through the thickening fog for the entrance to the narrow side road.

He missed it the first time and had to turn around.

When he finally found the road and jumped out to take a look, the gate was closed and locked. There were no tire tracks or any indication vehicles had passed.

Given the amount of time since they had escaped the house, though, the prince and his bodyguards could have come here, unlocked the gate, and gotten away ten minutes ago.

He closed his eyes for a second, his back to the SUV, pushing down the feelings of failure. He'd never been the brains of his SEAL team, despite learning a decent amount of Pashto. That had been more hard work, dedication, and a desire to improve himself than intelligence. But the mistakes he'd made—kept making, he reminded himself—

were inexcusable. He wasn't dumb. He knew that. At school, he held his own with the other teachers, and no one got far in the Teams by being stupid.

He was merely out of practice. And maybe the desire for revenge was clouding his judgement.

Bone shoved the feelings down. It was time to move on. Adapt and overcome.

He ran back to the SUV and drove up the street, focused on the present.

"Shit happens," Matthew said in an understanding tone from the passenger seat. "Maybe they haven't left."

Another half mile brought them to the house. The fog was thicker than ever and the tall privacy hedge blocked most of the house from view, but a few exterior lights were on and the large metal gate closed.

"Does it look any different?" Bone asked Yousuf.

"Not at all. It is the same as ever when I get home this late."

"Does that mean they're sheltering in place, counting on the police not taking us seriously, or did we lose them?" Matthew asked.

Bone checked his gut as he continued driving around the curve that would lead back to the main road. "I missed them," he said. "But by how much?"

He floored the accelerator, hoping no one was out walking their dog or jogging this early. He might not see them in the fog. He slowed just enough to be able to stop if someone appeared in the headlights.

"I have an idea." Bone fished his cheap burner cell phone from his fanny pack and handed it to Matthew. "Turn it on and find me directions from Del Mar, the city north of here, to the freeway. We can catch up to them."

Bone could feel the skepticism from both Yousuf and Matthew. He didn't care. If there was a chance at taking out the prince before he left the country, he'd try, no matter how unlikely.

SEALs weren't perfect. But they kept going through everything life threw at them—including their own failures.

He was never out of the fight.

102

THE CHASE

North La Jolla, California

The fog grew thicker as Bone raced north through streets deserted aside from the occasional vehicle: a few early morning delivery trucks, panel vans of contractors getting a jump on the day to beat the traffic, and some pre-dawn surfers, their boards strapped to the top of their cars—everything from beat-up vans to luxury sedans.

Bone had his own doubts this last-ditch effort would work. If he had truly lost the prince again, he could console himself with the rescue of Matthew and Yousuf. He'd saved two lives.

The two-lane road curved, forcing Bone to slow in the ghostly white morning.

"Anything?" he asked.

"Yes," Matthew replied, staring at Bone's phone. "The beach parking lot is at the bottom of this hill. After that, it's less than a mile to a sharp right turn, and a mile-and-a-half to the freeway onramp. Or, if you want to go straight, it's three miles to another right turn and a closer onramp."

"Copy," Bone said, focused on driving as fast as safely possible.

"Ahead on the left," Matthew said, checking the map.

Bone slowed to a reasonable speed for an early Monday morning.

He eased off the accelerator further as he reached the bottom of the hill. A large parking lot served a state beach to the left.

Barely visible through the thick fog was a concrete lifeguard tower on the sand. A small hut guarded the entrance to the lot—the place to pay for parking. Bone had visited once before, years ago. There had been a gate across the entrance and metal spikes at the exit; people could safely drive over them to leave after the lot officially closed, but not enter.

This morning, the lot was empty. No vehicles drove up the lifeguard access ramp from the beach.

There were no headlights on the street ahead, either, at least for the half-mile of visibility through the fog.

Bone pounded the steering wheel hard, needing to vent his frustration. He felt like screaming but held himself in check.

At least Matthew and Yousuf kept their mouths shut. Bone couldn't take an "I told you so," or—worse—sympathy.

"Maybe we can still catch them," Bone mumbled, but he had a tough time sounding upbeat. He sped up anyway, though not with the same urgency he'd rushed here.

"It'll be easier to see on the freeway," Matthew said, trying to be positive.

"They have to be headed to LAX or a nearby executive airport," Bone said, thinking out loud. "Where would he be able to get a jet out of first thing this morning? And where did you guys usually fly from—LAX or San Diego? Which do you think is more probable?" He needed to know whether to turn north or south on the freeway.

There was no answer from the back seat. "Yousuf?"

"Slow down without braking," Yousuf whispered. His tone had gone from quiet to authoritative.

Bone took his foot off the accelerator and glanced in the rearview mirror.

Yousuf had spun around on the seat and faced backward. "I thought I saw something."

Bone appreciated the positivity from both of them, but enough was enough. He would rush up the freeway on a last-ditch chance of finding the prince in the lighter morning traffic, but he didn't need to be babied.

"Guys, thanks for humoring me, but—"

"I think it's them," Yousuf interrupted, still whispering. "Two vehicles in the parking lot. There were no cars in the back section or anywhere, right?"

"Totally deserted," Matthew said, also whispering as if anyone in a car a half-mile behind could hear.

"Then it has to be them, right? Who else can it be?"

Bone refused to get his hopes up. "A trick of the fog? Could it be cars coming down the hill?" In the mirror, he now saw headlights but in the fog couldn't discern the make or model of the vehicles.

"No," Yousuf said, certain. "It's them."

At the intersection, Bone signaled and turned right. If they could see the two cars, the drivers could see them. Better to pretend to be just another early-morning commuter.

Once around the sharp corner, though, Bone counted to three before killing the lights and coasting to avoid the brakes lighting up the morning. He turned left into the parking lot of an upscale coffee shop. A white sports car was parked in the back corner and a single light lit up the counter inside. A young man moved slowly around in the shop, prepping for morning.

Bone pulled around back and parked facing the road, partly blocked by the building. "Hold still," he said. "Movement attracts the eye."

They didn't have long to wait. First, a high-end red electric sedan passed by on the road. Close on its tail was a small black SUV.

"That's them," Yousuf whispered.

103

THE STORIES

Bone risked losing the SUV and the electric car, staying far back on the northbound freeway, keeping them barely in sight.

As they moved inland, the fog disappeared. Visibility was fine and traffic picked up—more so headed south, but there were enough vehicles on the road to make ramming the smaller SUV and shooting Al-Najjar unrealistic.

Bone would have to bide his time and hope for an opportunity.

"If they go straight to an airport, we're screwed," Matthew said. Bone had already gotten there, but it felt good to talk things out. To be part of a team again, such as it was.

"We play it by ear. Adapt and overcome," Bone said.

"Adapt and overcome," Matthew repeated in a reverent tone, making Bone glance over at him.

Yousuf had confirmed the prince and his bodyguards were likely going to the private VIP terminal at Los Angeles International Airport. The drive would take a while, so they had time to chat—and Bone was flagging. He needed to stay awake and alert.

"Now that we have a minute, if you don't mind me asking," Bone said, "what's your story?"

After several seconds of silence, Matthew spoke, his tone filled with regret. "I wanted to be a SEAL. That's why I joined the Navy. I was in great shape, I promised my buddies back home I wouldn't give up, no matter what, but..."

Bone nodded in the glow of the dash lights. "I understand. BUD/S is nearly impossible. It's not for everyone."

"I didn't want to give up. One night, two thirds of the way through the first phase, I was so cold... so tired... We were lying in shallow water, right at the edge of the beach. Those damn waves were frigid, washing over us. We were side by side in a long line, arms hooked. You know?"

Bone knew all too well. The nights had seemed endless. The cold seeped deep into his bones; he'd been certain he would never feel warm again. But somehow he held on and stuck it out, one second at a time.

"I was at the end of the line," Matthew continued, speaking as if he were picking off a painful emotional scab. "If there had been someone else next to me... If I had to untangle my numb arms from two other guys instead of just one..."

He paused, staring ahead, his body slumped in the seat, his long, matted hair cascading around him. "I wasn't thinking clearly. It wasn't so much that I gave up. I just found myself ringing the bell. It was like sleepwalking. I wasn't even relieved; I was going through the motions. Twenty minutes later I had some hot coffee and a doughnut and was filled with regret. I begged them... I literally begged. I got down on my knees and pleaded with them to let me go back. I'd lay in the water by myself to make up the time, whatever I had to do." He paused and shook his head. "It was too late."

Matthew cleared his throat and sat up straight in the seat. "They said I could apply again. That was my plan. Later, though, I was deployed, assigned to a ship, doing my duty. I got out of shape. My motivation was gone and the years slipped away."

Bone said nothing. There were a hundred variations of the story. Only twenty percent of candidates at BUD/S made it; those that didn't ended up deployed in other roles, making a difference serving their country—but not in the way they'd wanted.

"Fast forward a bunch of years," Matthew continued. "I'm out of the Navy, I've got some issues with authority, get into money trouble, end up on the street. Middle of the night, I'm foraging for bottles and cans, to get the deposit money back, you know? A van comes down the road and swerves into my bags. Plastic bottles go flying. Two dudes jump out. One helps pick up the bottles and then jabs me with something. A sedative. The next thing I know I wake up chained to the wall in the room where you found me. I go two rounds as a human punching bag sparring partner for..." Matthew glanced back at Yousuf. "Him—or the guy who looks exactly like him, I guess."

He turned to Bone. "Thanks for rescuing me, by the way."

"Thank him," Bone said with a nod to the back seat. "He told me about you and guessed which room you were being held in."

Matthew turned and thrust his hand toward Yousuf, who shook. "Thanks for saving my life," Matthew said quietly.

"You're welcome," Yousuf said. "I am not at all like him."

"I'm glad."

A mile went by in silence as the traffic picked up and the hint of dawn crept into the sky.

"What about you?" Bone asked with a glance in the rearview mirror.

"Me?" Yousuf asked. He took a few seconds to compose himself before beginning. "Ten years ago I worked in my parents' restaurant. A man ate there and came back a few days later with another man—Khalid—who offered me a job and my parents and me a lot of money to hire me away from them. Khalid said I would be the household help for a Saudi royal. When I met him—Prince Rafiq—it was like looking into a mirror. Our beards and hair were styled differently, and he had a scar under his eye and a bump on his nose. But we were very similar—like brothers. He was excited to see me and gave Khalid his approval."

Yousuf paused and fingered the scar high on his cheek. "Khalid offered me a job, one with more responsibility than merely working as household help. It meant an ongoing bonus sent to my family. I would play the role of prince when Prince Rafiq didn't want to. My job was to smile and shake hands, saying little. His Highness hated to attend certain events, I was told, so I would be helping him a great deal."

"But you'd have to change your beard, learn about him, act like him, and get the matching scar?" Matthew asked.

Yousuf nodded. "I did it, of course. It was a great honor. I was good at it too. No one ever suspected."

"But they locked you up the rest of the time," Bone said.

"Yes," Yousuf agreed, his voice sad. "It has been a lonely several years. This is the most in-depth conversation I've had. The staff doesn't converse with the prince, and only Khalid and Nasir know that I am an impostor, though the others must suspect."

He leaned forward between the front seats. "Thank you for rescuing me," Yousuf said to Bone.

Traffic grew heavy as they approached Los Angeles, forcing Bone to close the distance between the prince's vehicles and theirs. The red electric car and small black SUV cruised along at a steady speed in the far right lane at only a few miles per hour above the speed limit.

"Okay," Matthew asked after a few more miles passed in silence. "What's your deal?"

104

THAT NIGHT

I-5 Northbound

Bone had expected the question and had an answer worked out that would protect Zia and Lamar's involvement, along with keeping Admiral Nalen's role secret.

"Long story short," he started. "Navy SEAL, retired. My whole Team..." He had to stop. He'd never said the words aloud. He had been interviewed for an after-action report, but it had been a professional, matter-of-fact recounting of the moment-by-moment actions of the Team and the enemy that night. Other SEALs had asked if he was doing okay, what he needed, all that, but he'd never sat down and told the story.

"We got ambushed," he said in a whisper, his emotions threatening to spill out. "All Afghans, except for three foreigners. One guy had a sniper rifle; he killed all of my buddies."

Bone focused on his breathing, refusing to let reality slip away while driving on the crowded freeway in the middle of the mission.

He could handle this. He had to.

"Last week, I was on my phone, killing time, and saw an announcement about a movie premiere," he said, going with the cover

Admiral Nalen had worked out for him. "I watched the trailer and it looked good, so I read the article, which mentioned the executive producer: Prince Rafiq Al-Najjar. It had a picture. I zoomed in because he looked familiar. It was the guy from that night. The sniper."

"Dude," Matthew muttered.

"He had the scar under his eye. Small but noticeable. I knew for sure it was him because I did that—right before they killed me."

Bone had to make a conscious effort to release his tight grip on the steering wheel. "From there, it was easy to find him."

"You were at the premiere?" Yousuf asked.

"Yes. Set up on a roof down the street, ready to shoot him. I assume that was you, though?"

Yousuf nodded in the rearview mirror.

Bone let out a long breath. "I had you in my sights and couldn't take the shot. Nerves. Maybe somebody was looking out for me," he muttered.

"And me," Yousuf whispered. "If you had taken that shot..."

"The real prince would still be alive. He'd have gotten away," Bone said.

"What did you mean," Matthew asked, "'right before they killed me.'"

"I flicked a stupid throwing star at the prince. It cut his face. As I went in to finish him off, the main bodyguard—who I recognized tonight: Khalid—pushed the prince away. The other guard shot me and I went down. I pulled my knife and hacked at someone first, though. Khalid, right?"

Yousuf nodded. "Khalid walks with a pronounced limp. His left leg is permanently damaged."

"Good. Hope it hurts every day. Anyway," Bone said, the story coming more easily now. "I woke up in a helicopter. A medic had refused to give up and brought me back." There was sadness in his voice he hadn't realized he felt until hearing it. "I was there," he said to himself, not caring if the other two heard it or not. "With my brothers. Heaven or someplace. All warm and peaceful. Then I was back in that damn helicopter."

He loosened his fingers on the steering wheel again, flexing one hand at a time.

"I lived. They died. I'm going to avenge them—or die trying."

The only sounds in the SUV were the drone of the engine and the tires on the road. Matthew and Yousuf digested the story while Bone fought to keep his emotions under control.

"Um," Matthew said after several seconds. "Now that we're along for the ride, do you mind if we avoid that last part?"

Bone chuckled, welcoming the release of tension. "I'll do my best," he said. He'd made several big mistakes so far on this mission. He better have gotten them out of his system. It wasn't just him any longer.

Anything that happened now affected them all.

105

THE FREEWAY

I-5 Northbound

Khalid worked the phone, doing research until he had what he needed. The original plan required only slight modification.

The prince snored softly in the backseat. Basoul leaned against the window on the other side, also asleep.

Nasir drove in the right lane, following Syed and Fahad in the electric car, safely staying within a few miles per hour of the speed limit as traffic picked up and vehicles flew past them.

Khalid checked his phone as a coded text came in. Daoud had made good time, leaving from north San Diego immediately after getting the text. He would arrive at the location before them, but not by much.

This morning would be the last of the risks, Khalid vowed. The police would want to ask the prince questions, whether they completely believed the homeless captive's story or not.

There would be no returning to the United States.

"The American president?" Nasir asked, his voice low to not wake the prince. He had helped Khalid with recon and planning for the original mission to shoot down the ex-president's plane.

"We cannot wait until Thursday," Khalid said.

Nasir nodded. "This will be better for him."

Khalid agreed, but given the prince's obsession with killing the former American president—the one most responsible for the increased presence of American troops in the Middle East—the president's long-planned Los Angeles speech had seemed perfect.

And despite Khalid's commitment to serve the prince, killing civilians didn't sit well with him. In his mind, American soldiers in Afghanistan and other Middle Eastern countries were fair game. The former president too. And the bikers the prince had killed over the years had chosen to fight him.

The homeless men was another step Khalid had reluctantly taken to appease the prince.

In the end, though, it was his role to protect, not question.

106

THE MOUNTAINS

Bone sped away from the intersection where he'd stopped at a red light, desperate not to lose the car and SUV, one of which had to contain the prince.

He'd fallen back, letting the two vehicles get far ahead of him to avoid being noticed. As the eastern sky turned pink, traffic had picked up even more. Leaving the freeway east of Los Angeles had made tailing the prince's caravan more challenging.

After stopping at the light, he'd lost sight of them entirely.

"Where are they going?" Bone asked Matthew, who had the cell phone out, examining a map of the area.

Bone accelerated, first ten, then fifteen miles over the speed limit, praying no police noticed them.

"Do they have another house in the area? A safe house? A secret place to hole up in case of emergency?" Matthew asked.

"Not that I have been to or heard of," Yousuf said. "Maybe, though. Khalid is very thorough."

"It could be in any one of the subdivisions around here," Matthew said. They continued north through an upscale tree-lined area filled with shopping centers, office complexes, and endless houses.

Bone slowed. A half-mile ahead, the red car and black SUV pulled away from a stop light.

"They're going straight north," Bone said. "What's around? An executive airport? A helipad?"

"Nothing like that," Matthew said, moving his fingers on the screen. "If they aren't bolting to a house, the only place that I can see is the San Gabriel Mountains." He pointed at the mountain range looming a few miles ahead, filling their vision from east to west.

"Definitely a good place to hole up," Bone muttered. "Few people, easy to defend. Get far enough away from other homes and cabins and gunfire goes unheard or disregarded."

"The prince hates nature, especially trees," Yousuf said. "He wouldn't hide out there. He would be more likely to have a large house in the desert or one of the nice areas here."

Bone hung back again, letting the prince's vehicles get almost out of sight once more.

"My gut tells me he's going into the mountains," he said.

"To lure us in? Maybe they know we've been following?" Matthew asked.

"That's what I'm worried about."

Bone turned off the SUV's headlights, though the sun wasn't quite up. The glow of lights from the overpopulated valley a few miles behind them and the faint pink of the coming dawn was enough to see by.

He dropped back farther. The narrow two-lane road into the mountains had no other traffic heading up or down. They drove in a mini canyon that the road had been carved from, with gravel and rock walls twenty feet high on both sides, covered in brush and bushes. The actual mountains were farther back, not high compared to Colorado, but tall enough to be majestic in the morning light.

"What if they turn into a trailhead?" Matthew asked.

"I hope the side roads are dirt so we'll see dust in the air if they do," Bone said. "Otherwise, we'll quickly check any big turnoffs and hope we get lucky."

He slowed as the road curved sharply right.

"Luck is not a strategy," Matthew muttered.

"It's all we have right—"

Coming around the bend, a red sedan blocked both lanes of the road, its hazard lights flashing brightly. Both front doors were wide open, but the car was empty.

"Get down!" Bone yelled as he slammed on the brakes.

Matthew and Yousuf both ducked as Bone shifted into reverse.

Before the truck moved, the passenger side window exploded in a shower of glass, followed an instant later by the SUV's rear window.

More gunfire peppered the truck as Bone floored it, reversing out of the ambush. Bullets followed them until they rounded the bend in the road, where Bone braked hard and put the truck into Park.

"Yousuf, stay down! Matthew, out now. Right side of the road. Shoot anything that's not me."

Bone opened the door and stepped out, pistol in hand, and advanced up the road in a crouch.

Hugging the right side of the road, nearly in the shallow ditch between the asphalt and rocky hill, Matthew kept pace with him, steadily putting one foot in front of the other, leading with the small 9mm, showing no fear.

107

THE GUNSHOTS

The San Gabriel Mountains

Syed scrambled along the top of the rocks overlooking the road, angling for a view of the SUV that had backed around the bend.

He had planned for the truck to brake hard, stopping to investigate their car blocking the road. The target might guess it was an ambush, but Syed and Fahad would have plenty of time to kill whoever had been following them.

Instead, they had been surprised at the quick reaction of the target.

Khalid had been clear: there should be no survivors. "Kill anyone in the SUV, pile the dead bodies in the back, and follow us to the trailhead," he had said, warning them that one of the men was a trained soldier.

Their shots had hit the vehicle, but when it quickly backed out of the kill zone, they had lost the advantage.

Across the road, on a matching hill through which the road had been cut, Fahad slipped and fell to one knee. Pebbles trickled down the slope to the road.

Gunfire came from directly below Syed, kicking up dirt near Fahad as he rolled away.

One of the targets was nearby and within range. Syed had the advantage.

He rose to a crouch, checking the far side of the road first.

The homeless man he and Fahad had abducted from a back street in Los Angeles pointed a small pistol directly at him.

Before he could drop to the ground, the prince's captive fired.

Syed flung himself down and rolled away, unharmed.

Another shot kicked up dirt near the edge of the cliff, followed by more.

He and Fahad had been in the Royal Saudi Land Forces—Saudi Arabia's army. He knew covering fire when he heard it.

Syed stayed prone, aiming for the lip of the small cliff and wishing he had a rifle.

Fahad fired three times from the other side of the road.

Answering gunfire came from Syed's side.

In the silence that followed, nothing stirred.

There were no more shots from Fahad.

Syed blinked back shock. They had worked together for fifteen years, first in the army and then for the prince. Was he really gone—or only reloading and preparing to reengage the enemy?

In his heart, Syed knew he was dead.

He focused his attention on the cliff edge, ready to avenge Fahad's death.

The ambush was no longer only about following orders. Now it was personal.

108

THE WARRIOR

The San Gabriel Mountains

Matthew moved as quietly as possible, inching the rest of the way up the hill. He hadn't understood Bone's quick gestures—they weren't the simple, common signals he'd learned in the Navy's basic training, and he'd never gotten far enough in BUD/S to learn small unit tactics and how to communicate detailed plans silently.

He was either supposed to crest the lip of the hill and shoot the second target or be the decoy while Bone handled the killing.

Either way, he thought he'd be nervous, but from the sudden stop of the SUV and frantic backing up, he'd slipped into a zone he'd only felt before when playing first-person shooter video games.

This morning, unlike in those games, there would be no reset or second chances.

Getting shot here along this road in the mountains outside of Los Angeles would be game over forever.

"Your partner is down," Bone called to the second tango from ten yards ahead.

Matthew moved under the cover of the words.

"Surrender now and we'll take you to the police. If you testify against the prince, you'll probably only be in jail a while."

Matthew reached the top of the hill. This time, Bone's hand signals were easy to understand. A finger at Matthew, a gesture which meant to go over the top and start firing at the tango who had to be somewhere nearby. Five fingers. Four. "Otherwise," Bone said, showing three fingers as he started calling out again. "I'm going to have to—"

Matthew didn't hear the rest as he pushed hard, crawling the rest of the way over the lip of the hill.

The tango lay prone only five feet away. He must have moved south after Matthew had him in his sights and missed.

The man—Matthew recognized him as one of the guards who'd abducted him a few days before—swung his weapon from the direction of Bone's voice toward Matthew.

Their eyes met as Matthew fired, his finger pulling the trigger repeatedly.

Return bullets whizzed by Matthew, close enough to feel.

He didn't move. Didn't stop firing.

Matthew's last shot hit home. His abductor's head snapped back as Matthew's bullet finally found its mark.

Just in time—the gun was empty.

He'd used the last of his ammo and they still had several men to kill.

———

Matthew stared at the lifeless body as Bone collected the tango's weapon and cleaned out his pockets, surprised to find himself feeling neither remorse nor shock.

He'd finally done what he'd set out to do so many years before.

He had become a warrior.

109

THE TALK

The San Gabriel Mountains

Bone drove the electric sedan away from the trailhead where they'd parked the SUV. The shot-out windows and bullet holes in the passenger-side body would attract attention at some point, but that was a problem for an hour from now—if they were still alive.

The two dead bodyguards went into the spacious trunk of the sedan. Another issue to deal with in an hour.

The most immediate concern for Bone was the lack of ammunition.

Both guards had used almost all their rounds, and Matthew had gone through the magazine in Bone's small backup pistol along with the spare.

Bone had one half-empty mag left for his pistol, and just enough ammo from the dead guys' weapons to refill Matthew's smaller magazine.

It wasn't enough firepower to take on Khalid and the other two guards Yousuf said would be with the prince.

They'd have to go with the obvious plan of using the enemy's sedan as a modern-day Trojan horse. It all came down to how capable Khalid thought the two guards from the car were—and whether he believed the guards would have easily taken out Bone and company.

"You handled yourself well back there," Bone told Matthew as he raced up the road in the nearly silent electric car. He slowed at every bend, wary of another ambush.

His first taste of combat, years ago, hadn't gone as smoothly as tonight's firefight. "You okay?" he asked.

For many people, Navy SEALs included, the first kill hit hard. No matter how much training or how many rounds fired at the range, shooting a living human being in the heat of battle took a toll.

"Good to go. Thanks for the plan," Matthew said. He sounded surprisingly fine.

"No regrets?"

Matthew replied immediately. "Only that I can't seem to shoot straight. It took five shots to hit a motionless target."

"Combat does that. The adrenaline, the stress, not to mention someone shooting back at you."

"Yeah, he almost took me out. I…" He trailed off.

"What?"

"If I make it through this, I need time on the range."

Bone glanced over at him. "Thinking of making this type of thing a regular activity?"

"Like a bowling league?" Matthew joked. "No. But better to have the skill and not need it, right?"

"Right." Bone needed more range time himself. The experience was there and the skills were coming back, but it had taken him too many bullets to kill the other guy on the hill across the road. Seven years ago, he would have nailed him on the first or second shot.

"Any idea where they could have gone?" Bone asked, back to the business at hand. They couldn't pretend to be the guards catching up to the rest of the crew if they didn't know where to go.

"This is the only road," Matthew said, back to looking at the map on Bone's phone. "There are multiple parking areas at hiking trailheads. More houses right off the road the higher up you go. Otherwise, it's up to the top where there's a road that branches off and winds around to the west and back to the city."

"Would he have a helicopter come pick him up here for some reason?" Bone asked Yousuf.

Bone glanced back when there was no reply from the backseat. Yousuf's face was ashen in the dawn light. "Hey, you okay?" Bone asked, knowing he wasn't.

He shook his head. "I… this is…"

"First time in a dangerous situation?"

"Aside from earlier tonight when you held a knife to my throat, yes," Yousuf managed. "And…"

"The dead guys?"

Yousuf nodded. "They weren't my friends, but…"

"I get it," Bone said. "You knew them and now they're gone."

"I am okay," Yousuf said. His voice sounded stronger. "It was the surprise. How did you know what was happening? One second we were driving, then next we were going backward and they were shooting at us."

Bone took the question seriously but wasn't sure how to answer. How to explain the prickling sensation on the back of his neck a second before the bend in the road or the instinctive solution to getting out of the kill box?

"Training and experience," he said, which seemed to satisfy the prince's lookalike. It wasn't the full answer but would do for now.

It made him realize the warrior skills he'd cultivated as a SEAL had gone from dormant and dusty a few days before to—finally—back to being instinctive. He was once again a finely honed weapon, and all it had taken was making a bunch of stupid mistakes, a firefight in a fancy kitchen, and a shootout on the road to get his mind back in the game.

"I don't know about a helicopter," Yousuf said, answering Bone's question.

"Might raise some eyebrows, a private chopper flying up here. But if he wanted that, there's a pullout ahead that looks pretty big. It's a parking lot for a bunch of trails and it has a nice vista looking south over the city. Otherwise, there are smaller trailheads further up that would involve hiking to the top of one of the mountains."

"He won't hike," Yousuf said. "That is for poor people, in his mind."

Bone checked that the car lights had turned off automatically as the sun came up. "How far until the big parking lot?"

"About two miles."

"You ready for another go-round?" Bone asked.

Matthew nodded. "I'll shoot better this time."

"You'll have to—we don't have rounds to waste." Bone turned his gaze to the rearview mirror. "What about you?" he asked Yousuf. "Do you need us to drop you off?"

"No," he answered immediately. "Maybe I'll be able to help this time."

Bone nodded but knew that wouldn't happen. Some people were born warriors, others—like Matthew, perhaps—could be shaped into them. Most were civilians, through and through. Brave—maybe. Willing—some. But all Bone needed from Yousuf was to stay low so Bone didn't have to worry about him.

"Just stay out of sight. If it sounds like things aren't going our way, jump in the driver's seat and get out of here. Go to the police and tell them what happened."

Word would eventually get to Stephanie back home.

Maybe she'd put a flower on his casket—or lie and tell people he'd been a good man.

110

THE PARKING LOT

Mid-Mountain Trailhead
The San Gabriel Mountains

Dust billowed as the SUV turned into the gravel trailhead parking lot. Khalid had scouted this location but discounted it for firing the missile at the former president's plane; it was too far away from the airport.

Khalid would put the recon effort to good use with today's change of plans.

A smaller parking lot lower on the mountain saw occasional traffic this early, but he had seen no one here until mid-morning during his previous visit. While this flat parking lot and open ground provided an excellent view of the sprawling city, the trails here weren't as popular as lower—closer to where people lived—on weekdays just after dawn.

The sun, still low in the sky, promised a bright, clear, warm day.

"Perfect hunting weather," the prince said, leaning forward from the back seat as they bounced across the bumpy parking lot. His eyes were bright and his face glowed with anticipation.

"Yes, sir." Khalid kept his misgivings off his face while his stomach churned. Hundreds of innocent people were about to die—and he was having second thoughts.

Picking fights with bikers or soldiers was one thing. Abducting homeless men to beat before killing them was another. He'd gone along with it all out of loyalty to the prince.

This, though…

Why had he suggested it?

He should have argued more. Demanded they leave for the airport immediately. Threatened to expose the prince's activities to the king. Even promised him another chance at the former president someday.

Anything but this.

And now it was much too late for regrets.

The lot was empty except for a white panel van parked near the far end of the lot, close to the grassy overlook. Daoud would be in back, waiting.

Nasir stopped the SUV a few spots away from the van, facing toward the road on the other side of a small hill.

The prince was the first out, hurrying to pound on the back of the van.

"Open the door," the prince called. "I want to see it."

Nothing moved in the cool morning. The prince scowled at Khalid as he rushed to join him.

Khalid knocked twice on the rear doors, paused, and knocked twice again.

The doors opened to reveal Daoud, Khalid's army buddy and fixer.

A thin, pale young man, college-age, with a ridiculously thin beard sat behind him on the metal floor of the van with a smartphone clenched in his hands.

Daoud's face behind the full gray beard was expressionless, his eyes hard.

Omar was terrified.

A thick blanket covered a long, narrow lump along the right edge of the van's cargo area.

"It is time," Khalid said.

The two men in the van nodded. Daoud pulled the blanket, revealing the prize underneath.

Prince Rafiq had a rapturous look as he gazed at the Russian-made man-portable surface-to-air missile.

"She is beautiful," Prince Rafiq whispered. "How did you acquire this one?" he asked Khalid, ignoring the two men.

"The same as the others in Yemen, sir," Khalid explained. "Your money plus my connections. The missiles are not hard to find. The real challenge was convincing the supplier to risk shipping it to the United States."

"That is why there is only one?" the prince asked. He had wanted at least two—preferably four—and had pouted when Khalid told him there wouldn't be more.

"Yes, sir. One was as many as they would risk," he lied. Khalid had only asked Daoud to have his contact send one. There was less chance of disaster that way.

"Do we have time for them to explain how they aim and fire it?" the prince asked like a child acting extra polite to get his way.

Khalid checked his watch. They were early. "Yes, sir. You can see how it works," Khalid said, feeling like the father he'd never been, humoring his child. "This is Omar," he said, introducing the young college student in jeans and a hoodie, who bowed his head in respect. "He has spent the past week learning everything about the weapon and how to fire it." He nodded at the young man. "Omar, please explain how to fire the weapon. I will hold the cell phone."

He accepted the cell phone Omar would use to record—and stream—the airplane exploding.

Nasir and Basoul joined the group at the rear of the van, fascinated by the weapon. Both had been in the Saudi army, like Khalid, but none of them had experience firing missiles. And they originally weren't supposed to be here, anyway. Omar was the expert.

"It is simple, sir" Omar said. "The range is approximately three miles. The target is best engaged below 10,000 feet in altitude. Omar glanced at Khalid for reassurance.

Khalid nodded. "We are well within those parameters."

Omar continued, sounding more confident as he walked the prince through tracking, aiming, and firing. The missile was simple—a fire-and-forget weapon that locked onto the heat signature of an aircraft.

Military targets had several defensive capabilities, while some civilian craft had a more basic defensive package, though those systems were expensive. Not many commercial airliners had them, especially planes that flew mainly between the United States and Europe, like the one they would bring down shortly.

"Show me," the prince demanded, gesturing for the weapon to be unloaded.

After checking the empty parking lot, Khalid gave a subtle nod to Omar. It was nearing time to prepare for the shot, anyway.

Khalid shoved down the feeling of dread in his stomach. He was a former Saudi soldier in the service of a Saudi prince. His duty was not to question orders but to follow them.

Daoud got back in the van to prepare for a fast getaway, while Omar carried the missile out of the vehicle and over the low metal guard rail marking the edge of the parking lot and the start of the grassy lookout area.

The prince walked with him, asking more questions about the weapon, while the rest of them followed, including Nasir, who was now in charge of the phone. He would use it to stream the footage to a private cloud account while recording the event for the prince to enjoy later in ultra-high definition.

Khalid glanced at Nasir and Basoul, searching for the slightest hesitation. Their faces were set; they'd been dedicated soldiers for years.

Ignoring the hitch in his step from the constant pain in his left leg, Khalid followed. The attack had to continue. To cancel the mission now meant the prince would turn on him—he would order Nasir to kill him. Or, worse, His Highness would beat him to death right here next to the dusty parking lot.

They stopped near a bench on the overlook. Khalid glanced at his watch. If there were no delays, the plane would be taxiing for takeoff now.

Hundreds of innocent civilians flying from Los Angeles to Germany were minutes away from death.

And it had been his idea.

111

LAX

Los Angeles International Airport
Los Angeles, California

"Welcome aboard Flight 843," Captain Perry said over the intercom. "This is your captain. Thank you for traveling with us. Our flight time to Frankfurt today will be ten hours and fifty minutes. We have clear skies and we should have smooth flying. We'll be on our way shortly," he said, and clicked off the intercom.

"Perfect day for a crossing," Ellen, the co-pilot, said.

"Beats working for a living," Perry said. At sixty-two, he was closing in on mandatory retirement age. Flying was all he'd known. He'd earned his private pilot's license during college, joined the Air Force right after, and had flown ever since.

He envied Ellen—she was in her early forties, divorced, and had plenty of years left.

While flying the big commercial planes had a few drawbacks— being away from home, jet lag—Perry loved the job. The wide-open sky, the joy of flying.

A few minutes later, they were loaded and all 467 passengers were settled.

"Ladies and gentlemen, this is the captain again," Perry said. "The doors are closed and we'll be pushing back shortly. Please settle in for your nearly eleven-hour flight to Germany."

Perry clicked off the intercom and got busy with the part of the job he enjoyed most: flying the airplane. He focused his attention as the plane got a push away from the gate. Takeoffs and landings were statistically the most dangerous part of flying. Even with the advances in technology, nothing could take the place of a steady hand at the controls.

"Before start checklist?" he asked.

"Before start checklist," Ellen said.

A few moments later, the checklist was complete.

"Start them up," Perry said.

112

THE RAGE

Mid-Mountain Trailhead
The San Gabriel Mountains

Rafiq's body felt like it was on fire. The missile waited, two feet away, carried by that... boy. A poor, worthless idiot from America who thought converting to a religion made him special.

Why should this fool be allowed the honor of killing the hundreds of people on the airplane?

The very idea was obscene.

Drawing himself up, Rafiq spoke to the men around him. "I will fire the weapon," he announced.

He saw the look on Khalid's face before his servant got himself under control and hid his true feelings. His long-time bodyguard would protest—as he often did when Rafiq wanted to have fun—but today Rafiq would accept none of his usual defiance.

At the parking lot entrance, his red car with the other two bodyguards turned onto the dirt lot. Its lights flashed quickly—the men had accomplished their mission and killed the intruder and anyone else in the SUV. Including, he hoped, the body double and the escaped captive he hadn't had the chance to beat to death.

Khalid turned from the distraction and, as expected, treated him like a child. "Your Highness, it is impossible. This man—"

"This man has never fired the weapon either. He has explained the process to me. The weapon is made for the untrained, correct?" he asked the American boy, whose name he had already forgotten.

The young man had the nerve to glance at Khalid as if he were in charge.

Rafiq felt a surge of rage. He'd dealt with so much the last few days. First his men failed to kill the Afghan cousins. Then the break-in at the house. His captive—taken. His body double—escaped. He'd been forced to flee from the police like a common criminal. And now this... serf... treated him like... like... a child?

He stepped forward and put all his rage into a strike to the young man's trachea. Rafiq snatched the missile out of his surprised hands before he dropped it. The boy grasped his throat, struggling to breathe —and failing.

His face looked so comical, with the ridiculous attempt at a beard and terrified expression. Rafiq had to giggle. He stopped after a second and turned to Khalid. "Now who will fire the weapon?" he asked.

Khalid only stared at him, his mouth slightly open, stunned.

The anger receded as quickly as it appeared, replaced by the joy of his success with the punch. Using only one blow, he'd harmed the boy severely and squashed the protests of the bodyguard who had kept him from his pleasure much too often over the years.

Rafiq wanted to watch the American die as he fought for air, but once again, one death paled in comparison to hundreds.

He hoisted the weapon to his right shoulder and turned south. "Point me in the right direction and tell me how long we have," he ordered Khalid. "Or I will tell Nasir to put a bullet in your skull."

He scanned the sky to the southwest, searching for the glint of an airplane, knowing his orders would be followed now that he'd demonstrated who was truly in charge.

113

THE PEPPERONI

Omar fell to the grass, clawing at his throat.

He couldn't breathe. The man in charge, whoever he was, had broken something inside there.

And laughed at Omar's pain.

The men on the grass ignored him.

He had been discarded.

All he'd done for the cause, for them, meant nothing.

He wasn't needed.

Wasn't special.

There would be no more missions for him.

He would never recruit and lead his own army.

Tears streamed down his face. The tiny amount of oxygen slipping through his broken throat wasn't enough to sustain him.

He had to get to a hospital.

When the prince walked away, toward the edge of the cliff to fire the missile—instead of him—he had his chance. He waved his hand

and struggled to make noise. Surely one of the remaining two men would help.

Neither of them would make eye contact with him.

In their eyes, he realized, he was as good as dead.

Omar felt darkness closing in.

He was sorry for everything.

Except for the pepperoni. He remembered the taste as the darkness took him.

114

BLUE SKY

Los Angeles International Airport
Los Angeles, California

Captain Perry grabbed the intercom for a final announcement. "Ladies and gentlemen," he said, "we are number three in line for takeoff. Please sit back, relax, and enjoy the flight."

Clicking off the intercom, he continued with his primary duty. "Before takeoff checklist," he said.

"Before takeoff checklist," Ellen responded.

They went through the list.

Finally, it was their turn to take off.

He had a few years left until retirement, but he'd already started to savor every flight. He never wanted them to end.

THE TROJAN HORSE

Mid-Mountain Trailhead
The San Gabriel Mountains

Bone drove the car at a slow, steady pace across the parking lot—a challenge given what the prince held on his shoulder.

"Is that…" Matthew muttered.

"Yes. A Russian-made man-portable surface-to-air missile," Bone said.

As they neared the metal guardrail between the parking lot and the grassy area, he passed a white panel van and the small black SUV the prince and his bodyguards had been driving, frantically forming a plan.

"The missile is our top priority," Bone said.

"Definitely," Matthew said.

From the backseat, Yousuf spoke up. "Agreed."

Bone glanced back. "Just stay down and out of the way."

The double nodded but didn't speak.

The prince and Khalid hurried across the grassy area, closer to the edge of the overlook. The city sprawled out before them. They were out of effective range for the pistol, even for Bone.

Bone slowed the car smoothly at the edge of the parking lot.

"That's Nasir on the left," Yousuf whispered. He huddled behind Matthew's seat but kept his head up, peering over the dash. Bone recognized the man from seven years before. He was the one who had shot him repeatedly when Bone rushed forward after flicking the star at the man he now knew as Prince Rafiq Al-Najjar.

"Next to him with the bandaged arm is Basoul," Yousuf continued. "I think he got badly burned the other night, but no one talks about it."

Badly burned—like while starting a fire at Zia and Lamar's restaurant. Bone wanted to shoot him first but would focus on Nasir, the greater threat. Basoul's injury would prevent him from getting to a pistol quickly.

"I don't know who the other man is," Yousuf finished. While they drove across the parking lot, the prince had hit the young man wearing jeans and a hoodie. He now lay on the grass, his eyes closed.

The electric car had an insane acceleration capacity. If Bone floored it, they would cover the remaining distance in a few seconds and possibly plow through the metal guard rail keeping people from driving on the grass.

Once the car broke through, he could run over the guards and maybe make it to Khalid and the prince before they shot him.

The car would plow into them from behind...

Right before it sailed over the edge and dropped a few hundred feet for the three of them to die in a fiery wreck.

It would be worth it, though, to stop whatever Prince Rafiq had planned.

116

THE REGRETS

Khalid's moment of doubt had come much too late.

He remembered Nasir's words in the security monitoring room a few days before.

"What of our souls?" he had asked.

One day, they would find out. Today's actions, surely, would weigh in their fate.

Every step of the way, Khalid had followed the prince's orders. In the early days, he had set up a bounty program, using the prince's money to pay Afghan and Iraqi fighters, farmers, or civilians to kill Americans.

He had escorted the prince to Afghanistan so he could use an expensive sniper rifle to shoot American soldiers himself.

Khalid had had ample opportunity to ask for help from more highly placed royals.

Recently, he could have sent a message to the new King of Saudi Arabia with word that Prince Rafiq had turned into a psychopath.

But Khalid had believed—wrongly—that he could control him.

He had acted out of loyalty to the man's father.

And hadn't wanted to risk reprisals for what he'd already done on the prince's behalf.

Now there was no turning back.

He followed the prince to the edge of the grass and surveyed the city below them.

"There," he said, pointing south and a few degrees west. A plane flew from west to east over the city, gaining altitude.

The prince brought the weapon up sharply, preparing to aim.

"No, sir," Khalid said, stopping him. "That is not the correct aircraft. It is too far away. The one for you will turn in this direction and fly much closer." He checked his phone. The flight to Germany was on time. "It should be taking off now or very soon, depending on how many other planes are in front of it."

The airport was too far away to see clearly, but the massive airplane would be obvious once it turned in their direction.

"Excellent!" The prince's voice couldn't hide his nervousness. He cleared his throat. "Your efforts in this will not go unrewarded," he said, softer and more in control.

"Thank you, sir. It is my pleasure to serve."

The other plane receded into the distance to the east.

The sun was burning away the morning's chill.

"And after this," the prince continued, so low Khalid could barely hear, "I promise I will be better. We will leave this country and I will no longer need to indulge in this sort of playtime."

He sounded sincere, but Khalid knew he would never be able to stop. Shooting down an airliner would only make him crave more.

What would be next? Khalid refused to consider it. He would go to the king instead of letting the man escalate again, no matter what the personal consequences of appearing disloyal to the Crown.

"Yes, sir."

Behind them, near the parking lot, Nasir cursed, a sound of anger, frustration—and fear.

117

THE EDGE

Mid-Mountain Trailhead
The San Gabriel Mountains

"I take Nasir on the left," Bone told Matthew.

"You shoot Basoul on the right, then we go after Khalid and the prince." They didn't need to worry about the dead kid on the ground.

"Copy that," Matthew said. He seemed focused and unafraid. He would have made a good SEAL.

Bone ignored the parking places along the hill to his right and stopped the car with the bumper nearly touching the low metal guard rail preventing the unwary from driving onto the grass and over the edge of the cliff.

"Ready?"

Before Matthew could answer, Nasir turned in their direction. His eyes widened and he called out in Arabic as his hand reached behind his back. The bodyguard recognized him—or at least understood that Bone wasn't one of the two guys who had originally been in the car.

"Now!" Bone yelled.

Bone fired as soon as he stepped out of the car, the *crack* of the pistol shattering the calm morning.

Nasir fired too, but his shot went wide.

Bone's didn't, hitting Nasir in the head. Finally, Bone's years of experience and time on the range were kicking in.

Matthew shot Basoul, only using two bullets to put him down.

Bone focused on the cliff edge in the distance in time to watch the prince—holding the missile launcher—disappear over the edge.

118

5,000 FEET

Aboard Flight 843
Over Los Angeles, California

Perry banked the plane smoothly as they passed five thousand feet, heading north-northeast. The San Gabriel Wilderness area opened up in front of them, surprisingly green after California's recent wet winter weather.

"Los Angeles Center," Perry said, keying the mic. "Flight 843 climbing through 5,000 feet for 10,000 feet."

The chipper voice of a young woman came back immediately. "Flight 843, Los Angeles Center, climb and maintain 10,000 feet. Expect further climb after passing 10,000."

"Climbing to 10,000 feet," Ellen said from the seat next to him.

"Roger, climbing to 10,000 feet and beyond," Perry said.

"Everything looks good," Ellen continued.

"Yes. Another beautiful morning."

They had about twenty more minutes of climbing to reach cruising altitude before they could relax and enjoy the day.

119

THE HILL

"Don't stop!" Khalid yelled at the prince. A narrow path ran down the forty-five-degree slope of the cliff. Switchbacks continued for about ten meters before another flat observation area for picnics. From there, the trail ran to the east, eventually disappearing around the mountain.

The prince scrambled down the trail, cradling the missile launcher, but he was not a runner.

It would be up to Khalid to eliminate the threats—the prince's former captive and the warrior who had broken into the house.

Khalid dropped prone on the downslope, his pistol instinctively in his hand, and prepared to defend the prince's escape, all thoughts of disloyalty—or stopping the day's events—forgotten.

120

BULLETS

Bone sprinted across the hundred yards of open ground toward where the prince had vanished over the lip of the cliff.

Matthew was several steps behind and to the right.

Khalid aimed a pistol at Bone from the edge of what must be a downslope, not the sharp dropoff Bone had expected. Khalid didn't fire yet, wisely waiting for a better shot.

One of the Navy SEAL's slogans popped into Bone's head: "Don't run to your death," but there wasn't much he could do about the situation.

"Spread out," he called to Matthew. If they were far enough apart, it would be harder to kill both. One of them might make it through.

At forty yards, Bone slowed and fired, making Khalid duck and reminding him that he faced death too.

The shot went wide and long—but Matthew gained ground.

Bone poured all he had into running toward the cliff edge while keeping an eye out, waiting for Khalid to pop up.

When his head appeared a few feet from where he'd vanished,

checking first on Bone before bringing his pistol up to aim at Matthew, Bone stopped and fired again. His shot hit the ground three feet in front of Khalid.

Matthew pumped his arms as he ran, but his injuries slowed him down.

He'd proven earlier he wasn't the greatest shot. Between the exertion from running and the adrenaline from the action, he'd be worse now.

But Bone only had a few rounds left.

Khalid turned to aim at Bone this time. Bone fired as he ran but Khalid didn't flinch.

A shot whipped past Bone's left arm, missing him by inches.

Matthew's pistol cracked from Bone's right.

Khalid vanished again.

Bone was twenty yards out. Matthew had farther to go.

Khalid appeared to the left of where he'd ducked down, closer to Bone.

Bone threw himself to the ground as Khalid fired.

Matthew fired twice. The second shot hit surprisingly close, forcing Khalid down. Bone sprang to his feet and ran.

For several seconds, Khalid was gone. Bone hoped he'd run down the mountain after the prince.

Khalid appeared ten feet closer to Bone's side, aiming right at him, getting a shot off as Bone dove to his left.

Bone felt the bullet blow past, low, right where he'd been an instant before. Khalid was a good shot.

Bone was now well within his effective range.

And Khalid was farther out of Matthew's.

Bone got a desperate shot off as covering fire before he logrolled further left, away from Matthew. Another shot from Khalid hit the ground nearby.

Bone stopped rolling and low-crawled as Khalid fired at Matthew. The two of them traded shots like gunfighters in the Old West, neither flinching nor taking cover.

Matthew sprinted and fired wildly, using up his precious ammo.

He cried out.

He'd been hit but he staggered forward, still firing, until his pistol clicked—empty.

Bone skidded to a stop. He had two shots left.

Khalid turned toward him, but Bone fired first.

Khalid's right shoulder jerked as Bone's bullet hit.

Khalid's shot went wide. He grimaced in pain as he fired again.

Bone dropped to the ground, anticipating the hit, but instead of a gunshot, there was the click of an empty magazine.

Khalid dropped out of sight again.

"He's out!" Bone yelled and jumped to his feet.

Khalid, however, surely had another mag—unlike Bone and Matthew.

121

NEVER AGAIN

Mid-Mountain Trailhead
The San Gabriel Mountains

Matthew moved forward despite the pain. Agony from the bullet to his shoulder competed with the pain throughout his body from the beatings he had endured.

He forced himself to ignore the pain—an impossible feat, but attempting it helped some other part of his soul shuffle his feet another step, and another.

He'd given up eight years earlier at BUD/S training.

Never again.

Bone needed him to keep running. To stay in the fight.

Khalid had been hit by Bone's shot and vanished over the edge.

Bone ran toward the cliff, closer to Khalid than Matthew was.

The pistol went into the pocket of Matthew's sweatpants.

In a few seconds, he would need his hands free to take on Khalid or go after the prince.

Or serve as target practice for Khalid, giving Bone a chance.

Either way, Matthew was in the fight.

They'd have to kill him before he quit.

122

TEAM

Bone ran flat out to beat Matthew to the edge of the cliff. Though Matthew had proven himself a warrior, he was injured and no match for Khalid.

Bone couldn't lose another team member.

Prince Rafiq was somewhere further down the slope, armed with a deadly surface-to-air missile. As close as they were to Los Angeles International Airport, he had to be prepping to shoot down a commercial plane.

Could Bone kill Khalid—saving Matthew—and still stop the prince?

All without dying?

Bone had one round left, two targets, and he was out of time.

123

THE RECOGNITION

Mid-Mountain Trailhead
The San Gabriel Mountains

Khalid finally realized where he'd seen the warrior he first traded gunfire with in the mansion's kitchen—and who had just shot him in the shoulder.

It had been seven years earlier, in Afghanistan—the ambush where Khalid had saved the prince's life.

On that night, his leg in agony, Khalid had turned to face the man who had stabbed him. The American was already unconscious. His night vision goggles had been dislodged as he'd fallen to the ground.

As the American helicopter drew closer, Khalid only had a second. Nasir hurried the prince and Khalid to safety—but the face of his opponent had been seared into his memory.

The warrior running across the field at him was that man—the face from Khalid's nightmares.

Khalid's shoulder burned, and the bullet might have nicked an artery—there was more blood than he expected. He would live—if he could stop the bleeding quickly.

He lay on his left side, swiftly changing magazines as the homeless captive and the warrior must be doing as well.

It would be a close call, but he'd be able to kill them as they came over the lip of the hill.

He might die as well—from another of their bullets or blood loss from the first shot—but the prince would live—and shoot down the airplane.

Khalid would do his duty to the end, no matter how much he regretted his actions.

He moved lower on the mountain's slope and limped through brush and native grass to his left. He'd be in the center of the two men as they came over the edge of the cliff.

The homeless man who had been the prince's captive was injured from Khalid's shot and not as much of a threat as the warrior—the man who had somehow survived the ambush seven years ago in Afghanistan and permanently injured Khalid's leg.

He'd kill them both. If he survived, he would get the prince to safety and never return to this country again.

124

THE PLANE

Scenic Overlook Picnic Area
The San Gabriel Mountains

Rafiq didn't let the gunfire from the upper overlook area deter him from his fun. Khalid would stop them.

He stood in the small lower picnic area, three meters down a steep hill from the parking lot and upper grassy lookout area, cradling the missile. He admired his little bundle of joy, as the Americans called their stupid babies.

The rumble of the jet's engines reached him as it flew northeast, growing closer as it ascended. It would pass to his left in a minute or two, making for the perfect shot.

It had to be the one Khalid had chosen.

Filled with Americans for him to kill.

He hefted the weapon and removed the cap at the front end. The tube rested comfortably on his shoulder.

This was going to be so much fun. After this, when Khalid had eliminated whoever dared interrupt his morning, they would have to discuss securing more of the weapons. Another attack in America might be difficult, but there were plenty of other countries where Americans flew on holiday.

As the plane drew closer, he savored the idea of taking more and more lives. Hundreds. Thousands. With his money, determination, and skill, he could single-handedly kill more Americans than any individual in history.

First, though, the approaching plane.

He had never killed more than one person at a time. At best, he had killed eight during a single attack—the night of the ambush seven years earlier. He'd shot seven American soldiers and an Afghan elder —eight people in only a few minutes.

It was his most cherished memory.

This morning would take the place of that special night—until next time.

The missile had two three-inch protrusions on its left side with small metal circles for aiming. He lined up the rear sight with the forward one, centering the airplane in them and tracking it easily, waiting for it to come into optimal range.

125

THE OPTIONS

Mid-Mountain Trailhead
The San Gabriel Mountains

Daoud sat in the white panel van and deliberated. He was out of the fight from the moment the men leaped out of the red car several meters behind the van, shot the nearest guards, and ran across the grass toward the prince and Khalid.

From where he was, in the parking lot, nothing he could do would have affected the outcome of the surprise attack.

He'd done his jobs, picking up Omar, the college student, from a cheap motel in the Los Angeles suburbs. He'd delivered the boy and the missile to this overlook at the last minute due to Khalid's change of plans.

If the prince died, Daoud would be fine. He'd stolen the panel van from Las Vegas a month before, swapped license plates with a similar van in Los Angeles, and wore gloves every moment he drove or handled the missile.

Khalid made the arrangements for the warehouse, shipping container, and missile.

Daoud could take his savings and return to Saudi Arabia or disappear into America to live a simple life under the radar.

No one would know of his existence, nor what he'd done.

But if the prince lived and he hadn't helped, the prince would kill him as surely as he had Omar, the college student.

When the two attackers reached the edge of the cliff, he slipped out of the van, pistol in hand, and started across the parking lot toward the guard rail.

He'd shoot the attackers in the back as they fought Khalid and the prince.

He would be a hero.

Or he would kill them as they returned with the missile.

With little effort, he could find a buyer for the device.

What extremists wouldn't want the power to shoot down an aircraft?

126

THE FINAL SHOT

Mid-Mountain Trailhead
The San Gabriel Mountains

Bone slowed as he reached the edge of the cliff, angling forward to get a line on Khalid.

To his right, Matthew ran without slowing. His left arm was covered with blood, but as he reached the edge of the cliff, he let out a fierce war cry—and kept running, angling down the cliff.

Bone rushed forward. Khalid waited twenty feet down the slope, halfway between him and Matthew.

Matthew's war cry and crashing descent caused Khalid to swing from facing Bone to Matthew, his pistol tracking the faster moving, more immediate target.

Bone skidded on gravel, desperate to stop.

He took a half second to steady himself for the final shot…

And fired.

127

THE TARGET

Scenic Overlook Picnic Area
The San Gabriel Mountains

Khalid staggered forward at the impact of the bullet to his lower back. The pain was intense and the blood flowed immediately.

His shot at the homeless captive had gone wild—and then the crazed man slammed into him, sending them both tumbling backward down the hill.

At least being wrapped up together prevented a kill shot from the warrior on the edge of the cliff.

But while Khalid dealt with the captive, the prince would be vulnerable.

"Rafiq!" Khalid cried, failing for the first time to call the prince by one of his titles and hoping it would surprise him enough to make him pay attention for once.

The rapidly approaching plane slipped out of the sights as Rafiq swung around at Khalid's desperate call.

His bodyguard, hand-selected by his father years before, rolled down the steep hill, locked in a struggle with the captive from the playroom.

At the edge of the cliff, a thin yet muscular warrior pointed a pistol at him. Rafiq didn't care.

He swung back to the plane.

The warrior was too far away, at a steep angle, and likely to miss with a pistol.

Rafiq needed only a few seconds to aim, then he could fake surrender to the man until he was close enough to fight.

But the missile had to be fired at the plane, even if he got shot doing it. The opportunity was simply too good to miss.

———

Matthew fought like a madman. His right hand grabbed Khalid, holding tight as they rolled. Sheer willpower made his left arm work long enough to grasp Khalid's right wrist and keep the pistol under control.

After a few seconds of tumbling, they slid to a stop near the bottom of the hill at a small, flat overlook.

Matthew accepted a blow to the head in exchange for getting his right hand on the pistol. As he fought for control of it, he got his finger in the trigger guard with Khalid's and wrestled the man's arm in the general direction of the prince thirty feet away.

Matthew traded a painful knee to the groin for a squeeze of the trigger before Khalid head-butted him, further damaging his broken nose and making him see stars.

———

The crack of a pistol and zing of a bullet near his head made Rafiq falter. The plane slipped from the sights.

He steadied himself and searched for it with both eyes before closing one and aiming through the tiny round sights.

Bone sailed straight down the severe slope, ignoring the switchback trail. He blocked out the worry about Matthew dying at Khalid's hands. He'd evened the odds by using his last round on Khalid instead of a longshot at the prince.

Al-Najjar's objective—a jumbo jet approaching from the southwest —made the perfect target for the heat-seeking missile.

Bone stumbled as he reached the bottom of the hill, his sole focus on the prince as the man tracked the plane. He had to distract him right now or it would be too late.

"How's that scar below your eye from my throwing star, Rafi-boy?" he called. "Khalid's not going to save you this time, you little coward."

128

THE FIGHTS

Scenic Overlook Picnic Area
The San Gabriel Mountains

Rafiq raged at the American's words.

Him—a coward?

Never.

And the rest... Nasir and Khalid alone knew that he'd needed saving that night. The Afghan fighters had been behind him and too far away to understand what happened.

Only the man who threw the small piece of metal that nearly took out Rafiq's eye could have seen, but he was dead. Shot repeatedly by Nasir, though he had still managed to stab Khalid as he died.

As he once again acquired the plane in the launcher's sights, Rafiq wondered if the man with the pistol at the top of the slope could somehow be the American from that night in Afghanistan.

It didn't matter. Rafiq would destroy the plane in front of the American—and then kill him for good. He smiled at the thought.

Bone struggled to stay on his feet.

His momentum carried him directly into the prince, flinging them both down.

The missile launcher fell to the ground, unfired.

Bone landed hard but struggled to his feet in time to take a roundhouse kick to the head, which dropped him like a sack of potatoes.

Al-Najjar knew how to handle himself.

Khalid fought hard, but he was rapidly losing blood—and the homeless man was an unpredictable, crazed opponent. There was no time to worry about the prince.

Khalid kneed the former captive in the groin. The younger man returned the favor of a headbutt. Khalid grunted in surprise, his nose broken.

Then it was back to wrestling over the gun. Khalid couldn't risk another errant shot at the prince.

He kept his head back, careful to avoid another strike to his face. He ignored the pain from the bullets to his shoulder and back, but the blood loss made the fight against the man who had been their prisoner only hours before harder than it should have been.

Slowly but surely, however, Khalid's experience made a difference. Inch by inch, he forced the pistol toward the homeless man.

The crunch of the guard's breaking nose and accompanying grunt had been music to Matthew's ears.

Out of the corner of his eye, he saw Bone and the prince scuffling. Distracting the prince with an errant shot from Khalid's pistol had bought the SEAL the chance he needed. Now it was time for Matthew to survive his own fight.

With his barely working left arm, Matthew had trouble keeping

Khalid from forcing the pistol closer and closer to his body. It wouldn't be long before the bodyguard brought it to bear, fired, and ended it all.

That would leave Bone thirty feet away, fighting the prince, with Khalid ready to jump in and shoot Bone in the back.

Matthew couldn't allow that.

There had to be something he could do. He was desperate for a solution, no matter what the cost.

With their hands fighting for control of the pistol and Khalid straining to keep his head out of reach of another headbutt, there was little Matthew could do...

Except the unthinkable.

Khalid's neck was exposed.

Matthew didn't need a knife or a gun.

Just the will to never quit.

To adapt and overcome.

To always be in the fight.

He lunged forward, brought his mouth down on Khalid's neck, and bit with all his strength.

Khalid screamed as his opponent ripped at his jugular.

He yanked at the pistol with all his strength but couldn't move it enough for a body shot. He pulled the trigger repeatedly anyway—hoping to somehow stop the horror at his neck.

Blood spurted, and as much as he wanted to believe it was the homeless man's from a lucky pistol shot, it was his own.

129

THE PARKING LOT

Mid-Mountain Trailhead
The San Gabriel Mountains

Yousuf slumped low in the driver's seat of the red car. Once Bone and Matthew had disappeared over the edge of the cliff, there was nothing to do but wait and hope.

After only a few seconds, he began to doubt. Khalid was extremely capable. And the prince was the prince.

What chance did a homeless man and a former soldier have against them?

He owed them everything—or did he? He'd had a safe, boring yet lavish life. One that could have lasted years.

He should leave. If Bone and Matthew lost, the prince and Khalid would find him.

If somehow the Americans managed to win, would they truly blame him for escaping? Bone had wanted him out of the way. Shouldn't he take the car partway down the mountain and wait?

At the very least, he could move to the parking lot entrance. He would be away from the danger yet close enough to move in if Bone and Matthew needed the car.

He'd also be far enough away for a head start if Khalid limped onto the grassy overlook area.

Yousuf slipped into the front seat.

On the grass in front of the car, the young man in jeans and a hoody lay dead.

Yousuf figured out the car's controls and managed to put it into reverse.

The rear-view backup camera activated.

A man hurried across the parking lot five feet behind the car.

Carrying a gun.

A friend? Or enemy?

There was no police car. Only the white panel van and the small black SUV.

Yousuf slammed his foot down on the accelerator. The tires flung gravel as they spun, then caught, and the car surged backward.

The back tire thumped once as it rolled over the man, followed by the front tire.

Yousuf stepped onto the brake, skidded to a stop, and switched from Reverse to Drive.

He ran him over again, then backed up once more for good measure.

With trembling hands, Yousuf put the car into Park, blocking the man's still body from view of anyone driving into the parking lot. He slipped out of the car and retrieved the dropped pistol.

He would wait here. If Bone and Matthew survived, they might need his help.

If Khalid and the prince lived, he would use the pistol on them.

130

THE BLOOD

Scenic Overlook Picnic Area
The San Gabriel Mountains

By the time Bone shook off the kick, the prince had the missile launcher in his hands again.

Bone scrambled forward, grabbed the prince's ankle, and yanked.

Al-Najjar stumbled, going down to one knee before spinning and slamming the end of the missile tube into Bone's head.

The plane continued over the mountains, but it wasn't out of range yet. Rafiq untangled his foot from the dazed American's grasp and didn't bother standing up. There wasn't time. With shaking hands, he lifted the weapon back onto his shoulder and tried to center the plane in the sights.

Bone acted on autopilot, drawing the knife from its sheath at the small of his back. With a desperate lunge, he threw himself forward and up, stabbing at the prince's spine.

The sharp, metallic tang of blood made Matthew want to gag, but he held on. It was his only way to survive.

After what seemed like an eternity, Khalid ceased screaming and struggling and lay still.

Matthew spat, yanked the pistol out of the dead man's grasp, and rolled, ready to shoot the prince if Bone had failed.

Rafiq tumbled forward and landed on his right side, his arms useless. The missile launcher fell, still unfired.

He watched the plane soar over the mountain range, unable to move. He should have focused on the fight at hand and not the hundreds of people in the airplane.

Still, even without the attack on the plane, he'd killed plenty of Americans. He was prepared for the afterlife, where he would get his reward.

But there would be no more fun in the playroom each summer.

No more killing.

His mood changed. What good was paradise if he couldn't have his fun?

There would be no eternal bliss for him. No, it would be hell.

He struggled to move but couldn't.

Two men stopped in front of him, standing so he could see their faces—the warrior from Afghanistan and the homeless man from the playroom.

The former captive handed the other man a pistol.

Once again, Rafiq fought his body, desperate to lash out or crawl to freedom.

It couldn't end like this. He was Prince Rafiq Al-Najjar.

Bone held the gun Matthew had taken from Khalid and looked Prince Rafiq in the eyes. The man was alive but couldn't move. Bone's knife had severed his spine.

The prince understood what was about to happen.

"This is for Tank," Bone started. "And Baldy, Bossman, Sneaky, Biscuit, Iron, and Dizzy," Bone said, and pulled the trigger.

131

FROSTY

Azusa, CA
East of Los Angeles, California

Matthew ignored the pain and struggled to stay conscious. He was exhausted from the long night, the beatings, the battle, and the blood loss.

Bone had coached him through bandaging his wound, but the blood still soaked out of the hole in his shoulder. "Through and through," Bone had called it, telling him he'd be fine as long as he got to a hospital soon.

The small strip mall on the road at the base of the mountains had a liquor store, a bakery, a pet groomer, and a dry cleaner. Both the bakery and dry cleaner had illuminated "Open" signs.

Most importantly, there weren't security cameras along the side street or anywhere else in the area.

"You sure you're up for this?" Bone asked from the driver's seat of the small black SUV they'd liberated from the dead prince. They were parked within walking distance—or crawling, if Matthew had to—of the bakery at the end of the strip mall.

"I will never quit," he muttered—or thought he did.

"Good man," Bone said. "You would have made a fine SEAL."

He offered his hand to shake and Matthew took it, squeezing as hard as he could, which wasn't much.

"As far as I'm concerned," Bone added, "you'll always be my brother."

Matthew couldn't fight back the tears, but he told himself they were from the pain—nothing else.

"Someday when things have calmed down, I'll look you up," Bone added. "Don't worry about all this," he gestured at Matthew's blood and wounds. "Stick to the story and you'll be fine."

Matthew nodded. "Stay frosty," he croaked, hoping it didn't sound stupid. He opened the door of the SUV and staggered out.

"Stay frosty, brother," Bone said before Matthew closed the door.

Bone drove away. He'd watch from down the street until Matthew got help.

Matthew stumbled toward the bakery, drawn by the smell of freshly baked food and the promise of an ambulance ride, clean sheets, pain meds… and lots of questions.

He'd tell the truth—or some of it. He was homeless, had gotten abducted, taken somewhere, beaten, and fought his way free, getting shot along the way. He didn't see or remember what his abductors looked like, where he'd been held, or what else had happened.

But he was a retired Navy veteran, and he never gave up.

132

BROKEN EAGLE

North Second Street
Alhambra, CA

As far as Bone was concerned, this part of the mission was at least as dangerous as everything else they'd been through. While neither he nor Yousuf would die if they messed up, they could get caught—which would have its own negative repercussions.

Bone sat in the driver's seat of the red car. It fit perfectly in the neighborhood; they'd seen a few exactly like it, along with several dozen others in white, black, and blue.

The license plates were in the front trunk of the electric car.

Yousuf sat straight and proper next to him like they were both normal, law-abiding citizens with nothing to hide.

A block ahead on the residential side street, the white van waited, driver's side door unlocked, with the Russian-made surface-to-air missile uncovered in the back.

It was a small risk. Bone could run the few hundred yards to the van before anyone could make off with the missile. In an emergency, the fast car could cover the distance in a few seconds, though doing either would blow their cover.

A buddy from Bone's BUD/S class owned a popular jiu-jitsu and MMA training gym two blocks to the east. They hadn't spoken in years, but he was a solid guy.

He'd do what was right.

Bone had a whole story worked out to get him on the phone if someone else answered, which proved unneeded.

"East-West MMA and Jui-Jitsu," "Big" Ben said after only one ring.

Bone whispered, hoping it would be enough for his voice to go unrecognized after so many years. "Broken Eagle," he said. It had been an emergency code phrase back in the day on his Team, and he prayed other Teams used the same one, taught to them all by the old-timers. It was a rarely used phrase that meant the shit had really hit the fan, the end was near, and everyone had to drop everything to help out a brother in need.

"Broken Eagle," he repeated, his voice as quiet as he could make it and still be heard. "White panel van, two blocks to your east. North Second Street. How copy?"

There was a pause long enough for Bone to wonder if Big Ben hadn't heard him or thought it was a joke.

Just when Bone was about to hang up and try again, Ben replied. "Solid copy," he said, focused and serious. "White panel van, two blocks to my east. North Second Street. What's the problem?"

Bone smiled sadly at the sound of his old buddy's voice and pressed the red button to disconnect the call on the burner phone.

He put the car in gear and made a U-turn, pointing away from the van but keeping track of it in the rearview mirror.

Less than two minutes later, a tall, muscular figure wearing a white gi with a black belt and black sneakers, ran around the corner. He glanced Bone's way for an instant before focusing up the road to the north.

Ben's hand went under his gi and produced a pistol which he kept lowered as he stalked up the sidewalk toward the van.

Satisfied the missile was in safe hands, Bone pulled smoothly away from the curb. They would follow a carefully plotted route, avoiding intersections that might have cameras, and eventually make their way back to the mountain overlook.

There were eight dead guys baking in the backseat of the SUV they had to get back to San Diego and somehow dispose of.

133

THE ROOM

33 Gold Road
La Jolla, California

Bone backed the small SUV into the garage bay closest to the house. He didn't want to have to carry the bodies any farther than necessary.

Yousuf pulled in next to him, looking exhausted.

"You're sure no one's here?" Bone asked as they exited the vehicles.

"No," Yousuf said with a worried look. "But this is our only option, yes?"

Bone nodded and clicked the key fob to lock the SUV door. If they encountered cleaning staff or anyone else, they might be able to bluff their way through—as long as no one opened the SUV and saw the real prince, his five bodyguards, and two other dead guys piled under the blanket on the folded-down seats in back.

Or smelled them. They were getting a little ripe.

Yousuf took a breath, stood straighter, narrowed his eyes, and... changed. He took on the air of a rich man who didn't need or want a thing—including conversation.

"Come with me," he ordered Bone, who marveled at the transformation from Yousuf to Prince Rafiq Al-Najjar.

Yousuf pressed buttons to lower the garage doors and used one of the keys on a gold keychain—taken from Khalid's body—to unlock the door into the house. There was an alarm keypad, but it obviously hadn't been activated the previous night. It made sense to Bone. The last thing the prince would have wanted was for the police to respond to an alarm and want to search the house. He'd figured the security cameras and on-duty guard to monitor them would be more than enough.

Yousuf led the way into the kitchen, turning on lights as he went. The setting sun cast a beautiful glow into the house, but it would be dark soon.

The home had a deserted feel to it as the two of them made their way through every room except the prince's suite, which they couldn't access without a code—and the prince's finger on a scanner. The second part would be easy, but Bone didn't want to take the time to guess the code.

They found the security room—small, dark, and filled with twenty monitors showing views of the exterior. In the corner of one from the roof, a sliver of black revealed the bag containing the glider Bone had used to arrive the previous night; it seemed like weeks ago instead of less than twenty-four hours.

Convinced the house was empty, they returned to the kitchen, where Bone grabbed a cola from the fridge and Yousuf drank water.

"You said disposing of the bodies would be easy," Yousuf said.

Bone nodded. He was convinced there would be an obvious way to handle the dead guys in the SUV. He wanted to cover the tracks of the operation as much as he could.

He'd thought of leaving the men in the van with the missile, but shot-up bodies of a Saudi prince and his guards, plus whoever the college kid was, along with the man Yousuf had run over several times, would be harder to cover up than what Big Ben was dealing with right now.

"The garage?" Bone asked as he guzzled the last of the soda and filled a large glass of water from the dispenser on the stainless-steel refrigerator's door.

Yousuf shrugged. "I've only walked through it to and from the vehicles."

They returned to the garage and found the room right away. A door at the far end led back to a large space, about twenty feet wide and as long as the garage, set up as a ceramics studio.

Thin sheets of plastic covered the walls, ceiling, and floor.

In the corner of the back wall was a large, squat silver ceramic kiln plugged into a 220 outlet.

"Brilliant," Bone muttered. Unless you knew what to look for, you'd only see the bags of clay, jars of glaze, the workbenches, the pottery wheel, drying racks, and the utility sink. You'd think of a rich guy with an interesting hobby.

Bone noted the high-end wet-dry shop vac and the large rolls of spare plastic.

The trash bags on a shelf near the kiln, the long-handled shovel like the one he'd used in a woodstove growing up to scoop out the ashes each Saturday morning.

The heavy-duty hook in the ceiling over the sink.

And the large bottles of bleach.

Lots of bleach.

Somewhere in the large storage cubbies, he was sure he'd find a supply of hazmat suits, rubber gloves, rubber boots, and high-end face masks.

He ducked his head into the garage. Arrayed neatly above a workbench on a pegboard wall right outside the door were several hack saws, a coping saw, and a reciprocating saw with a variety of long blades, all sparkling clean.

"Just a guy with a lot of tools, right?" Bone asked Yousuf, who looked sick.

"How many men like Matthew?" Yousuf murmured.

It was a rhetorical question, but Bone had an answer. "Too many," he said. "Let me grab more water, then we'll find some hazmat suits and get dressed.

Yousuf looked like he was about to faint, vomit, or both. "Don't worry," Bone said. "I just need help moving the bodies. I'll do the rest."

"The rest" took hours of gruesome work, reminding Bone of deer hunting with his father as a kid.

Most of the blood went down the sink, though there was plenty to clean up.

In the end, he had the kiln fired up, eliminating as many remains as he could fit into it. The rest waited in large trash cans sealed with duct tape for when the first batch finished.

He cleaned all the equipment and hung fresh plastic.

The splattered plastic and hazmat suit went into a trash bag along with large cleaning wipes from a supply near the door.

After stripping off his clothes, Bone locked the door to the "ceramics room," and put on the robe and slippers Yousuf had left on the workbench for him. He desperately needed a long, hot shower, food, and caffeine before the drive back to Los Angeles to pick up the large SUV safely tucked away in the back corner of a commuter parking lot, where they had moved it after turning the white van over to Ben.

Bone barked out a laugh and shook his head. Not once had he considered alcohol. He had no interest in it.

Coffee would be enough.

PART 7

TUESDAY

134

CHOICES

.

33 Gold Road
La Jolla, California

Bone woke slowly from a restful sleep. It took him a few seconds to remember he was in the upstairs guest bedroom he'd successfully infiltrated late Sunday night.

He'd slept for hours with no nightmares.

He opened the blackout curtains to another stunning Southern California day. The sun glinted off the Pacific several hundred yards away.

He felt foolish in the robe and slippers, but he'd left his filthy clothes in the laundry room several hours earlier. Stepping into the hallway, though, he found a paper bag next to his door with his laundered socks, shirt, and pants folded neatly, so he changed before heading down.

An intoxicating smell came from the kitchen of some kind of freshly baked bread along with exotic spices he hadn't tasted since his time in the Middle East.

Yousuf offered a small smile as Bone entered the kitchen. "Hungry?"

"Hell, yes."

"Good. I have made chicken kabsa with traditional flatbread. It's a lunch or dinner dish, but we haven't been on a regular schedule. Oh, and I used Khalid's cell phone to text the house cleaners. I told them His Highness was returning to Europe early and their services were no longer needed. They did not sound suspicious in their reply—possibly because I said I would put a cash bonus in an envelope and leave it in the mailbox Thursday morning.

That would be plenty of time, Bone figured.

They ate at the kitchen island where he and Khalid—whose bones were still baking in the kiln—had exchanged gunfire.

Bone nodded at the brown leather bag on the far side of the counter. They had grabbed it from the backseat of the small SUV. They'd been in too much of a hurry piling up the bodies to do more than glance inside.

"The bonus?" he asked.

"Yes. It's exactly what you guessed," Yousuf said. "Traveling money."

Bone raised his eyebrows.

"One could travel quite far on it," Yousuf added. He opened the bag and showed Bone the stacks of bound hundred-dollar bills.

"What are you going to do?"

Yousuf took a bite of kabsa and chewed slowly, staring into the distance. He shrugged. "If I stay here, someone will eventually wonder about the bodyguards. Khalid handled the prince's calendar. People will call him and expect a response. I cannot answer my own phone— as the prince, I mean. I would have to hire someone, train them—all things a prince does not do. And sooner or later, someone from the royal family would want to see me. They would know I wasn't really the prince." He shook his head. "It wouldn't last."

"Do you have identification?" Bone asked.

Yousuf frowned. "My passport may be in a safe in the prince's suite. I have this," he said, reaching into the bag and producing the prince's Saudi Arabia passport. "But using it for long would be risky."

"With that kind of money and the right connections, identification might not be a problem."

Yousuf nodded but still looked sad. "The money could buy a passport with a different name, I assume. But I would have to choose carefully where to settle down. A place big enough to blend in, to disappear. But what would I do? As much money as it is, it will not last forever. Paying for an apartment or house with cash looks suspicious. Carrying and hiding it is a problem, as well. Places where cash might be accepted—Mexico, for example—would expose me to criminals who could rob me. Having a bag full of cash and no responsibilities sounds perfect until you realize the difficulty of living like a fugitive. No friends, no job, no life. I've had my fill of reading books and watching television. I want to live." He paused, then added softly. "To work. To love."

Yousuf's words struck a chord in Bone. He thought it through, using the homemade flatbread to scoop up the last of the chicken kabsa.

"I have an idea," he said at last.

PART 8

WEDNESDAY

135

THE CLEAN UP

33 Gold Road
La Jolla, California

By Wednesday night, they'd taken care of all the business needed.

Bone painstakingly detailed the back of the small SUV and the trunk of the sedan with a small carpet-cleaning machine found in the garage, sucking up the blood.

Between the two of them, Bone and Yousuf shut down the security system and erased the recordings made since Monday—the ones prior to that had already been deleted.

They disabled the electric car's security camera feature and deleted footage from the past few days.

Bone climbed onto the roof and retrieved the paraglider gear.

It went into two large trash bags stuck together and into the back of the small SUV.

The double-bagged ashes from the kiln and the blood-splattered plastic and hazmat suit from the ceramics room ended up in the SUV too.

Long after dark on Wednesday, Bone drove the SUV until he found a dumpster behind a restaurant. It was unlocked and had no security cameras nearby. Bone threw all the bags inside as quickly as he could and drove away.

He ditched the SUV near the Mexico border in a run-down area. Bone took the registration, insurance card, and everything personally identifiable from inside and removed the license plates. He left the key fob on the dash, the windows down, and the door unlocked. It would be gone in an hour and across the border in thirty more minutes.

Yousuf drove them back to La Jolla in the red sedan where Bone picked up the shot up full-size SUV. After removing the license plates and other items, they ditched it a few miles away from where they'd left the first one.

They grabbed a few hours of sleep before washing the sheets from Bone's bedroom, wiping down anything Bone or Yousuf might have touched in the house, and cleaning up Matthew's blood in the playroom.

There wasn't much they could do with the chain bolted to the wall, but maybe it wouldn't matter.

Eventually, someone would question where Prince Rafiq was—probably one of the members of the royal family.

Yousuf didn't think they would get the police involved, but someone would look into his disappearance.

They couldn't predict how thorough that investigation would be, but they could cover their tracks as much as possible.

Shortly after dawn, Yousuf drove Bone to the 24-hour pharmacy parking lot and dropped him off at his car.

"No second thoughts?" Bone asked.

Yousuf shook his head. "You're sure this will work?"

"If it doesn't, we'll figure something else out."

Yousuf stuck out his hand. "In case I don't have a chance later. Thank you for everything."

Bone took the offered hand. "Thank you. Without your help…" He trailed off. He didn't want to think about what would have happened without the body double's assistance. "See you in a few hours. And don't forget—"

"Yes, I'll bring it," Yousuf said with a shy smile.

PART 9

THURSDAY

136

TRUST

Pacific Oasis BBQ & Smokehouse
San Diego, California

"It's going to be okay," Bone said, reassuring Yousuf. They sat in Bone's silver hatchback up the street from Zia and Lamar's restaurant. The barbecue place would open in fifteen minutes for lunch, but Bone hoped that Zia would already be there.

The sun shone, the sky was blue, and the breeze from the west brought the scent of the ocean into the car.

Yousuf ran a hand over his freshly shaved face and touched the scar below his eye before realizing what he was doing and pulling his hand away.

He looked completely different. The missing beard changed his look, making him seem younger than the forty-year-old man he was, but the shorter haircut made the biggest difference. Gone was the thick, wavy black hair styled just so. In its place was what could only be described as a young-executive, close-cropped professional look. He wore black jeans—some expensive brand, Bone was sure, but jeans were jeans. A black t-shirt and sneakers rounded out the ensemble.

"What if the cousin is dead?" Yousuf asked.

"I hope he's not. But if he is, he is. We'll just have to see how it plays out."

Bone held out his hand and Yousuf reluctantly handed over the package. "It'll be fine. I promise," Bone said. He had a good feeling about this. "Wait for my signal, then just be yourself," he added as he got out of the car.

He made his way up the street and knocked lightly on the restaurant's window.

He had to knock a second time, harder, before Zia's head poked out from the kitchen. Seeing Bone, he rushed to the repaired door and unlocked the deadbolt. "I thought you were dead," he said, looking up and down the street. "What happened?"

"How is Lamar?" Bone asked, slipping inside. Zia swung the door shut and locked it.

"He is alive and healing. The doctors are incredible." Zia glanced away and wiped his eyes. "He will be fine, but it will take a while."

Bone reached his hand out and set it on Zia's shoulder while the man fought off more tears. "That is great news." He leaned in close to Zia's ear. "Our problem has been handled," he whispered.

Zia's eyes grew wide. He rushed forward and grabbed Bone in a bear hug.

"Thank you for your help," Bone said. "I couldn't have done it without you and Lamar."

Bone waited until Zia eventually let go and backed off. "Now," Bone said, "I have a gift, a question, and possibly a favor to ask."

"Anything," Zia said.

"First, the gift. Please taste this," Bone said, handing over a small plastic food container.

Zia looked at him quizzically but walked to the counter, grabbed a black plastic spoon from a tray of other cutlery, opened the container, and took a bite. His eyes widened. "This is delicious. Chicken kabsa?"

"You know it?"

"Yes. I have had it before, but this is a better version. You made it?" he asked, doubtful.

Bone shook his head. "Next, the question." He paused, catching

Zia's eye as the man eagerly took another spoonful of the kabsa. "Do you trust me?"

Zia's eyes narrowed as he chewed. He nodded but said nothing.

Bone went to the door, unlocked the deadbolt, and waved up the street.

Several seconds later, he held the door open for the rich-looking man who entered hesitantly.

Zia's half-smile of greeting faded and his nostrils flared. He set the container of food on the counter behind him blindly, never taking his eyes off the man in front of him as Bone locked the door.

"Wait," Bone said. "This is Yousuf. He is not the man you think he is. Trust me," Bone added.

Zia's gaze flicked from Yousuf to Bone and back. "He is. You have only shaved him and given him a haircut."

"No. He was an actor. A body double."

Yousuf nodded and spoke, though that wasn't part of the plan. "It is true. I am not him. I could pretend to be," he said with a glance at Bone, "but sooner or later the lie would catch up with me. Instead, Bone said you might be in need of a chef temporarily. Before I did my latest job, I was a cook for my family's restaurant."

There was silence in the barbecue joint while Zia digested the information. "It's not him? You wouldn't lie to me?" Zia asked.

"I wouldn't and no, it's not."

"Where…?"

"He's dead," Bone whispered. "And that's the last we speak of it, agreed?"

Zia nodded slowly. "You made that?" he said, tilting his head to the food container on the counter.

Yousuf nodded modestly. "Yes. An old family recipe. It goes better with flatbread but…"

"Sorry, I ate all of the bread," Bone said.

They all startled when the deadbolt behind them clicked open. A young woman—Tiffany—smiled at them. The smile quickly faded as she realized she'd barged into the middle of an important discussion. "Zia? Should I come back in a few?"

"No, Tiffany, please come in. Meet…"

"Yousuf," he said, turning and extending his hand.

"Yousuf," Zia said. "We're going to try him out as a cook for a few weeks to see how he does."

ADVENTURE

Montclair General Hospital
Montclair, California

Matthew stuck to his story through round after round of interviews with the police.

First, patrol officers took copious notes. Detectives followed once the doctors patched him up and put him in a small room with a guy recovering from some kind of surgery. The patient in the next bed got an earful every time the detectives questioned his bullshit tale of abduction, defending himself, and escaping.

After three days, he was feeling fine and demanded to be discharged.

"You sure you're going to be okay?" the nurse who reluctantly wheeled him to the main exit asked.

"I'll be fine," Matthew said. He was a hundred miles from San Deigo, but he had some cash from Bone and felt better about life—and himself—than he had in years.

His first stop would be a barber to get cleaned up.

After that, he'd have to see. But he was alive, the sun was shining, and the next adventure awaited.

THE TARGET

Central Analysis Group (CAG) Headquarters
Arlington, Virginia

Wyatt tore the wrappers from two frozen burritos and dumped them onto a plate, his mind locked on the problem that had bothered him for the past few days.

Weeks before, he'd been forced to push aside his obsession with Prince Rafiq Al-Najjar when Gregory said he'd handle it; it was no longer Wyatt's problem.

Since then, he had opened his brain to the feed of intelligence data, speed-reading raw intel reports as they scrolled up his screen.

One report had caught his attention. He'd read it, filed the information away, and returned to the feed.

Last night, an unrelated scrap of data in another report caught his eye.

They were connected somehow.

He didn't have enough to take to Gregory yet.

But there was a dangerous target out there that required attention.

He could feel it.

THE WORK

71 Ocotillo Street
Sands, Arizona

In the setting sun, Bone's house looked the same as when he'd left it almost a week before. The high desert heat felt shockingly different than the cool ocean breeze of the past week, but it was home.

He parked in the driveway and made his way to the front door, expecting it to be broken open and the house vandalized again, but all was fine.

It still stank, an underlying scent the man at the big-box hardware store said would disappear with the enzyme solution he sold Bone, along with primer and paint for the walls, and all the supplies needed to get the house back in shape.

A long weekend of ordering carpet and shopping for furniture would be needed, but he had the time. The two stacks of hundreds from Yousuf—twenty thousand dollars total—would be plenty to make the house a home again.

His pistols, Lamar's AK, and the bodyguards' weapons had all been disassembled and disposed of on the long drive back from San

Diego, along with the burner phone and the whiskey from the LA rooftop.

His depleted go bag went back into the safe. He'd have to restock it but figured he had at least a little time.

Bone grabbed his favorite—and last—pistol from the safe and slipped the concealed-carry holster into his pants.

You never knew what the night might bring.

His personal phone chimed when he turned it on. There were two text messages from the past week and a voicemail from this afternoon —the school's number.

He checked the text messages. Both were from Stephanie hoping he was okay.

The voicemail was next.

"Hi, Thomas, it's Cathy Kaeler from school," the principal started, sounding apologetic. "This is rather awkward, but we received confirmation just now that you were right. There was some kind of computer or database glitch. You are, of course, exactly who you always said you were. We are all so sorry for the mistake. Please come to the school tomorrow morning. We have a few papers for you to sign and you can get right back to your old job. Assuming you still want it, that is. Anyway, sorry again." She paused, then said, "You'll still get paid for this past week. And I hope, despite the terrible circumstances, that you had a chance to rest and relax on your unexpected days off. We hope to see you tomorrow."

Bone slid the phone into his pocket. Admiral Nalen had come through and fixed the problem.

It would be great to get back to teaching—and helping Simon.

As he returned to the car to unload his purchases from the hardware store, life threw yet another curve ball at him.

Four pickups and one old car, loaded with twenty-something-year-old guys, coasted to a stop in front of the house.

Four guys per vehicle and five vehicles meant Bone was vastly outnumbered.

The weight of the pistol reassured him. He just hoped he had enough ammo.

He could take care of this by talking—or violence of action if necessary.

But his newfound sense of danger—or rather, his former senses rekindled by the recent mission—told him he was fine.

Still, he moved to the front door, set the bags full of brushes, paint rollers, and painter's tape inside, and readied himself for whatever the guys had planned.

The three asshats from the bar the week before slowly climbed out of the lead truck. The ringleader limped along on crutches, another had his arm in a sling, and the third had a bandaged nose.

A fourth stepped out and stayed near the truck.

The guy with the crutches had been the first one to rush Bone in the bar—the one he'd almost kicked when down. He stopped at the end of the driveway and awkwardly held up an arm with a crutch in greeting. "Mr. Marks? We just want to talk."

The other two glared at their friend who had led them astray.

"Actually," he said after clearing his throat, "we—I—want to apologize."

Bone stayed in the doorway, but this didn't feel like a trap or ambush. "Come on, then."

The kids came up the driveway and stopped at the end of the short walkway to the front door.

"Last week, I heard the story..." The ringleader paused and looked down, away, and reluctantly back at Bone. "My mom is the school secretary. She thought... she heard... We thought you were a fraud, impersonating a hero. Maybe even stealing the identity of a real Navy SEAL. But now..."

"His mom royally screwed up," one of the others said, cutting to the chase. "The school got a call this morning. There was some kind of computer mistake. Which I guess you knew."

"You're the real deal," the third said.

Bone nodded.

"We're all really sorry," the first one said quietly. "You're a hero." He glanced at the other two, got reluctant nods back and stood up as straight as the crutches and his broken ankle allowed. "If you want to finish kicking our asses, we understand and we're ready to accept the beating."

Bone stared at each of them in turn for several seconds, drilling into them with his eyes, letting the tension build.

"Your guys out there feel the same as you?"

The ringleader nodded. "They…" He couldn't say it.

"They messed up my house," Bone said, filling in the details.

The ringleader nodded. "But it was my idea. I put them up to it. Take it out on me, not them."

Finally, Bone nodded. "I've got a better idea." He stepped aside and waved the three guys into the house, along with the men in the vehicles. "Come on in. There's plenty of work to be done."

An hour later, the crew was spread through the house, hard at work. The floors had been treated with the enzyme solution, one kid had run for pizza, and primer was being painted on the walls.

Bone made sure that every last one of them took a turn loading the pile of trash into their pickup trucks for a dump run, standing upwind so he didn't gag or vomit like the kids when the smells they'd left behind—that had only gotten worse from baking in the sun—overwhelmed them.

"You boys good?" Bone called. He got reluctant nods from the pale faces in the dusk.

He headed inside to the ringleader.

"When the second coat of primer is done and the last load of trash piled up, you can call it a night," Bone told him. "What do you say you come back here first thing tomorrow after your run to the dump?"

"We'll be here, Mr. Marks."

"Good. Close up when you're done. I'm going to the Bar."

140

THE START

The Bar
Sands, Arizona

"Henry," Bone said, sliding into his usual spot near the right end of the bar.

"Thomas," Henry said with a pleasant smile. By this time of night, he was feeling no pain. "Back so soon?"

Bone nodded. "Took some time to get my head on straight."

"Good for you. First one's on me." Henry waved a hand at Stephanie.

Bone had felt Steph's eyes on him from the second he walked through the door, but she was busy with a few tables of tourists.

"Thomas," Stephanie said as she came to the end of the bar. Her bright green hair seemed to glow in the dim bar light, reminding him of the view from his night vision goggle Sunday night. She looked fantastic in her tight black jeans and t-shirt, both of which accentuated her natural beauty. "The usual?"

Bone shook his head. "An NA," he said, asking for a non-alcoholic beer. It earned a long, steady look from Henry and an arched eyebrow from Steph.

"One NA, coming up."

"On me," Henry repeated.

"Feeling all right?" Steph asked when she returned with his beer and a tall glass.

"Better than ever," he said, far more seriously than he intended.

Her eyes softened. "Glad to hear it. Where have you been?"

"Sorry I missed your texts. I was out in the desert, just clearing my head."

She saw right through his lie.

Steph picked up a white towel and used it to wipe down a perfectly clean portion of the bar. "Those boys came by earlier."

"They found me. They're painting my house as we speak."

Her smile lit up the room.

"I have to keep moving," Steph said, glancing around the bar. "Busy night. You going to be around?"

"Yep. I have to get back to the house, catch some sleep. Work tomorrow."

"Yes, I heard the news. What I knew all along—you actually are Thomas Marks, Navy SEAL, and all-around badass."

"Retired," he added with a chuckle.

"Yeah." Her eyes narrowed as she looked right through him again. "Retired," she said, her tone skeptical.

She paused a second, her eyes still searching his before she hurried to a table of tourists ready for another round.

Bone sipped his fake beer and enjoyed the vibe of the bar. He had no idea when or if Admiral Nalen would drop by to check on him. Until Prince Rafiq started missing appointments or the royal family grew concerned, no one would know he was gone, including Nalen.

He must have fixed the mixed-up Veterans Administration records assuming Bone would be successful—or he'd done the right thing like he said he would, not waiting for the mission's outcome.

No matter what, though, there wouldn't be an after-action report listing all the mistakes Bone had made—along with the ultimate success of the mission.

Bone had done a good job; he had righted a wrong and saved lives in the process. He didn't have any proof that Prince Rafiq Al-Najjar was responsible for the bounty program in Afghanistan and Iraq. He had to take Admiral Nalen's word for it.

But Al-Najjar had killed seven Navy SEALs one night in Afghanistan. Bone had seen that with his own eyes.

And, more recently, the prince had tried to shoot down an airplane full of innocent civilians.

The world was a better, safer place without him in it.

There would be no medal for Bone's efforts, no hearty handshake of congratulations, and no thank you from a grateful Admiral Nalen, let alone the commander in chief.

Bone could live with that.

It was good enough to have completed the mission. To be alive. To see Steph smile. To go to school, accept their apologies, and return to work.

This was a decent life. He was happy to be here.

He finished his beer and dropped some bills on the bar, enough to cover his beer and a few of Henry's, along with a decent tip. "Actually, Henry, these are on me," he told the older guy. "And thanks for your help the other day."

Henry nodded, his face suddenly serious. "Glad you got yourself sorted."

"Me too."

Bone left the bar, fine with making it an early night.

He still had plenty of demons to confront. Wandering the United States in his spare time, killing bad guys for his country, wasn't a realistic way to deal with all his issues.

But it could be a good start.

141

AUTHOR'S NOTE

Thank you so much for reading. I hope you enjoyed the book.

For a free short story about one of Bone's early missions and for information about my other series (*A Team of One, A Team of Two,* etc.), please keep reading.

First, the excitement continues in book two of the Covert Asset series with:

Target: Unknown

The United States is threatened.

Lives hang in the balance.

The president desperately needs a covert asset who is completely off the books to accomplish an impossible mission— quickly and quietly.

As a teacher, former Navy SEAL Thomas "T-Bone" Marks has the summer off, too much time on his hands, and the perfect cover.

Is he ready to return to his warrior roots?

To once again use his skills, focus, and dedication for the good of the country?

To answer the call and put his life on the line?

Or are his demons too big of an obstacle?

The risks too great?

Will he willingly put himself back where he belongs: under fire and out of time...

With the fate of the country in his hands?

Find out in the latest heart-pounding, page-turning book in the Covert Asset series.

Type this short link into your browser to see more details on Amazon:

https://geni.us/Target-Unknown

If *Target: Redacted* was the first of my books you've read, please check out my other series starting with book one:

A Team of One

New York City faces a fate worse than death, the president suspects a traitor in the government, and an intelligence analyst discovers a diabolical plot.

Former Navy SEAL "Axe" Southmark is enticed out of retirement to help the analyst and the president. But does he have what it takes to save the world?

As a Navy SEAL, Axe was trained to never give up. But after fifteen years on the front lines, it was time to let younger, faster men take the reins.

When he's enlisted to help the president's niece search for both a terrorist on the loose and a traitor in the government, he doesn't hesitate.

It's what he does: protects the vulnerable and hunts bad guys.

With New York City threatened by a virtuoso bomber, there's plenty of both to be done.

Will they be able to stop a madman before it's too late? And is there more to the plot than meets the eye?

Find out in this wild ride of a story.

If you like the adventures of Mitch Rapp, Scot Harvath, Jack Ryan, and Court Gentry, you'll enjoy "Axe" Southmark.
Type this link in your browser to view on Amazon:
https://geni.us/Team
Or visit Amazon and search for "A Team of One."
The books can also be ordered from your favorite local bookstore.

Finally, please note: in ***Target: Redacted***, I used the names of some real places but fictionalize many details. I also take inspiration from areas but change names and some features to improve the story. My apologies if you live in or are acquainted with one of the areas and think, "Wait, that's not right." You're correct.

License was also taken in describing technology, equipment, weapons, tactics, and military capabilities. Where location details, distances, or technical issues conflicted with the story, I prioritized the story.

- **Get a free Thomas "Bone" Marks short story by signing up for my newsletter.**
- **Go to: https://www.authorbradlee.com/story**
- If you enjoyed the book, please leave a five-star or written review. It helps new readers discover the book and makes it possible for me to continue bringing you stories.
- I'm active on social media, sharing photos and writing progress updates. I also occasionally ask for input on character names, plot points, or reader preferences as I'm writing, so follow me and help out. Find me here:
- Facebook: https://www.facebook.com/AuthorBradLee
- Instagram: https://www.instagram.com/bradleeauthor/
- Finally, please join me in thanking Beth and Crystal for their help. The book is far better because of them.